Adam Hall, also known to an international readership through novels published under his real name of Elleston Trevor, has been called 'the most successful literary double agent in the business' by *Life* magazine. The first novel in the *Quiller* series won the Edgar Award and was filmed with Alec Guinness. His subsequent Quiller novels (*Barracuda* is the fourteenth) and his many other books have been translated into eighteen languages, constantly reprinted by book clubs and reissued in hardback and paperback throughout the world. Born in London, he now lives in the Arizona desert, where the film of his novel *The Flight of the Phoenix* was shot. He is a black belt in Shotokan karate.

CONTENTS

1

HUSH

'Then they started to – ' Fisher began.

We waited.

He sat there like a schoolboy, legs together, head down.

I should have said no, I was busy or something. This wasn't my field.

It was very quiet. Tilson wasn't looking at me while we waited; he was looking at the ceiling, angled back on the chair with his thumbs hooked into his pockets. He didn't want to –

'Why the hell should I tell you?'

In a muted scream and we jerked our heads to look at Fisher and I said, 'You don't have to. We didn't – '

'You want to drag everything out of me – ' near tears, his voice stifled, his knuckles white and spittle on his chin. Christ, what was he, twenty-two, twenty-three? *'You want me to go over the whole fucking thing for you – '*

'No,' I said, 'we don't,' and I went over to him and sat on my haunches, so that I was lower and less threatening and he could concentrate on me and forget Tilson was in here, two against one. 'All we want to know,' I said, 'is how you feel now, now that it's over and you're back safe and sound. Just how you feel, that's all, about the future.'

The problem was that *he* wanted to know how *we* felt, and he didn't understand that it was totally beside the question. The question was: if you send out a man this age on his first mission in Beirut and they pull him into the camp and put a hundred and twenty volts through his testicles and keep him awake for six days until he breaks, what have you got when he finds a gap in the wire and gets a lift on a US army truck and comes back to London? Anything you can use again?

'We're not worrying – ' Tilson began but I cut across him.

'You couldn't have told them anything important, and that's the – '

'*I told them everything.*'

'I know, but it wasn't critical and it doesn't concern us.' I didn't point out that you don't send a green executive into the field with anything in his head that's worth getting at. We'd got to save what was left of his pride.

He was sitting on his hands now, rocking on them, as if he'd just been bashed over the knuckles with a ruler, oh those schooldays, those bloody schooldays, they last you all your life, but his eyes weren't squeezed shut any more and he was looking at me with the patience of a trapped animal, waiting to know what I was going to do, kill him or let him go.

'*Everything.*' In a whisper.

'Most of us do,' I said.

Tilson had moved on his chair, making it creak, and I thought if he meant to start talking again I'd have to shut him up somehow. He'd caught me coming out of the Caff about half an hour ago:

2

Fisher had just got back from Beirut, in a bad way, would I mind giving a hand, so forth. Tilson had been moved up into Debriefing and I suppose he was competent, but he wasn't sure how to handle a wrecked schoolboy. I wasn't either, but I suppose he wanted someone who'd been through the same thing somewhere along the line, and now that he'd brought me into this thing I wanted to do it alone.

'That's not true,' Fisher said in another whisper.

'I've done it myself.' Not *absolutely* true, but it would help him.

'*You?*'

He thinks you're God, Tilson had told me on our way here. They need their mythic heroes, the young ones, the new ones, and we never tell them about the feet of clay bit because they crave belief, otherwise they'd never go out there.

'We're not expected,' I said, 'to be superhuman in this trade. We're expected to try holding out and you held out for a whole week, and on top of that you made your own escape and you got back here. We think that's – '

'*You know what they did to me?*'

'Yes, but that's – '

'Don't worry,' I heard Tilson say and I got onto my feet because Fisher was off the chair and it rocked back and hit the floor and he was standing with his face in his hands and shaking badly and a lot of what he was saying got lost in the sobbing . . . '*Told me . . . never see . . . mother again . . . light in my eyes . . . then they . . . wires all over me . . . kept screaming for them . . . stop but it went on and on . . . syringe with stuff in it . . . give me AIDS . . . something, do you know something? They could've eaten me . . .*'

That bit was familiar because it's the feeling you

3

get after a while when there's nothing more they can do to you: they're not human any more; they're just creatures with huge jaws and you go into the final phrase where you lose identity and you wait for them to swallow you up. *The worst fear*, the instructor had told me at Norfolk, *is that of emasculation*, and it had taken five missions before I found out that he was wrong: the worst fear is of *annihilation*, of being eaten, swallowed up.

He was still sobbing, Fisher, swaying on his feet with his face blotted out by his thin white hands, his hair sticking out, button off his cuff, his narrow shoulders hunched over the rest of his body to give it shelter. Someone tapped on the door and looked in and went out again, making a point of being quiet, and I glanced at Tilson once – he was just standing there miserably with his arms folded and I think he'd got the message: we'd have to let Fisher go through it all again because he still couldn't believe what they'd done to him out there, taken away his identity day after day until at last he was nothing but a piece of food. And if he could get over it, day after day and in front of other people, it would save him from the nightmare that could goad him into picking up a knife or wrenching a window open. But in any case he wouldn't be allowed to sleep without someone else in the room, perhaps for months. We'd lost Claypool like that, and Froom.

'What do you think?' Tilson was beside me, unsettled.

'He needs time.'

'Is this all right? What he's doing?'

'It's all he can do. He's got to get to the other side of what they did to him.'

'But I mean – ' he thought about how to put it.

4

I said, 'You can't throw him out.'

'It won't be up to me.'

'Standing behind me . . . I could feel it . . . back of my head . . . kept pulling the trigger . . .'

Rocking and swaying: it might have looked as if we weren't even here, but that wasn't true – he remembered we were here all right; he needed us for his survival. This was the confessional we were listening to, the confessional and the statement for the defence and an appeal for the court's clemency, the whole thing coming out as fast as it could because if it stayed locked in there for much longer it was going to kill him.

'You won't get anything useful out of him,' I told Tilson, 'until he can face himself again. Could take weeks.'

'He sent in quite a bit of stuff before they got him, stuff we can use. I suppose,' he said, watching Fisher, 'we ought to have some kind of resident shrink, for people like this.'

'I've told Loman that till I'm sick. Policy is, if they can still stand up, send them out again, and if they fall down, throw them into the street. They've lost good people like that.'

'They're going to do it again,' Tilson said, didn't look at me.

I could feel anger quickening. 'What have they said?'

'Give him the rest of the day, and if he's no better, sign him out. He – '

'*Shit*. Who said that?'

'Mr Croder.'

'Quick,' I said and left it to Tilson because he was nearer the boy and he caught him halfway to the window and Fisher went mad, then, and Tilson couldn't hold him so I went over to help and had to

5

work on the median nerves, get them numb enough to stop him using his hands, and then I said, 'Listen, I'm taking you to my place and tonight we're going to get smashed out of our minds.'

'What time?'

'Eleven.'

'What does he want me for?'

'I don't know.'

I put the phone down and went along to the Caff and found Tewkes chatting up Daisy by the tea urn, reeking of that bloody cologne.

'Croder was looking for you,' he said.

'I know.'

'How's the lad?'

There isn't a grapevine in this place, it's more like a fast-burn fuse.

'Very good,' I told him. Not, however, in point of fact, very good at all but *that* was the message I wanted to disseminate throughout the whole of the Bureau. Fisher was *better*, yes, but he'd been born with a thin skin anyway without the Beirut thing, and if they put him through it again today they'd draw blood without even using their nails.

I'd got him smashed on vodka by midnight and he'd more or less surfaced at the Key Club during the early hours and didn't remember, for a minute or two, anything about Beirut, and it hadn't been the ego suppressing it – the tension was off at last and he was on the other side of what they'd done to him and that was where he was going to start living again. Then he messed up the carpet in the Jensen and said he was terribly sorry and I could have wept because he was so bloody *young* for this game, and yet so very good, from what I'd seen of the stuff he'd sent into Signals from his base out there – I'd asked Tilson for a look at it this morning.

He was still at my flat: I'd phoned Harry and asked him to come round and look after him. I told him that if anyone from the Bureau located him there he wasn't to report to the building – that was an order and I would take the responsibility. Tilson knew where he was, and might have leaked it.

'Mr Croder,' Tewkes said, 'yet.'

'Oh for Christ's sake shut up.'

It hadn't totally escaped me that when Croder sends for a shadow executive it's reasonable odds that he's got a mission lined up and that soon after eleven o'clock this morning I'd be taken off standby and put into operations and cleared and briefed and sent out to God knew where, and the prospect was touching the nerves.

'Cuppa, love?'

'Yes.' Red, chafed hands at the big tea urn, powdered wrinkles, what would we do without our Daisy, the gentle dispenser of the universal anodyne? 'How's the arthritis?' It had been pouring for days on end, October rain.

'Gives me gyp now and then. What about that poor young man, though?'

'He's fine now.' Keep on saying it, telling people. The Caff was the only place where we could talk without the gag on and Daisy was an information centre second only to Signals itself.

There was no one in here I wanted to talk to and I'd had enough of that bloody cologne and it was still only 10:45 so I went along and kicked Holmes' door open, not exactly, but I was a fraction quick with the handle and he noticed.

'What are they going to do,' I asked him, 'about Fisher?'

'Steady, old fruit. Take a pew.'

You can't rush Holmes. He keeps his cool, and that was why I'd come to see him. He was also in Signals and Mr Croder was his chief and he might have heard something definite.

'I've only got a few minutes,' I said.

'Yes, you're down to see Mr C, aren't you?' Steady eyes under heavy brows, watching me carefully. He'd felt the anger as soon as I'd come in here. 'I can't tell you anything,' he said, 'about Fisher. Sorry.'

I had to start using control, not a good sign. 'Have they been looking for him?'

'Yes. Would you like some tea?'

'Has *Croder* been looking for him?'

'Not specifically. Various people have been sort of popping their head in to ask if I knew where he was.'

'Do you?'

'Tilson said you'd sort of taken the chap under your wing.' Eyes very serious now, concerned. 'That could be tricky.'

'They're going to waste him,' I said, not particularly to Holmes, just thinking aloud, not quite sure why I was letting this Fisher thing rankle, not sure I wasn't simply using it as a focus for other kinds of anger in me, other kinds of fear, not sure whether I was afraid for him or afraid for myself, drifting in the limbo that isolates us between missions, bringing loneliness, uncertainty, while you find yourself looking at the calendar, at the clock, killing time on the way to the countdown.

'I don't know,' Holmes was saying, 'if Mr C has got anything for you.'

'I didn't ask.'

'I thought you might.'

I would have, of course, and he knew that. Staring

at me gravely from behind his neat, orderly desk, worried about me, silver-framed picture of a deceptively-pretty girl, other pictures on the wall, some nice Arabians by Chaille, some sketches, a Henry Moore, a Chinese watercolour, *will I see them again*?

'It'd be better,' Holmes said after a while, 'not to fight with Mr C. He's a bit upset today.'

His voice sounded faint, and I realised I'd slipped into alpha, and that I would have to get some control back. It had been –

'It's been almost two months,' Holmes was saying. 'That's a long time.'

'Beginning to show?'

He moved a hand, placatingly – 'Not to most people. The thing is,' leaning across the desk, his tone quietly urgent, 'I'd be very careful with Mr Croder. If he's got a mission for you, and you're in this – ' avoiding the word mood – 'frame of mind, you could lose it.'

'Or turn it down.'

We can do that. It's in the contract, because we don't take anything on that might find us, somewhere along the line, in a red sector where the odds against our getting out are not worth counting. They can't force us, in other words, to sign away our life.

'I don't think you'll turn anything down,' Holmes said. 'He wouldn't offer you anything less than interesting.'

I was half-listening to him, half-listening to the voices that whispered urgently in the dark of the spirit, the thin, whining voices of fright, alarm, paranoia. It wasn't anything new: since the last time out I'd been moving on a collision course with the next one, and it doesn't get any better.

He was waiting for me to say something, Holmes, sitting patiently at his desk, long fingers interlaced, his eyes attentive. *Will I see him again, be here in this room again?* That was the essence of what was going on, the sense of seeing things, doing things for the last time.

Pre-mission nerves, enough to make you sick. 'I don't know how I stand you,' I said, 'you and your bloody intuition.'

Sudden white smile, head on one side. 'You made the choice, come in here or not come in here. Lesser of evils, or am I being self-indulgent?'

Then the chrome-framed government-issue clock on the wall moved to the hour and I got up and tapped my fingers on his desk to make contact with it, with him, *in case it was the last* –

'God knows how you got a girl like that,' I told him, the one in the photograph, and went to the door and saw him, as I turned to go out, sitting there looking solemn again.

'Heed the gypsy,' he said.

'Do you know what you're asking?'

'Not very much.'

'But it's not even your concern.'

'Everything that happens here is my concern.'

'That gives you no right to meddle.'

'It gives me the right to a hearing – '

'Not at present. Later on, you – '

'But this can't wait, you know that.'

Heed the gypsy.

'It's for *me* to know whether it can wait.'

'I want to be told, that's all, what you're going to do with him.'

'It is *not* your concern.'

He swung away, his shadow moving across the wall, thrown by the bright green-shaded lamp on his desk, the curtains drawn against the rain outside, night before noon, typical of him, Croder, thin and sharp-shouldered like a predator busy in the dark, his black hair brushed close to his head as if by the force of a stoop, his black eyes buried in the bone and lost in shadow, his nose cut by the sculptor's knife in a single stroke and jutting sharply, scenting carrion, a trifle, yes, a trifle exaggerated but it gives you the gist I hope, he's simply, shall we say, a man untouched by the humanities and therefore brilliant, admittedly, at his work, which is to bring his executives back in safety if he can manage it and throw them out if they don't match up to his own exacting standards and with no slightest thought of a second chance.

The thing is, I'd be very careful with Mr Croder.

A little too late for that.

He'd offered me a chair when I'd come in, how was I, so forth, the niceties, he's not an unmannered man, but I decided to get the Fisher thing over before he told me why he wanted to see me, told him I was worried and asked him if he'd let me look after the new recruit for a day or two, didn't, as you may have noticed, go down at all well.

'Look, I'm not talking about giving him charity. He did a good job out there – '

'And came to pieces the moment he got back – I tell you this is *not* a refuge for burnt-out apprentices.'

'That's not burn-out, it's delayed shock. I've been through it myself – '

'And so have I – ' swinging back to face me with his head down and his eyes hooded – 'and so have I,' his artificial hand catching the light.

'Then you can understand – '

'But I did *not* go to pieces as soon as I came home.' Stood with his eyes on me, black, glittering,

11

green-flecked with the reflection of the lamp.

'Look, they took away his identity but he'll get it back in time. The real – '

'You will please – '

'The real problem is *guilt* because he broke and spoke and he can't live with himself unless he's given a chance to atone. Send him to Norfolk for a couple of weeks, run him through the survival course and then run him through it again, tell them to flay him alive. He's desperate for *punishment* and until he gets it he won't be able to find his self-esteem and if *you* don't do it he'll do it on his own – he's tried the window trick already and he'll try it again. But if – '

'That is self-pity – '

'It's self-*disgust* but if you'll give him a chance he'll make a first class shadow executive and God knows they're rare enough. It's not as if – '

He was looking at his watch and I turned and went to the door and pulled it open.

'Quiller.'

I looked back at him.

'You know Proctor, don't you?'

Conversational tone.

'*Czardas?*'

'Yes.'

'He did a couple with me.'

'So you know him rather well.'

I didn't think he wanted an answer; if you go through a couple of major ones you know your contact in the field rather well, yes.

There were some people coming along the passage and a woman's voice said, 'I think someone's in there with him' and Croder said, 'You'd oblige me by closing the door and sitting down, if you've got a moment.'

Oh Jesus Christ he was in a towering rage but all you could hear were the words, give him that much, he knew how to get control. What he was really saying was that if I didn't come back and sit down in the next five seconds flat he'd hit the second telephone from the left and blast me straight into six months suspended operations and leave me to rot.

But that wasn't why I pushed the door shut. I didn't think we'd finished with the Fisher thing.

'Thank you. Proctor has been doing sleeper in Florida for the past eighteen months.'

'I didn't know.' I thought he'd been laid off, because *Czardas* had left him with a 9mm slug behind the heart they couldn't get at – he'd caught a side shot at Ferihegy Airport in Budapest when he was taking off in a Partenavia P.68 Victor with half the Defence Ministry's ultra-classified files and one of their younger secretaries on board.

'He's very good,' Croder said, and picked up a phone that had started ringing. 'No later than eighteen hundred hours, and they are *not* to be armed – that's very important.' He put the phone down. 'He's been sending exemplary material through our routine-grade lines without cessation except for periods of leave, when Hayes took over. But in the last few weeks his signals have – Proctor's, that is – his signals have taken a slightly strange turn. Moreover, he's begun sending material through the diplomatic bag.'

Verboten, in the absence of exceptional circumstances. I didn't say anything.

'I've decided not to call him in for investigation because I believe it's already too late for that. There was a certain amount of delay before I was consulted.' Below in the street a bus throttled up, making a sound just like the rolling of heads. 'It might also seem wise to leave Proctor to go on as he's going, and send someone out there to take a look at things without alerting him. I thought of asking you, because you know the man rather well and there's nothing we can offer you at the moment, unless Krinsley's operation in Dakar comes unstuck, which is unlikely.'

'What's he doing?'

'But then,' Croder said, 'Africa's not your preferred field, is it?'

'It's time the whites got out of there and left it to the natives. It's their land.'

A phone rang again and he picked it up; it wasn't the red one. 'Switch calls to Costain.' I thought that was interesting, considering the Proctor thing didn't sound terribly urgent. And there was another thing: I wouldn't have thought the Chief of Signals would have been asked to send out a top-echelon shadow executive to the United States to check out a sleeper with a screw loose. But I didn't give it a lot of attention because I was coming down from the anger about Fisher and the adrenalin was washing around and leaving the system sour, a taste in the mouth.

'Have you been there before? Miami?'

I said I hadn't.

'Not unpleasant, this time of the year.'

'It's too risky.'

'In what way?'

'I mean I could be out there nursing Proctor and you could have a mission come onto the board and you'd give it to someone else. And I need one.'

'I understand that.' He looked down. Carefully: 'You are normally less sensitive.'

Let it go. 'I'm down for the next one in, and I've got to be here. I'm on standby.' He couldn't do

14

anything about that; it's recognised that if they leave a shadow too long with nothing to do he's going to claw the wallpaper off.

'There might be time,' Croder said, 'to call you in from Miami.' Looking up, 'I would consider it a personal favour, if you'd agree to take this on.'

'I'd like to oblige.' I don't take charm from a vampire.

His expression didn't change. 'It was Mr Shepley, I should perhaps tell you, who asked me to send someone out.'

Bullshit. Shepley was Bureau One, king of kings and host of hosts, and he wouldn't give his Chief of Signals a thing like this to play with when there were five missions running on the boards. I suppose he knew I was giving him some bullshit too: I certainly didn't want to be way out there in the States when a new mission came up in London because I couldn't trust them to call me in, but I *could* ask for a formal guarantee and expect to get it. But I wasn't going to ask, because it was giving me a certain amount of dark joy to keep on saying no to the man, considering he wouldn't give me even a minute of his time on the Fisher thing.

'I'm sorry,' I said. 'I don't want to leave London.'

'You make it difficult, Quiller,' hooded eyes brooding on my face in the greenish light of the lamp.

'With regret.' Politesse for tough shit.

'I could of course *require* your acquiescence.' For require read order, but as I say he's not unmannered.

'Of course.'

'But I would prefer to persuade you.' Dark head sinking lower onto his shoulders, I could see the feathers.

15

'There's no chance,' I said.

He pulled a drawer open and dropped some papers onto the desk, some kind of forms on top, I think. Then he reached for a pen. 'To put it formally, then, you decline to undertake this assignment, despite my repeated request?'

'Yes.'

'What if I kept Fisher on and sent him to Norfolk?'

'I'd go to Miami.'

'I have your word on that?'

'Yes.'

I looked in on Holmes before I left the building.

'He's going to keep Fisher on,' I said.

In a moment, 'Yes. He told me this morning. I'm sorry I couldn't say anything – for some reason he put me under strict hush.'

2

MONCK

'Gin?'

'Just some tonic.'

Glass crashed again, musically.

'Good flight?'

'Bit bumpy coming in.'

'I'm not surprised.' He gave me the tonic. 'There's still a bit of turbulence about.' Baggy alpaca jacket and trousers, cracked suede shoes worn to a shine along the sides, fifty, I suppose, thin silver hair across a peeling scalp, name of Monck. 'Lost my boat.'

'I'm sorry.' I'd seen litter across the bay as we'd come into the approach, two or three yachts wallowing in the dark sea, capsized. Maria, the captain had told us, was approaching the Florida coast by now and well out of our way, but she'd done some damage, with an estimated death toll of fifty.

'Good timing,' Monck said, 'on your part,' and gave a slow winning smile. 'Cheers.'

More glass fell: a huge Bahamian was at the top of a ladder clearing away the smashed window panes, a trickle of blood down one arm, which I didn't think he'd noticed.

'You really mean she was a write-off?'

'What?'

'Your boat.'

'Oh. Pretty well. Salvage some of the interior teak and brass and so on, perhaps. *Pretty Polly.*' A quick brave smile. 'Long may she sail the Elysian seas, what? Let's go and sit over there.' We were in a kind of conservatory where they'd put a bamboo bar and filled the rest of the place with huge palms and hibiscus and birds-of-paradise. Some of the floor was still flooded where the coloured tiles had broken over the years, leaving hollows.

Wicker creaked under us, and Monck balanced his drink on a leaning stool. He'd met me at the airport and brought me here in a clapped-out Austin, no air-conditioning, any more than there was in this place.

'How long do you think you'll be here?'

'A few days.'

'You're going to see Proctor, I believe.'

'Yes.' I hadn't been formally briefed in London but Croder had said that Monck was *persona grata* and would give me any help I needed.

'Then you'll be more than a few days. He's back in Florida. You just missed him – he was on the last plane out before they stopped traffic because of the hurricane.'

'Where's his base, here or – ?'

'Miami. He shuttles a bit; quite a few people do. Judd was here last week; he's got a place. Have you studied Judd?'

'No, if you mean the senator.'

'Don't worry,' he said, and got a crumpled packet of cigars out of his jacket. 'You're not politically inclined, as I know. Proctor *is*, at least he is *now*, and that's the main problem.' He scraped a match. 'You can consider this as interim briefing, you

18

understand, filling you in a bit before the other people arrive.'

His face was pink in the light of the flame; the lamps weren't on in here yet and the place looked like a jungle, the plants beginning to crowd in as the dying sun fired the walls and windows.

'Other people?'

Monck let smoke trickle out of his mouth, watching the huge man on the ladder. 'You'll be taking a look at Proctor, but it won't stop there. You didn't bring much baggage, but you can do a little shopping when you've the time.' He faced me suddenly, the wickerwork creaking, his faded blue eyes resting quietly on mine. 'I'm fully conversant with your record, and it must have occurred to you that Mr Croder wouldn't lightly toss you the chore of checking on a sleeper who's started sending in funny signals.'

This man, for all his baggy suit and thinning hair, wasn't coming across as a semi-retired staffer put out to grass in the dependencies. For one thing I knew the tone: he was telling me precisely what he wanted me to know and that was all, and he answered only those questions that called for it.

But I decided to take him head-on: 'Did Bureau One want me out here?'

The big overhead fans sent the smoke streaming away on the sticky air. His eyes were still on me, and when he was ready he said, 'Surely Mr Croder told you.'

'At the time, I wasn't ready to listen.'

Softly, 'Then I hope you're listening now.'

Glass crashed again and it sent a flicker along the nerves. It hadn't been bullshit, then, on Croder's part: the *head* of the Bureau had told his Chief of Signals to send this particular executive out here and

I hadn't believed it because there wasn't even a mission on the board, but Monck had spelt it out for me a minute ago: *You'll be taking a look at Proctor, but it won't stop there.*

But Croder must have known that the mention of Bureau One would have got me out of London with no trouble at all – he hadn't needed to use Fisher like that.

'You say it won't stop,' I told Monck, 'at Proctor. But are we talking about an actual mission?'

He looked away, picking a bit of cigar-leaf off his lip and studying it with abstract care. A plump woman came through the doorway with her arms on her hips.

'Justin! You come on down from there, I need your he'p in the kitchen, man! Now you jus' come on down!'

'This stuff gonna fall on people's heads!'

'Ne' mind about they heads, they have to watch out for theyselves. You c'm'on down now, y'hear me?'

Monck didn't say anything until the huge man had got down the ladder and gone out. 'An actual mission . . . well I'm not sure, you see. My job – ' he faced me again with a sudden swing of his head – 'is to keep you out here in the Caribbean until such time as things develop. Until we know where best to deploy you. Does that – ?' He waited.

'Not really.'

'I didn't think so.' Shifting his weight in the chair, 'I'll put it like this. Vibrations have been coming out of this region over the past few months and they've started to reach London. All departments have been working into the night for a long time now, especially Signals and Data Analysis and of course Codes and Cyphers. At first it had the look

20

of a major narcotics development, understandable in this area; and then we thought it was something political involving Fidel Castro – again understandable, given the geography.' He dropped ash, watching it blacken on the wet tiles. 'We still don't know *much*, but we know differently. What it does concern is the upcoming American election, in which of course Senator Mathieson Judd is actively engaged. It also concerns the balance of power between East and West as it exists at the present time, which is precariously. So we're talking about something rather more than the requirements of a *mission*.' His faded blue eyes still on me, 'Let me put it this way. If the extent of things proves as far-reaching as we've begun to believe, I shall find it difficult to sleep soundly in my bed.'

Black girl, extremely pretty, more than that, vibrant, demanding male attention, petite in a silk dress that you could have hidden in one hand, watching me as I came in, so that I hardly noticed him in the shadows between the hanging brass lanterns, noticed him only when he moved slightly. I'd rung the bell and he'd called out for me to come in; they were standing quite a few feet apart, as if they'd been talking but not intimately.

'Here you are,' said Proctor, as if he hadn't quite expected me to come, though I'd phoned him ten minutes ago from the hotel.

I would talk to him, Monck had said at the airport in Nassau, *with extreme caution. It's not out of the question that he's been turned*.

And was wired, or had a bug running.

The door swung shut behind me; it was probably on a spring, though I hadn't felt it; there was no draught; the air in Miami tonight was deathly still:

they said we were in the eye of the hurricane, the eye of Maria, though it had been downgraded to a storm after blowing itself out across the ocean.

'Monique, this is Richard Keyes.' I'd told him my cover name on the phone. 'Monique.' He didn't say her last name. She stood with one dark slender arm hanging with the hand turned for effect, like a model's, as she studied me, her eyes a sultry glimmer set in the black mascara.

'Good evening,' she said on her breath, then looked at Proctor. 'Call me?'

'Of course.' He didn't go to the door with her; as she passed me she left the air laced with *patchouli*.

I thought I heard a shutter bang in the wind, but it must have been someone upstairs, perhaps slamming a door: it was too soon for the storm to start up again.

'When did you get in?' He didn't offer to shake hands.

'Earlier on.'

'You come direct?'

'Through Nassau. You look good. Long time.'

'I'm all right. What'll you have?'

'Tonic.'

He went to the built-in bar where there was a ship's lamp burning; the glint of mosquitoes passed through the light. He didn't actually look all that good but I didn't think it was because of the bullet in him; Monck had said it didn't trouble him providing he didn't get into any kind of action. It looked, I thought, more like natural wear and tear: booze and late nights and girls like that one, a bit of a man, Monck had said, for the ladies.

'Lime or lemon?'

'I don't mind. Nice place.'

'It's all right.'

Lots of wicker and bamboo and big cushions mixed up with some Miami Beach art deco mirrors and wall plaques, fixtures, I would have thought, they wouldn't be his. Not much light anywhere, the walls mottled by the filigree work of the lamps hanging all over the place on chains, a Moorish touch. Big-screen TV set and VCR cluttered with boxes of tapes, a pile of glossies spilling onto the Persian rug – *Vogue, Harper's, Elle, Vanity Fair*. He'd established deep cover as an advertising rep, working through the major US east coast and Bahamian stations.

'Still on the wagon?'

'Pretty much.' I took the glass. It was more, I could see now as he stood close to a lamp, than natural wear and tear. He had a good face, unusually well-balanced, the dark eyes level and the nose dead straight and the chin squared, but the skin had started to go, even at his age, forty or so, because of the stress, which had made him start losing weight. It was in and around his eyes, too; they were less steady than they'd looked when we'd been waiting there in the cellar in Szeged near the Yugoslavian border the last time out together, waiting ten hours for them to find us and throw a bomb in and leave the pieces there for the rats to pick over. *Czardas*.

He didn't look as if he could ever go into the field again, although I couldn't tell whether some of the stress he was showing, or all of it, wasn't to do with me: he might not always be like this.

We sat on cushions on the floor – the only chairs were grouped around the bamboo table – and I went into the routine according to briefing, just thought I'd look him up, heard he was out here, so forth.

'Sure, it's good to see you.' He'd poured bourbon

for himself, a big one, neat. 'Some kind of vacation?' The accent was still English but he was picking up the US vernacular.

'Not really. We think Castro's putting in some new off-shore listening posts on instructions from the Komitet. The High Commission signals room's been getting crossed lines.'

In a moment, 'Not your usual pitch.' His smile had a certain confiding charm, and it was there to take the danger out of the comment. It didn't.

'It's not on the board,' I said. 'There was no one else they could send out here. But I got a guarantee from Croder.' If there was a bug running I couldn't do anything about it. I was meant to be out here on the Castro thing and thought I'd look in on Proctor for old times' sake: that was the script and I had to stay with it.

'Guarantee?'

'That he'll pull me back to London if a mission comes up.'

'How long has it been?'

'Getting on for two months. You know what it's like.'

He scratched at the black hairs on his chest through the vee of his shirt. 'I used to.'

'You miss it?'

'Things are all right here. This election's warming up, you know. What do you think of our Senator, Judd?'

'Politics aren't my bag.'

'They can be quite amusing, the way they play them here. Someone started a rumour last month that Judd had been a pot addict, and they finally pinned it down to a single drag on a joint in high school, thought it was an ordinary cigarette. But it could have crippled his campaign – these good

24

people don't care about a man's foreign policy, so long as he's Mr Clean.'

'Bit puritan.'

'Of course. Then the Anderson crowd started a rumour that he'd been AWOL in Vietnam for three months, but it turned out he'd been in a military hospital with honourable wounds. Judd's war record is unimpeachable, and they know it. Then last week, by way of a riposte, the Republican tabloids came out with pictures of Tate on a friend's yacht, cruising off Fire Island, and – '

'Tate?'

'Oh for God's sake, do you live down a hole? Senator Tate from Connecticut, running for the Democratic ticket – they got zoom pictures of him with Patsy Stiles perched on his lap in a bikini on the afterdeck. The shock waves rattled the whole of Washington and of course Tate was kicked straight out of the running – and in case you're going to ask me who Patsy Stiles is, she's a celebrated Mafia moll. I tell you, politics can be quite fun in these lively climes. Is it too hot in here?'

'No good opening a window – '

'No, but I can notch up the fan a few revs.' He uncrossed his legs and got off the floor and went across to a wall switch and I noted that he was still supple and moved well and was obviously in some kind of training. It didn't fit in with his job: sleepers tend to get soft.

'I notice you're reeking,' he said, 'of citronella. That's good, they're buggers.' Mosquitoes. 'But mark my word, Mathieson Judd is not to be underestimated. He's a statesman with a world view that we haven't seen since Nixon, and he's not a megalomaniac. He'll get in. He's *got* to get in.'

So this was why they'd sent me out here. I'd been

shown some of the 'odd' signals this man had been
sending in to London and some of the stuff he'd
been putting through the diplomatic bag and we had
a case of a first-class shadow executive getting shot
up in the line of duty and sent out to the Caribbean
to operate as a sleeper and becoming engrossed in
US politics to the extent that it was interfering with
his job.

The whole picture was totally out of focus and I
began listening very attentively because I had to
catch everything I could – a false note, the wrong
tone, a word out of place – and I hadn't forgotten
that first warning with its disarming smile when I'd
told him why I was out here in the Caribbean – *Not
quite your pitch*.

This man had been given some of the really big
ones, usually in the Middle East because that was
his preferred hunting ground, and he'd done some
critical reconnaissance work inside the PLO headquarters in Tunisia the week before the Israelis had
blown the roof off and he'd infiltrated the Libyan air
defence system and the Soviet shipment programme
funnelling arms, missiles and material to the Arab
states. He was too trained, too experienced and too
professional to let anything get in the way of the
work he was doing – I mean okay, yes, it was perfectly acceptable for him to fill me in on the local
scene over drinks and make his pitch as an interested
armchair campaigner for Senator Judd, but *this* was
the kind of stuff he'd been sending the Bureau
through signals and the diplomatic bag. It didn't –

The phone rang and he stretched full length across
the rug and picked it up.

'Yes?'

The earpiece was bound with soiled adhesive tape
and the cable was in knots and I wondered if this

was his main line to London.

It was a woman's voice at the other end, too faint for me to hear any words or even make out if it was Monique, the woman who'd just left here.

'Not long,' he said in a moment and dropped the receiver back and got onto his haunches again. 'When I say that Mathieson Judd has *got* to get into the White House I mean he's the only man in this country who can give it a new direction – and I'm not quoting the standard rhetoric. This time, with this man, it's for real.'

I put in a question and let him go on talking and consciously took in what I could while at the back of my mind a sense of unreality was creeping in and a bizarre question flashed suddenly – *was this man actually Proctor?* Bizarre because I knew without any doubt that he was; he'd changed a bit since I'd seen him last and he'd lost some weight and was showing signs of stress but he was the same man I'd been with throughout two very nasty missions and I knew him to the bone. But the question echoed in the mind.

'. . . Very much hope the Thatcher government realises what we've got in Mathieson Judd, because the outcome of this election's going to have a major effect on the UK . . .'

It was almost word for word from one of the signals he'd sent in the week before – *repetitive*, the communications analyst had noted in the margin, *a major theme*. I went on listening, but couldn't shake off the feeling of unreality, of lost focus. The air in the room was sultry, electric, even with the fan stirring it: the whole town was held in the eye of the storm and charged with tension, and that didn't help.

'. . . His understanding of the internecine struggle

27

for power inside the Kremlin is infinitely deeper than we've seen before in any US president – thanks partly to the partial lifting of the veil by *glasnost*, sure, but Judd isn't missing a trick. The thing is – ' he brushed the air with a hand and this time the smile was rueful – 'the thing *is* that since politics aren't your bag I'm boring the hell out of you. Now listen, can I give you a hand with your mission until – '

'It's not exactly – '

'Your *assignment*?' his dark eyes narrowing as he smiled, the mouth, the teeth alone showing evidence of friendship, false evidence.

'Good of you.'

I said it straight away but it had taken some fast thinking because he was throwing me at every turn – it's *right* out of character for *any* shadow executive to offer to 'give a hand' to one of his own kind because when a mission goes on the board it's circumscribed and sacrosanct and the briefing is ultra-classified and totally verbal except for the maps and the frontier papyrus and the relevant documents, and the same goes for an assignment or *any* official undertaking for the Bureau necessitating a cover name for the field and the cover itself. But I'd said it was good of him to offer his help because it was the answer he'd obviously expected.

Listen, please: *He didn't realise that what he'd said was completely out of character, and I was instinctively aware that I mustn't let him know.*

Beginning to sweat but it wasn't the heat of the room, it was the nerves. Something was appallingly wrong with Proctor and I was having to talk to him as if he were someone else, as if I had to humour him, and it was a bit like playing Russian roulette because the next wrong word could trigger a full chamber, and I knew now why Croder had picked a top shadow to come out here: someone like Fisher would have blown the whole thing before he'd known what was happening.

I would talk to him with extreme caution.

Monck.

Yes indeed. I'd given this man my reason for being out here and he hadn't accepted it – *Not quite your pitch* – and in a minute or two he was going to bring the subject back, had *already* brought it back, *lend a hand*, so forth, and I was perfectly certain now that every word I said was going on tape, *it's not out of the question that he's been turned*, noted.

Bang of a shutter somewhere: the wind was rising again at the rim of the eye and the night was stirring across the town.

Every word, and the sweat was running because this man too had been a top shadow and had been put through Norfolk and been trained to interrogate, put through a dozen major operations with the ability and the experience to face another man alone in a room and draw him through a minefield of traps and tripwires with question after question and that bright, treacherous smile under the hanging lamp.

'Tell me,' he said, 'about your assignment.'

Bang of a shutter.

3

CONTACT

A tile crashed and the pieces whined through the dark near my face and I got closer to the buildings, not wanting to cross the street to the sheltered side because there was debris flying on the wind and it was difficult to see anything coming through the driving rain. The storm had knocked out the power station feeding this area and the only light came from the few late cars making a run for home.

He'd tried two or three numbers, Proctor, for a taxi, but they weren't turning out.

Something hit a big shop window and the glass burst like a bomb and I ducked and found a doorway and stood there soaked by the rain with my back to the open street as the gale took the shards of glass and flung them through the air. A car forced its way past the doorway against the gusts, throwing silvered beams of light as it wallowed through the floodwater surging at the storm drains, a woman screaming somewhere, inside the car I suppose, terrified or just excited, the sound whipped away by the wind.

It was less than half a mile to my hotel and I got back onto the sidewalk again with my head down, leaning against the force of the rain, fingers against the face as a shower of debris hit me with the dying impetus of shrapnel. More sirens, and the crimson flicker of lights in the distance as a firetruck ploughed through the intersection with its sirens going, a police car taking up station.

Assignment, kept calling it an *assignment*, just because I'd said there was no actual mission running for me.

Strong wind-gust and I braced against it, the rain beating, lights throwing my shadow in front of me across the littered sidewalk, sound of an engine and a sudden shout – '*Wanna get in?*' – speeding up again as I made signs for *no* and *thank you*, not easy, I must have looked like a soaked scarecrow trying to keep the birds away. The hotel was only half a block now and I started a slow run to raise the odds against catching something really lethal on my head.

'There's not much to it,' I'd told Proctor. 'There's been no briefing yet.'

'I see,' with the bright understanding smile, the eyes no more than a shimmer between the lids, half his face in shadow under the lamp. 'But I'm sure it'll turn out pretty interesting.'

'Not necessarily – '

'I mean they didn't send someone like *you* out here just for a bit of housework. I'm surprised – ' taking another swallow of bourbon – 'I'm surprised I didn't get wind of it. After all, this *is* my bailiwick.'

'Got lost in all the buzz.' Signals term for heavy traffic. Nassau and the Florida peninsula formed a tight network with its own console at the Bureau, since the US stations presented a major information exchange between London and Foggy Bottom, and Cuba's proximity offered a rich lode of signals traffic for infiltration and analysis, providing a window on Moscow's interests in the region.

'I'm very good,' Proctor said, chin tucked in, 'at sorting out buzz.'

'They're very pleased,' I said. 'I got it from Croder.' *Slip* but it was too –

'I send to Bracknell.'

'He's on Croder's watch.' It was true and he knew that but it had been a close thing. But use the chance – 'You still happy out here?'

In a moment, the smile not there any more. 'Is *that* what you're here for, in fact?'

'Not sure I'm with you.' Sweat itching on the skin.

There was no danger, of course, no physical danger unless he'd got a gun and I'd already walked into a trap, *not out of the question that he's been turned*, it's a rotten word, frightening, with its sense of turning to show a different face, once an ally's and now an enemy's, with trust knocked away and betrayal springing suddenly to life, betrayal and treachery. But if Proctor had been turned I didn't think there was a case for trapping me into anything, not physically: I'm not *that* paranoid. Yet in a way it could be worse than that: I could be moving into territory where I could become lost before I had time to see the danger.

I knew at least that Moscow wasn't involved. Proctor had never liked them over there since they'd put him through five weeks in a psychiatric ward in an attempt to make him break and speak; it had taken him six months to get the shock out of his system. But he could have been got at by any one of a hundred international factions in need of a spook of his experience, and these days the money was big and the girls much more sophisticated.

Who was Monique?

'It's just that it occurred to me,' Proctor was saying, 'that they might have sent you out here to

33

check up on what I'm doing.'

Out in the open now.

I needed time and there wasn't any. 'Not quite that. They asked me to look you up while I'm out here on the Castro thing, to see if you're happy.'

Tilting his head a fraction: 'Is that how they put it?'

'No. It was Croder. He called it a psychological evaluation – you know bloody Croder.'

In a moment: 'I see.' The tone was icy now and even that false bright smile was dying away. 'And why would he want to have me psychologically evaluated?'

'I think it makes sense. Otherwise I'd have told him to let someone else do it: Cheyney's still in the area. But we've done a few jobs together, so I know you better than most people – that was their thinking.'

And now I'd found out it was wrong. I'd known Proctor, not this man. This wasn't Proctor. Fencing with him, having to listen with every nerve and watch every word, I didn't have time to think what could have happened to him, but the obvious answer was drugs.

'You know me better than most people,' he said. 'You think that's true?'

'In this trade no one knows anybody else too well, do they? It's relative. But look, if you'd rather Cheyney or someone else talked to you, all you've got to do is signal Croder. I didn't ask for the job.'

'Quite so.' He was on his feet suddenly and moving around with his thumbs hooked in the pockets of his worn blue jeans, his shadow swooping on the walls as he passed the hanging lamps. 'To see if I'm happy, yes, that's how *you* put it, not Croder,' swinging to look down at me, 'but why shouldn't I be happy?'

I got up too because we were about the same calibre and I didn't want to be on the floor if he decided to start anything; his tone was silkily hostile and if he was on angel dust or something he could suddenly take fire.

'Look at it this way, Proctor. You were into a *lot* of action in those missions and you were bloody good – I know you *that* much. But since the bullet thing you've been doing what amounts to a desk job and frankly if it had happened to me I'd have blown up by this time.'

Coming close suddenly, watching me with the glimmer between the lids – 'Do I look as if I'm about to blow up?'

'With you, it wouldn't show.'

But that wasn't true: it was showing very clearly; he'd lost the ability to keep his nerves under the skin. In *Czardas* and *Lighthouse* we'd both come as close to Christendom as we'd ever been but he'd had a face like a mask the whole time, even when they'd taken him out of the interrogation cell in Zagreb and he'd looked back at me with his eyes absolutely steady and the signal perfectly clear but only to me: *Don't worry, they didn't find the pill.* Capsule, potassium cyanide, the instant exit.

'Then let me assure you,' he said with the accents honed, 'that I am not about to blow up. I'm perfectly happy here and I can quite believe that Croder is pleased with the product I'm sending in.' His blunt head turned as the shutter banged again and some glass crashed somewhere in the street. A wind was getting up, fluting through a crack in the door.

'Here we go again,' Proctor said, his tone suddenly normal. He went to the phone and sat there

35

on his haunches, pressing out a number and looking up at me. 'You said your hotel's ten minutes from here?'

'Yes.'

'You mean walking or driving?' I said walking and the line came open and he asked them to send a taxi but it obviously didn't work and he tried some other numbers, looking at the pad by the phone, then getting up. 'We've left it a bit late; they're all staying put.' Looking at his watch, 'I'd ask you to stay for some spaghetti or something, but – '

'I've got to go anyway.' *Not long*, he'd said to the woman on the phone.

'Let's keep in touch, then.' The tone still normal, no trace of hostility, no bright smile. I found it unnerving – it was like suddenly talking to someone else.

'Let's do that,' I said. He came to the door with me. 'In the meantime I'll tell them you're perfectly happy, is that right?'

In a moment he said, 'Perfectly happy', as if he wasn't sure what I was talking about but felt it was the right answer.

The rain had started soon after I left him but there was nothing I could do about it and for most of the journey I was hardly aware of getting soaked because the chance of fetching something conclusive on top of the head was more of a worry – that, and the knowledge that the Bureau had a sleeper out here manning a sensitive network and going through some kind of personality change.

And there was something worse, something that had a degree of horror to it that I couldn't quite identify as the rain whipped through the streets and the sirens began again in the distance. And then as the blacked-out facade of the hotel loomed up the chill truth came into my mind and I broke my run as if I'd hit something.

It wasn't only that Proctor had started to go through some kind of personality change. There was this: *He didn't know it.*

The red light was blinking on the phone in the hotel room and I asked for messages but there was only one. The name was Mr Jones, code identity for the Bureau, with only an extension number, 59. I used the prefix and dialled long distance direct. It was coming up to 05:00 hours in London.

'Are we clear?'

Holmes' voice. He meant were there any bugs.

'As far as I know.' There could be a lot of stuff all over the place but it was unlikely because I'd switched rooms as soon as I'd booked in, as a matter of routine.

'A couple of things,' Holmes said. 'Mr C wanted to tell you himself but they've had a wheel come off with *Snapdragon* and he's at the console now. First thing is, he wants you to meet Ferris. He's – '

'Spelling?' There was some lightning around but the line wasn't too bad: I just wanted to make absolutely sure. He spelt it and a flicker went through the nerves.

Ferris.

'He gets in to Miami in thirty minutes,' Holmes said, 'your time, unless that storm's still on. Is it?'

'They've started traffic again.'

'All right, he's British Airways Flight 293 direct from Heathrow. I'm sorry I couldn't give you more notice, but you weren't there earlier. Can you meet him?'

'Yes. Is he alone?'

37

'That's right.' His tone was overly casual: Holmes enjoys understatement at a time of tension and he knew exactly how I'd reacted to the name *Ferris*: he was one of the elite directors in the field who were sent out only to look after something really major, the only DIF I always asked for but didn't always get. 'The second thing is,' Holmes said, 'we've opened a new board, *Barracuda*, and it's yours.'

Lowering in the night sky.

'What's the ETA?' the driver said.

'11:37. British Airways.'

'Sure, that could be it.'

The nose coming up, the lights of the town silvering the wings. 'How long can you wait here?'

'Maybe a minute. Fuzz here don't have no patience.'

'Then go in and check the arrival time for Flight 293.'

'I can't leave the cab.'

'I'm a generous man.'

He came back and said the flight was on time.

'All right, make a circuit.'

'A *what*?'

'Go round again.'

'Come back here?'

'Yes.'

Reversing thrust, the roar waking the night. The cop said something as we pulled out but I only heard the driver.

'Gimme no shit, man, I wasn't no more than a half-minute.'

Reek of kerosene blowing through the driving window.

Ferris.

I nursed his name, going over all the things it

38

meant: a major mission, for one thing, because of his status and his track record and because I'd seen his name on the board for *Catapult* when I'd looked into the signals room before I'd left, so they'd pulled him in from Paris overnight and sent him out here direct with no local briefing from Monck unless it had been done on the phone between Nassau and London. Monck would have given Ferris everything he knew without keeping selected material back as he'd done with me, because that's the way it works: the shadow executive in the field is told *only* what he needs to know at any given time; the background to a major mission can be infinitely complex with areas of ultra-classified material on a government level right up to your-eyes-only files exclusive to the Prime Minister.

'Go round again.'

Even Ferris wouldn't have *all* of it in his hands. His job was to direct the shadow in the field, see that he was fed and watered and kept in signals with London, give him the information he needed to know and send him wherever he had to be sent, wherever the mission took him, protect him from the opposition and from his own paranoia when things got rough, and finally bring him home with enough life left in him to stand up to debriefing for days on end, weeks on end, while they turned off the light over the board in the signals room and got on with something else.

'Shit, man, I'm getting giddy.'

'How does this bloody window open?'

'It's broke.'

There was reflection on the glass but I could see him now, Ferris, coming through the arrival area but not from the baggage claim; he'd have only one case, prepacked for him and stored by the travel section in the Bureau and marked *F.I.P. – For Immediate Pickup*.

'Can you pull in here?'

Between a limo and a dirty red VW, luggage all over the place, two men with sideboards and black coats and padded shoulders and Panda-style smoked glasses ducking into the Lincoln, a college boy lurching under the weight of a surfboard and scuba gear, somebody's maiden aunt with a carnation corsage and blue hair. And Ferris.

'That man there,' I said, 'Tall, thin, glasses – '

'I got him.'

'Fetch him in here.'

Exhaust gas thick on the air as the door came open and I shifted over.

'Where we go now, man?'

Ferris said the Flamingo on 30th street and the driver pulled out and gave the cop the finger and I told him to turn up the radio nice and loud.

'It's two blocks from your place,' Ferris said, but I told him I'd need to move out because someone had searched my room at the hotel and I'd been tagged there from Proctor's in the storm.

'You've made contact already?'

'Yes. Or they have.'

4

PATCHOULI

'While you were at Proctor's?'

'Yes.'

'He sent someone round to your hotel?'

'He could have. I phoned him when I left there, to say I was coming. No one else knows me here, and there was no tag from the airport when I got in.'

'No contact until you called on Proctor.'

'No. But I suppose Monck could have been blown.'

The light caught his glasses as he turned his head. 'No. He keeps his cover in the bank.'

Meaning that Monck was unblowable; so no one had got on to me from there. 'Then it was Proctor. Monck said he might have been turned.'

'Who by?' Ferris dropped a pair of new socks onto the bed. 'I do wish they'd get it right. Look at this, dogshit brown.' He was already half unpacked. We hadn't talked much in the taxi, even with the music. Ferris is impeccable with his security.

'I don't know. Anyone could've turned him, especially out here.'

He glanced at me again, a black shoe in his hand,

brilliantly polished. 'Out here?'

'It wouldn't have to be anyone political. There are people here earning a million dollars a week running cocaine in from the south. A good sleeper with Proctor's communications could monitor the US Coastguard rather efficiently, and make a pile.'

'I see. Look at the polish on these bloody shoes, they think I'm Loman?' He had a soft, rather sibilant voice, like a snake shedding its skin. I wouldn't want to be whoever it was in Travel who'd packed his bag. 'All right,' he said, 'you know Proctor well. That's why they sent you out here. Would he be likely to bust his career for big money?'

'I can't say.' I got up to walk about, not near the window blinds: there was only meant to be one of us in here. 'He's changed. He's changed a *lot*.'

'Oh really.' He took a black leather toilet bag into the bathroom and came back, fingering his thin straw-coloured hair. 'Then who'd be sending the product in?'

'Possibly Cheyney. He – '

'But you don't mean *turned*.'

'I've been out here,' I said, 'for twenty-four hours and I talked to Proctor from ten till eleven tonight, thereabouts. I can't give you processed feedback.'

'I don't expect it. First we've got to beat the air.' He put a Kent brush on the dressing-table, setting it at a precise angle. They hadn't moved surface things in my room at the hotel but they hadn't remembered that the second drawer down in the bureau had been left half a centimetre open, for one thing.

'Where are you going to put me?' I asked Ferris.

'The Cedar Grove, near the airport.'

'Is that the reserve base?'

'Dear God,' he said, 'would I do a thing like that?'

'Sorry.' I wasn't thinking fast enough.

The reserve base could have been vetted by Cheyney or even Proctor himself and passed on to Travel for recommended use. Tonight it could be a trap, or bugged, or both.

'I've stayed,' Ferris said, 'at the Cedar Grove. It's small, clean and secluded, even though it's near the airport. Good access, egress and rear-view vision. And cheap, so Molly will be pleased.' He dropped a green-striped shirt into a drawer.

Molly is that acidic old bitch in charge of Accounts.

'What about cover?' I asked Ferris.

'We don't know yet.' Zipping the empty bag and dropping it onto a chair, 'Listen, it's late, so I'm going to give you the basic scene as it looks at the moment, but realise this: Proctor is the key.' He sat on the end of the bed and leaned his elbows on his knees. 'The *overall* picture is vast and as yet undefined. Only three people have seen the actual print-out that comprises the essence of weeks of signals, sleeper-data and private-line conferences that have been shoved through the computers for analysis and evaluation. Only three. I'm not one of them. So what I've got to do is funnel you a selected breakdown of what London gives me, and your position is this: you're in the field to give *us* the access we've got to have before *Barracuda* can begin running. That's the code-name for the mission as you probably know because Holmes has doubtless told you.' He ran his fingers through his hair. 'Proctor is therefore the key and he's also the access, because *this* is the information I've been given to work on and I can give it to you *in toto*. Do *not* think of Proctor as a possibly-turned or renegade sleeper who's conceivably been feeding *dis*information to

London for an unspecified time – or I should say don't think of him *only* as that. He is more. He is *much* more.'

This was briefing. He hadn't debriefed me yet on the meeting I'd had with Proctor and that was the next thing he'd do but he wouldn't necessarily do it tonight. 'Question,' I said. 'Has *Barracuda* got anything to do with the American elections?'

I think it worried him a bit but I didn't know why. Possibly I'd touched on part of the information he'd been instructed to hold back from me. 'Indirectly,' he said in a moment, 'yes.'

'Because that's the Proctor connection. He's gunning for Senator Judd, and it sounds as if he's right.'

Ferris was watching his hands. 'Yes, London knows that.' A beat. 'I mean that he's gunning for Judd.'

He was watching me now instead of his hands, and I felt a tremor in the nerves. I'd missed a point somewhere but Ferris hadn't. I didn't flinch when the telephone rang but it felt like that.

He swung across the bed. 'Yes?'

I couldn't hear the voice at the other end.

'When?'

His thin body was bent over the phone. I don't think he was looking at me but I couldn't tell: the light was across his glasses. I'm never completely comfortable with this man, even though I've always asked for him as my director in the field every time out and even though he's handled me with total expertise and brought me home still functioning. Opinions and preferences vary among the shadow executives but I count him the most brilliant DIF in the Bureau, and there are seven or eight of them in operation at any given time.

'It's running now?'

What makes me uncomfortable is the man him-self, the way he treads on bugs and the way he'll look at you with his quiet amber eyes for so long without blinking that you start getting paranoid. It had happened just now.

'No. But there's been contact made.'

Searched my room, yes, and tagged me from Proc-tor's place. This could be Monck on the line.

Quite a few other people don't like him either – I mean Ferris. They say that when he's bored with the telly he strangles mice.

'I'll tell him.'

He put down the receiver and got off the bed, pushing his long pale hands deep into his pockets and moving around, stooping like a don.

'Other questions?'

Not going to tell me who'd phoned or why. Not good for the little ferret he was about to shove down the hole, down there in the dark where the tunnels were, a chill along the nerves still because of the slip I'd made.

Had it been a slip? What kind? What did I have to hide?

'Yes,' I said. 'What are we doing out here in the US?'

'You mean where do we stand *vis-à-vis* the FBI?'

'And the Company.'

He gave a sigh, releasing tension, and I knew that in one second flat he'd had to scan right through the not-for-my-eyes material and decide how much it was safe to unclassify.

'They could have been compromised.'

Mother of God.

'You weren't meant to know that,' Ferris said with his head at an angle, 'at this stage. But it was a good question and I've got a certain amount of

leeway in terms of discretion. We don't *know* the
FBI and the CIA have been compromised at any
particular level, so I want you to keep things in
perspective; but there's a risk, so we're not liaising
with them or reporting to them or requesting their
help at this point.'

The scene was coming into focus for me now. *Let
me put it this way – Monck – if the extent of things
proves as far-reaching as we've begun to believe, I
shall find it difficult to sleep soundly in my bed*. And
Ferris, a few minutes ago – *The overall picture is
vast, and as yet undefined.*

'Can I get some water?'

Technically he was my host.

'What? Yes.'

I went into the bathroom and unwrapped one of
the glasses.

'Would you like some tonic or something? There's
probably some in the fridge.' He was in the doorway
and I caught sight of his face in the mirror, watching
me as I turned on the tap, and I didn't know what
he was thinking, what was on his mind.

'It's just a thirst.'

When I came back into the room he said again,
'Other questions?' That was all right; he normally
briefed like this – the general picture and then questions, to save time.

'Yes. The two major intelligence organisations of
the United States of America could possibly be
compromised, and London's sent one little ferret in
here to check up on one little sleeper?'

'I know what you mean, but life is a local affair.
The problem, you see, with *Barracuda* is that there's
so much going on in the background that the communication data's started to jam the computers.
That's why London – Croder, under Shepley's per-

sonal direction – is working the analysts round the clock before the networks start crossing wires and picking up other people's signals and going to ground. One by one,' he said with soft emphasis, 'the stations are switching codes and channels and frequencies as they get scared of leaking their data, and at any time at all the analysts in London are going to be sitting there on their hands with the computers shut down for want of input. The onus is already on you to provide it.'

I said faster than I meant to – 'I'm not signed up yet.'

'I've sent for someone,' Ferris said.

'For someone?'

'To clear you and get your signature.' Watching me all the time, his thin mouth set in amusement, not quite a smile, the way it looked, I could easily believe, when he was busy strangling mice. 'But I'm expecting more questions, before he comes.'

Drank some water; the nerves have got a thirst of their own.

'You could be wasting his time.'

'Possibly. We've got Meddick standing by – they pulled him in from Stuttgart tonight.'

'Meddick's all right,' off-hand, 'so long as he can keep his sphincter muscles under control when it comes to the crunch.'

This man Ferris laughs through his teeth, you know, like a snake hissing. 'The questions,' he said, and glanced at his watch.

But I still didn't like it. This, all right, yes, was the moment of truth we all go through when they offer us a mission and it's never easy, because you've got to decide whether to play it safe and turn it down and wait till something more attractive comes along or go for it and pick up the pen and commit yourself to the high likelihood of walking into the cross-hairs or taking a curve too fast or hitting the floor before they can get at the capsule and rake it out of your mouth, the moment of truth, yes, and the point of no return.

But this time the nerves were nearer the surface than usual and I didn't know why. Correction, *I did know why* but I didn't want to face it. Not yet.

Questions, yes. 'All right, what's the field for *Barracuda*?'

'The Caribbean.'

'Is it exclusively mine?'

'Exclusively.'

'There must be concurrent operations running if this thing's as big as you say.'

'Yes, in Zurich, Capetown and Hong Kong. But they are financial and political, not active.'

Behind the closed teakwood doors and in the private international clubs, not in the midnight streets or the interrogation cells. 'Am I the only active shadow in the whole of the enterprise?'

'Yes. But don't let it phase you. Bureau One is in charge and Croder is in Signals and I am directing you in the field. You can have, of course, any kind of support you need, without number. This', he said softly, 'is Classification One.'

I suppose I should've expected that, with Shepley and Croder running the board in London and Ferris out here with me in the field, but it came as a surprise and I was impressed because Classification One gives the shadow executive in the field *total* support and facilities – communications, courier lines, the strategic deployment of paramedical units and liaison with the local British embassy or consulate and diplomatic status in case of unavoidable transgression of the host country's laws.

Very few of the top shadows have been offered a C.1 – Thorne, Fosdyck, Barrett and I believe Tasman – because in any case a mission of this size doesn't often break.

'I don't want it,' I told Ferris, and finished the glass of water.

'Too posh for you.' Watching me carefully, 'Even with your degree of arrogance.'

No takers. 'Too bloody *busy*. Look, I haven't changed, Ferris, and you know I can only work if you bastards leave me alone.' No heat in the tone, but I wanted him to get the message.

'But if you *do* need help?'

'Then you'd better be there.'

'Well it's nice,' he said, 'to know we're of some comfort, even if you don't want to admit it.'

'Bullshit.'

He was trying to rile me but it wasn't just to amuse himself; the man he'd sent for to clear me for *Barracuda* could be here at any time and Ferris would need my signature straight away because if I turned this thing down he'd have to bring Meddick in from London to take over – if in fact they'd got that man standing by, which I somewhat doubted *because they'll do this to you*, you know that? They'll drag every nerve out of your body if it suits their book. I've seen them kick a man headlong into a mission with the absolute certainty that when he'd done the job he'd never get back through the frontier alive *and then* they'd pulled off the impossible and brought him in still ticking and debriefed him just in time before he went and walked under a bus.

The Bureau is the Sacred Bull and our heads, my friend, are never far from the sacrificial stone.

'So if I'm going in,' I told Ferris, 'I'm going in alone, and if I want help I'll ask for it.'

'Understood.'

Questions. 'What about Proctor? Are you going to put tags on him? Bugs in?'

He got his lean body off the bed and went into the bathroom and broke the plastic off the other glass and turned the tap on. 'I've got a thirst too. You're driving me too hard.' Joke. 'We put a tag on him yesterday and we're mounting a round-the-clock watch. And we put bugs in.'

I asked him: 'At what time?' And waited.

Watching me from the doorway, the glass of water in his hand. 'Just before you went there.'

'On whose orders?'

'London ordered it when – '

'*I mean whose orders locally* for Christ's sake, who told the man with the screwdriver?'

'I did.'

'And did you know what time I'd be there?'

'Yes. They – '

'*You bugged my phone too?*'

'I do wish you'd sit down. You'd be much more comfy.'

I had to centre to get the control back before I spoke.

'Not very good manners, was it?'

A sigh. One of his characteristic and calculated sighs. 'I really think this is a job for Meddick, you know. He'd be so much easier to handle.'

I moved around a bit and came back and sat on the floor with my back to the wall, slight smell of carpet and a shift in the acoustics: less traffic noise from the window. 'Fuck Meddick.'

'Now that'll make you feel better.'

'So you've got the whole of my meeting with Proctor on tape?'

'Yes.'

'And you don't, therefore, need to debrief me.'

'Except for the visuals, and the ambience.'

'He's in good shape, works out.' I went on talking normally to let the angst dissipate of its own accord. The only physical alternative for getting rid of the adrenalin would have been to hit Ferris and he'd saved my life too many times for me to touch him and in any case that too would have been bad manners. 'He started off all right but turned hostile. He – '

'Did you antagonise him?'

'No. I played him very carefully. He's lost some weight and he's living on his nerves – you'll pick that up in his voice too. Shabby flat, renting it furnished, air-conditioning not working – this was before the storm hit the power off. Very pretty black popsy who left without a word. He's – '

'Tart?'

'No, unless she's flying extremely high, Washington or somewhere like that. She's sophisticated, and potential dynamite. Raw silk dress, platinum Pinochet watch.'

'Yes, the tag reported on her. Did Proctor introduce her?'

'Yes, the name was Monique.'

Talking about her, thinking about her, brought the hint of *patchouli* back to me and by association something else that had been there in Proctor's flat, something I hadn't seen or heard, some kind of presence, an element, and it was *this* that had got my nerves strung up, and what I was afraid of most was a question about it from Ferris. He hadn't asked me yet and he might not ask me at all but if he didn't I'd know the worst.

Paranoia.

'Did you arrange to see him again?'

'What? Yes. We're meeting for lunch tomorrow at the Oyster Pick.'

'Despite his hostility.'

'He wants to know more.'

'About?'

The phone rang.

'Why I'm here. He suspects I'm checking on him.'

'Oh really.' He picked up the phone and listened and said, 'Come on up.'

He dropped the receiver back and I asked him where Monck fitted in.

'He's very seasoned,' Ferris said, 'and quite high in the overseas staff echelon, so if he contacts you, listen with care.'

'Is he directing anyone over here?'

'You mean plumbers and people?'

'Yes.'

'He is not. He's too far away and he is *much* too elevated to look after plumbers. Think of him as a liaison figure between *Barracuda* and the operations in Zurich and Capetown and Hong Kong, and in direct signals of course with London – which is why you were sent to Nassau for local briefing.'

'Who's looking after the plumbers?'

Knock on the door and he went over there. By plumbers we mean engineers of some kind, mostly electronic and mostly concerned with bugs and counter-bugs. 'We've got a man called Parks who does that,' Ferris said, and opened the door.

I got off the carpet as he came in, a small man with quick movements, clerical, deferential, terrible tie.

'Truscott,' Ferris said, 'this is Mr Keyes. It shouldn't take long, I know it's late.'

We nodded and Truscott looked around for a chair and got his briefcase unzipped and then Ferris looked at me and said, 'Why do you think, by the way, that Judd should get in?'

Sudden chill and the skin crawling, the senses of reality drifting away.

And the faint scent of *patchouli*.

'Judd?' *Quick*. 'Oh, Proctor was full of it – you've got it on the tape.'

'Of course.' As if he'd forgotten.

He hadn't forgotten. 'Actually – ' *be careful, be very careful* – 'anyway, it's all on the tape.'

Ferris had turned away and I said to the man, Truscott, 'You're here to clear me?'

'Yes.' He looked surprised. Well of course, Ferris would have told him but I suppose I was just making conversation while I waited for Ferris to turn round again – I wanted to see his eyes, see what was there. Sweat cold on the skin.

Then he was looking at me, and of course there wasn't anything at all I could see in his eyes because he wouldn't be showing it.

'Is it on?'

As if nothing had happened. Had anything happened, or was it just in my head?

'On?'

Reality creeping back.

'The mission,' he said, watching me all the time.

'Yes.' Said it without thinking, but there was no question, because I wanted him, Ferris, and the Bureau, wanted their help. 'Yes of course.'

'Hot in here,' he said, and went across to the thermostat. Over his shoulder, 'Get him cleared, then, will you?'

I suppose it took ten or fifteen minutes, I don't remember: there's not a lot to do at this stage, just forms to sign.

'Next of kin?'

We started into it, while I watched for Ferris'
reflection to come into the bathroom mirror through
the doorway, into the glass of the picture on the
wall, the seascape, because I didn't want to look at
him directly. But the worst was over now and I
wouldn't have to think about it until later, in the
night perhaps, in the still of the whinnying dark
when the dreams bring demons –

'The same bequest, sir?'

'What was it last time?'

'Shoreditch, the battered wives' – '

'Yes, right, let it stand.'

Took it from there and got through by 01:00
hours, no weapons drawn, no courier requested, no
support, so forth. Signed all the bumph.

Went off, Truscott, bobbing his head, briefcase
under his arm, almost too big for him.

'In terms,' Ferris said before I left him, 'of final
briefing, your primordial task is to latch on to Proctor and get everything you can from him, get right
inside his head and work from there.' His hands
held out in front of him with the long fingers spread
– 'Proctor is the *access* we've got to have before we
can even start running *Barracuda*', and I said yes I
understood.

But in the morning he phoned me and said that
Proctor was missing, cleared out during the night.

5

LANGOUSTE

She was below me, looking upwards through her mask.

Two of them had worked all through the night.

Down, with her hands beckoning. I pretended not to see. Looking at all the sea fans, very pretty, so forth.

They'd gone through the flat with counter-snoop equipment and hadn't found a thing, nothing of his, anyway, only the bug that Monck had ordered put in there *without telling me*, but I'd stopped worrying about that by now because this wasn't going to be like other missions; this was a Classification One they'd got on the board and they were going to run me like a rat through a maze and I couldn't expect any manners.

Down, she was saying with her hands, encouraging me, nodding slowly, her light hair streaming in the current, so I tilted and went down to where she was waiting just above the sand, four atmospheres on the gauge. *Okay?* with her thumbs up. I made a bit of token fuss with the faceplate and then nodded *yes, okay*.

I've never seen Ferris move so fast, though he

didn't seem to hurry: he just got a lot more done, calling people out of the woodwork and signalling London and Monck, telling me to get to the Cedar Grove on South River Drive and make certain I was clean when I got there; my hotel was blown and Ferris had got my things collected and sent to the new place.

This morning he'd used every trick in the book and got hold of Proctor's phone bills for the last three months and we'd gone through them and the most frequent local number we'd turned up had been called in the period of August 3rd to 19th and it was hers, Kim Harvester's, the woman drifting beside me with her long greenish eyes watching me through her mask.

Okay, so let's go on up now, her hands palming upwards and her flippers beginning to stroke, the stripes on her suit rippling in the underwater light and her hair drawn straight and then billowing as she slowed, waiting for me, then drawn straight again like pale seaweed in the current.

They'd known he'd gone for good because the peep Ferris had stationed in the building opposite had seen him pile a lot of his stuff into the seven-year-old soft-top Chevrolet in the street below; he'd even taken the stereo and the rowing-machine.

Up we go. Feel okay? Bubbles rising against the flat white surface.

They should have known the man they were handling. He'd seen the tag in the Toyota three cars behind him along Biscayne Boulevard and stopped at an Arco station to make a phone-call and then got back into the Chevvy and driven on, and the police car had moved in before they'd gone three blocks and put the tag through the breathalyser while the Chevvy had kept on going.

Sunlight bursting against the eyes, the body heavy again.

'You did very well,' she said when she'd pulled off her mask.

'Thank you.'

I'd told Ferris I wanted him to play the tape they'd made when I'd been in the flat talking to Proctor and do it now: I didn't want London to think I'd frightened him off with anything I'd said. Ferris had cleared me, called it a model exercise.

'How did you find me?' she wanted to know; we were stripping off our wet suits on the quay, where she'd got a shed full of equipment and lobster pots and some deep-sea fishing gear. 'I'm a bit out of the way.'

'Someone I was talking to yesterday said you were good. When did you leave the old country?'

'Years ago.' Shaking out her wet hair, 'My father was a small-boat skipper in Dover, but he finally couldn't stand the winters.' She hung up our suits and hosed them and then the air tanks, sluicing out the masks. 'What about you?'

'I'm just visiting.'

Looking down, then up again. 'You don't need scuba lessons.'

'It's been a long time. I'd lost confidence.'

There was a squawking of seagulls suddenly from the water beyond the boats and she swung her head and looked across at them, a square face but small, with a firm mouth, marks on the cheeks still from the mask, thirty, I would suppose, her skin ageing too fast in the sun. 'No,' she said, 'you haven't lost confidence. You were just making it look like that.' She smiled for the first time since I'd come down here.

'How long have you been teaching?'

'Oh, years.' She put a brush through her hair. 'So who told you where to find me?'

'George Proctor.'

She straightened – 'Oh.'

'He said you were a good teacher.'

'He's trash,' she said off-handedly as she looked away and then began stowing the air tanks.

'Can I give you a hand?'

'I do it in my sleep.' Lean-bodied and strong, turned-up khaki shorts and a tee-shirt, its back dark from her wet hair.

I was waiting for her to ask me how he was, Proctor, because he'd phoned her every day, sometimes twice a day, the last time nearly a month ago, but she just said, 'I didn't catch your first name.'

'Richard.' But then I suppose you wouldn't ask about someone's health if you'd dismissed them as trash.

'Since,' she said, 'you don't need scuba lessons and you haven't lost your confidence in the water, why did you come down here?' With a full frank stare.

'I hoped you might know where he's gone.'

'Oh.'

Someone was bringing a Chris Craft in, throttling the diesels down, two or three people on deck, very tanned, one of them with a line ready, and she waved back to them when they saw her. There was still a lot of flotsam swirling on the surface from the storm. There was flotsam all over the bloody place as a matter of fact: Ferris had put *three* men on me as an exercise in caution. A lot had happened last night – my room at the hotel had been gone through and someone had tagged me back there and then Proctor had got out very fast indeed and left no tracks, so anything could happen now and if anyone picked me up again and moved in, Ferris would want to know who they were and where they came from.

'*Proctor is the key*,' he'd said. '*He's also the access.*'

Croder, at the board for *Barracuda*, would not have been pleased with that signal. *Subject missing, no trace.*

'Would you like some lobster?' the woman asked me.

'To eat?'

'What else would you do with a lobster? Don't tell me you're that kinky.' With a freezing smile, loathing me for even having known Proctor, but still too interested to let me go.

I said I liked lobster.

'Actually she's a tug,' Kim said, 'still is, really, though I've made a few changes.'

We'd put out a couple of miles, as far as the warning buoys on the reef, and dropped anchor.

'She was my father's, his one great love, apart from me. Two-inch oak on double-sawn oak frames, my God, the way they used to do things! She's still registered for coastwise and harbour work. Are you starving?'

'There's no hurry.'

'I've got to catch it first. There's some Scotch in that cupboard, unless you'd like wine. Help yourself.' She went into a berth and came back in a black bikini, hooking the bra and shutting the door with her bare foot. 'Aren't they handsome?' I was looking at the blown-up photographs of sharks all over the cabin. Brushing against me in the close quarters she said, 'I was rude to you back there on the quay.

59

Sorry, but he really is such an absolute bastard. I won't be long – you can get some water on the boil if you like, that pan there, half full.'

Over the side in a perfect curve, no splash. The lobster-pot marker bobbed in the ripples.

I kept in the shade, under a canvas awning she'd rigged up aft of the cabin; the sun struck out of a full noon sky and the deck was giving off the smell of pitch. There was the glint of field-glasses again from the stern of the motor-launch that had nosed its way along this side of the reef soon after we'd dropped anchor.

Things had gone better in the night than I'd expected; the hags of Morpheus had been kept back by Ferris's telephone call reporting that Proctor had gone, and there'd only been a couple of hours after that, sometime before dawn, for sleep or night-mares. But there was still a sensitive area in my consciousness that I was deliberately avoiding, because it frightened me. It was about Senator Judd, and the way Ferris had put his question.

I'd face it later, when I had to, when I was forced to: and I would be, I knew that.

'*Langouste à la Sétoise*,' she said, 'but I think I should have marinated it. Garlic, tomatoes, oil, mainly – the olives are extracurricular because I dote on them. I had a French mother, not *French*, actually, Belgian. She met my father on the Dover ferry one night in a storm. Lonely people talk a lot, don't they?'

'Do you talk a lot?'

'You haven't noticed?'

'Are you lonely?'

'My God, four questions in a row. Is this any good?'

'*C'est exquise*.'

After a silence that wasn't obtrusive – 'Lonely in a way, yes, I suppose. Or this is the aftermath. He dropped me flat, only a few weeks ago.'

For Monique.

'You're well rid, aren't you?'

She looked up at me, her green eyes deeper in the shade of the cabin. 'It never really matters, you know, what they're like. He was the only man I've ever loved. Not *loved*, actually – been obsessed by. Why didn't you just – ' waving her fork – 'come to me and tell me what you wanted?'

'I didn't know how sensitive you might be feeling.'

She watched me for a moment. 'That was nice of you. But it cost you fifty dollars.'

Flash, flash from the launch near the reef.

I hadn't answered, and she said, 'You told me he's "gone". You mean cleared out altogether?'

'He took all his things.'

'But you said you'd been talking to him yesterday. He went last night?'

'Yes.'

'This really calls for the Chablis, you know.'

'I have to keep off it.'

'Oh. Are you some sort of official, then? I mean is he wanted for anything?'

'Not as far as I know.'

'That's a bloody shame.' Laughing on the outside, crying on the inside. With a big effort that only showed in her voice, lightly, casually – 'Did he talk about me?'

'We were talking business the whole time.'

A gull swooped and perched on the aft rail and she swung her head, then looked back at me. 'But you said he told you I was a good scuba teacher.'

'That was a lie. I couldn't think of a better introduction.'

'An honest liar – that's unusual. Then how did you really find me?'

'He'd cleared out in a hurry and left the flat in a mess, papers all over the place, including some phone bills.'

She was looking at me less often, and listening carefully, her eyes down. 'So how many numbers did you call? The whole lot?'

'The one he'd called the most often, first.'

'Mine.'

'Yes'.

Looking away, 'There wasn't another number, since then, that he'd called often?'

'No.' She didn't want to know about Monique.

'Well it won't be long.' Pouring herself some more wine – 'So you found my phone number, but you didn't call mc.'

'I got your answering machine.'

'And didn't leave a message.'

'You're listed.'

She drank some wine. 'I'm a careful soul, you see, and when a man comes here for lessons and uses his gear like an expert I want to know more.' She looked up at last. 'And I think I believe most of what you've said. Have you ever been rejected, Richard?'

'It happens all the time.'

'I doubt that,' holding my eyes for a moment. 'It's not the *missing* so much, the sex and all that. It's the colossal blow to the ego. You know? I mean I can find another man, the place is full of them – but even that isn't certain any more. He's made me suddenly feel unattractive, and I sense you're the rare kind of man who knows what that does to a woman.'

'It doesn't take a lot of imagination. But you

ought to get that thought right out of your head. I've never been so close to a more attractive woman in my life.'

'Look, I wasn't – '

'I know.'

'Well it's always nice to hear.' She looked away at the reef. 'He's dangerous, did you know that? I don't just mean to women.'

'All I know is that he's in my debt.'

'Owes you money?'

'Yes.'

'That's why you want to find him?'

'Can you think of a better reason?'

'No, but there might be one.' She put down her knife and fork. 'Did I pass?'

'It was superb.'

'You can thank my mother. Does it sound as if I'm always fishing for compliments?'

'No, but women have to in a man's world.'

'God's truth.' She began clearing the table. 'There's some fruit in the fridge. Smoke if you want to. Are they friends of yours?'

'Who?'

'The people over there with the field glasses.'

'In the launch?'

'Yes.'

'I hadn't noticed.'

'I think you had.' She brought a bowl of peaches.

'I don't want to sound cute, but with you diving for lobsters I'm not surprised there are some field glasses around.'

'My God, that was the fifties. They do it, these days, they don't just look.'

'Then they'll have to start just looking again.'

'That's true. It's frightening.' She sliced a peach. 'I suppose it's a way of keeping the population

63

down. Are you in the same kind of business?'

'The same – ?'

'As George Proctor.'

'Advertising, yes.'

'You live in the States?'

'No.'

'So you're not interested in the election. These aren't ripe, I wouldn't bother.'

'I don't know a lot about it, but I hope Judd gets in.'

She looked up quickly. 'He's got to. Mathieson Judd is not to be underestimated. He's a statesman with a world view that we haven't seen since Nixon, and he's not a megalomaniac. He'll get in. He's *got* to get in.'

She stopped, but I didn't say anything. She didn't want me to, wasn't looking at me: she'd withdrawn into herself. 'It's not just the Americans who are concerned, this time – the whole world's involved, and much more than usual when there's a change of administration here. I very much hope the Thatcher government realises what we've got in Mathieson Judd, because the outcome of this election's going to have a major effect on the UK.'

Stopped again. I still didn't say anything. She was poising a short chopping-knife vertically above the peach-stone on her plate, holding it carefully and taking little stabs, trying to split it, I suppose; but then if I'd asked her what she was meant to be doing with it she wouldn't know, would even wonder who I was, what I was doing here. She looked psyched out, robotic.

That area, the area of consciousness I was afraid of touching, exploring, was making demands on me now, moving right into the forefront of my mind, and I almost recoiled physically.

Stab with the knife, chipping at the peach-stone. 'His understanding of the internecine struggle for power inside the Kremlin is infinitely deeper than we've seen before in any US president, thanks partly to the partial lifting of the veil by *glasnost*, sure, but Judd isn't missing a trick.'

The short sea lapped at the sides of the boat, and a lanyard fretted in the wind. I didn't know if the launch had gone from the reef, wanted to know but didn't want to turn my head or do anything to break the silence, because I was into the zone of consciousness now, the one that made me afraid, and I lost the sense of time – the past and the present overlapped, leaving me in an eerie wilderness of the mind.

Then the knife split the stone and she looked up at me with her eyes blank for a moment; then she focused, and said, 'They're not ripe, are they?'

'I don't know.'

Glancing at my plate, 'You haven't tried.'

So I made a gesture, and when I spoke again it was with the feeling of pulling the pin from a grenade. 'George Proctor feels the same way.'

She frowned. 'I wouldn't know.'

'He didn't talk to you about Mathieson Judd?'

'God no.' With a hurt smile, 'that wasn't our relationship. Just heavy sex and . . . what I thought was love.'

'Lucky escape,' I said. 'Think of it that way.' I got up and helped her clear the rest of the table.

'Yes, but it's not so easy. Do you like my sharks?'

'I was looking at them earlier.'

'There's a special one out here somewhere.'

'That you want to catch?'

'That I want to kill.' She ran the tap in the small metal sink, brushing against me sometimes, still in the bikini, her skin tanned, copper-coloured in the light from the portholes, with a powdering of dried salt on her shoulders.

'Isn't it the same thing?' Catch, kill.

'No.' She looked up at the photographs on the bulkhead. 'It's one of those, a thresher. It took my father, here in these waters. I was there.'

'When?'

'Eighteen months ago. Eighteen months, a week and two days.'

'How did it happen?' Talking about the tug, she'd said it had been the one great love of her father's life, *except for me*.

'We were just off the reef over there. The anchor got fouled and he went overboard to free it. The shark saw him.'

'I'm sorry.'

'A whole pack. We hadn't seen them.' She dropped the last plate into the rack and dried her hands and turned away, padding on her bare feet to the shade of the awning, looking across at the launch and waving, turning back to face me, 'maybe they'll stop gawping now,' her green eyes wet as she said, 'have you ever seen anyone eaten alive?' Before I could think of anything to say, 'I'm sorry. It's okay now, really. We've come to an agreement.' She came towards me slowly, her face hard now. 'They won't come for me until I find him, the male thresher, and kill him, or try.'

In the glare of the sun on the sea behind her she stood in silhouette, her short legs braced to the motion of the boat, her feet splayed a little and her arms hanging loose, her eyes alone catching the back-light from the portholes, glimmering in the dark of her skin. She looked primitive, naked, as she stood there speaking of primitive things.

'I go to meet them, you see, whenever they're in

these waters. I go and swim with them.'

In a moment I said, 'Alone?'

'I took a friend once, with a camera.'

'*This is you*?' I was looking at the blow-up near the gallery, under the swinging lamp. 'In this one?'

'Yes.'

I'd noticed it before, and had meant to ask her about it because it looked unreal, surrealistic: the figure of the swimmer wasn't perfectly clear; it could be another shark, because of the surface reflection.

'They won't attack, you see, if you swim the right way – unless of course they're hungry and then it doesn't matter what you do. But my Dad was making a lot of fuss with the anchor – we'd got no idea they were anywhere near the reef or he wouldn't have gone down. *Oh Christ* – ' I went to hold her as she broke suddenly but she shook my hands away – '*I'm okay now*, but sometimes I've got to talk about it to someone and it's your bad luck today, you see – because there was my Dad down there fooling around with that fucking anchor and then there was just a lot of blood on the surface, a lot of threshing about and then the blood, Christ, it was a beautiful red – ' shaking and with her breath moaning – 'he was a beautiful man, he coloured the whole sea like a flag, like a banner,' sobbing now but still standing straight with her arms hanging by her sides, refusing to bring her hands to her face, 'and that was all I could see of him, all that was left, a sunset on the sea in the early morning light, and you know what I don't understand? I don't understand why in God's name I didn't just go over the rail into all that beautiful red, so he wouldn't be alone.' The tears bright on her dark face, 'so *I* wouldn't be alone.'

The waves hit the boat and the lamp in the galley

swung; the door of a berth creaked. After a time I said, 'A wonderful man.'

'*How do you know*?' on a sob.

'For you to have loved him so much.'

She swung her head, her hair flying out – 'Love isn't enough, is it, not powerful enough, however big it is, it can't guarantee anything.' She turned and leaned her back to the bulkhead and the tension went out of her and she looked across the sea, across to the reef. 'A wonderful man, yes. It was just over there.'

Where the short waves broke along the reef, tossing up flotsam. 'You can't keep away?'

She turned her head quickly. '*I don't want to.*' Looking across the sea again, 'that's where I swim with them, and that's where I'm going to find it, and kill it.'

'How will you know which one it is?'

'I'll know. We think words are all there is.' She came back into the shade. 'Writing, speaking, we think it's the only kind of communication. We talk about vibes, but we don't really understand how deep they go, how strong they are. When I see *that* one, touch it, I'll know.' She went and found some tissues.

'Is this your father?'

'Yes.'

Laughing, in the photograph in the centre of the bulkhead, holding up a big fish, a tuna or something. A handsome man, not young but youthful, lean, tanned.

'I'll make some coffee,' she said.

'What time do you want to be back?'

'Whenever you do.'

'As soon as you like, then.'

She came and leaned her head against me, closing

her eyes. 'It was nice of you to listen to all that. Not that you could help it, captive audience.' Moving away, 'D'you know how to get an anchor up?'

'Yes.'

'Okay, I'll put the coffee on and start the diesel. You look after the winch.'

More gulls now, and the din of a donkey-engine on the quay, the wail of a siren from deeper among the streets.

'I'll try and find George Proctor for you,' she said, 'if you like.'

'It'd be a great help.'

'How much does he owe you? Or maybe I shouldn't – '

'More than I'm ready to lose.'

'I can't promise anything.' She brought the engine down to slow and span the helm; she'd put on the khaki shorts again, with a sweater over the tee shirt; there'd been a cool breeze off the sea. She was easy in her movements, capable, in charge of herself, not the sort of woman who'd try killing a man-eating shark out of revenge.

I asked her, 'Why is he dangerous?'

She watched me for a moment, wondering, I think, whether to tell me. 'The last time I was in his flat, I was just leaving when the phone rang, so I told him I'd see myself out, and he went back to answer it. He couldn't see the door from where he was, and I stayed a minute to listen, to see who it was. It's not the sort of thing – ' she shrugged – 'but I'd started to think there was "someone else", as they say. But it wasn't a woman. You can tell, can't you, even when they don't say their names, whether a man's speaking to another man or a woman?' She swung the helm hard over and shifted to full astern.

'Can you make a line fast round a capstan?'

'Yes.' The launch hadn't followed us in but it had left the reef and was moving towards the marina further along the shore. 'So what was he saying?'

'I don't remember much, really, because it obviously wasn't a woman. But I know he said something about "going over". "They suspect I've gone over", something like that.'

A gull swooped, screaming, sighting flotsam.

'Anything else?'

She glanced up at me from the line: something in my tone. 'Was that important? He mentioned an embassy, "your embassy", I think. The reason why I think he's dangerous is that he *sounded* like that, on the phone. You know how his voice can sometimes sound sort of – I don't know – menacing? Goes sort of silky. It always gave me the shivers. And there *was* a name he used, I remember now. It was Victor. Look, we're set up – would you jump down and catch the line? It'll save me whistling for someone.'

I dropped onto the quay and waited. Not Victor. *Viktor*. There was a phone on the tug but I didn't want to use that one. I'd have to find a booth as soon as I could and do it in private, signal Ferris: *Proctor has been turned. Contact's first name, Viktor, at the Soviet Embassy.*

6

LIMBO

There was the long black weatherboard wall of a wharf on the right side and a row of capstans on the other side with the sheer drop to the water just beyond them and when I gunned up the rear wheels met a wet patch and slewed and sent the front end smashing through a stack of fish crates and I did what I could to get back on track before I killed someone but it wasn't easy because I was crouched as low as I could below the seat squab because they'd probably try again.

Pickup truck on the left and I grazed the side and tore some metal away, someone shouting, a two-tone cab pulling out from the gap between the wharves but keeping its distance as I pulled the rear end straight and looked for a clear passage but there wasn't one – three or four people with bags and fishing rods were walking down from the street and I hit the brakes and we slid and I let them off but the speed was still too high and I chose the only way out that wouldn't hurt anyone and put the car between a capstan and a rusting trailer and flexed the seat belt to make sure it was tight and then they tried again and after that there was just a lot of metal screaming as we ricocheted and hit the trailer at ten degrees and dragged the wings off and the car windows on that side burst into snow and we bounced and corrected and hit the rear end of a private car and swung it round, glass smashing again and the pop of a tyre bursting and then there was a shed straight in front of me and at this speed it was going to be a jolt and I sank lower into the seat and settled the belt again and waited with my foot hard down on the brake and the tyres shrilling across the concrete.

Hit the shed with an explosion and the daylight got shut off and the impact pitched me at an angle but I was ready for that because of the belt's diagonal and I used my right hand against the facia as the deceleration phase came in and there was the ripping of metal again and then flames bursting in the dark with an orange light and I was feeling for the belt release and the door handle but it was going to be awfully close because we'd hit some kind of flammable tank and all I could see was a mass of bright orange.

Waves of heat now and I got the door open and dropped and crawled to the rear of the car because we'd come straight through the wall and I wouldn't have to look for a door, but the fuel tank was at the rear and I got across the ground as fast as I could with the heat washing down across my back.

Someone yelling, *In there?* something like that, broken glass under my hands and I shifted them, pulling my legs after me, a face staring from the near distance with the eyes shielded by the hands, a man shouting again, *Get you* or something and then I was into the daylight, *Roll over, roll over, roll!* Clothes on fire presumably, then hands grabbed me and the face was close and the mouth said *Barracuda.*

Rolling and rolling and his hands beating at me, 'Okay now, that's it.'

'Get me clear,' I told him, 'I don't want the police.'

'I don't think there's time.' I could hear a siren from somewhere quite close, or maybe it was echoing off a wall.

'You've *got* to cover me and get me out.'

He turned away and I could see the two-tone cab turning broadside on to the flames and I crawled that way through the debris until the man turned and said, 'Wait – *wait* there.'

I couldn't see anyone else in the area because the whole shed was crackling and there were beams coming down and sending out sparks and I had to crawl further into the open but I kept my face down because I'd have to go to ground at this stage and hole up and work things out but that *bloody* siren was closer now and it didn't look as if –

'*Come on – in here!*' A man grabbing for me in the black rolling smoke. '*Make it quick!*'

The door of the cab had swung open and I went for it with the man helping me because my eyes were streaming. 'Show them the bullet holes,' I told him, 'two of them from the rear – *bullet holes*, you got that?'

'Got it.' He slung me into the cab. '*Keep right down.*'

'*Listen*,' I said, 'this is for Ferris, immediate. *Proctor's been turned* by the Soviets.' Said it again because of the choking, I wanted to make sure. 'Got that?'

'Yes, I've got that,' he said and slammed the door shut and told the driver to move it.

Throat still raw, kept drinking water.

Decker, name of the driver, one of ours, a Bureau cab – Ferris had kept it standing off with Decker on the peep even though I'd told him I did *not* want support. I'd sent Decker away after he'd brought new clothes for me and taken the old ones, *old*, Christ they were more than *old*, more like the coat off a scarecrow after a lightning strike.

The phone rang and I picked it up.

'Who? . . . All right.'

Cardinal rule: we can't refuse.

There were two windows, north and west, because this was a corner room, and while I was waiting I took a look from both of them – the airport control tower a couple of miles away and some three-storey buildings nearer than that with billboards, *United Overnight To These Ten Cities, Marlboro For Those Who Like To Smoke, Coors Is The Champion*, no windows overlooking mine at a distance of less than fifty feet on the north, thirty on the west, a man in the doorway near the bus stop and another one at the corner and two more on the north side twenty yards apart and looking in shop windows and of course there'd be more of them on the south side of the hotel where the entrance was, prisoner of bloody Zenda but they weren't there *only* to give me moving cover whenever I left; they were also scanning the environment for possible pollution: field glasses behind windows or the hump of a magnum with a laser sight or an infrared night lens, so forth.

They would also note any opposition peeps standing off in the environment or coming into the hotel, leaving it, hanging around, it was ironic, if you will, that the *first* thing I always ask for at the start of a new show is that Ferris should direct me in the field, and here he was blocking me in with so much support that I wouldn't be able to move without saluting the troops.

'Come in.'

'Greenspan,' he said, a soft handshake and Charlie Chaplin eyebrows, dropped his bag on the bed and looked me up and down.

'Does anything hurt?'

'Bit of sunburn.'

'I'm not surprised. That was a gasoline fire, wasn't it?'

'Something like that. Are you from the consulate?'

'I look after their staff. I'd like your shirt off.'

It's a cardinal rule: you can't refuse a medical checkup after you've been through any kind of traumatising action, otherwise I wouldn't have let him come up, because I wasn't in the mood for coughing and saying ah when there was so much to think about, so many questions, *did she set me up for those shots*?

'Take a full breath. Another one. Now, did you feel you were filling your lungs to capacity?'

'Yes.'

'Well you were lucky with that seat belt. I've seen osteo-chondritis of the cartilage around the sternum you wouldn't believe. You must have taken some of the shock with your right hand, even though there's no echymosis. I've had people with the belt go halfway through the side of the rib cage. Have you seen *The Rainbow*?'

'What?'

'It's a movie. You should see it. This hurt?'

'No.' The launch had moved in to the harbour parallel with the tug and they'd put me in the cross hairs from there, or come closer in a car or gone into one of the quayside buildings and climbed, though not more than two storeys because the first shot had smashed through the rear window and hit the speedometer at not much more than a fifteen degree angle from the horizontal. They –

'Rock your head – gently. Now this way. Feels good?'

'There wasn't any whiplash.' I'd got my head back on the support before we'd hit the other wall of the shed and bounced back. *Are they friends of yours?* With the field glasses. Friends, perhaps, of hers. But if –

'Look, I'm going to give you some Aloe Vera gel for these burns, and some propolis. I've brought some, because they gave me a rough idea what happened.' He raked around in his bag.

The sun was lowering across the ocean, reddening the wall in here. I would need to wait for dark before I moved.

'Use the propolis sparingly – it's quite sticky. You're sure you don't have any pain anywhere?'

'No pain.' Just a blinding impatience to find things out.

'You must keep yourself in pretty good shape. I'm going to leave you with some D-Phenylalanine, 500 mg. Take two tablets fifteen or thirty minutes before a meal and make it a total of six per day – it's on the label here. I want – '

'No drugs.'

'It isn't a drug, it's an amino acid, no toxicity, no side-effects. If you'd wanted aspirin and antibiotics and all that horseshit you'd have had to see someone else. It works with L-Phenylalanine to stimulate the neuro-transmitters and the body's own pain-killers.' Shutting the bag, soft hand-shake. 'Her Majesty's picking up the tab – is that how you guys put it? Two numbers there on the bed, the second one's my beeper. Call me any time, midnight, 3 am, whenever, if you need me – you can expect a bit of delayed shock in the night when the blood sugar's low. *Call* me, okay?'

Said I would.

At the door – 'And get to see *The Rainbow*. Make time. Trust me.'

The phone rang a minute after he'd gone and I let it go on ringing till it stopped. It would be Ferris, wanting to make a rendezvous for debriefing, and I wasn't ready yet. There'd been too much data coming in and I wanted to do some analysis first on my own.

Flat on the bed with my eyes shut, but the muscles wouldn't let go and I couldn't shift into alpha waves because there is *no* excuse, there is no *conceivable* excuse for putting off debriefing by your director in the field at any given time during the mission.

Delayed shock, just as the man said.

Bullshit. There is *no* excuse.

Sweating a little, cold on the skin, you must surely allow me to express at least a token reaction to being shot at with a trajectory two inches from the back of my skull before that thing smashed into the speedometer, to being shot at *twice* and hitting a shed full of petrol cans, maybe *more* than twice – they could have put half a dozen more shots into the inferno and I wouldn't have heard them above the crackling.

Proctor?

The muscles still tensed, the beta waves still whipping me along when all I wanted to do was rest, and wait for nightfall.

1330 West Riverside Way.

Nightfall because I'd need to go there alone, leave them all down there watching the hotel.

The crimson light in the room deepening against the closed lids, the nerves sending multicoloured firecrackers across the retinae, the blood singing through the tympanic membranes, the sweat coming faster now and more copiously because there was *no* excuse to delay debriefing and yet I knew it was what I had to do.

Question it.

Accept. Don't worry.

But the muscles wouldn't let go because the subconscious was in panic, aware that the organism had gone out of balance, that something was wrong, appallingly wrong.

Those are your instructions.

Hearing voices, send the poor bastard to the funny farm before he starts foaming at the mouth and rolling over the floor embarrassing everyone, *are these my thoughts*, get him to a cool white ward with gentle nurses and the goodnight kiss of an anodyne, *give him another Valium*, shivering in my sweat now, *they are not my thoughts, no*, hallucinating perhaps, they're not *always* wrong, those bloody medicos, *you can expect a bit of delayed shock in the night*, so that's all it is, my good friend, there's no need to worry, just relax.

It is not all it is.

Deep breaths, deep regular breaths to stem the high wild racing of the heart, the eyes open now because when the organism is in extreme danger we must tune the senses, deal how we may with the onrush of desperation to know, to understand what is happening, to divine how to rescue the beleaguered self, how to survive.

1330 West Riverside Way. At any time before midnight, but not later than that.

All, then, in that place, would be answered.

Some kind of sleep came, a swirling world of random phantasmagoria, carrying me along through the dark and keening streets of nightmare and throwing me at last onto the bedrock of reality, the sweat running as I woke and caught a breath and let it go, drained and bereft of strength but somehow purged and at ease again, ready to accept, and follow the instructions.

On the way to the bathroom my legs faltered and I knocked into the door but didn't fall, ran the cold tap and filled the basin, leaning on it and burying my face, my head, as I drew water into the parched body, seeking to quench the insatiable thirst that burned in it now – because fear does that, terror does that, it leaves the mouth dry as a husk.

Back in the room the wash of ruddled light had gone from the wall and in its place was the acid sheen from the street-lamps outside the north window, and it was nightfall.

'As far,' I told him, 'as your next stop.'

He didn't answer, but got another crate and took it into the building. The engine of the van was still running, stink of carbon monoxide filling the yard. It served both buildings, the yard – the Cedar Grove and the restaurant next door.

I was feeling all right now. Not perfectly balanced, but all right, I mean not terrified any more, with only a shred of consciousness telling me that I should be, nothing had changed.

'Which direction?' he wanted to know, a shock-haired blond boy with a half-grin on his face the whole time, amused, perhaps, or almost certainly, by this weirdo he'd found in the yard.

Did I look so odd?

A mirror would do nothing, though, I don't mean

look, I mean *behave* – am I *behaving* oddly?

'Any direction,' I said.

'You don't mind where you're goin'?' Humped another crate. Fish, by the smell.

'I just need to get away.'

'Got cabs, in front.'

Shivering in the warm humid air, but not enough to show, I believed. 'I need to get away discreetly.'

He never looked at me. He refrained from looking at me in the way that we refrain from looking at a drunk or some poor cretin child, because our sense of inadequacy in the presence of the abnormal troubles us. He looked at me in that way, Billy. *Billy*, it said on the name-tab stitched to his overalls.

He took another crate in and I stood there in the yard and later remembered standing there in the yard like a figure in a surrealistic painting, as I waited for this *bloody* fish peddler to come back, taking his *bloody* time while the deep indigo sky roofing the yard rang with the clamour of drums and alarms as the little lamps winked across the board for *Barracuda* in far Londinium and the whole of the network trembled to the urgent tenor of the signals going in, *Subject is missing . . . Reported to have gone over to the Soviets . . . Executive in the field has failed to appear for debriefing following attempted hit . . . Director requests instructions re procedure . . .* while the executive in the field, this hapless weirdo, stood waiting for assistance, God help him, and those dozen people out there in the streets stood ready to give him all the assistance he could ever want.

But I couldn't ask them. Not now.

'Discreetly,' he said, Billy said, not looking at me. 'I can't take anyone in my van, see.'

'Look, I'm going to be frank with you, Billy. I

80

can't use a cab because they're out in front of the hotel and he's waiting there for me.'

'Who is?'

'Her old man.'

Big grin now, bright with the light of understanding.

'You Australian, are you?'

'Limey.'

'My dad was over there once, in the war. Kenley. See, I can't ride anybody in my van. Rules.' Taking for the first time a glance at me, conspiratorially, emboldened by my not being, after all, abnormal, 'little bit of love in the afternoon, was it?'

I started with twenty but he didn't give it more than a flick of his eye, taking two more crates in and coming back whistling, a man with a sense of covert communication. I gave him fifty and he looked at it long enough to make it seem he was giving it his careful consideration, and then folded it and put it into his worn plastic wallet.

'Mind you don't slip, okay? It's a metal floor.' Gave me a push and slammed the two doors and dropped the bar and went round to the cab and got in and started up.

Darkness and the ammoniac reek of fish, the empty crates shifting as the van took the turns, a faint whistling from the cab, and deep within me the feeling of having missed the road, of going in the wrong direction, the nagging urge to turn back.

'Cab rank across there, mate,' stressing the 'mate', proud of the bit of Cockney slang he'd picked up from his dad. We were four blocks from the hotel, on NW 6th Street. 'Wanna take a bit of advice? Go for the single chicks, they're cheaper in the long run.'

This was at 8:14.

'The 1100 block at Riverside Way.'

'You don't know the address?'

'That's close enough.'

Cracked black vinyl and the scent of stale cigarette-stubs, a blue silk garter thick with dust hanging from the driving mirror, *Albert Miguel Yglesias* on the identification plaque, the photograph nothing like his face.

'You wanna good place to eat?'

'No.'

'I know a good place to eat. Fillipo Grill, fantastic, oysters *this* big!'

Said really.

In twenty minutes we turned east into the 1100 block and I got out.

'Open till midnight, great bar too, fantastic!'

8:41. The street was quiet, the restaurants full.

I began walking.

They would expect me there, at 1330 West Riverside Way, sometime before midnight, not later. But they might also expect me to hesitate, as I grew close, even to change my mind. They might, then, have people out here in the streets, in the rendezvous zone, to trap me, cut me off, if in point of fact I decided to turn and go back the way I had come. So I took in the environment as I walked. In the cab I would have had no chance of going back, if Albert Miguel Yglesias had dropped me anywhere in the 1300 block. Approaching on foot, I would have a chance.

Step after step, observe.

A late signal going in, perhaps: *Attempted to phone the executive between 20:05 and 20:40 hours but received no answer.*

The evening air sticky on the face: the noon temperature had been ninety-three degrees and the hygrometer touching seventy-five. Under my clothes I was shivering again – it came in spasms, triggered by each new onset of nerves. Do you know what I felt like on this warm Miami evening? I felt like a man on his way to be hanged.

Attempted to have a visit made to the executive at 20:45. There was no answer to the knock. Forced entry revealed the room empty, no sign of disturbance, no message left.

People window shopping. The sidewalks were wide here and observation was easy because of so many reflecting glass surfaces and the lack of shadow. He was a white Caucasian, thirty, medium build, a slow walk with a certain degree of strut.

So what decided you, Ferris would ask me, to leave the hotel without notifying the support?

But I wouldn't be seeing Ferris again.

The sky bore down across the tops of the tall buildings, its weight buckling them, bearing down through the thick and steamy air to press on my head, to crush me, while the street's perspective widened, bellying out like a scene through a fish-eye lens, but then I suppose it had been a long day and the bullets had come very close and there's always, you know, a shift in the state of consciousness when you're still walking about, still doing ordinary things, when by a small margin you have just missed being carried to the ice cold slab and filled with formaldehyde. I was feeling the reaction, that was all.

Not feeling reaction.

The voice of panic, vigorously to be ignored.

He was very close now and I moved to the left along the sidewalk and picked him up again in the window standing at an angle in a shop entrance way.

I hadn't seen him before, on the quay or anywhere in the street.

On my way, yes, to be hanged, in other words following a course that would take me to an imminent death, a course from which there was no possible deviation. A feeling of inexorability, of karma being fulfilled. It didn't take away fear, terror, but it took away responsibility.

These were my instructions, to make the rendezvous.

Your instructions come only from the Bureau.

But things have changed.

I swung round very fast and he almost walked into me, had to jump sideways, his eyes round, surprised.

'Are you okay?'

The way, I suppose, the way, I am certain, actually, I was looking at him.

'No.' That is what I said to him, and I heard it. I was not okay, and things had gone terribly wrong.

'You need some help?'

But he was already eager to go, not wanting contact, involvement, with this cokehead, this junkie. He was, you understand, no more like an opposition agent of any kind than Mickey Mouse, and it had just happened that we'd been moving at about the same speed along the street. It happens all the time.

'No.'

No help.

But he'd already gone, and I stood there with my head bared to the overwhelming weight of the sky and knew that I couldn't in fact shrug off *all* responsibility, because that would indeed lead to the mortuary and the formaldehyde, but oh my God you can have no idea how far it was to the telephone at the end of the block, how many desperate encounters were played out as the insubstantial figures leapt from nowhere and from everywhere, how many times they came for me, squealing for my blood as they dragged me to the hangman, the stink of fish sickening to the stomach, his madman's inane grin, *go for the single chicks, they're cheaper*, lurching on my nerveless legs to the end, all the way to the end of the block with oysters *this* big as the sky crashed at last across the roaring chasm of the street and I reached the phone-box, smashing away the flimsy aluminium panel with my shoulder to break the momentum, digging for a quarter and forcing it into the slot, a pale girl with pimples staring for a little time before she hurried past, so that I buried myself against the phone-booth, into it, in it, my back to the street and the people, hunched like a pariah dog, like a leper –

'Yes?'

Ferris.

1330 West Riverside Way. At any time before midnight. Not later than that.

'Yes?'

Those are your instructions.

Of course. Put the phone down, make the rendezvous. Of course. Without question.

'Who is that? I am listening.'

I tell you I had to use *physical force* to keep the phone pressed to my head while the other force did everything it could to pull it away and slam it across the hooks. I remember that very clearly.

'I need – ' the breath blocking in my throat.

'Yes? You need?'

Force countering force while I waited in limbo for the outcome, the sweat drenching my body as the street reeled, roared, swept over me.

'I need to debrief.'

Clinging to the broken booth like a drowning man

to a raft. '*1200 block and Riverside Way. West River-side Way. Hurry. For God's sake hurry.*'

7

DEBRIEFING

Four men.

The clock – a jade clock in a gilt frame, standing on the desk – showed 11:56. A little before midnight. 1330 West Riverside Way, not later than midnight, so forth. No longer important.

One of the men was Ferris.

It was a big room, ornate, in a way. Dark heavy furniture, velvet curtains, a pile carpet, all very substantial, reassuring. I felt reassured. I felt as if – let's get it absolutely straight – I didn't just *feel* as if. I *had*, in fact, come through something and reached the other side, and the other side was here, the here and now, the true reality. But dear God it had left me weak, punch-drunk.

Greenspan was another of them. He was the only one standing up.

'Did you pee in the jar?' he asked me.

Ferris was in one of the deep leather chairs, a thin leg draped over one of its arms.

'What? Yes.'

'Great.'

'And what is so fucking great,' I asked him, 'about peeing in a jar?'

He watched me quietly. No one spoke. It had helped, a little, the rush of anger, but had left me exhausted again. In a moment I said, 'I'm sorry.'

'No problem,' Greenspan said. 'What is so great about it is that you remember doing it. And we took a little blood, right?' The Chaplinesque eyebrows lifting.

'Yes.' Needle in the arm, out there in the hall, I think.

'Very good. Your memory's fine.'

'My *memory*?'

'You bet.'

'Why shouldn't it be fine, for Christ's sake?'

'Well I guess – ' a shrug, a glance across Ferris – 'you've kind of had a busy day.' A hand on my shoulder, 'Feel okay now?'

'I have never,' I told him carefully, 'felt better in my life.'

'Well I can take a hint,' Greenspan said brightly. 'You don't need me around here any more.'

He fetched his bag from the desk, leaning across Ferris for a moment, saying something; then he slapped my arm with an excessive amount of good cheer and left us. It occurred to me that I wasn't quite straightened out yet, too aggressive, too defensive; but then he was damned right – it had been a busy day.

I shut my eyes for a while, less than a minute, and the firework show died down behind the lids and left mostly black. Then I opened them and saw Ferris watching me.

'What's this place?'

'A safe-house,' he said.

I looked around the room again. Big geographical globe, a glassed-in case of ivory elephants, massive tomes on dark mahogany shelves, *Existential*

Psychotherapy, Noyes' Modern Clinical Psychiatry.

'It's a what?' I got up and looked at the shelves, at some of the other titles. 'Is this a psychiatrist's office?'

'Yes,' Ferris said. 'It's also a safe-house. That's why we're here.'

I had an urge to walk out and slam the door but a certain degree of reason stopped me. A Bureau safe-house can be anything and anywhere – there's one in the basement of the British Consulate in Marseilles and there's one in Madame Labhouet's bordello in Abidjan on the Ivory coast and there's one in the Horacio Escobar Clinic for Enteric Diseases in downtown Santiago – so a psychiatrist's office in Miami, Florida, wasn't untypical.

Jade clock: midnight, the gilt hands together at the top of the dial in a prayer of thanksgiving. Rendezvous aborted.

It is also a sacrosanct rule that once the opposition has made contact with the executive in the opening phase of a mission he is *not* to approach his director in the field at that director's base, since it risks exposing him. The DIF can only function from an ivory tower, controlling the shadow from a distance and keeping clear of the action. Directors in the field, by their nature, amass an infinite store of intelligence data every time they go out, and their value to the organisation is beyond the price of pearls. Most retire after sixty and take up golf; most shadow executives are dead before thirty-five, or if not, uninsurable.

So it was entirely reasonable that Ferris had ordered me brought here from the 1200 block on West Riverside Way for debriefing. Entirely reasonable.

'What's his name?' I came away from the bookshelves and dropped into the armchair again, a dead weight.

'Whose?'

'The shrink's.'

'Dr Xavier Joachim Alvarez.'

'Are you going to have him check me out?'

'Only if you ask.'

The quietness came back into the room. Everyone seemed to be listening. 'I'm in first-class condition.' Said it straight to Ferris, carrying the weight of it in my eyes, the shadow executive formally reporting to his DIF that he was able to take on any kind of action if the need arose. 'He didn't put anything in, did he?'

Ferris turned his head a fraction, and I realised I was tending to talk in ellipses, my thoughts jumping ahead. 'Again?' he said.

'Greenspan. I mean he only took some blood, is that right? He didn't give me any dope. Sedative or anything.'

Quietly, 'Would you like a sedative?'

'No. What the hell for?' *Be warned*: this was the second time it had happened. A minute ago I'd thought they were going to have me checked out by the shrink but it'd only been in my mind, not theirs – *Only if you ask*. And now it had been in my mind that they might have wanted to sedate me and I'd been wrong, dangerously wrong, putting ideas into their heads. *Did I really want a shrink, sedation, but didn't have the guts to ask for them?*

Paranoia. Relax. I was much better now, less scared about what was happening to me. It was going to be all right.

'What is he going to test me for?'

'Drugs.' Ferris watched me steadily. There was a

chandelier over the desk and that was where I was facing.

'Can we have that thing out? Bloody bright. What sort of drugs?'

Ferris turned his head and one of the other people got out of his chair and went to the wall switch. 'Oh,' Ferris said, 'any sort, really. We'll come to that.'

He looked less cold now in the softer light from the wall lamps, less hostile. So we will come to that, will we? Meant, I suppose, that I'd been behaving a bit oddly of late. Damn his eyes, I'd nearly got my head shot off, enough to shake anyone up.

The man sat down again and I said to Ferris, 'Who are these people?'

'Upjohn,' he said, turning his head again. 'And Purdom.'

'I need to know more than that.' Said it with an edge. The director in the field calls the shots at every phase of the mission but he is also there to succour, support and sustain the executive, who may indeed look like a snotty-nosed little ferret down in the catacombs but who is nevertheless the *only* man who can bring the mission home, and when I'm brought into a room to debrief and there are total strangers hanging around I want to know who they bloody well are, if you'll be so kind.

'Upjohn,' Ferris said, 'is a sleeper here. He knew Proctor, though not well. It's possible that he can help us find him, if he listens to the debriefing. Unless you object.'

A small man, Upjohn, with a spotty skin and a slanting eye and a pucker in the face for a mouth, terrible haircut, stuck up like bristles, the kind who can surprise you, former lieutenant-colonel in the special services or something like that.

'I don't object,' I said.

'Thank you. Purdom,' Ferris said evenly, 'is here from London to get experience in the field.'

I jerked my head to look at the man, saw red suddenly – 'Experience in the *what*? You were in China, weren't you, on *Pagoda*? You did *Mirage*, didn't you, for that bastard Loman in Morocco? Jesus Christ, what sort of *experience* – '

Watch it.

It mustn't happen a third time. This was the *last* thought I wanted to put into their heads – that I couldn't keep my control.

Silence opening like a grave.

Then Ferris said gently, 'Experience in the United States. He hasn't worked here.'

Of course. Entirely reasonable. But the thought was still there, chilling the nerves. I'd heard of Purdom, seen him in the Caff now and then, seen his name on some of the boards, certainly the board for *Pagoda* and the one for *Mirage* and possibly others: he was one of the high-echelon shadows and *no one* had sent him out here from London just to 'get experience'.

Looking at the wall, not at me, the wall or the door or whatever was there behind me, a dark man, big-boned, his body hunched in the chair, thick hands folded and his legs crossed, almost twisted together, a quietly-ticking bomb with some clothes round it and some hair on top, an exaggeration, of course, but you get the picture – it was his nerves I was picking up on, his held-in energy. I watched him for a moment, taking him in, not wanting to look at Ferris because if I looked at Ferris I was liable to put it straight into words, get it over with.

Is Purdom out here to replace me?

Someone was speaking, his voice very soft, reaching me as if from a distance. It was Ferris. 'You're among friends, Quiller.'

He didn't know what he was saying because he hadn't been there in London when that bastard Loman had said *exactly* the same thing: You're among friends.

Friends? Loman had flinched. It was the time when they were trying to get me to think twice about resigning because they'd put that bloody bomb under the driving seat of that truck in Murmansk, deciding that I was expendable. *I still couldn't trust these people.*

Not even Ferris?

'Am I?' Among friends.

'But of course.' His voice still gentle as he watched me with his pale honey-coloured eyes. I'd have to think, you know, think a little more carefully, because this man had saved my skin so many times – Berlin, Hong Kong, Murmansk – where other people would have left me to rot in the red sector and vouchsafed their sleep with a lie. *Communications compromised, opposition in control, executive unreachable..*

Trust, then, perhaps, this one man among them all. Because, in any case, if you can't trust your own director in the field you're dead. I'd proved that in *Northlight*: I hadn't been able to trust Fane and I'd come close to getting blown into Christendom in that truck.

'All right,' I said, heard myself saying, meaning all right, I was ready to believe I was among friends. 'I'm a bit tired, that's all.'

'Of course.' His voice still gentle. 'And there's a bit of delayed shock hanging around, according to Greenspan.'

'Possibly.'

'So you might not feel quite ready for debriefing.' Paused, giving me a chance to say no, not quite ready. I said nothing. 'But if you're willing, we could make some progress. London's a tiny bit fidgety.'

'Why?'

In a moment, 'First Proctor was missing. Then you.'

I sank into the chair, letting the muscles go, trying to centre. It wasn't going to be easy. 'You sent signals?'

'I had to. I didn't know where you were.'

'It was only for a short – ' and left it. I didn't remember how long it had been, didn't want to.

'I need to know,' Ferris said, 'why you left the hotel covertly.'

'I wanted to walk for a bit, without a whole troop of people around me. You know I hate support.'

The other two were looking at me now; I'd noticed their heads turn, the light catching their eyes. They shouldn't watch me. It made me nervous. Ferris ought to tell them not to watch me. He was unzipping a flat pigskin briefcase and getting a book out, a ballpoint from his pocket, opening the book.

He asked me: 'To walk where?'

'Oh, just around, for the exercise.'

1330 West Riverside –

'You were shot at,' Ferris said, 'and were therefore revealed as a target for the opposition, whose intention it was to kill. Having been recognised, then, and set up as that target, you obviously realised that this town has become a red sector for you.' A beat. 'Yet you went for a walk in the open street, "for the exercise".'

I got out of the chair and turned my back on him because it was the only way I could talk to him without letting him see my eyes. 'Is this a debriefing,

94

for Christ's sake, or an inquisition?' Wheeled on him, anger in the eyes now and I wanted him to see it. 'You don't consider that the executive hand-picked by Bureau One himself for this mission isn't capable of deciding whether he can safely walk in the bloody streets or not?' Folded my arms, wrong posture because defensive but too late to change it, not *one* of these bastards looking at me, all looking down or into the middle distance, embarrassed perhaps because my voice was hitting back from the glass panels of the display case and the lacquered Chinese screen in short-range echoes, shouting, you might call it, you might call it that. 'I'd been cooped up in that stinking hotel for hours on end and I was still full of adrenaline from the lark on the quay and I wanted some *exercise*, yes, and I didn't want half a regiment keeping me under mobile surveillance because it could have attracted attention.' Tried to keep my voice under control, failed. 'I think that makes sense but if you think I'm out of my mind then you'd better send for your bloody shrink.'

Watching me now, Ferris was watching me.

'Why don't you come and sit down? You'll feel more comfortable.' Turning his head to the man on his left, Johnson, no, Upjohn, saying quietly, 'See if he'd mind joining us for a few minutes.'

The man got up and went out through the door behind him, not the one I'd come in by, leading to the hall, the other one. I looked down at Ferris. He was making notes in the debriefing book.

I said: '*The shrink?*'

'Yes,' Went on writing.

A quietness on me suddenly, the anger fading. 'You said you weren't going to send for him.'

He looked up. 'Only if you asked. I think you just did that.'

I turned away, moved about. He was perfectly right. *Then you'd better send for your bloody shrink.* It had come right out of the subconscious because I knew I needed help and I'd been frightened to ask for it in so many words. I could have gone on lying, trying to protect my ego, but I didn't, because we'd got a mission running and something had gone terribly wrong and I had to face it, deal with it somehow. Listen, if nothing else I am a professional, for God's sake give me that.

'Can I have a drink?'

The thirst still burning.

'But of course.'

Ferris got up and went over to the table by the couch, where there was a decanter and a glass. I suppose that was what it was, the classical psychiatrist's couch; I'd only ever seen them in cartoons. If he asked me to lie down on it I would twist his head off at the neck and – *steady, lad*, you need this man, you need him.

'Thank you.' Glass of water. He looked at me, Ferris, with his pale amber eyes, concerned that I should understand, if I read them right. 'All is well, my dear fellow. There will be no misdirection.'

A word normally used in the context of a courtroom, but within the Bureau the connotation is different: a director in the field will sometimes, if he's incompetent or devious, misdirect his executive, and if things are running close it can be fatal.

'I'm Dr Alvarez.'

A short man in striped pyjamas and a dressing-gown, dark eyes not smiling, serious. Taking me in, evaluating me, reaching for my hand.

'This is Keyes,' Ferris told him.

'Good, yes,' not taking his eyes off my face, 'why don't we all sit down? You have some water. Would you prefer a glass of wine, some whisky?'

'This is fine.'

'You're thirsty?'

'Dry mouth.'

'Of course. You had a nasty experience, I'm told. Do you mind if I sit behind the desk? I'm not trying to look authoritative, you must understand, it's just that I can think better there – it's my *querencia*. You are not sleepy?'

'No.'

'It would be understandable, if you were – it's late.' He swung his legs onto the desk, tilting the leather-padded chair back, folding his strong square hands, watching me for a bit longer and then turning his head to Ferris. 'Well now.'

'What I'd like to do,' Ferris said, looking at me, 'is to go through a routine debriefing, and if you find any trouble with it, Dr Alvarez will make things easier. You should know that he's on the Bureau's overseas roster and provides us with this safe-house in emergencies. His clearance status is Prefix 1.' Meant totally reliable, even that being an understatement. I could therefore, Ferris meant, go through a debriefing in depth with nothing barred.

I took a slow breath. It still frightened me, the memory of what my mind had been doing in the time period following the quay thing, and the debriefing wouldn't be easy, even with Alvarez here.

Ferris glanced at him now, and I think Alvarez nodded, only the slightest movement of his head. Then Ferris looked back at me.

'All right, I'm going to ask you again. Why did you leave that hotel covertly?'

It went on echoing in my mind, *covertly* . . . *covertly* . . . and I realised that something was happening to me, something I couldn't control. But my

97

voice sounded all right, a fraction terse, that was all.

'I didn't go there. Isn't that the important thing?'

Ferris watching me. 'Didn't go where?'

And then the whole thing blew up and I was on my feet and standing over Ferris shouting at him – '*I can't tell you –* ' the other two men suddenly on their feet as well and moving towards me very fast – '*I can't tell you, for Christ's sake, don't you understand?*'

8

SACRIFICE

Her breast brushed against me, her skin copper-
coloured in the subdued light, a powdering of dried
salt on her shoulder.

There's a special one out there somewhere.

That you want to catch?

That I want to kill.

Green eyes alighting softly on mine, the eyes of
a mermaid, of a succuba.

*You will go to 1330 West Riverside Way, at any
time before midnight.*

Flash, flash from the field glasses across the water.

Not later than that.

Her skin bronzed, the down silken above her
breasts, the light flashing, flashing on the cylinder
of the syringe.

'Can we use your phone?'

Watchful amber eyes, the tick of the jade clock.

'But please.'

The sea had calmed. There was no movement
now.

'Get them onto it straight away.'

A man, one of the men, Johnson, no, Upjohn,
blotting a wall-lamp out as he passed across my line
of vision. The faint beeping of the push-buttons.

'Make a note. 1330 West Riverside Way.'

A shadow across my eyes, then its substance, Alvarez.

'Well now. How do you feel?' His dark face with its black silk beard, his gaze intent. 'How do you feel now?'

'All right.'

'Good!' He rolled my sleeve down.

'What was in it?' The syringe on the tray.

'Valium.' He took the tray away.

'We want you to check out that address.' Upjohn, phoning.

'Utmost caution,' Ferris said.

1:20 on the dial of the jade clock. An hour and twenty minutes' time gap. *I can't tell you, for Christ's sake, don't you understand?* The last thing I remembered.

'Use utmost caution,' Upjohn said into the phone.

It's an esoteric Bureau term reserved strictly for when, for instance, you're defusing a motion-detonator bomb.

I looked at Ferris, but he was at right angles. Everything was. They'd put me on that *bloody* couch.

'Ferris.' I got onto my elbows and swung my legs down. No shoes.

'Hello,' he said.

'*Did I tell you?*'

'Yes.'

'The address?'

'Yes. But tell me again, just to confirm.'

Silence, and time going by.

'Where are my bloody shoes?'

'Tell me again,' he said gently.

'Oh, for Christ's sake. 1330 West Riverside Way. Now where are they?'

100

Somebody fumbling around with my feet.

'Take,' I heard Upjohn saying, 'as many people as you need.'

Alvarez, pushing my feet into my shoes. 'I can do that,' I told him.

'Did you hear that, Doc?' Ferris was asking.

'Oh, yes. We are ourselves again!' Sounded terribly pleased.

Ferris said to Upjohn, 'Strictly observation. No entry, no contact.'

'I can tie my own laces,' I told Alvarez. 'Listen, how did you get that needle into me? I don't like needles.'

'Report directly to me,' Ferris said. He was making notes on the debriefing pad the whole time.

'You lost consciousness. We had to catch you.'

'*Before* you put that thing in?'

'Yes. The stress had become overwhelming. You didn't want to answer his question, do you remember?'

'Report directly to the DIF,' Upjohn was saying.

'I don't know. I don't know what I remember.'

'I think you do. It's a little alarming to you, that's all. But there's no more block.'

'Block?'

'Psychotraumatic inhibition. You'll feel better now. It's all behind you.' Small pearly teeth showed in the black beard.

Behind me? That'd be a relief. That would be, dear God, a relief. 'Can I have some water?'

'Round the clock?' Upjohn was asking.

'Yes,' Ferris told him, then looked at me. 'When you phoned for us to bring you in, you sounded in a bad way. What had happened?'

It was like thinking back through a veil, having to reach for the past. 'Nothing.'

'But you sounded dead beat.' Amber eyes watching me.

'Thank you.' I drank the whole tumbler straight off. It tasted odd.

'Did I? It tastes a bit odd,' I told Alvarez.

'Everything will, for a little while. Your body chemistry has to adjust. There was a great deal of adrenaline in the system, and then there was the Valium. I'm so pleased,' he said, 'to see you in such good shape.'

'Thank you.' I got off the couch and found a chair and dropped into it. Purdom, the top-echelon shadow, got up and went across to the decanter and filled my glass again, which I thought was nice of him. 'Yes,' I told Ferris, 'I was dead beat, that's absolutely right. I was fighting something off.'

'And you won.' Alvarez, at the desk again, his feet on it. 'But it left your reserves critically depleted.'

Ferris asked: 'Fighting what off?'

It meant going back, and it frightened me. I had never known such a force applied against me, such *dominance*. 'I – I'd been told to go there, and I knew I shouldn't. But I had to. Kind of – compulsion.'

Upjohn came back from the phone and couldn't find a chair; I think I was sitting in it now. 'You did well,' Alvarez said, still pleased. 'Others would not have resisted.'

'You've no idea how *strong* it was. The compulsion.'

'Oh, but I have. It was so strong that your resistance left you "dead beat", to the point where you couldn't resist any further. When you were asked why you left the hotel covertly, you lost consciousness rather than explain.' The intercom on his desk began ringing. 'It was a remarkable manifestation.'

He picked up the phone. '*Sí, mi querida?*'

Ferris got up and dragged the carved oak chair closer to mine and sat down again with his pad. 'You also said, when you were coming out from under, *Those are your instructions*. Do you remember that?'

'*Todavía no. Es una emergencia.*'

'Yes. I was following instructions.'

'Don't worry,' Ferris said.

I'd started shaking, hadn't thought it showed. More water.

'*Date vuelta y duermete, mi querida.*'

Alvarez put the phone down. Ferris asked me quietly:

'Where did they come from? The instructions'

'*I don't know, damn you, I don't know.*'

They all brought their heads up. It had sounded very loud. Alvarez hadn't moved. Perhaps I'd woken his wife, upstairs, shouting like this: he'd just told her on the phone it was an emergency case. *I had to get control.*

Alvarez said to Ferris, 'He really doesn't know, you must understand. It's very frustrating for him.'

Ferris was watching me. 'Don't worry. Take your time.'

'We haven't *got* any time.'

The mission had been running only forty-eight hours and Proctor had gone to ground and the opposition had put the executive into the cross-hairs and *got right inside his mind* and left instructions there and I'd come appallingly close to walking straight into a trap. There wasn't a chance to –

Run that through again.

'Ferris,' I said, 'there's something that doesn't match. They wouldn't go for me with a hit and get inside my head with subliminal instructions at the same time.' Ferris was making notes. 'They wouldn't have told me to go to that address if they didn't mean it. They'd set it up as a trap, and I couldn't walk into it if I'd been shot dead first.'

Upjohn said, 'Unless you were given the instructions after they'd failed with the hit.'

'What? No, I was given them before we were back in harbour. Before the shooting.'

Ferris asked quickly – 'How do you know *when*?'

'Because of her breasts.' Straight from the subconscious.

He tilted his head. 'Say again?'

Alvarez was leaning forward now.

'When I was coming to, I had visual impressions of the girl on the boat, Harvester. But I don't – '

'There was a voice,' Alvarez said, 'overlying the visual impressions?'

Feeling of panic suddenly. I reached for the glass and drank, hand not quite steady, did they notice? 'Yes, the voice was in the background. She was talking, too, but in the foreground.'

Panic because it had just occurred to me that *there could be other instructions still inside my head*, like a worm in an apple.

'There was music?' Alvarez. 'A radio playing?'

'No.'

Purdom looked across at him. 'It could be radionic. Remote beamed.'

'At what distance?' I asked him.

'I'm not too conversant.'

'I'll talk to Parks,' Ferris said. He was the electronics man who'd checked Proctor's flat for bugs.

'There was a launch,' I said, and told him about the field glasses. 'It followed us into harbour.'

'Noted. But this inconsistency – they *wouldn't*

have put those instructions into your head and *then* put you under that gun.'

Upjohn said, 'Be unwise to assume it was the same cell. I mean the whole thing's open, isn't it? The drug scene's very big here – eighty per cent of the cocaine used in the States comes in from Cuba, a lot of it by sea. The Harvester girl could be running stuff herself or for one of the cartels. They might've thought you were an undercover man for the Coast Guard or something, bang bang. Happens all the time.'

'Do you think she's in drugs?' Ferris.

'Christ,' I said, 'I wouldn't know. If – '

'She's American?'

'English.'

He turned the top sheet of his pad over and said, 'All right, can you take a debriefing on Harvester?'

'Yes.'

It took forty minutes, because there was a lot of material: her relationship with Proctor and her present feelings about him – *he's trash* – and the phone call she'd overheard and everything we'd said on the boat and of course the points Ferris picked on:

'Did she try seduction?'

'No.'

'But you mentioned her breasts.'

'She was in a bikini and bra.'

'There would have been,' Alvarez said, 'a certain amount of dream content surfacing when you were coming to. We tend to undress women in our sleep.'

Ferris thanked him and turned back to me.

'The launch,' he said. 'Did you think she knew what it was doing there?'

I got out of the chair, weakness in the legs, getting

up quickly to make it look all right, but Ferris caught it.

'When did you last eat, Quiller?'

'Lunch. On the boat.'

'Protein, then,' Alvarez said at once and came out from behind his desk. 'You need some protein. Cheese, yes? Would some mozzarella appeal?'

Debriefing went on.

'The field glasses. You say she noticed them.'

'This is complicated.' I thought it through and then said, 'One scenario is this: I noticed them and of course said nothing. She saw them, innocently, and called attention to them, a bit annoyed. Or: she noticed I'd seen them and called them to my attention to clear herself in case I thought she'd seen them and wasn't saying anything because she knew all about them. Knew all about the launch.'

'Did she make anything of the fact that the launch followed you in?'

'No.'

'Do you think she saw that it had followed you in?'

'I was watching for that but I can't be certain. I was tying up the boat.'

'We've got photographs of her, of course. I had a man with a zoom on the quay.'

'When did you put her under surveillance?'

'Before you got there.'

'You're keeping her under surveillance?'

'But of course.' His amber eyes on me. 'I know it hasn't escaped you that she might have set you up for that hit, on Proctor's orders.' In a moment, 'Does that trouble you?'

'No.' But I said it too quickly and he caught it. He can catch flies in flight.

'Perhaps a little.' Making a note. 'She's not unattractive, and you've got some sympathy for her because of what happened to her father.'

'Are you putting down what I think or what you think?' Tone with an edge. I was leaning with my back to the bookshelves, wanting to move about, restless, not able to because of the weakness, not wanting to sit down because I was being put on the defensive – debriefing always has that element in it because you're asked to give reasons for things you said and things you did, to justify every move you made and take responsibility for every signal, every strike, every mistake, and what makes it difficult is that you said those things and did those things in hot blood with the dark coming down and nothing between you and the unmarked grave but a random blow or a desperate last-ditch run that in the cold light of enquiry are seen as ill-advised and potentially hazardous for the mission: the one sin above all others.

Debriefing can leave the spirit naked, and sometimes we rebel. *Are you putting down what I think or what you think?*

He didn't answer, and with good cause. As the director in the field he had the right, the sacrosanct *obligation*, to record events as he saw fit, because when the executive's back is to the wall he'll say anything to protect himself.

Some morose and mission-weary shadow with a penchant for statistics has worked it out, slumped over a tea-stained table in the Caff with his busy abacus, that in the first three phases of a mission the executive in the field has been pulled out and replaced on four occasions out of ten because his debriefing proved that he couldn't handle the demands on him, couldn't control the field, couldn't proceed without increasing the risk of blowing his own operation or half the Bureau's ultra-classified files. And whoever they are we forget their names because it scares us to remember them.

'When you asked her for a diving lesson, did she get you to sign a waiver in case of accident?'

'What? Yes.'

'What address did you give?'

'The hotel. The first one.'

'She phoned you there.'

'When?'

'Twenty-three minutes after the shots were fired.'

'What did she say?'

'She left a message, asking you to phone her back. She sounded – ' he checked his pad – 'agitated.'

'Then she must have seen me pushed into the cab.'

'Not necessarily. She could simply be living in the hope that you'd got clear in some way.'

'No one,' Upjohn said, 'saw him getting into the cab. I was there.'

'Her number?' This was Purdom.

'You'll get all that,' Ferris told him, 'if there's anything you can do.'

Purdom shut up again. I wished he wouldn't just sit in that bloody chair and brood. I could feel vibrations coming out of him that jarred the nerves and I tried the whole time to ignore the man because the truth couldn't be faced: he could have been called out here to replace me the minute the debriefing was over, and he'd seen what the opposition had already done to the shadow in the field, and didn't like it.

What would I do, then, if London sent instructions to pull me out of *Barracuda*?

Go to ground.

Vanish and work from the dark, from the silence

of the catacombs. A pox on them.

There is nothing worse, my friend, for the executive in the field than to be replaced, to be sent home crippled with his inadequacies, bringing nothing with him but the news of a lost cause and leaving behind him nothing but his bloodied tracks. Nothing worse, you understand, than professional ignominy, the irretrievable loss of face.

Correction, yes. There would be, at this phase of this particular mission, one thing worse.

'You said – ' Ferris – 'that Harvester repeated word for word a political diatribe you'd heard before, from Proctor.'

'Yes.'

I noticed Alvarez shift in his chair.

Ferris said quietly, 'How could you remember it *word for word*?'

'I – ' and left it. I didn't know.

'Could you repeat it now – ' Alvarez – 'word for word?'

'Yes.' Beginning to sweat because I remembered how Kim Harvester had looked when she'd gone through the same material on board the tug, stabbing at the peach stone with the knife, withdrawn, robotic.

Ferris looked at Upjohn. 'Tape?'

'Sure.' He got the recorder and waited with his finger on the button.

'When you're ready,' Ferris said.

It was frightening because I went straight into it without any hesitation, bringing it out at a measured pace, *He's a statesman with a world view that we haven't seen since Nixon* . . . half his face in shadow beside the brass hanging lamp . . . *very much hope the Thatcher government realises what we've got in Mathieson Judd* . . . the first stirring of the wind as the eye of the storm began moving across the town . . . *his understanding of the internecine struggle for power inside the Kremlin* . . . my voice distant-seeming, the words unnaturally paced, until it was finished and the voice stopped, and I looked up to see Alvarez watching me, leaning forward, intent.

'Finished?' Ferris.

'Yes.' The skin crawling.

Upjohn shut down the recorder. No one spoke so I said, 'What did I look like?'

Short silence and then Upjohn said, 'Bit switched off.'

'You were in an altered state of consciousness,' Alvarez said, 'somewhere between alpha and theta waves.'

I got the decanter and emptied it into the glass, only half full, took it at a gulp while Upjohn asked Alvarez where the tap was. 'That was where I picked it up,' I told Ferris. 'I got visuals with it.'

'Proctor.'

'Yes. But I mean it wasn't just that he'd told me that stuff viva voce. I wouldn't have remembered it word for word. I was picking it up from the background.'

'Just as he had, before.'

'Yes. The same subliminal source.'

'Again,' Alvarez asked, 'was there music playing?'

'No. Nothing in the background.'

Ferris was making notes. 'Is that all you've got in your mind about Mathieson Judd?'

'Yes.' Poured some more water and drank it.

'You don't know anything about the elections?'

'No.'

'You haven't followed the news.'

'Christ,' I said, 'I haven't had much time to read the papers.'

110

'So you have no ideas,' Alvarez said, 'about Senator Judd's chief competitor, Governor Anderson?'

'No.' The water was cool, and I savoured it. 'Except of course that he's trying to tell the voters that there's so much wrong with America after the Republican four-year term that the country needs taking apart and rebuilding,' the water cool in a dry mouth, a quietness in the room as deep as the quietness that snow brings, 'whereas Judd's theme is reassuring – the country's in good shape and all we need to do is consolidate the gains that have been made under the present administration,' the glass making a small musical sound when I put it back on the silver tray, the quietness settling.

'Go on,' someone said gently.

'So it's not a question of whether each argument is right or wrong, but a question of which message is the more likely to appeal to the nation. Obviously, Senator Judd's.'

And then after a long time I couldn't hear my voice any more and I saw Ferris leaning across the desk talking to the psychiatrist and Purdom watching me from his chair and Upjohn switching off the recorder. I'd been walking about, I think, and now I sat down.

Ferris was facing me suddenly. 'Do you know how long you spoke for?'

'No.'

'Nineteen minutes, with no interruption.'

I felt drained, emptied of something. Looking up at Ferris, not wanting to believe it. 'That bad?'

'Do you know what you were talking about?'

'Yes. Anderson's campaign theme. And Judd's.'

'There's nothing buried,' Alvarez said, 'you must understand. The material is quite near the surface, an integral part of the conscious, even though it was

111

ingested subliminally, by the subconscious.'

Ferris sat down again and got his pad. Off-hand-edly, not looking at me, 'Have you any more instructions?'

The nerves sent a tremor through the organism. In a moment, 'What instructions?'

Still not looking at me, busy writing, 'I mean is there anywhere you've got to go, anything you've got to do? It's only a thought, you don't need to worry about it.'

Time going by, while the skin chilled under the sweat and their faces watched me, not with their eyes, with their heads turned, listening.

Instructions.

After a long time, 'No. I don't think so. I don't know.' And then I was on my feet suddenly and looking down at Alvarez. *'How much stuff have I got in there, for God's sake? How much more?'*

He said: 'We may never know.'

03:14.

Ferris made a final note on the debriefing pad and put it into his briefcase and looked at Alvarez. 'May I use the phone, Doctor?'

'By all means.'

'I need to call London.'

'I understand. The switch is just under the desk here.' At the door he said, 'I shan't be far away, if you need me.'

Did he expect me to go berserk or something?

Control, yes. *Mea culpa.*

Ferris went behind the carved redwood desk and picked up the phone and sat with it, elbows on the big green blotter, his eyes nowhere, thinking. Then he dialled.

I got up again, not wanting to go on sitting there

waiting, moved about a little, took another look at those bloody elephants, God what a waste of a good tusk.

We may never know.

Like an echo in the mind. How big, then, was the worm in the apple, how healthy, how vigorous? As big as a snake? As a dragon?

'Miami,' Ferris said. 'Get me Board 3.'

Board 3 was for *Barracuda*.

8:15 in the fair city of Londinium, with the double-deckers jamming Piccadilly Circus and the taxis dodging through the gaps, their black tops bright with rain.

'Yes, good morning. I'm switching to scramble.'

I have no wish, not the slightest wish, to go to London, whatever they say, whatever they decide.

Purdom moved now, got out of his chair. He was like me, couldn't just sit still nursing his nerves. If you were to ask me for whom the bell tolled, I would tell you that it tolled for him too.

'Is Mr Shepley there?'

He would make a good psychiatrist, this man Ferris, looks the part, thin, ascetic, totally calm, though perhaps he is a shade too cold-blooded, and of course might even find it not abnormal for a patient lying there on that bloody couch to explain that his problem was that he couldn't stop strangling mice.

'Yes, sir. There's been an unexpected development, and I've asked Monck to fly in from Nassau. He'll be here in twenty minutes. I haven't worked with him before, and I need to know whether he qualifies for major Classified One decision-making.'

Purdom was standing by the bookshelves looking at the titles, if that's what you want to believe. I suppose I hated him in an infantile way, because there was nothing in his square balanced-looking head, I mean nothing coiled there, no worm.

'Yes, I can give him the whole picture. We've just interim-debriefed the executive.'

Upjohn hadn't budged from his chair. I didn't like him much either, not because of his acne or his broom-head haircut of course; I disliked his detachment, or rather his ability to detach himself from what was going on. I could believe his blood was colder than Ferris's, if there were any in his veins at all.

'All right, sir. Understood. Do I fax the debriefing?'

He said a few other things that weren't important. The important bit was over now, I knew that, but I hadn't heard Shepley's answer to the question. I wasn't looking at Ferris when he put the phone down, had my back to him. I heard him flip the scrambler switch and get out of the chair.

'Monck was in Croder's place,' he said, 'before he left London. He's still on that level, overseas section.' I'd turned round and was facing him. 'Whatever decisions have to be made, he has the power to make them.' Getting his briefcase, looking at his watch. 'I'm meeting him at the airport, cutting it a bit fine. Why don't you catch up on some more sleep at the hotel? It's still secure. Upjohn will take you there.'

Didn't really want an answer: these were orders.

Then everyone was moving about and Ferris called Alvarez back and thanked him for his hospitality and then came with me to the alleyway at the back of the house where there were two cars standing in shadow.

'Try not to give it any more thought,' he told me. 'Just try to sleep. When I've talked to Monck and asked him what we're going to do, I'll contact you, probably in an hour or so.' Got into his car.

'But I like the town, because it's crazy.'

Upjohn drove through the lit streets, knew his way. I sat beside him, like an aristo in a tumbril. Ferris knew what was going to happen already, but couldn't give London the whole picture without faxing it and there wasn't really time even for that. *Barracuda* couldn't go on running without an executive and the only executive it had was a man who might at *any* time break loose and start following instructions he wasn't even aware of at this moment – and instructions that could tell him to blow the whole thing up.

Shivering a little, not unexpected.

'It's got everything, after all. Drug trade, casinos, refugees, the mafia, you name it. Sight more interesting than Streatham.'

I suppose I answered him now and then on the way, but I don't remember clearly. When we got to the hotel he opened the gates at the back and drove the car through and got out to shut them again before I left the car.

'Feel like company? Play some poker?'

I thanked him and said I needed some sleep, and he nodded and stood there in the half-lit yard until I was inside the hotel.

Lying in the dark with my clothes on, watching the reflection of the traffic lights at the corner of the street below, listening to the creak of the plumbing and the thin whistling of the first jet landing as the night drew towards dawn, I looked at this thing in the face and got rid of illusions.

There would be only one thing worse, yes, than being sent back to London and seeing my name gone from the board and the final entry on the form I'd have to sign, *executive recalled from mission*, only one thing worse than losing *Barracuda* and handing over to Purdom, and that would be for them to order me to stay with it and do what I could.

Because the *only* reason for their doing that would be to find out what I would do if they gave me room, where I would go if they set me running again, how they could profit if the worm in the apple went on eating and drove me across hazardous ground, into a red sector, into a trap.

And that would be terrible, to run through these streets not as the shadow for the mission but as a rat in a maze, an experiment, a subject for sacrifice.

That would be their only reason for keeping me in.

Red to green, amber to red, a toilet flushing on the floor above, a jet turning onto the taxying lane with its sound and the echoes fading, red to green and the silence settling in and then the explosive shock of the phone bell jarring the nerves.

I reached for the receiver.

'They're leaving you in,' Ferris said.

My hand clammy on the smooth plastic, the dark room crowding me, a sense of disbelief. I suppose I wanted it spelled out for me, so that there shouldn't be any misunderstanding.

'My name is still on the board for *Barracuda*?'

Someone was whistling, down in the yard, as daybreak came.

'Your name is still on the board for *Barracuda*.'

So help me God.

9

NEWSBREAK

She's petite, strawberry blonde, violet eyes, great cheekbones, very trim. Age thirty-one.

11:03.

Make-up. Highlight the cheekbones, deep eye-shadow, hairspray. She applied her own lipstick. Impatient with her cosmetician, small curt gestures, eyes on the mirror, on her face.

Most people hate her, especially men who have to work for her, under her – the show's director, technicians, those people. She enjoys emasculating them.

The hand of the big clock moved to 11:04 but there was no significance attached to this: she wasn't going out live tonight – this show was to be pre-taped.

I don't know why. She normally goes out live. There was some mess-up, I guess. You may find out when you're there.

I could only see part of her, waist up, through the glass partition. Two of the monitors were blank; the third was showing a Buick ad.

She can use that kind of clout, you see – Chuck Baker, called in by Ferris to brief me on her – *because some people say she's arguably the single*

117

most accurate and important source of information on current events for one-fifth of the American people, through syndication programmes. Okay, other people say that's just hype, but I'd say it's a close guess. The Nielson Media Research figures give 'These Are My Views' twenty-one million households per broadcast.

She threw off the make-up gown and crossed into the studio, moving with care to preserve the fluffed-up, Luster-Gel coiffure. Looked at her hands, set the tourmaline ring facet-uppermost, checked her nails. Other people came in now, two men and three women, some of them technicians with audio-gear, clipboards, papers. One of the men switched on the TelePrompTer and checked the display.

I could see her better now. This was one of the monitor rooms and someone had come in a minute ago and asked where Harry was and I told him I didn't know. I'd got the studio lapel pass from Chuck Baker. *But I guess it's up to you to tell people what you're doing there, if they ask, okay?*

At this hour most of the studio was dark, and the man who'd asked about Harry was the only one I'd seen.

She and Brokaw were called the sexiest anchors in the industry, by a poll conducted last June. TV Guide printed a joint opinion of influential critics that puts her as the first most trustworthy anchor on the screen, in terms of news accuracy and her own deeply considered views. She's strictly non-partisan, and that comes through for her, though at this time of course she's down here from the National Newsbreak network in Washington to pitch for Florida's Senator Judd.

I could hear her voice faintly now through the panel as she began rehearsing. The other people were moving about the whole time now, checking equipment, and one of the monitor screens lit up and began showing her image as a camera started shifting its angles, zooming in on her face, pulling back to head-and-shoulders.

In the last quarter her show cost $80,000 a night and brought in $150,000, giving a profit for the network of more than $4,500 a minute. They pay her a million dollars a year and she's obviously worth it, with all the syndications thrown in.

One of the technicians was taking a quick bite at a sandwich as she worked, and the anchorwoman said without turning her head, 'No food in here, you know the rules. This isn't a goddamned construction site.' A man looked in from the corridor and one of the crew put his thumb up and the man went out again.

'Cameras?'

'I'm ready, Jeff.'

'Where's Harry?'

'He took a day off and forgot to tell anyone.'

'Jesus. Get Phyllis in here.'

'Erica, what's our timing?'

'When I'm ready I'll tell you.'

She's a legend in her time already. She can go into a studio cold turkey and in ten minutes you can start the cameras and she can hit thirty or forty million people with the kind of charm and authority and sheer presence *that hasn't ever been seen before. Offstage she's gotten a reputation for being a real personal bitch, but on-stage she's got a red-light reflex you wouldn't believe. The minute the light goes on, she projects herself right into those twenty-one million households and stops everything right there, and all people can do is watch. You know something? She could stop a family fight, knives, guns, you name it,*

119

without even leaving the studio.

'Bennie.'

'Uh?'

'Cut those lights.'

'Sorry, Erica.'

The backdrop behind the anchor desk was a map of the United States covering the whole flat, with a backlit transparency of downtown Miami by night. One of the on-screen monitors lit up with a still head-and-shoulders shot of Senator Mathieson Judd, smiling and waving.

She is also – and this is pretty rare in the industry – she's also of what they call good family. They came over on the Mayflower *and Jonathan Cambridge II is the founder and president of Marlborough Chemical Bank. She doesn't mix very much in high society – she went through a leftist kick just out of high school and left the ancestral home to live by herself in a sixth-floor cold-water walk-up on Lexington for two years – but the pedigree's there if she needs it. She could walk in to just about anyone's country house and they'd ask her to stay.*

Some people were moving one of the theatrical flats and adjusting the lights. A man was kicking cables clear and using duct tape. Another monitor screen came live with a tight head shot of the woman at the desk and the camera pulled back. The girl who'd been eating the sandwich loaded the Tele-PrompTer and checked it and stood away, not looking at the woman at the desk but just waiting. Others were standing back, one of them twisting a rubber band round and round his fingers. There was no sound now.

'Bennie, is that your stuff hanging there?'

'Yes, I'll – '

'For God's sake put it somewhere else, it's distracting me. Jeff, are we ready?'

'When you are.'

'All right, let's go.'

A flood of light, no movement anywhere until her eyes had reacted to the glare, then her head tilted to look straight up at the TelePrompTer and the red lamp came on at the main camera and she flashed a brief, brilliant smile.

'Good-evening. I'm Erica Cambridge, and these are my views. Yesterday in New Hampshire it looked as if Senator Mathieson Judd was for the first time pandering to the dictates of those on his campaign staff who have been trying to persuade him to "throw in a little healthy theatricality", as Josh Weinberg of *The Post* has put it, to counterbalance the Republican candidate's serious and perhaps solemn approach to the matter in hand. But in my view, ladies and gentlemen, the matter in hand is indeed serious and indeed solemn, nothing less than the task of your goodselves, the people, of choosing the man who will become one of the two – and I say this advisedly – one of the two most powerful statesmen on this planet.'

Pause, a glance to the papers on the desk to give weight to the silence, the violet eyes lifting again. 'And Senator Judd himself knows the seriousness and the solemnity of this occasion, and had more than once declared himself categorically disinterested in cheapening his respect and regard for the electorate. So what happened yesterday in New Hampshire was not rehearsed, was not premeditated. It was real. Some of you were there, I believe. You saw the little boy with the childishly-lettered placard on his chest, reading I HAVE AIDS BUT IT'S OKAY TO HUG ME. You saw Mathieson Judd's instinctive move towards him in the crowd,

121

brushing aside his bodyguards. You saw him hug that little boy, and if you were close enough you saw the sudden springing of tears on that man's face as he stood with his arms around his small, suffering fellow-American for those few seconds of amazing grace.'

And again a pause, but this time her eyes remained on the TelePrompTer. 'I do not think, ladies and gentlemen, that I need to translate that scene into the banality of mere words for you. Allow me to say only that those who consider Senator Judd a figure of almost majestic dedication to the serious and solemn business of leadership, those who consider him as no more than an intellectual devoid of feeling, should now rejoice in the knowledge that he is also a man of heart. And it is this, above all, that we must have in the White House – a man who will not only lead this nation with the high skills of management and statesmanship, but a man graced with humanity.'

Her eyes on the TelePrompTer for two seconds, three; then she looked down and shuffled the papers.

'Haven't seen you around here before, Mr Keyes.'

Faint smell of sweat.

'I'm not surprised.'

He'd come in quietly a minute ago and I'd checked his reflection in the glass panel without looking up. Thick-bodied, bland-faced, moved like a cat. Sitting beside me now, been working out somewhere and hadn't had time for a shower.

'You're not surprised?'

I wished he'd go away. 'But Governor Anderson's theme – ' Erica Cambridge on the monitor screen – 'is that there's so much wrong with America after the Republican four-year term – '

'Mr Keyes?'

He didn't know me; he'd read the name on my lapel pass.

'If you want to talk to me you'll have to do it when Miss Cambridge has finished.'

' – Whereas Senator Judd's theme is reassuring. The country is in good shape – '

I could have read this for myself. Word for word.

The chill came creeping, hadn't expected it. I'd been trying to think it was all over now, done with, the subliminal infiltration of my mind.

'I have to check up. Are you with the crew?'

He was nothing to do with the studio. He was probably her bodyguard. Blue suit, black shoes, rubber soles.

' – to consolidate the gains that have been made under the present administration.'

Word for word.

I remembered Ferris, leaning across the desk, talking to the psychiatrist, Purdom watching me from his chair, Upjohn switching off the recorder.

Then Ferris had turned to me. *Do you know how long you spoke for?*

No.

Nineteen minutes, with no interruption. Do you know what you were talking about?

Yes. Anderson's campaign theme. And Judd's.

I sat for a long time watching the woman with the violet eyes, listening to the words she spoke, the words that I had spoken before.

When had she thought of them, written them?

The man had gone out.

' – is to thank you for letting me be with you this evening. I'm Erica Cambridge, and these are my views.'

Brilliant smile, hold, fade, credits.

I waited until most of the people had left the main studio; then I went in there.

'Who are you?'

The bodyguard hadn't followed me in. Either I'd cooled him off or he didn't want to start anything that could bring Cambridge down on him for being stupid: for all he knew I could be the head of the studio.

'My name is Richard Keyes.'

'I don't know you.'

'We need to talk.'

Getting her long slim snakeskin bag, checking her watch, swinging towards a door – 'Bennie?'

'You want me?' Voice off.

'Where did you put the transcripts?'

'I sent them for copying.'

'*All* of them?'

'He's doing them tonight. They'll – '

'Oh for *God's* sake, I need the originals to take home.'

His face in the doorway, patient, enduring, 'I sent them ten minutes ago, Erica, and they'll be back here practically *now*.'

'Next time, Bennie, get it right.'

She picked up one of the phones on the desk, remembered me and said: 'You can make an appointment through my secretary.'

I said, 'We need to talk tonight.'

'I don't know you. Please leave.'

She dialled, and I went to the main door. 'George Proctor sends his regards.'

The bodyguard was waiting for her outside and she came past him and caught up with me at the elevator. 'Who?'

'I haven't time,' I said, 'to make appointments.'

She wasn't biting her lip but it looked like that. Her make-up girl had taken off the heavy studio masque and fluffed the gel out of her hair and she looked younger and more human. 'How much time do you have?'

'We'll play it by ear.'

'I need to make one short call, okay?' Turned to the man in the blue serge. 'Is the car there?'

'Yes, ma'am.'

'Go down and wait.'

It was 11:40 when we came out of the building into the street and got into the limousine.

She leaned across the small marble-topped table. 'When did you see him last?'

Ferris had told his people to check on the second most frequent number on George Proctor's telephone bills and it had been unlisted but they'd got around it through contacts and the name they'd come up with was Erica Cambridge.

'Two nights ago.'

She looked away. 'Was he with anyone?'

I think she regretted it immediately but of course it was too late.

'Yes.'

She'd learned already, and just went on watching the people. 'Has he contacted you since then?'

'No.'

'Have you contacted him?'

'No. He's missing.'

I was watching her carefully and there was a lot of reaction in the eyes as she brought them back to me and looked down, too late again. 'You can't say someone's missing when you saw them so recently.'

'He took everything with him.'

'I see.' She straightened up, pulling the white silk stole round her bare shoulders. 'Have you been here before?'

I suppose I'd looked interested in the environment, which was true enough: two of the Bureau people had come in here soon after we had and taken up station near the doors. I didn't recognise anyone else but that didn't mean I was safe. I hadn't seen the marksman on the quay or anyone else in his cell and they could be in here now, sitting with a coffee, playing the juke box, using one of the payphones.

'No,' I told her. Hadn't been here before. The neon sign outside had said *Kruger Drug*.

'It's rather like Schwarb's Pharmacy,' she said, 'on the Strip in LA, but that's gone now. This was just a drugstore at first but it stayed open all night so people came in here for company – night-club types looking for something different, late-night workers, actors, that kind of crowd. Now there's just everyone – Cuban traders, cops, drug dealers, the survivors of family fights, you name it. Coffee?'

'Yes.'

'They have nineteen different kinds.'

She waved to someone and the brilliant smile flashed and died again, leaving the nerves showing just under the skin. It could have been because of her job, or her temperament; I didn't know anything about her, except that she might know where Proctor was.

That remains your immediate objective. Ferris.

Not really. My immediate objective was to stay on my feet and run through this town while they watched me, followed me, waiting to see if there were anything left inside my head, any traces of the subliminal material that had been put in there, waiting to see if the worm were still in the apple, eating its way through.

Waiting over there by the doors.

Sat here feeling the chill but I'd have to get used to it for Christ's sake, deal with it. Find Proctor and the rest would take care of itself. Proctor had been turned and gone to ground and for all I knew he'd been the principal who'd set me up for the kill down there on the quay.

'Hi, Dorothy.' The smile flashed again.

She liked being seen, came in here, probably, to be seen, but at the same time wanted privacy, which was why she'd chosen this table right in the corner and put her bodyguard close enough to fend off anyone she didn't want to see.

'I liked your show,' I said.

'Thank you. Which of the nineteen?'

'What? Oh. Whatever you're having.'

The girl went away with the order. 'I had to tape it because there's a meeting tomorrow evening with the Senator's campaign manager and I'm invited.'

The presence of her bodyguard two tables away would not, of course, do me any good if anything started; nor would the presence of the two Bureau people. The whole town had become a red sector two days after the mission had begun running and that put me at great risk but there hasn't been a single operation in the Bureau records that didn't go through the end-phase with the executive working on the very edge of extinction: it's the nature of the trade; and there was the obvious possibility that if I could find Proctor at some time during the last hours of this night I could turn him in for interrogation and give them a chance to shut down the board for *Barracuda* if they could get him to break.

'That little scene,' I said, 'in New Hampshire. Was it true?'

She looked down. 'In this business, truth is what you make it. That's the only way to play. Who else was there, that night?'

'With Proctor?'

'Yes.'

'A friend, just leaving.'

'A woman.' It wasn't a question.

'Yes. I think they'd been having a row.' As a gesture.

'And she doesn't know where he's gone?'

'I haven't asked her. I don't know where she lives.'

The bodyguard stood up suddenly, turning two women away. In speech at a distance the vowels stand out better than the consonants, and when we'd come in here I'd heard *ameidge* from several tables, and now there was *au-oh-ah* from one of the women, with small moans of disappointment.

The guard sat down again.

'Sugar?'

'No.'

'I want,' she said without looking at me, 'to find George Proctor, very much.'

'So do I. Perhaps we can help each other. If you want to tell me the places where he used to go, I can have them checked out.' It wasn't necessarily a thin chance. Proctor was a top-echelon executive and he knew how to go to ground without leaving a trace, but he could be operating as part of a cell or part of a whole network and he'd have to keep in contact and that would be where I could find him: by catching a stray signal, tripping on a wire, crossing a courier line and working inwards from there.

I knew one thing: it could be fatal to under-estimate Proctor. Monck, briefing me in Nassau three days ago: *What it does concern is the upcoming American election, in which of course Senator Mathieson Judd is actively engaged. It also concerns the balance of power between East and West as it exists at the present time, which is precariously. Let me put it this way. If the extent of things proves as far-reaching as we've begun to believe, I shall find it difficult to sleep soundly in my bed.*

Proctor had been turned and gone over to the Soviets and for all we knew he could be at the very centre of the opposition network, the centre of an organisation that had moved in on me the instant they felt I was a danger – the instant when I'd tele-phoned Proctor to say I wanted to see him. They'd searched my room and tagged me through the streets and put me in the cross hairs and infiltrated my brain within hours of my arrival in Miami. Whoever Proctor was operating for now, they were important, perhaps international, even multi-national, and he would have a major role to play.

'I can tell you,' Erica Cambridge said, 'the places where he used to go, yes, but I doubt if you'll find him there.'

'We could find traces. That's all we need.'

'I think I should tell you – ' a moment of hesi-tation, but she decided to go on – 'I think I should tell you that my need to find that man isn't . . . personal.'

She was looking down again; she did it a lot. I said, 'Are you sure?'

'Oh yes. Yes, in spite of my asking you – ' she left it.

Asking me about the woman.

'If it's not personal,' I said, 'it's political?'

'In the United States of America within ten days of the presidential election, the way a dog scratches a flea is political. But with George Proctor – ' hesitation again – 'it's something even more than political. There's something going on that – ' this time she broke off and her eyes became wary. 'Mr Keyes – did I get your name right? – I don't have the slightest idea who you are or what you were doing in the *Newsbreak* studios.'

'I'm looking for George Proctor.'

'Sure, but a minute ago you said that "we" could perhaps find traces of him.'

'My organisation.'

'There's no deal, Mr Keyes.' Her eyes were hard now. 'Unless you're prepared to name names.'

'I may do that later,' I said. 'Not now.'

Her head turned to look at the bodyguard, then back to me. 'I have to go soon, Mr Keyes. I come here sometimes to – you know – unwind, be by myself.'

I didn't get up. 'You won't find him,' I said, 'by yourself.'

'Will you?'

'Not immediately. Not for a day or two. But we'll find him.'

'Then why did you come to me?'

'Because you might have helped us to find him sooner. If we pooled our information we'd shorten the time. We'd rather not wait two days, but it won't be more than that. You'll need longer, and you may be too late.'

Looking down, running a fingertip round and round the rim of the little espresso cup, her breath quickening, the lift and fall of her breasts under the white silk catching the light from overhead, a vibration in her that I half-caught through the

130

senses, half-felt across the space between us at the small round table, an emanation from her etheric body, from her nerves.

Then she looked up, and I caught a touch of fear. 'Only two days?'

'No more than that.'

'When you find him, what will you do?'

'We'll get him out of the country, very fast.'

Watching me steadily, the fright still there. 'It's – important for me to see him first.'

'We couldn't allow that.'

Looking away now, trapped. I waited.

'Hi, Erica!'

A woman waving, the bodyguard on his feet and turning for instructions, Cambridge giving a quick little shake of her head.

It was going to be all right but I put three dollar bills onto the check as a gesture.

'It would be very helpful to you,' Cambridge said, leaning closer, 'if you let me see him before he leaves. I have a great deal of information on him.'

'Then give it to me now and you'll see him before he leaves. That's guaranteed. I'm sorry, it's the best I can do.' Stood up, buttoned my jacket.

'Mr Keyes, is your "organisation" the British government?'

'I would have thought it was rather clear. Proctor's a British national. But look, get in touch with me some time tomorrow, if you want to – though I'm not easy to reach. We – '

'May I see some kind of ID?'

I chose the card with the Foreign Office crest and dropped it onto the table and she looked at it carefully.

'May I keep this?'

'By all means.'

Took a purse out of her snakeskin bag, put the card away. 'It's difficult to talk to you if you're standing up.'

'We've talked enough, I think, and you were working late. It was a pleasure – '

'Mr Keyes.' The fright in her voice now. She was looking down again, her small hands flat on the marble top of the table with the fingers spread, the voilet nail varnish glinting under the light. 'I'd be glad if you'd sit down for a moment – is that too much to ask?'

I was surprised because I hadn't expected her to break so completely, but this was simply because I didn't know the Proctor background and her connection with it. It looked critical, because as I sat down again I could see that she was having to make an effort to keep control, and her voice was shaky now.

'Look, you've caught me at a crucial time. I – I need help, if that doesn't sound too melodramatic.'

She waited for me to say something.

Said nothing.

'There's no one I can trust, you see. I mean I've got friends, sure, associates,' pressing the table hard, 'and they're all good people but – but I don't know how strong they'd be if things got really rough. And none of them know about George Proctor – okay, we were close, yes, but they don't know about – this thing that's happening.' Driving her hands against the marble, her eyes wide now, then changing, narrowing as she caught an inward glimpse of herself and looked up at last and around her in case anyone were watching, her eyes coming back to me, her voice soft, suddenly, fierce – 'Are you listening to me, for God's sake?'

'Yes.'

'You goddamned British, you won't give an inch

will you?' Her hands off the table now, restless, brushing the air – 'But I'm going to take a risk and trust you because I'm gullible enough to feel reassured by the Queen of England's crest on the card you gave me.'

No. Going to trust me because she desperately wanted information on Proctor and I'd guaranteed her a meeting with him as soon as we found him.

Looking around her, then back to me, 'The next ten days are going to be critical for the United States of America and by extension for the rest of the world. Not politically critical because Mathieson Judd is a Republican and if he gets into the White House there won't be any change. But critical internationally, globally. I have a question, since you know George Proctor. Is he a small fish, or a big fish?'

'It depends on the pond.'

'It's a very big pond, so let's try this: would you say he's capable of becoming a big fish, in a very big pond?'

I looked away. One of the Bureau men near the doors was different. Midnight shift. 'Proctor,' I said, 'is capable of anything that requires cold courage, risk and endurance. He shouldn't be underestimated.'

'That's also my opinion. He and I – ' she looked down, spreading her hands on the table again, perhaps wanting to feel its stability, wanting to borrow from it – 'he and I were close personally until – quite recently, close enough for me to be quite sure he wasn't the advertising man he purported to be – though he used his connections with *Newsbreak* pretty well as a front. But he still had a reserve I couldn't get through, and I believe he was doing things unknown to me that would have surprised me

– correction, alarmed me, frightened me – not just personally, I mean on a geopolitical scale.' Pause. 'I want to get this right. On a *clandestine* geopolitical scale.'

'For instance?'

'I'm not saying he's the *biggest* fish in this thing, by any means, but I believe he's being used as the prime mover. You remember a man called Howard Hughes?'

Said I'd heard of him.

Someone over there was pointing in this direction, one of the waitresses.

'He had a mad dream,' Cambridge said. 'He wanted to buy America.'

'In what sense?'

'He wanted to control it, by buying up its major companies, the machinery behind the throne. He went a long way, but it was the wrong way, the hard way.'

The bodyguard was getting to his feet again.

'There's an easier way.' Her voice quieter, intense, her eyes on me the whole time now. 'To buy America, all you have to do is buy one man. The president. But first you have to – '

'Excuse me, ma'am.' The bodyguard held out a remote telephone. 'You taking calls?'

'Who is it?'

'Mr Sakamoto.'

'Yes, I'll take it.' Surprise but no hesitation. 'Excuse me, Mr Keyes.'

I picked up a menu.

So first they'd tried her home and been told Miss Cambridge was at the studio, and then they'd tried the studio and been told that if she weren't home she could be anywhere, but she sometimes went to Kruger Drug, and then they'd tried Kruger Drug, so they must have wanted to talk to her quite urgently, at five minutes to midnight.

'You mean right away?' Looking at her diamenté watch, 'Oh sure, no problem. Has anything – ' then she corrected it and said, 'I'll be there in fifteen minutes,' and gave the phone back to her bodyguard. 'I'm sorry, Mr Keyes, it's something I'm unable to pass up.'

'Of course. This isn't the place, anyway, to talk.'

We left the table, the bodyguard ahead of us. 'When can we meet again?' She sounded torn, under pressure. A woman called *Hi, Erica*, but she didn't turn.

'Tomorrow,' I said. 'I'll phone you.'

She gave me her card and as we got to the doors I passed close to one of the Bureau men, '*Car*,' and he left his table and went out in front of us while I was talking to Cambridge in the lobby.

'It's absolutely vital,' she said softly, 'that we get together as soon as possible.' Her eyes with fright still in them. 'I'll make a point of staying in until noon. Call before then.'

The limousine was at the kerbside with a chauffeur at the rear door. 'Can I drop you somewhere?' she asked me.

'I feel like a walk.'

A last glimpse of her face at the smoked window, no more than a featureless smudge, leaving me with the odd impression that she'd been trapped in the big black car, obliterated.

Midnight plus seventeen, the late-night traffic rolling with very little sound through the streets, gathering at the lights and waiting, finding release, changing lanes to go round the work gangs still clearing debris left by the hurricane, the black Lincoln ahead of me with two other cars between until the limousine slowed, letting them past and turning into the driveway of 1330 West Riverside Way.

10

CONTESSA

There was nothing I could do.

This was a residential street, large balconied houses, stucco and porticos behind trimmed hedges, wrought iron gates, the residences of old Miami money. Shadows everywhere thrown by the trees and hedges, one of the tall ornate street lamps out, like a dead eye in the night. Heat still rising from the stones and the tarmacadam after the day's unremitting sun, the air moist from the vegetation, from the sea.

I wish to *Christ* it didn't affect me but it always has, always will, and don't try telling me it's all in the day's work, I'm not standing for that.

Seed pods dropping, big ones, spiralling down through the lamplight and hitting the sidewalk with the sound of autumn hail.

12:34.

He must have been under their own surveillance for quite a time because they didn't ask any questions – they used one car and two men and the snatch didn't take more than ten seconds and the car was gone again, *more than a snatch*, because the first man to reach him had broken his spine at the first vertebra and they'd dragged him across the sidewalk and thrown him into the back.

There was nothing I could do because the distance was something like a hundred yards and it was over before I could have got out of the car and started running and in any case the executive in the field is strictly forbidden to go to the aid of anyone at all because he'd reveal his presence and that's what they'll sometimes go for, attacking one of the support people to bring the shadow out. It was the only thing about this killing that gave me any comfort: they couldn't have known I was anywhere in the environment or they would have worked more slowly on him to give me time to get there.

What was his name, then, and where was he from and who would tell her? One of the personnel staff, a woman, they did it better, I'm sorry, love, but there's some bad news about Bob, the tyres whimpering under the brakes and the doors flying open and the rush of feet and then death in the warm Miami night.

He'd tried to run, I'd seen that much, turned and tried to get clear somehow because the support people don't carry arms and there were two of them and they were quick, very quick.

I checked the three mirrors again, the one inside and the two others; I'd been checking them at short intervals since I'd passed the limo and made a square and put the Trans Am in the shadows of trees on the far side of the street, and the nerves were raw now because of the death. They weren't in any kind of intelligence, these people; their methods were too direct and they had no interest at all in pulling one of us in for interrogation; they went straight for the kill.

I would have to telephone as soon as I could, to report what those snivelling creeps in Records would call a terminal incident and to warn Ferris that 1330 West Riverside was no longer surveilled. It looked like a one-man station and there wouldn't be a relief until eight in the morning because this was the graveyard shift, and not thus named for nothing.

He'd been nearer the house than I was, and on foot. No blame to anyone, except possibly to himself; I'd no means of knowing whether he'd made some kind of mistake. Put it into the computer and you'd come up with fifty recommendations for doing a surveillance job on foot: you're faster, more mobile, less easily seen, so forth, and fifty recommendations for doing it with a car: you've got permanent cover and armour plating and even though a car makes a bigger profile than a man it attracts less attention parked in a street than a man on foot just standing, doing nothing.

The armour plating hadn't done me any good on the quay but if there's a long shot set up for you it doesn't much matter what you're doing, you're in the cross-hairs and that's it. They could do the same thing again without leaving the house, any second from now, but the risk was very slight because no one had come close enough to see me, to recognise me. I was only running *one* calculated risk and that too was low: they were keeping surveillance on the street from the house as a matter of routine, and that was how they'd picked up the Bureau man just now; and they might have noticed this dark blue Trans Am pulling in to the kerb and staying there *with no one getting out*.

Fingers on the ignition key.

They could in point of fact be watching me now as I sat here, with night-lenses and a tripod, beginning to wonder why the pale blur of the driver's face was still behind the windscreen after twenty minutes; they could in point of fact have sent a man out to check on me, but he would double and approach from behind and he couldn't stay out of the mirrors.

Turning the key, a spasm along the nerves in the right arm, from the fingers to the shoulder, and the odd sensation of the mind dipping away from reality, nothing dramatic, just dipping away, *but don't start the car for God's sake, they'll pick up the sound*, turning the key but slowly, the mind working on the muscles with its subtle, omnipotent demands, the message perfectly clear: *You will go to 1330 West Riverside Way at any time before midnight. Not later than that*.

Turn the key and wait for the bang of the starter dog against the flywheel and the beat of the engine, *turn the key*, with half the mind issuing its unquestionable orders and half swinging full-circle in a dizzying attempt to get control, full control.

Logic startled me, saved me. *It's gone midnight. No later than midnight, they said*.

The hand, the fingers coming away, and for a little while a sickening wave of fright bearing down, *it almost happened, they've still got control of you, there's nothing you can do to –*

Bullshit.

Yes, let us be forthright about this. Sat up straighter, both hands crossed on my lap, the moment over, the danger done with. Because listen, it was only last night when I was one block from here, as close as one block, and fighting for survival, reeling against the telephone box and forcing a quarter in, hunched like a pariah dog – *I need* – *Yes, you need? – I need to debrief – Where are you? – 1200 block and West Riverside Way. Hurry – for God's sake hurry*.

The wave of fright bearing down, bearing away, leaving me with my hands cold in the warmth of the night, my breath steadying. Progress. Progress, you understand. Report to Ferris, briefly and with confidence: *Lingering effects of the subliminal programming now diminished; no major problem in combating.*

12:47.

Man in the mirror.

I'm sorry, Mr Keyes. It's something I'm unable to pass up. Her phraseology formal, correct; that was her *métier.* She'd sounded surprised but didn't hesitate – yes, she'd be there in fifteen minutes.

Was there now.

All you have to do is buy one man. The president. But first you have to –

First you have to what?

The man was coming down the sidewalk on the side of the street where I was parked. He was alone and walking steadily, his size increasing in the mirror as I watched.

Question: what had turned Proctor? He'd been dug deep in the ground on *allied* territory, an established sleeper nursing his wounds, a soft job, a steady job. Had he got bored? Some of us get bored; we work for a bureaucracy and that can drive us straight up the wall. But I didn't think he'd got bored, Proctor. It had been something much more critical than that. He'd done good work for the Sacred Bull, gone out on some of the major missions and come back with honours, put his life on the line time and again and got away with it, and in this he wasn't dissimilar to me. Then what had changed him, turned him? He wasn't a man to fall for the usual male chauvinist toys – money, power, women. He liked women, yes, but he didn't lack their com-

141

pany – Kim, Erica, Monique, perhaps others, of *course* others.

I would find out who had turned him when I found him. They were probably in that house over there with its gracious old-world balconies and wrought iron gates. We already thought we knew *how* they had changed him: by some kind of subliminal programming, and the thing that made me really frightened was that I'd been exposed to the same influence and felt its insidious power, the subtle, devouring power of the worm in the apple.

And might be exposed again.

His footsteps now audible, his humped body moving into the chrome rim of the mirror. My driving window was down but the one on the passenger's side was closed, and I could see him more clearly than he could see me because the facia was dark and the street lamps overhead were throwing reflections on the outside of the glass.

His dark figure came into the edge of the vision field and then the details began to clear; he walked with his head down and his hands in his pockets, his gait tipping him forward a little as if he were being pushed along, away from somewhere he wanted to be or towards some place where he didn't want to go.

I didn't move. With my head at this angle I could see all I needed to see but there wouldn't be anything I could do if he turned within the next second and smashed the window in and fired and kept on firing. I didn't think he would do that. I thought that one day, perhaps tomorrow, in a few hours, they would do that, or something like that, because they knew by now that their first attempt had drawn blank, walking on, he was walking on, and they would try again. But not tonight, or not, at least, at the present moment because he didn't turn to look into the car, didn't know I was here, knew only that he was unable to do more than keep moving along the sidewalk, pushed steadily from behind towards an undesired destination, his humped body arched forward and his head down, a lone unwilling traveller in the night.

And my well-loved and unwitting friend, because he had not in fact come to smash the window in and fire and go on – *but there'd been no risk of that* – oh really well how do you bloody well know – *you said yourself there was no* – it doesn't matter what I *say*, for Christ's sake, it's what I *think*, it's what the *fear* thinks, it's *always* like this when there's a threat to life, don't you understand?

Relax, yes indeed, relax, the moment is over and all is well, we live on our nerves, for God's sake give us a break.

But Governor Anderson's theme is that there's so much wrong with America after the Republican four-year term that we need major changes, whereas Senator Judd's theme is reassuring – the country is in good shape.

Her eyes lifted to the TelePromTer, her attitude serious, informed. I could have given it to her word for word, so when had she written it? I would have to ask her; it could be important, the timing. And there she was.

Coming out of the house on the opposite side of the street. At this distance I couldn't see her face clearly and in any case she was now wearing dark glasses and a headscarf; but I know people by their walk and this was Erica Cambridge, crossing the sidewalk under the magnolia tree to the limousine at the kerb, her bodyguard with her and another man, short, deftly moving, also with dark glasses on, ushering her into the car and getting in after her. Chauffeur and bodyguard to the front, the doors slamming and the lights coming on.

12:56.

The moon in its third quarter, lowering across the heights of the city; a helicopter's lights tracing a path along the east horizon over the sea; the masts of yachts riding on calm water in the lamplit marina; the smell of seaweed that had been torn by the hurricane and brought to the surface to lie rotting under the day-long sun.

I stopped short of the quay, finding shadow. The limousine was nearer the row of power boats, the engine idling for a moment and then dying away. The bodyguard got out first, scanning and moving a little away from the car and standing with his back to it, containing the environment. Then the chauffeur got out and opened a rear door and there was Cambridge again, and the short man, a Japanese, both of them still with dark glasses on. He touched her elbow and they moved quickly across the flag-stones to the first boat in the marina, a motor launch with the crew in white ducks and a name at the stern in gold letters: *Contessa*. Cambridge and the Japanese were handed aboard with a lot of courtesy, a flurry of salutes. They didn't move into the cabin but stood waiting near the rail, turning to face the quay.

The chauffeur and bodyguard had got back into the Lincoln and now it turned and headed towards the ramp and the street. At first I thought it was coming back, but this car was smaller, a black sedan, slowing and stopping just beyond the motor launch. Four men got out the moment the wheels had stopped rolling; they all faced the way they had come, towards the street, two of them buttoning their dark blue jackets, tugging at them, not speaking to each other, watching the ramp. The limousine came past me less than fifty feet away; I turned my head to darken the image as a matter of routine. As it rolled to a stop by the launch three men got out, the driver and two bodyguards, and a third car came down the ramp and took up station behind the limo, four men getting out and scanning immediately, all well-trained, well-drilled.

The chauffeur was standing at the rear door of the limousine and another man climbed out, tall, slightly stooping, bareheaded, dark glasses, moving at once to the motor launch as the crew snapped into the salute. I recognised him from the photographs that were all over the town: Senator Mathieson Judd, the Republican candidate for the presidency.

11

NICKO

*'Get your fuckin' ass outa here right now or you'll
get your fuckin' brains blown all over the place, you
know what I mean?'*

Black, heavy-barrelled Suzuki, an inch from my
face.

He smelled of chewing-gum.

'Which way?' I asked him.

The quay was narrow here; this was more than a
mile from the boat marina; there were three other
cars standing further along towards the warehouses,
figures near them, the glow of a cigarette in the
shadows thrown by the cranes.

'Turn around. Make a U-turn. C'mon now!'

A jerk of the big gun. Lights came behind me
and I stopped halfway through the turn. An engine
idling.

'Who's he?'

'Just a guy.'

'What's he doing here?'

'Gettin' his ass out.'

Slam of a car door, footsteps. I left both hands
on the wheel in plain sight. One of the men standing
by the cars further along the quay broke away and

started walking towards us, dropping his cigarette, head up, alerted.

Blinding light in my eyes – 'Turn this way – *this way*!'

Couldn't see a thing, just the dazzling white fire of the light.

'Who are you?'

'Charlie Smith.'

'What're you doing here?'

'I'm looking for the marina.'

'There's ten thousand marinas in this place. Listen, I've seen you before somewhere.'

I shut my eyes against the glare.

'How long's he been here?' To the other man, the black.

'Listen, I'm doin' my job, man, I told him to get his ass – '

'Jesus, I think I know.'

The glare blacked out, leaving an after-light under my lids. I'd taken this route because there weren't so many overhead lamps; the streets up there were day-bright and my face was known to a few people, among them the man who'd had me in his sights yesterday.

'Is this you?'

Holding a black-and-white photograph, shining the torch on it.

'No.'

'I think it's you.' The light dazzling again as he moved it.

'I know my own face.'

'Goddamn,' he said 'this is you.'

Said nothing. These weren't intelligence people; I'd simply walked into some kind of drug-trade situation. *But they had my photograph.*

'Hold him there, Roget.'

'Okay,' The Suzuki swung up again. 'Cut them lights, an' the motor. *C'mon.*'

It was the other man I watched, the white man. He was walking down to the group of cars, his gait busy, energised. He'd sounded pleased when he'd looked at the photograph, as if it were something to eat: he was a fat man, with small delicate hands for picking currants out of cake.

I started thinking about egress, about, yes, getting my ass out of here, but the front of the Trans Am was pointing straight at the water between the rusting mass of a dredger and a timber jetty and even if they let me go it would take a couple of bites with the wheel to get me facing the other way and if they'd wanted me in a rat trap they couldn't have done a better job.

'Tomorrow,' I told Ferris on the phone, and he'd agreed: I hadn't got anything urgent to debrief tonight and I wanted some sleep. 'But you've lost one of your people.'

'Lost?'

The connection wasn't too good; the phone box had taken a battering and the armoured cord was frayed. I spelled it out for him and his voice was icy when he spoke again.

'I didn't realise we'd invited that much attention.'

'There was the long shot,' I said.

'But that had a specific target. Tonight it was over-reaction.'

I knew what he meant. In the course of intelligence operations we don't kill off the infantry just for being there; a beating-up as a warning would have been the normal response. But these people weren't in government-style intelligence, and that made it even more dangerous because they behaved unpredictably and there weren't any rules.

'You'll need to be very careful,' I told Ferris, 'if you're going to replace that man.'

Telling him his job I suppose because he just said, 'What about Erica Cambridge?'

'I'll give you a replay tomorrow, but you should know that she went aboard a motor-boat tonight in the company of a Japanese from 1330 Riverside. And Senator Judd.'

Silence, then: 'Name of the boat?'

'*Contessa*.'

'That's a cutter. The *Contessa* is a 2,000 ton yacht anchored in the Bay.' I think he was going to say more about it but changed his mind. 'We're getting a lot of information in with a direct bearing on *Barracuda*. I'll brief you tomorrow.'

Over and out. He wouldn't sleep well for the rest of the night, with a death on his hands. He'd feel responsible, but more than that, it would change his whole approach to the running of the mission: he couldn't afford to deploy support for the executive or even passive surveillance people in these streets without risking their lives, and he wouldn't be prepared to do that.

It's an ill wind. I didn't want support.

He was coming back, the white man, someone with him, a woman. He shone the torch on me again and I contracted the facial muscles to bring the ears back and pushed some air into my mouth to fatten the cheeks, all I could do.

'Is this the guy?'

I couldn't see her face because of the glare.

In a moment: 'No.'

'Don't give me that shit!'

He shook the photograph.

'I haven't seen him before.'

'But he was *there*, for Christ's sake. At the *apartment*.'

'This is someone else.'

A hint of *patchouli* on the air.

'How long were you with him?' Anger in his voice, frustration, wanted his currant cake.

'Long enough to remember what he looked like. This isn't the man.'

'Well Jesus Christ this is the face of the guy in the photograph!'

'You'd better take care, Nicko. Don't kill too many, for your own sake.'

'Get back to the car.'

Walking away – 'I'm warning you, Nicko.'

The scent of *patchouli* . . . a link with Proctor, subtle and tenuous but a link. And a question: why had she lied? She'd said nothing more than *good evening* that night in the apartment but I recognised her voice, just as she'd recognised me. A black girl, petite, slender, more than attractive, vibrant, her arm hanging like a model's in the light of the brass lamps, the hand turned outwards a little for effect, her dark eyes taking me in. So why had she lied? *I haven't seen him before*.

'Out!' He jerked the door open. 'Out of the car!' He turned to the other man, the minion. 'Frisk him.' Then he squeezed himself into the car and rummaged around for guns, taking the keys from the ignition and opening the trunk and throwing things around, the jack and the breakdown kit and the fire extinguisher, half pleased with himself, I thought at this stage, and half worried that he'd got it wrong and I wasn't the guy, the guy in the photograph.

Don't kill too many, she'd said.

Had Nicko killed the man on surveillance in

Riverside an hour ago? He couldn't have done it himself; he wasn't quick enough on his feet, with his hands. But I didn't think he'd even ordered it. The setup with 1330 Riverside and Erica Cambridge and Mathieson Judd and the cutter for the *Contessa* was strictly political. The setup here was cocaine.

'He's naked, Nicko.'

But there was the link with Proctor. Was Proctor on cocaine?

'Okay, take him down there and put him in the car. In the Linc, not the Chevvy. Keep the gun on him. You let him go, Roget, you're dead.'

That would explain Proctor's changed personality, if he'd got himself into cocaine.

We started walking and the black boy hit the muzzle into my spine two or three times because he'd seen it done in the movies I suppose but it was annoying because he could chip a vertebra and I was tempted to spin on him with the right forearm doing the work. There wouldn't be any risk because when a gun gives a man the type of cocky confidence this one was showing then you know he's not paying enough attention and you can take it away from him like a toy from a boy. But he wasn't alone here and it wouldn't do any good: I needed to get clear as soon as I could and I mustn't rush anything.

'Keep movin'!'

Another prod, though I hadn't slowed. He was young and fresh out here from Jamaica or Haiti, recruited from some cardboard city on a mudbank by an entrepreneur with a gold watch and a diamond pin and stories of fortunes to be made, hey big daddy here I come, and I didn't want to spoil everything for him but it would have to come to that.

Behind me I heard Nicko swinging the Trans Am straight and rolling it down the quay on the wall side, parking it and cutting the engine, slam of a door. Catching up with us, 'She's parked okay for you, limey, we don't want anything illegal going on around here,' a thin wheeze, something like laughter, pleased with himself. He was the pseudo manic-depressive type and I would have to watch him because they're the most dangerous, they'll kill out of caprice.

I said it was decent of him because I didn't like tickets and we reached the Lincoln and the black boy pulled the rear door open and pushed me inside and slammed it and stood away and his voice came through the glass – 'Stay in the car, mister, you wanna live, you know?'

He had a point because that Suzuki was big enough to blow the whole of the Lincoln through the wall without even being selective.

There wasn't anything I could do for the moment. There were three other man standing near the cars, all in dark clothing – a navy sweater, a jump suit, no shirts, nothing white. Two of them were smoking; they didn't talk; sometimes they turned slowly to look at Nicko and then they looked away again. It was important for me to get the hang of their relationships so that I could work with it; at this stage my thinking was that they were all traders except for the boy Roget, that Nicko was in charge but they didn't like him, were even afraid of him, perhaps because he'd killed people – *don't kill too many, Nicko* – and would be ready to kill more.

I couldn't see Monique; she must be in the Chevrolet parked in front of the Lincoln.

2:14 on the facia clock.

It looked as if they were waiting for a boat because they stood watching the sea, the strip of water between the dredger and the jetty. It wasn't

153

dark out there; the moon was throwing a milky light across the swell left by the hurricane, and ships lay silhouetted at anchor. A helicopter was working a course from north to south across the Port to Virginia Key, presumably a US Coast Guard patrol. If these people were –

Lights and the squeal of tyres under the brakes and the three men stood back, nearer the wall, one of them bending to look through the windshield; then Nicko came past the Lincoln from behind and was there beside the grey Pontiac when it stopped rolling and a door came open and two men got out, one of them holding the other in a police grip with an arm twisted behind him, both Latins.

'Where's Martinez?' This was Nicko.

The driving window of the Lincoln was down and I caught most of what they were saying, patching a word in here and there to construct the sense.

'He's on his way. Toufexis had some business.'

'We're running late, for Christ's sake. Put him in the big one.'

'What's Roget doing there like that?'

With the gun.

'We've got someone else in the car, same kind of thing.'

For the first time I began to worry. It's easy to think, when there are guns around and the talk is tough and they're confident to the point of inattention, that you won't find it very difficult to get clear. I've got clear in situations totally controlled by field intelligence people, sometimes KGB, people trained and drilled and capable, so that in this kind of lax crime-world setup the danger was in under-estimating the odds. These men were shipping coke and they were doing it in competition with twenty or thirty major narcotic gangs and that meant they had to carry firearms, but they hadn't been trained to use them and they hadn't been through unarmed combat instruction and they wouldn't have fast reactions, but to underestimate them could be fatal because it only needed one stray shot and *finis*.

And there was the fat man, Nicko.

I knew his kind. He'd been spoiled by his mother and he'd grown up to take what he wanted and hurt if he had to hurt when they wouldn't give it up and later kill if he had to kill, and it had begun with cake and now it was wealth and power and women and sometimes death if someone's death would give him one of those things or all of those things. But the thing about him that warned me, frightened me, was that he'd started to enjoy killing and had probably begun to want only those things that would give him the excuse for doing it. This was my impression.

He wasn't uncommon in the terrorist world or the narcotics world but that was no comfort to me: he was here now, tonight, and the cake he wanted was another death. My own.

'Not there! Put him in the front!'

Roget moved away from the rear door, backing off and keeping the gun levelled and ready to swing: he at least knew the rudiments. The Latin – I would have said Cuban – moved in front of him with loose jerky steps and his hands crossed over his head as if he knew exactly what had to be done, tugging open the front passenger door and climbing in, slamming it shut, putting his hands on the ledge below the windshield now and leaning his head forward. I could hear that he was praying.

'*No talkin' between you two bastards!*'

Roget's face at the window. But it was the other face that worried me, the fat man's. He was standing a few feet from the car with his hands hanging by his sides, the little pink fingers bunched like the legs of hermit crabs. He looked at the Cuban, taking his time, and then looked at me, taking his time, his fleshy red mouth in the faintest of smiles, his small eyes shining.

We've got someone else in the car, same kind of thing.

Chill rising up the spine, reaching the nape of the neck. The fat man turned away, and I seemed to hear the echo of shots.

'What's your name?' I asked the Cuban softly.

He didn't answer, went on leaning his dark head on his arms, the tremor in his shoulders never stopping, as if he were in fact bending forward under the lashes of a whip. I could hear his prayers now, tumbling in Spanish from his lips, his prayers and his plea to *madre mia*, a plea for help, *madre mia*, the sibilants throwing echoes back from the facia panel, soft as the rustling of dead leaves.

I left him to it and watched the quay, the men standing there. Nicko had his eyes on the water now, like the others, and sometimes looked at his watch. The others weren't talking together, nor to Nicko. The black had his back to them, his gun still levelled at the Lincoln, his jaws working on the chewing-gum.

When the Cuban took his hands off the ledge I asked him again, 'What's your name?'

'It's too late,' he said. I think he was at the stage where he realised he wasn't alone in the car, and wanted to voice his thoughts, and that was more important than my question.

'Too late for what?'

'For anything.'

The quiet despair of the damned in his voice. He didn't turn in the seat to look at me; he looked at my reflection in the windshield. Roget had said no talking.

'Is your name Juan?'

'No. My name is Fidel.'

'You mean it's too late at night?'

'Too late for anything. He will kill me.'

'Nicko?'

'Yes. It is why I am here. Is it the same with you?'

'Yes.'

Same kind of thing.

'Maybe he'll change his mind,' I said.

'How long have you known Nicko?' His tone calling me a fool.

He was perhaps forty, this man, short but I would have said muscular under the dark seaman's jacket, his face weathered, less by the sun and the wind than by the demons in his head. He looked as if he'd come a long way through the years, missing the right turning and having to go back. He was shaking a little as if cold, on this warm tropical night; I don't think he was on cocaine, on a downswing.

'What happened to your hand, Fidel?'

He didn't answer.

'What are they waiting for, out there?'

His eyes, reflected, widened a little, perhaps surprised by how little I knew of things.

'The boat,' he said.

'Where is it coming from?'

He went on staring into the windshield for a time and then his eyes closed. '*Juanita*,' he said, kept on saying, whispering, '*Juanita*', and was weeping now, his head going down and the tears coming freely, '*Juanita, oh, Juanita . . .*' in a tone of such desolation that I saw her in the distance, a red rose on her black dress and her face waxen white as she turned and waved, her hand no higher than her shoulder, and turned away, walked away, his woman I would suppose, Juanita.

My nerves jerked as he moved suddenly, hitting the door open and swinging it against the wall, his bunched body projecting itself out of the car as Roget swung the gun and shouted at him – *'Freeze! Freeze right there!'* – and Nicko and the others turned to watch, one of them giving a short laugh, having seen this sort of thing before, perhaps, having expected it.

Nicko said nothing, didn't make any move towards the car. He was smiling.

'Back in the car! Back in the car, you wanna get fuckin' shot?'

Fidel the Cuban stood turning, writhing, his head in his hands, moving as if he were struggling to get out of some kind of restraint, a strait-jacket, struggling but not succeeding.

I knew what he felt. I had no Juanita, but I knew what he felt. I wasn't doing the same thing because I had done the same thing in my mind a long time ago when I was new to things, before I learned that a trap cannot be sprung by allowing the onset of panic, which sounds stuffy, perhaps, considering this man was approaching his death, but it doesn't mean that I had no feeling for him, do not ask for whom the bell, so forth.

'Back in the fuckin' car!'

And the man came, Fidel, back into the car, his crouched shadow leaving the wall as he dropped onto the seat and pulled the door shut, leaning his head back against the squab, his eyes closed.

I began waiting until I thought he might be ready to listen to whatever I had to say, and while I was waiting, lights came from the dark sea, lifting and falling to the swell.

'Fidel. Is this the boat?'

He turned his head a little. 'Yes.'

'What are they going to do with you?'

'They will kill me.'

'Listen, Fidel, I might be able to do something to stop them but I'll need your help, so brace up, get your head together, you know what I'm saying?'

'Do something? With *him* there?'

I think he meant Nicko but he could have meant the black, Roget. Roget would be easy to work on.

'Listen, there's no point in giving up, Fidel, it won't get us anywhere. You've got to – '

'Who are you?' interested for the first time.

'I can get you out of this but you've got to help, now understand that. We – '

'You know *nothing*,' he said, 'you think you can do anything against *him*, against *Nicko*, then you know *nothing*.'

Not a lot of use. I wanted information out of him so that I could get something together and set it in motion but there wasn't going to be time because the arrival of the boat would change things and I wasn't ready.

'Where will they take us, Fidel? *Quick*.'

'Across the sea.' His eyes watching me in the glass.

'Across the sea to *where*?'

'They will take us out to sea, and then shoot us, and throw us to the sharks. That is the way it is done.'

Jesus Christ it sounded like a regular programme, sweating a little, I was sweating a little now because the time frame was narrowing, closing on us, and once they'd got us on the boat there'd be nothing we could do, *finito*.

In my trade I've seen one or two deaths, caused one or two deaths, all right, *killed* if you want me to spell it out for you but listen, this is the point, I've never taken it lightly, a man's death lightly, even when he was at my throat before I managed to beat the odds, even when he'd been doing everything he could to blow me away, I've never thought of it as all in the day's work, although to many that's all it is, a trick of the trade, a necessary inconvenience. But I would have to get perspective: this was Miami Florida and the drug trade here was a multibillion-dollar industry and the stakes were high and life was cheap and that man over there, the fat man, Nicko, had probably made this trip a dozen times, fifty times, and thought of it as no big deal, and if I got the correct perspective on what was happening tonight, if I pulled back from the environment as you pull back with a zoom lens, all I would see would be a miniature black Lincoln down there with some tiny figures standing around it and two tiny figures inside it, and they would be the two tiny figures who would be dropped into the sea in a little while from now, to float for a time on the slow lifting and falling of the swell until the dark fins broke through, accelerating and closing in, *and then there was just a lot of blood on the surface, a lot of threshing about and then the blood, Christ, it was a beautiful red, he was a beautiful man, he coloured the whole sea like a flag, like a banner*, and that was all it was going to be about, given the correct perspective and the background of a multibillion-dollar industry with its primal laws and its murderous checks and balances, a whorl of crimson blossoming on the moonlit breast of the sea.

And this perspective, I knew, was necessary to me: it would give me a tool for getting inside Nicko's mind, so that I could see if there were anything I could do to it, if there were time.

They will take us out to sea, and then shoot us, and throw us to the sharks. That is the way it is done.

'Fidel,' I said, 'why will they shoot us first?'

'Because otherwise we might swim to shore. It will be only a few miles.' His eyes watching me in the glass, interested in me now, perhaps because I wanted to know all about this thing instead of wailing to my mother. 'It is their way because they do not have to get rid of our bodies. There will only be bits and pieces found, perhaps.' Impatiently – 'You are not afraid?'

'I don't intend to be thrown to any sharks; I wish you'd understand that.'

In a moment, 'You are not American, I think?'

'No.'

'You are English?'

'Yes.'

'It explains things, then. I have heard that the English cannot see the nose on their face.'

'We try to look beyond it, you see. Have they sent for this boat especially to take us out there?'

'Of course not. There will be a pickup.'

Some of the fear had gone out of his voice; he'd got over his *madre mia* bit and his prayers to the almighty God who had decided understandably to drop him in the shit, and now he was fatalistic, but that wasn't really any better, any more useful to me. I would need to get some feeling back in him. Anger, perhaps. Anger towards Nicko. That could be dangerous because this man was a Latin and liable to shoot the whole chamber dry before he took aim, but I'd have to make the best of the material. I would much rather have worked alone, but he might get in the way and it was probably safer to bring him into the act than risk his messing it up.

The boat was riding at the jetty, a line taut round a capstan with a man keeping it secure. Another man had come down to the quay to meet Nicko, and they were talking now. *We've got a couple of guys to take care of,* so forth.

There were questions, of course, that would have to wait, because I needed all the time I could get to structure some kind of survival; they would be asked later and perhaps answered, if ever at all – where had Nicko got that photograph? Why was he so ready to blow me away without checking my identity more than he had? Was it Proctor who had thrown this net out for me, with photographs all over the town? Questions like that.

But more immediately: 'A pickup of cocaine?'

'Of course.'

'This boat is carrying the cash?'

'The cash is in the other car.'

'How much?'

'I do not know. I am not on this run. When you say you might do something, what – '

'I'll tell you when the time is right. How many runs have you done, Fidel?'

'Many.'

'With Nicko?'

'Sometimes.'

'How much cash is usually taken on board?'

'It depends. Different sources, different deals. Maybe half a million, maybe a million.'

'American dollars.'

'Of course.'

Nicko was nodding to the other man; then he turned and began walking towards the Chevrolet. The two men on the quay started scanning the environment, each with one hand tucked inside his jacket. Nicko brought a black suitcase from the Chevrolet, ducking to talk to someone inside, Monique perhaps. Then he nodded and slammed the door and began walking with the suitcase towards the jetty. Almost as an afterthought he turned his head to look at Roget, the black, and jerked his free hand, gesturing towards the boat.

It was then that the reality of the thing hit me and I was made to know that I had been whistling in the dark in order to keep panic away because there was *nothing* I could do if I got inside that man's mind, *no* argument I could use to stop his hand. I was one of the two tiny people who would be dropped into the sea and that was it.

The only chance of getting clear would be in some kind of action between the Lincoln and the boat and Roget would have his big black Suzuki trained on us and even if I could get it away from him the other men were armed and would be too far away for me to work on them. If the –

'*Outa the car!*' Jerking the Suzuki. '*C'mon, outa the fuckin' car!*'

I saw Fidel go into spasm as if a bullet had hit him; then he opened the door and its edge caught against the wall and he had to pull it away, walking round the front of the car with his eyes on the sky, praying again I suppose.

'*You! Outa the fuckin' car!*'

I opened the door and pushed it shut after me and noted everything I could as I walked to the jetty. Roget was of course at our backs; Nicko was halfway along the jetty with the suitcase, leaning a little backwards as fat men have to, leaning a little to the left to counter the weight of the suitcase in his right hand, not looking back, or towards us, towards Fidel and me, taking care as he got hold of the boat's rail and stepped aboard. Monique was still in the Chevrolet: I wouldn't expect her, or any woman, to be present at an execution.

'Keep walkin'!'

I think Fidel had slowed his step, understandably; when I glanced at him I saw that he had paled and was walking with that jerky motion, head down now, that I'd seen in him earlier, as if he knew exactly what had to be done. He'd been here before, not like this but behind a gun, herding some other man to the slaughter-house.

We were on the jetty now with the boat twenty, twenty-five feet away and black water immediately on my left. It was inviting, because once I was under the surface I could move a long way unseen; but there wouldn't be time to dive; Roget would pump the big Suzuki as a reflex action.

That was the last chance that offered; once on the boat there would be no more, and as I followed the Cuban onto the deck I caught some of the aura, and felt the fear wash into me, chilling me to the bone.

12

DIAMONDS

Seen from the ocean Miami is beautiful by night, a blaze of light floating from horizon to horizon on the water and reflected there. The night lends a semblance of purity to most cities; their light flowers from them as if from unsullied soil.

I saw the bright frieze of the skyline at intervals, when the swell dropped the boat into the long indigo troughs: Fidel and I were sitting in the scuppers on the afterdeck, our knees drawn up, Roget standing with his back to the opposite rail with the big gun trained on us. When I could see the water I noticed that flotsam was everywhere, the detritus of smashed pontoons and jetties and small boats thrown up by the hurricane and strewn across the sea. Perhaps there were bodies there; I looked for none.

She was a single-deck motor yacht with twin diesels and a cluster of antennae on the cabin roof; I estimated our speed at fifteen knots, and we were a mile from the shore, heading out.

'*We don't tolerate thieves!*'

Fidel didn't voice any reaction to the kick; his limbs jerked and were still again. It displeased Nicko. I think he'd wanted a scream.

'You know Mr Toufexis. *He doesn't tolerate thieving!*'

A hiss of breath as the kick raked across his legs, leaving him spilled on the deck with his groin exposed, and the fat man went for that and got his scream.

'There's got to be *trust*, you understand me? *Trust*. With this kind of money around and this kind of merchandise, we've got to trust everyone else, and they've got to trust us. You understand what I'm saying?'

Fidel the Cuban was prone now and vomiting, couldn't answer, wouldn't have answered anyway. I'd seen the two men in the control cabin look around when Fidel had screamed. They didn't like Nicko: I'd noticed it before. I would have said they were more like professional traders than men of the criminal type as such; they weren't here to take their revenge on society but simply to make money, a great deal of money. They were business men, not thieves; hence Nicko's nice distinction. This didn't mean they weren't dangerous.

'*Get up!*' Standing over the Cuban, hands on his hips, his face red with rage, a show of monstrous petulance. '*Clean that up!*'

The swell lowered us smoothly into a trough and there was the city again, looking beautiful. The throb of the diesels was low and sensual, the warm air rich with the scent of seaweed.

'You're too fat, Nicko,' I said.

He looked down at me.

'What did you say?'

'You're too fat.'

He was a short man, didn't carry his weight with majesty like Sidney Greenstreet or Orson Welles. Nicko was just a dumpling of a man, spoiled, a cake-

166

seeker. I thought he might be sensitive about it and he was. It was as quick as he could manage but it was done in rage, which lowered the muscle tone, and I had a lot of time to monitor the kick as it came, and when it came I caught it, nothing more than that, caught it and held the ankle until he began losing his balance, because I didn't want him to fall – the moment had come and gone.

It had been an essay, that was all. Nicko was standing over me and blocking Roget completely, and it might have been possible to use the fat man for my purposes, which were of course to avoid death. But I would need to make physical contact with him before I could do anything to him, and I couldn't have got to my feet and started work because there wouldn't have been enough time – he would have come at me right away. So I'd had to get him to make the first contact, and things had come very close because I could have done a lot more than just hold his ankle – I could have straightened up and pitched him back against the man with the gun and Roget would probably, would *very* probably have loosed off at least one shot in his surprise.

I wouldn't of course have stopped there: that would have been the beginning, with two people off balance and wide open and the ship's rail immediately behind them. It could have been quite elegant in a way, though somewhat too easy to claim any credit. I didn't attempt it because there were some unpredictable factors. Nicko and the black would have had their throats well exposed and would have been dead before they went over the rail; but I couldn't have told where that first impulsive shot would have gone: it could have gone straight through Nicko and into me. There had also been no predicting how fast the two men in the control cabin would have reacted and got to their guns. In the end, within those few milliseconds when I was holding the fat man's ankle, I let the subconscious make the decision for me because it could scan the whole range of data very much faster than the forebrain and it would be much more accurate.

I am just telling you this, my good friend, to let you know that I was not just sitting there on my bloody rump awaiting the grim bloody reaper; I was not intending to offer this fat little tick the high privilege of despatching me with a shot from his bloody little gun without first culling whatever grace and favour the gods might have for me and turning it to my cunning advantage, without in simpler terms trying *everything*.

But there is nothing to try, my good friend. You know that. You've heard of whistling in the dark.

'*You want to be funny?*' In almost a scream, a scream of rage, getting his balance again and bringing his right leg back and starting another kick, not having learned, and this time I parried the foot and turned and straightened up and let his momentum carry him against the rail and when he span round I slapped him with the back of my hand across the eyes, across, more significantly, the pineal gland. Then I waited while he got his orientation back, and it took a bit of time: he lurched about with a hand to his forehead and his other hand reaching out to grab the rail and then my arm, and when he grabbed my arm I chopped gently across his wrist to make him pay attention, to make him understand that I didn't like to be touched with those little pink hermit-crab fingers.

'*Freeze!*'

Roget, of course, getting excited, waving the gun.

'Oh fuck off,' I said and went on watching Nicko, waiting for him to get himself in order again; but the pain in his wrist was occupying him so I took the opportunity of talking a little.

'Look, Nicko, there are things we've got to discuss and they could be to your immediate advantage, but you're putting me in the wrong mood with all this fidgeting. Are you listening to me, Nicko? I hope you are, because otherwise you could make a very grave mistake in taking on the whole of the British Government.'

He got his eyes focused at last but their expression showed only confusion. I didn't expect him to fall for the British Government thing but I could be wrong and he might be thinking about it. There were also the other problems he'd suddenly been given to work out – he'd tried to get through with a couple of kicks but it hadn't got him anywhere and he was bright enough to know that if I'd decided to use more force I could have snapped his wrist and knocked him out cold with a backfist instead of stunning the pineal with a slap. People with guns aren't ready for any kind of resistance and it phases them, but I could be making a mistake with this man and he could get rid of his angst by going for his gun and putting a bullet right through my own pineal gland, *touché*.

'The British Government? The fuck are you talking about?'

An intellectual question: he'd got his emotions under enough control to let him think straight and I liked that because it made him more predictable.

'They're the – '

'Wait a minute.'

He was watching something across the water, something behind me, presumably a boat. We'd passed half a dozen lying at anchor as we'd left the shore, no more than their riding lights burning, the moonlight throwing the shadows of their masts across the surface. There had also been another vessel moving under power with lights flooding the control deck.

I didn't look behind me: he might be trying that one.

'Roget,' he said, 'get lower with that thing.'

The afterdeck wasn't lit but the black made a sharp silhouette against the moonlit sea and the Suzuki had a substantial profile.

'Coastguard?' I asked Nicko.

That would be nice.

He didn't answer, just went on watching the boat. I could hear its engine now. One of the men in the control cabin looked round, hearing it too. The waters off this coast were heavily patrolled by the US Coastguard on the watch for drug runners, Cubans and Haitians, and they could stop any vessel they weren't happy about and ask questions.

They were all watching the ship behind me, Nicko and the men in the cabin, and when I looked at Roget *I saw that his head was turned away from me and the nerves went into the full-alert phase in that instant and the adrenaline hit the bloodstream as I worked out the distance and the two strikes that were called for, one to deal with the Suzuki and the other to the man's throat* – and then it was over and his head was turning back to watch me and I found that my breath was still blocked to power the necessary movement and my right foot was dug against the deck to push me past the inertia and get me across the deck.

Relax.

But Jesus Christ that was –

170

Relax, it's over now. Deepen, calm the breathing, let the muscles go loose again. There might be another chance and more time to take it. The three other men had guns but there'd be nothing I could do on board this boat while that Suzuki was here: it could put out four shots a second and blow me overboard if that man starting firing.

'Nicko.'

The man in the cabin, the one who was watching the boat out there.

'What?' He didn't turn, went on watching the boat.

'You'll have to get it over with before we get there.'

Nicko didn't answer. Presumable meaning: you'll have to shoot those two before we make the rendezvous with the supplier.

Nicko still silent. Fidel the Cuban had finished sluicing the deck; he was on his haunches again, his face still pale, his head back and his eyes closed. I would have said he was wishing it were over, wishing for an end to pain.

'Nicko.' The man in the cabin again.

'What?' He turned round now. 'It's okay, they're just a – '

'Nicko, we want you to do what you have to do before we get there. We don't want bodies around, you listening, Nicko?' The man at the helm said something, and the first man nodded. 'And you'll have to do it quietly, Nicko. No guns. There's too much traffic out here.'

'That wasn't Coastguard, it was – '

'You don't listen, Nicko, I said there's too much traffic out here. You do like we say or we don't come out with you the next time, are you listening to me, Nicko?'

Patience in his tone, spelling it out, no four-letter words thrown in for effect, just the message, listen to me, Nicko. Patience and a certain authority. He was a dealer and he was out here on business and he didn't want anything to get in the way. He and his partner, then, the man at the helm, the dealers; Nicko the heavy, the hit man, bringing the half million or the million on board, seeing to it himself, for the others a necessary evil.

'You don't know these people,' he said, his stomach jerking as he pushed the words out. 'I know them. You didn't have me, you wouldn't be out here to meet them, the fuck are you talking about, Vicente?'

I didn't know if they would have started arguing if it weren't for the fact that murder was to be done. Perhaps it worried them, even though they were used to it. I could feel the same kind of tension that develops in a prison when everyone knows that not far away there's a man preparing a rope or a syringe or the straps on the chair and that the clock is moving towards morning.

'No noise, Nicko. And do it soon, or you'll get us in trouble out here and Mr Toufexis wouldn't like it – have you thought of that? Think of it, Nicko.'

The man in the cabin, Vicente, turned his back. He and the man at the helm carried guns holstered on the left side, and Nicko was wearing his the same way. There was no one else on board except for Roget with the Suzuki and Fidel the Cuban and of course Nicko. The two men who'd brought the boat to the jetty had stayed ashore. The main problem in terms of timing was Roget, the young black: his finger was inside the guard the whole time and he was seven, eight feet distant from me.

So I began work with that as the fulcrum.

'They're the people who employ me, Nicko.'

'What?' Turned to look at me, the small eyes squeezed almost shut, as if a wind had got up, a cold wind. The man up there, Vicente, had started to worry him.

'The British Government,' I said. 'I'm in Miami on a special assignment.'

'Fuck does that mean?'

'It means I've been assigned by the Thatcher administration to represent the United Kingdom's interest in the presidential election, under the aegis of Senator Mathieson Judd.'

He watched me. 'You're full of shit, you know that?'

'The thing is, Nicko, you're getting into something very big, and you're not aware of that. I think it's only my duty to tell you. Everyone can make a mistake, but what worries me is that this one is going to blow you right out of the water.'

In a moment, 'Mistake?'

'That's right. For instance, who gave you the instructions to kill me?'

'Mr Toufexis. Who else?' More quickly than I'd expected, perhaps to shift the blame. The blame, not the guilt; there wouldn't be any guilt, just the memory of sadistic pleasure.

'Then you'll have to tell Mr Toufexis he's making the mistake.'

The pink fleshy mouth became stretched slightly and there was a soft wheeze, a kind of laughter. 'Mr Toufexis doesn't make mistakes. Give me your wallet.'

I thought he'd never ask. *But I'm going to take a risk and trust you because I'm gullible enough to feel reassured by the Queen of England's crest on the card you gave me.* Erica Cambridge. Perhaps it would work with this man too.

Gave him the wallet, and as he took it I moved another two inches towards Roget, the man with the big Suzuki. I had moved more than a foot closer to him in the last three minutes.

Cash, credit cards, driving licence, taking his time.

'Foreign Office. What's that?'

'You call it the State Department.'

'Richard Ainsely Keyes. Right, that's the name. So there's no mistake.'

'Not on your part, no. But I think you should telephone Mr Toufexis and tell him about my assignment for the Thatcher administration. I'm sure he's no wish to get involved in Senator Judd's election campaign. The Senator wouldn't be pleased.'

Another two inches to the left, simply as an exercise in case there was something eventually to be done.

A green light was moving across the sea, at the starboard beam of a vessel. Nicko had seen it and stood watching it for a moment, then turned and went into the control cabin. I judged we were now three miles out, three at the least. Fidel the Cuban had said the rendezvous was to be made seven miles out, and the arithmetic was simple enough: at fifteen knots cruising speed we would be there in approximately fifteen minutes.

No noise, Nicko. Do it soon. Do it before we get there.

That was logical enough: there'd be other people at the rendezvous and I might get a chance to kick and scream, so forth, create confusion.

'Senator Judd?' Nicko looked up from the wallet.

'The candidate for the presidency.'

'Fuck are you talking about?' He turned and went

into the cabin and I watched him go to the radio unit.

Sound of a vessel, the one moving past us to starboard, heading for port. Roget heard it too and wanted to turn round and look at it, but he was only shifting his eyes, thinking about it, and I didn't get ready to do anything. I wasn't close enough to him yet, and I'd have to wait until Nicko came back before I could shift a bit more to the left again. The best thing would be to get to the Suzuki and swing it down but give him time to fire a few shots. It would make a lot of noise and if the Coastguard had a patrol out here they'd come and ask questions.

No noise, Nicko.

Telephone to his head. I could only hear a word or two as his voice rose and lowered against the throb of the diesels, but I think he was asking to speak to a man called Joshua. Or Foster. Or of course *Proctor* because the vowels carried more clearly than the consonants. Perhaps *Proctor*.

The immediate objective for *Barracuda*.

He was holding my card up, turning it aslant to catch the light. I think I heard *Foreign Office*, but that could have been because I was listening for it. Then there was *Mr Toufexis*, and then *Proctor* again and then *Thatcher*, be it given that I was only getting snatches.

It was really very frustrating because the executive for the mission was only a telephone number away from the objective and he was three miles out to sea with a man on one side of him with his testicles out cold and a man on the other side waiting to blow his head across the bay if he did anything wrong and a man in the cabin there with orders for his immediate execution.

All I want, Nicko, is that telephone number, you little fat bastard, the one you've just called, and if I ever get you alone you're going to tell me what it is.

The deck rose and fell away to the slow undulations of the swell; the Miami skyline was lifted suddenly from the dark and strewn across the horizon in a cascade of diamonds, then was lost again, blotted out by the profile of the cabin. *Assignment . . . government . . . janitor* – no, *Senator . . . Senator Judd*, more clearly now as the man at the helm throttled the diesels back, slowing us.

Nicko cradled the telephone and there was no more to listen to, as I asked the black, 'Are we nearly there?' I wanted to know how he was feeling, how confident or how nervous.

'Keep your fuckin' mouth shut, you know what I mean?'

No reliable data. Nicko was coming back and Roget turned his head a little to look at him so I shifted my feet again, three inches this time because it wouldn't be much longer now.

'You're full of shit.'

Nicko, standing in front of me, the small eyes glinting.

'Did you talk to Proctor himself?'

Got a reaction: we hadn't mentioned his name before.

'There isn't any mistake. There isn't any assignment. You wasted my time, and I don't like that.'

But I'd got the answer. Only *Proctor* knew enough about me to know I wasn't on an assignment for the Thatcher government in connection with Senator Judd. This man had just been speaking to the objective. I was that close.

'I suggested you telephone Mr Toufexis,' I said, 'not Proctor.'

'What's the difference?'

Perhaps I could have gone on from there, kept him talking if there'd been time, tried a few oblique questions about Monique, Kim Harvester, Erica Cambridge, 1330 Riverside Way, the yacht *Contessa*, to see if I could get any more information to work on, to give to Ferris, but there wasn't a chance because the man in the cabin, Vicente, was turning round.

'Hey, Nicko. You have to do it now.'

13

DANCE

This was the scene. This was the scene of the execution.

We were moving at less than cruising speed and there was less noise from the diesels. The wake bannered from the stern across the sea towards Miami. There was a vessel a mile off, perhaps less; it was difficult to judge distances by moonlight on a reflecting surface. The vessel was marked only by its riding lights. Two or three more stood off our port quarter, farther away, one of them with lights shining on deck and from a line of portholes below. Another looked as if it had way on, and showed both red and green lights. It was heading obliquely in our direction but wouldn't pass close, no closer than half a mile.

Water slapped below the bows; the night was peaceful.

The man Vicente was still turned towards us in the cabin, looking at Nicko. Fidel the Cuban wasn't aware of the moment; he sat humped against the bulwark nursing his pain, his eyes closed and his head on his chest. Across from him, five feet from where I was standing, Roget the black leaned in a crouch to keep the profile of the big Suzuki below

the rail. He also was looking at Nicko. The fifth
man was at the helm, his back to us. Above the
cabin roof the radar scanner swung, and a penant
flew against the stars.

This was the scene.

Nicko pulled his gun.

'Fidel.'

Kicked the Cuban's foot to get him conscious.
Fidel lifted his head and looked up into Nicko's
bright little eyes, and shrank.

'Get up.'

Didn't move. He couldn't look away from the
man above him. His lips began forming words that
made no sound.

'*Get up!*'

It took a little time, a few seconds, because he
was in a lot of pain; but he got to his feet and Nicko
looked into his face.

'Turn around.'

We rose on a crest and there was Miami again,
jewel-bright in the distance, riding out the night. I
wished Fidel could have turned his head and seen
it, because it was so pretty. It might have reminded
him of Juanita.

'Kneel. On your knees.'

Somewhere a lanyard was slapping timber to the
wind of our passage, strumming in the quietness,
passing the time. Flotsam drifted past, a cement
bag, I think, or a life-jacket.

'Nicko. Not with the gun.' Vicente, from the
cabin.

Nicko turned with a jerk. 'Jesus Christ, we're
miles – '

'*Not with the gun.*'

The tone almost quiet, but with a lot of emphasis,
a lot of authority.

Fidel didn't hear them, or didn't follow the meaning; he knelt facing the bulwark, his back to Nicko, praying softly in Spanish. There was nothing I could do for him and I don't think that in any case it would have been wise. If anything happened he would be in the way, fatally, perhaps, in the way.

'Listen, for Christ's sake, one shot won't make any – '

'Nicko. If you use a gun, Mr Toufexis is going to know. He is going to know from me. You've seen Mr Toufexis with people, Nicko. He will be like that with you. So do it now, and not with a gun.'

'Jesus *Christ*.' But in capitulation.

I suppose Vicente was thinking in terms of numbers, physical numbers. If he didn't want anyone to make a noise there was no point in Roget's holding the big Suzuki on me any more. He'd be better off putting it down and getting his hands ready in case I tried to do anything. Fidel wouldn't do anything: he wasn't in Vicente's reckoning. The way he was working his numbers out, there were four men against one, and that would be enough in the event of trouble.

'Do it, Nicko. Now.'

I don't think Vicente had thought about Roget and the Suzuki yet. He was too concerned with Nicko and the need to get this over soon, at once. He watched Nicko go to the chain locker and come back with a marlin spike.

'Christ sake,' he said, looking up at Vicente in the cabin. 'Think of the fucking *mess*.'

I thought his tone was interesting. To take a gun away from a man like this, a man who cleans it, loads it, wears it wherever he goes, is like taking his clothes off him. It feels like a different world to him, a world in which he feels exposed. And I believe

181

there was another thing. Nicko was squeamish. To shoot another man from a distance, however short, is to enjoy the remoteness of the act, the technical sophistication of moving the safety catch off, of aiming, holding still, and moving the trigger against the spring. But to take a man's life with the bare hands or with some crude instrument as an extension of the hands is an act of intimacy, of an intimacy greater by far than the act of love, involving as it does the plundering of life itself.

He stood there, Nicko, holding the spike, not sure how he was going to do this without getting blood on his expensive khaki suit. He was holding the thing in both hands, in the horrible semblance of a golfer about to make a stroke.

'Time, Nicko,' from the cabin, 'you're wasting time. Do it.'

I thought I heard Roget's teeth chattering, on my left. Perhaps he didn't really like the act of slaughtering when it came to it; or perhaps he was excited, I don't know.

'Nicko,' I said, 'let the poor little bastard jump overboard, give him a chance to swim. He won't steal again, after this.'

Nicko turned his head to look at me, and the look was murderous, I think because I'd offered him a get-out he couldn't take.

'*Fucking shuddup.*'

His fat little face shone with sweat. I could smell him from where I stood. Then he looked back at the man kneeling in front of him, at the back of his head.

The timing wasn't right: I couldn't make a move. If I tried making a move the timing would have to be perfect, and I would need to use Fidel the Cuban and I would need to use him in the moment of his death.

'Nicko.' From the cabin. 'You want me to come and do it, Nicko?'

I think Vicente knew the fat man well enough to know that he would be stung by that, would feel unbrave, unable to kill a man without his gun.

Do you know how to turn?

The swell moved under us all, lifting and letting us fall as if to the rhythm of our mother's bosom, the bosom of Mother Earth, as if we were brothers, Nicko, Vicente, Roget, Fidel and the man at the helm whose name I didn't know, as if they were my brothers.

Very fast? Do you know how to turn very fast?

Which in a way I suppose they were, my brothers, born with me on this little piece of interstellar rock, to be nurtured by the same essences of water and of air, the same magnetic waves, the same vibrations, and then to die. But I was not going to think about that.

He stood there holding the marlin spike, my little fat brother, smelling of sweat, mine own executioner.

It might amuse you, my good friend, if I tell you how to make a very fast turn, in case you don't already know. It will make an interesting digression in my stream of consciousness, because I always feel a certain lightheadedness when faced with the prospect of mortality; it has happened before.

Well, then, let us to the matter. It is performed sometimes in *Shotokan* karate, in *Heian Shodan*, when one moves from *zenkutsu-dachi* to *kokutsu-dachi*, turning completely through two hundred and seventy degrees. There are six things to do, each of them making the turn faster and faster, and it doesn't make any difference whether you're in *zenkutsu-dachi* or standing normally, though it's better if you have one foot forward a little, say the right foot, because this will be the pivot for the turn.

The lights swing upwards into view, brightly bedecking the night's horizon over there as we fall away to a hollow in the sea.

Nicko stands tensely now. He is very tense, his knuckles white as he grips the heavy spike. Only a second has gone by since Vicente spoke to him, daring him, though it seems much longer.

The right foot, yes, will provide the pivot, and the first thing you have to do is push off with the left one, if you are turning backwards to the left. The second thing is to swing the hips in that direction, to be conscious only of the hips in this millisecond of our little game, and the third thing to do is to swing the left arm in the same direction, to lend centrifugal force, and here it is worth mentioning that the left arm and hand provide a potent weapon at the end of the turn, if, say, the hand forms a fist with the knuckles vertical and the thumb uppermost.

Fidel is praying, as he has prayed before; he kneels as if in his church, and of course appropriately, since he is about, in his mind, to meet the personification of infinity he calls God. Nicko is starting to lift the marlin spike, swinging it in an arc above his head. It is heavy. He is sweating copiously. He stinks.

Vicente is watching from the cabin, hands by his sides. He looks Italianate, as his name suggests. I think he is a cool man, confident in himself, and therefore dangerous. The other man is of course looking ahead of him across the milky moonlit sea, maintaining the diesels at something like a quarter throttle with the bows cutting the horizon. The night is warm as we sail on in brotherhood, sharing its warmth.

But that is not quite true. The night has no warmth for me, because when the fat man has split the head of the Cuban he will come for me and if I do anything to stop him they will shoot, the others, and risk calling attention.

I am not, however, forgetting you, my good friend, as you wait agog to perform this totally spectacular turn, or so my totally inexcusable degree of self-indulgence allows me to believe. The fourth thing to do, then, is to use the right arm in the same direction, again using centrifugal force, and yet again, if the right hand is formed, say, flat and with the palm upwards and the fingers closed to provide a cutting edge, it will offer an effective strike at the face or throat or clavicle, should you wish to defend yourself against attack. The two last requirements for the turn are not physical. The first is mental, the second almost spiritual. You have to think *Get there*, and finally you have to feel *Be there*.

He is lifting the heavy spike, Nicko, swinging it back and upwards, his small pink mouth puckered and the material of his expensive jacket going into folds at the shoulder, the single button pulling at the waist.

. . . *Que Dios se acuerde lo bueno que he hecho en mi vida y se olvide lo malo* . . .

The lips of Fidel are moving, though I don't see them from this angle; I know they are moving because I can hear the sibilants of his last prayer. Vicente is watching from the cabin; he hasn't moved. Time has slowed, as always happens when the mind, brought to a high degree of stress, becomes aware that time is a man-made artifact,

185

and subject to contradiction by the infinite.

The marlin spike swings higher. I watch it.

The turn, yes, we must not forget the turn, the expression of my sense of lightness, of unreality as my life nears its seeming close. But you already have it all, my good friend, and you should practise each segment of the turn one after another, and you will find the speed increasing, and to the point where you are carried off balance – a sign of progress. Then you should put all those segments together, and let them happen at once, like an explosion, and in the instant of completion, tighten the abdomen to preserve the balance and land squarely at whatever degree you wish to – it doesn't have to be at two hundred and seventy, there's no magic in that number. The last requirement, to *Be there*, has to be made with the muscles relaxed and the mind in alpha waves, and this may not happen at the fiftieth turn of your practice, but could well happen at the hundredth.

The deck trembles a little beneath our feet. The lanyard slaps to the wind of our passage. The sibilants fall from the lips of the kneeling Cuban as the little fat man brings the marlin spike to the top of its arc and it comes fluting downwards to the Cuban's fragile skull and his executioner grunts with the effort.

It strikes. It strikes the skull.

Be there.

A whirl of lights as the city of Miami span across my vision field and the black was suddenly close to me and my right arm swung through the turn and the right hand lifted a degree to line up with his throat and even now the surprise was only just coming into his eyes and of course too late because the sword-hand was in contact with its target and beginning to bury there at the site of the thyroid gland.

What I had started to do was over now and it had taken very little more than one half-second, though the planning had taken longer. From this instant there would be chaos of a kind and there'd be no way for me to control it. There were risks, appalling risks to this desperate enterprise but it had been a question of choice, of letting myself get into a sordid little confrontation with Nicko and having to kill him an unknown number of seconds before Roget blew the heart out of my ribs with the Suzuki, or of going for this trick, getting rid of the black before anything else and taking the others on later. If I could reach the black's motor nerves fast enough and freeze them he wouldn't fire the gun and Nicko and Vicente and the man at the helm would opt to maintain silence on the boat and come for me with their hands or a knife and I might have a chance of dropping overboard before they could reach me, dropping and diving deep and turning for the long journey to the shore.

But there was nothing I could do now to control the moment. I would have to watch for a chance if ever it came and use it for what it was worth. A very great deal of data was coming in to the left hemisphere for analysis: the Cuban was collapsing onto the deck with his blood colouring the air as it flew from the site of the blow. I saw Nicko's face, saw the grimace, the mouth drawn back and the eyes widening in an expression I'd no time to interpret, though it was shock, I believe, perhaps because it was the first time the man had killed without using a gun, had killed personally, intimately, leaving blood on his hands that would not be easy to wash away.

In front of me was Roget, and he still hadn't pumped the gun, presumably because I had indeed reached his motor nerves in time. He was already dying as the blood began filling his windpipe and his body was beginning to swing back from the force of the strike. It wouldn't take more than one hand to tip his spine across the rail and send him overboard, but –

Began firing and I wasn't ready for it because I thought the moment had come and gone and all I could do was push at the barrel and he swung faster and the shots went raking across the cabin and the sound banged in the confines as glass shattered and the man at the helm was pitched across the controls and the diesels began racing at full throttle. Nicko was shouting something and I didn't know if he'd been hit. Vicente was tumbling down the three steps from the cabin with his eyes on me and his hands ready, not reaching for his gun.

Six shots, rapid fire, the last of them from a dead man's finger as Roget tilted backwards over the rail and I pushed the big Suzuki with him, stink of cordite on the warm night air and the deck keeling as the unmanned helm swung over and we began weaving across the sea with the engines still at full ahead both and then Nicko was at me and we locked together and I tried for his throat but missed because my shoes were slipping on the Cuban's blood so I tried for the solar plexus with the fist rising to get under the ribs for a direct kill but the area was thick with flesh and he only grunted and I changed the fist into a heel-palm and struck upwards but didn't do more than graze the side of his head.

'*Get him.*'

Vicente, as he reached us and Nicko got an arm

round my neck and put pressure there until I found the thumb and broke it and he screamed and the other man came in close for me with a knife and I hadn't expected that, the glint of the blade in the glow from the cabin lights, hadn't expected it because he hadn't been reaching for anything when he'd started his run.

Tried an elbow-smash into Nicko's face but he was half-turned away from me and off-balance, going down and dragging me with him and I let him do it because there was a chance of a strike and I straightened one leg with the foot angled to make a blade and thrust hard for Vicente's groin and did some damage and felt him spin sideways and strike the deck with his head, not making a sound, a different breed from Nicko and therefore the more to be wary of.

Cordite sharp in the lungs, someone coughing, the fat man coming in again and surprisingly fast and I couldn't do anything with him until he made a mistake and left himself open and I found his face exposed and went for the eyes and reached one of them but it galvanised him and he insisted with me, an arm round my neck again and squeezing as Vicente came in with the knife and I waited until it swung up and then turned and left Nicko as the target.

I don't remember when it was that they began gaining. It took time and much had passed. Vicente was losing blood because I'd managed to turn the blade and rip into him somewhere before I lost my grip on the handle and let it go. I had injured Nicko, perhaps with one of the nerve strikes I'd been working on, but he was still surprisingly strong and very quick, vicious in his anger because he wanted his cake and he'd been looking forward to it and I was trying to take it away from him, take my death away.

They had both spent a lot of time trying to reach their guns. At first they hadn't wanted to make any more noise after the hammering boom of the Suzuki, but then they'd realised I might get them both under control and they'd stopped worrying about making a noise. I'd sent the first gun – Vicente's – over the rail without any trouble because he was so busy with the bloody thing that he forgot about the combat and left himself open and I'd gone in with an eye strike and got the gun away from him while he was protecting himself.

Nicko was more difficult and we'd fired a round with his finger on the trigger and the gun pointing nowhere, but then I'd found his throat and he'd panicked and I'd got the gun and lobbed it overboard and this worried them and they became excited. I could have killed Nicko when I'd found his throat exposed but I didn't want to. That had been Proctor he'd phoned from the cabin and I wanted the number because it had become the focus of the whole mission, the only access to Proctor we'd got.

The stars were swinging through the black reaches of the sky and when the boat heeled as it sped across the surface I began losing orientation, just momentary flashes of knowing nothing, being nowhere, momentary but critical, potentially lethal. I didn't know where the boat was taking us; we knew it was running wild, that was all, the helm free and the throttles open, and the first thing Vicente or Nicko would do if they could get clear of me would be to break for the cabin and get control. I didn't want that to happen because if we hit another vessel and didn't totally smash up I'd have a chance of getting away.

The stars swung and the bows hammered across the swell and I lurched sometimes, mentally lurched into the oblivion that was waiting for me out there, a limitless void that was there to gather the end of things, the bric-à-brac of lost endeavours, the tattered rags of hope, where – *for Christ's sake stay with it don't give up stay with it* yes indeed, perhaps I'd taken the blade in somewhere and was losing blood, it felt like that, the onset of lassitude, *stay with it*, exactly so, but they were gaining, I tell you, they were gaining on me. Twice I found an arm exposed and worked my thumb into the median nerve with force enough to produce great pain but there was no sound, no jerking to free the arm, and after a time I realised that we were locked together, these two men and I, across the body of the Cuban.

'*Nicko,*' his voice, Vicente's voice, sounding stifled, with not much breath to spare, '*we've got him, Nicko,*' speaking perhaps to boost the fat man's morale, or not speaking to him at all but to me, knowing the value of despair if one can instill it in one's adversary.

He failed, because I knew the danger, but the thought stayed in my mind on an intellectual level, the thought that they could have got me now, they could be within seconds, shall we say, of bringing me my doom, here under the swinging stars as –

Dazzling lights swarming against us in the night, their brilliance rising in a wave, towering, the lights of the city breaking over us as the boat hit and the night exploded and I was flung headlong as the hull burst open and glass from the smashed windows in the cabin flew in a bright shower in the light from the shore, then the sensation of falling and the flat sheen of water below and I hit the surface shoulder first and the lights flared and then darkened as I went under.

Nowhere.

It wasn't dark down here, not now. They'd set up a generator and floodlights, or perhaps it was one of the fire trucks with its search lamps going. The coloured flashes of the police cars dappled the surface above me and I could hear sirens dying towards the quay. I could see sharp outlines close to me, debris turning as it sank, and blurred shapes farther off, the huge body of the boat angled bows down with the stern breaking the surface.

But he was nowhere, Nicko.

I was, yes, losing blood: I could see it now, blackish whorls forming in the water as I moved, blowing like smoke. But it couldn't be anything serious, worth surfacing for. I had already been up a dozen times to breathe, for a while floating face upwards to reorientate, having to take the risk of being seen. I didn't want to be hauled out and questioned, at least until I'd found Nicko, or they had. If they found him, I'd know: I was watching their progress every time I surfaced.

I would rather find him myself. I had something to ask him: the telephone number. The access to Proctor. It wouldn't be easy to ask him if they found him first and put him into an ambulance; I'd have to make out I needed medical attention so as to go with him, stay with him. But I would have said that the chances of finding him alive by now were thin, unless he was bobbing on the surface somewhere among the debris and they hadn't seen him yet.

Sound of a helicopter vibrating through the water, then more light came flooding down, silvering some of the bits and pieces that had been blown out of the boat. I dived lower, using the light, one hand on an anchor chain to keep my bearings, and there was Fidel below me, his arms and legs opened out, his face turning towards the light and then vanishing, the dark smoke of blood still curling from his skull. He would be going down there to wait for his little Juanita, to wait a long time for her in the limbo of the lost, his arms and legs windmilling slowly, disturbing the slime where a fish flashed in the light, then another, scenting his blood.

I surfaced again and floated, drawing flotsam around me and sighting along the surface. There was more noise here, the thin wail of the sirens piercing the boom of the chopper's rotors; the surface was ruffled by the airstream and the debris was tossed in circles. Then it rose suddenly: I suppose it had come lower to look at something, ready to deploy the salvage net. On the jetty a frogman was settling his mask and flip-flopping towards the water.

I took a final breath and went down again into the half-lit netherworld and saw him almost at once, Nicko, his arms stretched out as the Cuban's had been, the current tugging at the cloth on his little fat legs, and as I swam towards him the light was mottled with the slow drifting of leaves, rising and whirling and spreading out, some of them touching his hands, Nicko's hands, then drifting away, turning and catching the light and darkening again, hundreds of them, puzzling me until I saw they were banknotes, the suitcase on the surface somewhere among the other things, burst open and empty now.

Still losing, I was still losing blood, the muscles languid and the mind starting to wander a little, mesmerised by the whirling of the banknotes, but I went for him, scissors-kicking through the light and shadow and missing him the first time as the current turned him so that for a moment he was upright, standing there with his arms reaching to touch his windfall, to play with it, while fish darted at his face, at the hollows of his eyes. I got close to him at the second attempt, and danced with him as I caught the folds of his clothes and began searching the pockets; but the lungs were pulling for air and I had to surface and float there taking in a snatched breath and then another until I could breathe rhythmically, taking the necessary time but worrying because he could drift away, Nicko, and I might lose him.

Down again and I couldn't find him, had to go deeper, as far as the mud and the litter of cans and tyres and broken spars and then look upwards, catching his silhouette against the light and rising for him, working on the pockets again, the light troubling me now, flooding into my head and staying there when I closed my eyes, the weakness spreading from the muscles to the will, the will to go on moving instead of letting go, drifting in the shadows, dancing with my little fat friend as he – *watch it* – dancing among the leaves – *wake up for Christ's sake* – yes, no time for dancing is there, taking his keys and his wallet, drifting with him as he turned, wallet in my hand, wallet with perhaps the telephone number in it, the access to Proctor, drifting and turning in the eerie underwater light with the mind hallucinating, weaving patterns of its own, the scene swinging as I turned again and looked into the face of Kim Harvester.

14

GRACE

Honing the knife.

The noon heat pressed down from a brassy sky,
and the glare off the water hit the inside of the cabin
like a floodlight. The sea was mirror-smooth, with
a long swell running. We were somewhere south of
Cape Florida, she'd told me, ten miles from the
mainland. We didn't want, she'd said, anyone looking at us through field glasses again.

Honing the knife, turning the blade on the stone,
a big knife, long, curving to a fine point. One of her
breasts showed inside the loose turquoise bra, the
nipple raised. She wasn't sitting like that, leaning
forward, to invite my interest; she was just used to
being alone on board.

'I shall have to make it a clean kill,' she said.

The swell lifted the tug, lowered it. I could see
the Cape, north by north-east, and two other ves-
sels, one of them moving out of the bay under limp
sails, and a motor yacht on the south horizon. She'd
said it was the *Contessa*.

'Right into the brain, through the eye. If I don't
do it cleanly, he'll flash away. They don't like being
hurt – and he'd remember.' Looking up, her green

195

eyes seeing the shark, not me. 'Don't underestimate those beasts.'

She hadn't wanted to bring me to the tug, early this morning. She'd moved with me through the pale underwater light but I hadn't gone straight to the quay; there were a lot of people milling around there, silhouetted against the floodlights, and the Coastguard helicopter was still hovering above the sunken boat. I'd surfaced to breathe and then dived again, leading her past the end of the jetty before I climbed onto a moored boat well clear of the action and reached the quay.

'Are you all right?' Her mask off, watching me.

'Yes. Can you get me away from here?'

'You need an ambulance,' she said. 'You're hurt.'

Blood reddening the water trickling from my clothes. 'Look, get me away, will you? I don't want people asking a lot of questions.' It was dangerous, perhaps, to trust her, but I'd been losing blood and hadn't slept and if I dropped suddenly she'd go for one of the ambulances and I didn't want that. There'd be some of Nicko's friends in that crowd along there and my photo was in circulation. I didn't want a police enquiry either because it'd hold things up.

'Why don't you want them to ask questions?' Not letting it go, not taking anything for granted, watching me hard with her green eyes.

I'd said the wrong thing, you see, not feeling terribly bright at the moment. 'In any case, I don't want anyone to see me. They're still trying to kill me.'

She'd remember the shooting, yesterday. Swaying a little now, swaying comfortably, enjoying the rhythm, the lights of the city swinging away, swinging back, *watch it*, yes, don't want ambulance.

196

'Who are? The police?'

Oh Jesus Christ, what made her think that? The drug scene, I suppose, she was so used to it, thought I was a dealer, man on the run. 'No. Toufexis. His people.'

'*Toufexis?*' Didn't take her eyes off me. 'All right, I'll take you out of here, but I want to know who you are.'

'Government.' The whole city swinging, swinging back, the lights dizzying. 'HM Government.'

'You'll have to prove that, or I'm turning you in.' She searched for the knife wound, somewhere under my shirt, left side, found it. 'Handkerchief? Okay, keep it pressed there while I get the car.'

On the way to the tug I showed her my identity and told her there were two bodies back there, Fidel's and Nicko's, and perhaps a man still alive, Vicente, in the water, she could phone the rescue team and tell them that. Then I lost the whole thing and woke up on the boat.

'I was a nurse,' she said, 'for seven years. Does that hurt?'

'No.' Morning light across the sea. I'd slept nearly five hours and woke feeling successful, in a way, because I'd got that man's wallet and it had Proctor's number in it, or the number of the place where he could be reached, where Nicko had reached him from the boat.

'I liked it,' she said, 'being a nurse. But those male chauvinist pigs finally got under my skin and I quit, slammed the door of the emergency room in one of their faces, as a matter of fact, broke his nose. They think we're just their assistants, but nursing's a profession too; we're professionals like they are, and we spend a *lot* more time with the patients, and get very much closer, and that matters, you know, it's

197

very often a question of life and death if you hold someone's hand at the right moment. But those bastards just think we're scullery maids. Keep your arm away, this is the last one.' Curved needle, going into the flesh and out again across the wound, she might have been sewing a sock, very expert. 'I keep this kit for me, really. How do you feel?'

'Good shape.'

'Because you've lost some blood, as you know, but we can't tell how much. You're a bit white still, but that could be shock hanging about. Hold absolutely still while I get a bandage.'

Came back and I said, 'Are you a police reservist or something?'

'Volunteer diver, that's all. They beeped me. So I want to know all about it, Richard, because I could be some kind of accessory after the fact or concealing evidence or a dozen other things.' Looking at me straight. 'I took a risk, bringing you here, and you owe me. But all I want is the truth.'

Told her the whole thing and there wasn't any danger in that because she already knew I was looking for Proctor and the only thing I was adding now was that Proctor was looking for me.

'When you say he's "looking for you", what exactly does that mean?'

'He'd like to find me.'

It wasn't an answer and she knew that. In a moment – 'Is he trying to kill you?'

'I think so.'

She dropped the unused bandage into the medical kit and snapped the lid shut. 'Was that him, shooting at your car?'

'No.'

'How d'you know?'

'He's no good with a gun.'

'All right, then did he set you up?'

'Either he did, or whoever he's working for.'

'Is he working for Toufexis?'

'I don't know.'

'Look, if you'd rather – '

'I don't honestly know. But I'd like to.'

'Well that's the point.' She'd seen the yacht with the slack canvas coming out of the bay, and watched it for a moment. 'If you want to find Proctor, maybe I can help. But you'll have to tell me more about things, and if you'd rather not, then say so.'

'Why would you want to help me?'

In the labyrinth, where you can't see much more than the next corner, it's nice to know which side people are on, and even nicer to know why. People change their minds sometimes, and that's because their motivation isn't strong enough to keep them stable: it happens all the time.

'I think I want to help you,' she said in a moment, 'because I like you. Not like, exactly. I find you intriguing. First you get shot at and bloody nearly burned alive and the next time I see you it's six fathoms down with bodies and banknotes all over the place.' She held her gaze for a while. 'Turns me on. And as I told you, he's an absolute shit and I'd very much like to see you put *him* in the gun sights and drop him stone cold dead.' Looking down, 'I phoned your hotel, after that shooting, to see if you were still in the land of the living.'

'Kind of you.'

In a moment she said, 'I did a year in bomb disposal when I was still in England. It – '

'That was before you lost your father?'

She looked up quickly. 'Yes. Why?'

'I mean you had these – ' wrong start, had these suicidal tendencies was not very flattering – 'these urges to push things to the brink quite a while ago.'

She watched me quietly and when she spoke again her voice was lower. 'I suppose so. We're a bit alike, aren't we? It used to turn me on – and this is why I mentioned it, actually, about bomb disposal – it used to give me a real kick to sort of be in their presence, just sitting quietly in front of those things, knowing how much awful power there was in them. And being close to you gives me the same feeling, I mean the tension comes off you in absolute waves. And I like that.'

She got up and took the medical kit to the other end of the cabin and put it into a cupboard and then went into the head, and this was the first chance I'd had so I went over to the phone and dialled the number.

'Yes?'

'Shadow safe.'

I left it at that and hung up. He would have had support people watching my hotel and they would have expected me there after I'd called him last night from the quay, and they'd have started worrying by first light and Ferris would have signalled the board as a matter of routine, *executive missing*, and that boat had made a lot of noise with all the police and everything and he might have put things together and started a search.

When Kim came back she said, 'I want you to rest for a bit longer,' and dropped a pile of magazines onto the bamboo stool, 'just till you get your colour back.'

That had been hours ago and now she was honing the knife and not talking very much. She'd gone into a kind of shell, and I didn't disturb her, spoke only when she spoke.

'Sometimes you won't see one for weeks, then

you'll see a whole group, moving in to feed on something.'

Something like Roget, the black, still floating out there, unless his finger had got jammed inside the trigger guard of the big Suzi and he'd gone all the way down.

'Have you seen one today?'

'Couple of dorsal fins. Over there, look.'

Cutting the surface a hundred yards away, splinters of light flashing as they turned and caught the sun. I hadn't noticed them.

The noon heat pressed down, its weight seeming to calm the sea. The glare came up from the water blinding bright, flooding the cabin and bouncing, flashing on brasswork and reflecting in barbs of light. The silence was absolute and there was no motion except when the swell rolled under the boat; we floated here in isolation, trapped between sky and sea under the burning-glass of the sun.

'Did you expect them to be there?' I asked her.

Sound carried, and we spoke in murmurs.

'In a way, yes.' She turned the blade again on the stone. 'I've been getting a feeling, lately. A feeling it won't be long.'

I watched the two fins. I think there was a third now but the light was tricky, the whole surface shimmering. 'Before you find the one you're looking for?'

'Yes.' Looking up at me, 'Do you get feelings like that? Presentiments?'

'Yes.' It was a third fin, I could see it clearly now. 'What kind are they?'

'I'd say they're nurses. Not grey ones, but still aggressive.'

'How big?'

'Maybe three metres, fully grown. I've seen – '

she broke off as the water flashed over there and a slim metallic body broke the surface. 'No, they're threshers – that one's over four metres. It was a thresher that killed him. I got a close look.' She was silent for a time, her eyes on the rhythmic stroking of the blade. 'They hunt in packs.'

'How many is a pack?'

'It varies. Anything from ten to thirty. They've got large eyes,' she said, 'green ones, like mine.' She was watching them all the time now, the knife still in her hand.

'What's attracting them?' There were more of them now.

'They come and take a look at boats, quite often. People throw garbage out of boats.'

She was sitting totally still now, her eyes on the sea, her head angled a little, the knife lying in her cupped hand, her brown legs tucked under her, the toes flexed. They were circling the whole time but slowly coming closer to the boat, and we could hear the sudden sharp splash as one of them flicked a tail, scattering white water.

Five, six of them now.

The water was clear below, and I could see the dark line of a reef running across our beam, with shadows moving as the rest of the pack circled, fathoms down.

'Could you skipper this boat if you had to, do you think?' She was speaking slowly, only half-aware of me.

'I could work it out.'

There wasn't anything I could say that would change her mind. It was her own affair.

'As I said, some people say I just want to follow my Dad, be with him again. One man, I think he was into psychiatry or something like that, said that

202

sticking a knife into a shark was penis envy. Takes all sorts, doesn't it?'

They were close now, seven or eight of them, their bodies darkening the water just below the surface. She didn't move, looked carved out of bronze under the hot weight of the sun, the knife in her hand. *It used to give me a real kick to sort of be in their presence, just sitting quietly in front of those things, knowing how much awful power there was in them.*

I got out of the deck chair and stood at the rail and looked over the side. They were closer than I'd been able to see before, and one of them came right in and nosed along the beam of the boat and I felt its tremor as it grazed the timbers.

She was wiping the oil, Kim, the oil from the blade, and dropped the rag on to the stone and kept hold of the knife, moving to the rail and looking down into the water, and when she remembered me and looked up against the glare of the sun her eyes were narrowed to slits of pale green in the bronze of her face, watching me for a moment before she said, her voice clear in the unearthly quiet, 'If he's there, I'll know. I'll know the one.' Then she reached behind her and unhooked the turquoise bra and let it fall and tugged the bikini down her legs and over her long narrow feet and swung herself across the rail and broke the surface quietly, sinking as far as her head and then bringing her legs up to lie flat, just below the surface, not moving her arms or hands but only her feet, fanning with them to move away from the boat.

They were charcoal, the sharks, and she was a light bronze and of course much smaller, but she looked less alien among them than I would have imagined, floating with her body aligned to theirs as they closed in, slowing to get the measure of this other creature.

I didn't move, could not, I am sure, have moved. She was holding the knife behind her back, that is to say underneath her, so that it wouldn't flash in the light like a lure and attract their attention, and as she took a breath and turned slowly and dived the last I could see was that she was holding it in front of her now, the knife. Then she was gone.

Fear crept in me, contracting the scrotum, tightening the throat, as I watched those things from the safety of the boat, fear of them, certainly, of their huge size and their latent primitive force, and fear for her, the suddenness of her going from sight leaving a sense of shock, a sense already of loss and appalling danger, of murder down there where I couldn't see, of feasting as they closed in and their curved jaws opened and they ripped and began ravaging.

Too much, yes, too much imagination, very well, let us regain a little of our control, so forth, she must have done this before and she knows those ghastly things from long experience and all she's doing is playing with life and death and maybe putting on a show for me, proud of her obsession, flaunting it. But even so, even so, my good friend, I didn't relish this, you may well believe.

And then there was just a lot of blood on the surface, a lot of threshing about and then the blood, Christ, it was a beautiful red, he was a beautiful man, he coloured the whole sea like a flag, like a banner.

Forty-five, I would have said, it must have been forty-five seconds since I'd seen her. The great shapes were still circling slowly, not so near the surface now, as if something below were attracting them, their long tails fanning in the clear water, the light of the surface ripples playing along their smooth metallic flanks.

Could you skipper this boat if you had to, do you think?

The sun beat down on the sea, pressing it flat, spreading its heat and its molten light from horizon to horizon while I dwelled here on this gilded mote and came as close as I have ever come to praying.

Fifty seconds, sixty, perhaps, as they circled the slim bronze other-creature in the depths.

It's not my vessel. I brought it in. And I want to report a death.

More than a minute, she'd been down there more than a minute now, her lungs beginning to feel the need for oxygen.

You did nothing to stop her?

What could I have done?

You could have talked to her, surely, talked her out of it. You could have restrained her, if necessary.

She was a responsible adult with a mind of her own.

A confused adult, surely, intending suicide.

How do we know? I think she was following her karma.

Her what?

Her karma.

What is that, exactly?

Movement suddenly in the water there, over there, a fin cutting the surface and flashing in the light, the others circling wider for some reason, *oh for Christ's sake come up will you, it's a minute fifteen, a minute and a half.*

What is karma?

It means fate, loosely translated. Destiny. She was following her destiny. People meddle too much, you know, with other people's lives, we are not our brother's keeper when it comes to the crunch.

Slowly, very slowly from the depths there was this smaller shape now, a dull gold creature rising with its long hair rippling at its sides until the head broke surface and the body followed, turning gently to float as the weakness flowed into my legs and the breath came out of me and I shut my eyes against the brazen light of the sea.

And even then you didn't try to dissuade her?

No. It was her wish. Her will. I do the same thing myself, sometimes.

You go swimming among sharks?

No, but it's just as dangerous. We like the brink, you see. We like being there.

The great gray shapes circled, some of them just below the surface with a fin cutting through it here and there like a knife through silk, some of them deeper, no more than dark shadows, and there she was, the female biped, lying in the middle of them with her face to the sky and her eyes closed and her mouth moving as she breathed, breathed deeply to replace the oxygen she'd used down there, a human being with a history and two dead parents and a few boyfriends around and a job to do and a life to live or simply, if you looked at it that way, the way nature looked at it, a morsel of food for these fish, a delicacy with rich sweet-tasting blood and tender flesh, a small feast for them in the heat of noon, an offering in the celebration of life.

A tail threshed at the surface close to her but she didn't move, didn't turn her head. Perhaps they were playing. Perhaps, I thought with my breath blocked and my blood chilled, they were playing.

And then she moved at last, rolling gently until she was face down and then jack-knifing, her legs coming out of the water and poising vertically for a second and then sliding out of sight, leaving a small ring of ripples that melted away as the big fish drew closer and I knew what I would finally say when they pressed me to it, yes, I should have tried to talk her out of it, tried to save her life.

She came up three times to breathe and dived three times, surfacing closer to the boat than before and breaking the pattern, floating across the circle they were making *and lifting suddenly from the surface as one of them rose from below and glanced across her back* and I had a rope ready in my hands before she got her balance and crawl-stroked to the side of the boat and I helped her across the rail, 'He wasn't there,' with the water streaming from her body, 'the one I was looking for wasn't there,' streaming from her hair as she faced me with her green eyes shimmering as she lived through this little time in that particular state of grace that comes with a release from close communion with death, and then her hands were on me and she drew me down with her and the knife dropped to the hot scented timbers of the deck and lay beside us.

Blood on the deck.

'Yes?'

'I'm at sea, south of Cape Florida, ten miles from the mainland.'

In a moment: 'Condition?'

'Fully active.' The knife wound I'd taken last night had slashed the hip but hadn't cut deep muscle. I could still run if I had to.

She was wiping the blood off the deck over there by the starboard rail – the shark had grazed her shoulder blades when it had lifted her from the surface.

'The chief of the Miami Mafia,' Ferris said, 'has

put out a contract on you, effective immediately. Did you know?'

'I could have guessed.' It explained the Nicko thing.

He caught the tone. 'They've made contact?'

'Yes.'

Another pause and then he said, 'In any case it's too dangerous for you to disembark at the quay as you did before. You're on board the tug?'

'Yes.'

He was keeping the exchange of information as brief as he could: we weren't using a scrambler. 'Stay there till dark and I'll have you taken off. They'll ask for your exact position later. Understood?'

'Yes.'

'Anything to add?'

'Yes. We're under surveillance.' The motor yacht with the limp sails had furled her canvas and had come within a mile of us under power and I'd caught the glint of twin lenses.

In a moment he said, 'Wait for the dark.'

15

NIGHTFALL

'So who was firing on you?'

She was splicing a rope, making a loop-end, sitting on a box; she had a pair of khaki shorts on, nothing else, letting her back heal; all she'd asked me to do was throw sea-water over the abrasions.

'I don't know,' I said.

'I saw the whole thing. The fire and everything.' She worked at the rope. 'Did you think I'd set you up, Richard?'

'Why should I?'

'You were so wary of me, that day, is what I mean. So untrusting.' With a brief glance at me, 'But then I suppose you're wary of everyone, in your business, whatever that is.' Her tone changed, became more formal. 'There's nothing you want to tell me, and I understand that, but I need to know enough about last night, the boat crash, to satisfy myself that I'm not an accessory after the fact or concealing evidence or harbouring a criminal. I've got a good record and I work for the Miami police whenever they can use an extra diver, so I want to make sure I'm not getting involved in anything illegal. You've shown me your Foreign Office card but you can get those printed by some backstreet forger if you know where to find one.'

There were two steps down into the cabin and we were sitting at the forward end, out of sight from the sea. She knew about the surveillance: she'd seen the field glasses too.

'The head of the Mafia,' I said, 'has put out a contract on me. Hence the shooting on the quay and hence my boat trip last night.' I told her about it. 'Hence also the surveillance they've put on us again. I want you to know,' leaning forward, 'that as soon as I'm taken off this boat I shall keep well out of your way.'

She looked up. 'Why?'

'Because it puts you at risk.'

'I know that. But I want to see you again.'

'One day.'

'Look, I'm hardly a tender blushing rose. I know Luigi Toufexis. I've met him. I did – '

'He's the Mafia chief?'

'Yes. I did a bit of undercover work for the police here once, got involved by accident and made myself useful. Toufexis is deadly, but you don't need telling that. Look, I pick up quite a bit of scuttlebut in my job – I know most of the boat owners and some of the Coastguard crews.' She looked down, making another splice. 'And the rumour that started going around a couple of days ago is that you're an international cocaine dealer working under UK Government cover and you came here to put Toufexis out of business. Hence, as you say, the contract.' She looked up to catch my expression. Wasn't any.

What she'd told me fell right into place: it had Proctor's signature on it. He wanted me blown away and he'd picked the most powerful weapon in Miami to do it with. Logical Bureau procedure.

'Is it true?' Kim asked me.

'No. George Proctor put that story out to bring Toufexis down on me.'

'You know that?'

'I know Proctor.' He would have preferred to make the kill personally, as a matter of honour, but he was obviously too occupied with other things. 'Does he use cocaine?'

'Yes. Or he did when I knew him.'

That fell into place too. Proctor had been known for his integrity, and that was why Croder was concerned about his lapses in signals to London. And he wasn't a man to blow his mind on cocaine just for kicks, so it must have been a response to his increasing frustration: the bullet near the heart had left him unusable as a shadow executive and he'd felt out of it, a has-been, felt emasculated, and the coke had given him back the strength-of-ten-men feeling, the grand illusion.

'Was he subject,' I asked Kim, 'to illusions of grandeur?'

'Sometimes. He told me once that he could run for the presidency if he weren't a foreigner.'

For the *presidency*. Fell into place again: he'd been exposed to subliminal influence and knew enough about Senator Mathieson Judd to imagine himself in Judd's position as a presidential candidate.

'Tell me about this man Judd, will you?'

Her mouth came open and for a moment she seemed disoriented; then she said without hesitation, 'Judd is not to be underestimated. He's a statesman with a world view that we haven't seen since Nixon, and he's not a megalomaniac. He's got to get into the White House because he's the only man in this country who can give it a new direction . . .'

211

My own thoughts dipped away and her voice sounded fainter; then I surfaced to the full light of consciousness and knew without any question that there hadn't been any time lapse: I hadn't missed anything she'd been saying.

'. . . It's not just the Americans who are concerned, this time – the whole world's involved, and much more than usual when there's a change of administration here. I very much hope the Thatcher government realises what we've got in Mathieson Judd, because the outcome of this election's going to have a major effect on the UK.'

It was word perfect: I could hear the echo of my own voice in my head. 'His understanding of the internecine struggle for power inside the Kremlin is infinitely deeper than we've seen before in any US president, thanks partly to the lifting of the veil by *glasnost*, sure, but Judd isn't missing a trick.'

She stopped, and in a moment looked down and pulled another strand into the splice. The swell lifted the boat again and I leaned lower, sighting along the stern rail. The yacht was still at the same distance. I couldn't see the light on the lenses this time.

'Go on,' I said.

She looked up. 'What?'

'Tell me more about Judd.'

'That's all I know.'

A point, then, for the debriefing: Kim Harvester had come under the subliminal influence only in Proctor's flat, and not for very long. We could assume there was no radionic device on board the tug. She was not therefore a target, like Proctor. My own exposure had been different: I'd picked up some background material on Judd and also picked up *instructions*, which hadn't necessarily been for me.

The swell lifted us again and I checked the sailing yacht. It hadn't moved. It was nearly sundown, and I said, 'Are you heading back to port after they've taken me off?'

'Yes. I've got three morning lessons, the first one at six.'

'Is this boat faster than that one over there?'

'Quietly she said, 'I can look after myself, Richard.'

'Do you keep a gun on board?'

'Of course.' She dropped the spliced rope and leaned back, stretching, her slight breasts touched by the light of the setting sun. 'It's rather nice,' she said. 'You know I've played about with bombs and done some undercover work against the Mafia and you've seen what I do with sharks, but you still seem to think of me as a woman, and in need of protection. I like that.'

'Dates me, I suppose.'

'No. Becomes you.'

'We're going to Nassau,' Ferris said, 'to meet Monck and a few other people.'

He was watching me steadily with his pale champagne-coloured eyes, watching for nerves, fatigue, signs of disorientation. I'd told him I'd been in that wreckage down there. We'd seen the Mafia boat hanging from a crane at the quayside when we'd taken off.

Toufexis would assume I'd been killed with the others because no one had seen me come ashore, but it was risky to rely on that because of the surveillance they'd mounted on the tug out there: I could have been recognised. I'd never seen such tight security and for once I was glad of it. Two of the Bureau people had picked me up at sea in a con-

213

verted motor torpedo boat at nightfall and got me
from the harbour to the airport in a short-bodied
limo with tinted windows and brought it across the
tarmac and right up to the Cessna 500 Citation and
I didn't see Ferris until I went aboard.

'When did you eat last?'

'A couple of hours ago.'

'Sleep?'

'I caught up.'

'Injuries?'

'Minor.'

'Morale?'

'Very good.'

Because I'd got the diary from Nicko's wallet, and
it could give us access to Proctor. I gave it to Ferris
and he began peeling the pages apart: it had got
soaked and dried again.

'A Mafia type used it when he phoned Proctor.'

'He got the number from it? Proctor's?'

'Or a number where Proctor was, at the time.'

He went through the pages, taking care. Some of
the ink had run. Light spread against the cabin roof
as we banked over the city's brilliance.

'G.R.P.,' Ferris said, and snapped his belt open
and got out of his seat.

'Are you going to use the phone?' I asked him.

'Yes.'

'Then do me a favour. I want some protection for
Kim Harvester – can you manage that? Two men?'

'When?'

He didn't ask why, because that could wait. And
he didn't cavil. It would mean diverting the services
of two men in shifts round the clock and London
would want a very good reason indeed and Ferris
knew that and he'd have to take the responsibility,

and this was one of the things I liked about him: he trusted the man he was running and he didn't ask questions. That little bastard Loman would have wanted forms in triplicate sent from London with a ten-sheet questionnaire and a request for notarisation and God knew how I could ever persuade him to push all that lot past his sphincter muscles.

'As soon as you can arrange it,' I told Ferris.

'Two men, taking shifts?'

'Yes. And they'll need a boat available. Could they use the MTB?'

'Yes.'

'She's bringing the tug in to port early tonight; she would have started back as soon as I was taken off. Berth 19, at the place where they shot me up. Decent of you.'

He went forward into the cockpit and I loosened the laces of my shoes because they'd shrunk a bit when they'd dried out and I'd have to get another pair as soon as I could, because if your feet aren't absolutely comfortable it can take the edge off your speed at a run and that can be fatal if you're pushing things.

Ferris came back. 'I didn't phone that number direct. I'm having it checked for the address.'

'The odds are,' I said, 'that it's 1330 Riverside.'

'It could be anywhere.'

Point taken. The executive tends to get tunnel vision the deeper he goes into the mission, while his director in the field can keep a more open perspective and see things the shadow can miss.

'I haven't,' I said in a moment, 'picked up any more instructions.'

I'd seen it in his eyes when I'd mentioned Riverside. He didn't look relieved. He didn't necessarily believe me. I could have had further subliminal instructions piped into me with an injunction to keep them secret.

He didn't say anything.

'I'm fairly certain,' I told him, 'that there's nothing electronic on board Harvester's boat. She didn't have any more to say about Mathieson Judd; I checked her for that and she just gave me a repetition of what she'd given me before.' He pulled out a mini-recorder and pressed a button. Debriefing had started. 'So she'd picked up that bit at Proctor's – it was the same thing I'd picked up myself when I went there that night. The reason I want her protected is that they're still surveilling the boat and they might make a snatch and force her to give them all the information she'd got about me. None of it's vital but I don't want her to go through interrogation at the hands of people like that.'

In a moment he said without looking at me, 'What's the personal relationship at this point between you and Harvester?'

'None of your bloody business.'

He hesitated a fraction and then pressed rewind and play and got the tape back to *hands of people like that* and reset for record.

'You ought to know I don't let personal relationships cloud my judgement during a mission.'

'Except for the man you wiped out in the Underground three – '

'That wasn't during a mission. Look – ' I hitched round in my seat to face him – 'if you want to make an issue of my relationship with – '

'I don't,' he said, and his eyes stopped me dead.

'What time do we get in?' Making bloody conversation, you notice, to bring the tension down. What annoyed me was that you can't ever win a point with this man. The way I'd reacted to his question about Harvester had told him precisely what he wanted to know.

'Seven,' he said, 'give or take a few minutes.' In the same tone, 'How close did you come to buying it, in the Mafia boat?'

'Oh for Christ's sake, I got my nerve back hours ago.'

Easy, now. You see, my good friend, what I mean? He'd got his answer. I had *not* got my nerve back hours ago, despite Kim's tender ministrations.

'Do you feel like a little more debriefing?'

'Of course.'

He pressed for record again and I told him about the execution thing on the Mafia boat, naming names and getting the timing right as close as I could remember.

'This woman Monique,' Ferris said at last. 'What about her?'

'I don't know. She was with Proctor that night when I went to his place but we didn't say anything more than hello and goodbye – he made it clear he wanted to be alone for the meeting. But on the quay last night she did her best to convince Nicko he'd got the wrong man. Did her very best.'

'Check on the woman Monique,' Ferris said into the mike. To me: 'So you came out of it with the diary. Anything else?'

'My life.' Bridling again, quick to anger.

'It's well understood,' he said courteously, 'that the diary could locate Proctor for us. It's understood that even if you'd brought nothing out of the incident, the life of the executive for *Barracuda* is of inestimable value. We – '

'You've got Purdom,' I said, 'standing by.' Came out with it very fast and the tone was bitter and the

217

instant it was over I was appalled, because the bloody thing was still running and there was the loud, clear and irretractable record of my hitherto hidden fear: that Purdom had been brought in to follow the mission in the background in case I bought it and he had to take over.

Sweating a little, the nerves heating the blood, debriefing, you see, is not always easy; they'll dig right down into your soul and drag it into the sour light of inspection.

Ferris said quietly, the expression in his amber eyes guileless and to be trusted, 'If Purdom had been down as the executive for *Barracuda*, I would have refused it, and if he is ever obliged to take over, I would ask London to replace me as the director in the field.'

16

BREAKTHROUGH

'Quiller,' with a nod. 'How are you?'

Croder.

'Good enough, sir. And you?'

'Quite well.'

And at this stage of the mission when we didn't yet have certain access to the objective and they'd sent the *Chief of Signals* out here from London without warning anyone the nerves can get a bit on edge and I was already reading significance into the slightest word: by *quite well* did he mean considering the executive in the field had made so little progress that the Chief of Signals himself had been sent out here to ask what was happening?

He was the *last* man I expected to see here, watching me with his black eyes buried into his skull and his thin body held tightly within itself to hide any expression. The last time we'd met we'd had a row over that poor devil Fisher and I wasn't in a mood to put up with any bullshit.

His eyes briefly noting the state of my clothes, 'Shall we sit down, gentlemen?'

She didn't even keep an iron on board, *I just hang everything out in the sun, sorry.*

Creaking of leather as people moved the chairs

around, six of us in here, Ferris, Croder, Monck, a
man I didn't know, Purdom and myself, *Purdom*,
dark, big-boned, silent, simmering with frustrated
energy, come here to sit on my shoulder like a vul-
ture on a tombstone, damn his eyes, *I was not in
the mood, I tell you*, for being rubbed the wrong
way.

'All is well,' Ferris said quietly from the next
chair.

My nerves had been showing and I can't stand
that: it's appallingly poor security. It had been
nothing more than a brush with the infinite out there
in that boat last night and I was still alive and it was
time to get back into gear for God's sake.

'You've met Mr Monck, of course, but not Tench,
have you?'

I hadn't seen him before: short, studious-looking,
glasses, almost as held-in as that man Purdom, just
nodded to us as we said hello.

'He's here to assist me,' Croder added, which
could of course mean anything: he could be a
Bureau shrink sent out here to check my condition,
note whether my eyes were flickering, whether I was
putting out sweat, things like that – they do this
sometimes, people like Loman do it, they'll send
someone out to the field to give an opinion as to
whether the shadow is showing the worse for wear,
whether he ought to be recalled before the rot sets
in.

But listen, I was still in good shape and Ferris was
still in control and I didn't want these bastards –
watch it, you'll have to watch it, he's probably
nothing more than a cipher clerk sent here to look
after signals. Steady the breathing, loosen the hands,
go into alpha for a couple of minutes, calm the ego
down.

Nice room, it was a nice room, bit modern but not too institutional for a place like this – we were in the Deputy High Commisioner's office in East Street, no one else around or at least not visible: a security guard had shown us in and gone off again. There'd been more security on the way here from the airport, four men deployed at a distance with their jackets bulging and their heads constantly on the swivel, one of them worried when Ferris had wandered off track a bit to tread on a beetle, *I wish to Christ you wouldn't do that*, but he never takes any notice, *It was instantaneous*, he's got a laugh like a snake shedding its skin as you know.

'If you'll give me a little time,' Croder said, and began turning the sheets of the debriefing book.

I think I reached alpha but only for a few seconds, felt too restless, got up and walked about to look at the pictures on the wall, tugged at the laces and pulled my shoes off and walked about like that, what a bloody relief, saw Ferris making a note on his pad, *new shoes*, I suppose, he doesn't miss anything.

The phone rang and Tench picked it up at the first ring and said yes, but was it urgent, and then listened for half a minute and finally said all right and passed the phone to Croder.

'*Cocktail*, sir.'

I'd seen it on the board before I'd left London: it was Jowett's thing, one of our first in Sri Lanka.

'When was this?'

You can't tell anything from Croder's tone; he talks like a lawyer reading a will. I saw Ferris watching him.

'What are his chances?'

This I didn't need. Jowett had had a wheel come off and his chances weren't worth a damn because the man at the board didn't know how to help him

221

and you do not, you do *not* raise the Chief through Cheltenham when he's in the next hemisphere with a major mission already on his hands, unless there's a life in the balance.

'Has he got it with him?'

The product. The poor bastard had pushed it right into the end-phase and he'd got the product and he'd been running like hell for the coast on board a plane or in a Hertz or buried under a sack of oats in a truck and someone had blown him or he'd left traces behind and now he was holed up in a telephone box with blood in his shoes and the fear of God in his soul and ringing London, tugging on the lifeline to see if it was still there, still strong enough to get him home, to get him home alive while –

'Have you informed Hallows?'

I tell you I did *not* need this, it wasn't exactly what you'd call reassuring was it, I mean Hallows is the man they send for when something has got to be done extremely fast, not, in my private opinion, in a last-ditch attempt to succour the executive but as a gesture of concern, so that it can be spelled out in the final report that they had tried, at least they had tried.

'Tell him,' Croder said, and I knew the words by heart, 'that every endeavour will be made but that he is confidently expected to use his own discretion.'

Discretion, capsule, yes.

He gave the phone back to Tench, who dropped it on to the contact with the sound, I swear, of a coffin-lid closing.

Silence in the room for another ten minutes while Croder got through the rest of the debriefing book and Tench stroked the back of his untidy-looking head and Purdom stared at his hands and Monck sat like a crumpled-looking buddha in the biggest chair and I talked to Croder in the soundless confines of the mind, *don't you care about that man Jowett, is that all you can do, send for Hallows to disinfect the final report so that we can all sleep in our beds? You ought to be on that bloody telephone raising all the support you can get for that poor bastard, you should be –*

Oh for God's sake spare us the melodrama, there's a ferret in a trap and he can't get out, that's all, it's not the first time it's happened and it won't be the last, RIP, so forth, and let us get on, gentlemen, with the job.

'Very well.'

The coil-spring spine of the debriefing book made a faint discordant medley of notes across Croder's steel hand as he closed it and dropped it onto his lap and looked at me and said, 'Proctor, then. I would value your opinion.'

First obvious question and I'd had the answer ready in my mind. 'I've only met him once, but I'd say he's been suffering the increasing strain of being taken off the active list because of the bullet in his body. It looks as if he's been exposed to some sort of subliminal radionic suggestion, which could have changed his personality at the subconscious level, destroying his sense of loyalty – which used to be very high – and turning him against us. I also found out today that he's been on cocaine for quite a while and manifested illusions of grandeur; he once told Harvester he could have run for the US presidency if he weren't a foreign national. He – '

'Harvester,' with a glance at the book, 'is she a reliable source of information?'

Ferris hadn't moved in his chair but I felt the waves. I think he was expecting Croder to ask me what sort of relationship I had going with Harvester. Ferris likes his fun.

'She was a nurse in England for seven years, she's done some undercover work for the Miami police in their investigations into Mafia operations, and she's currently a civilian volunteer diver the police can call on if they need an extra hand – she was working for them last night when a boat smashed into the quay. I've talked to her over a period of seven or eight hours and in my opinion she's reliable in terms of information and can be trusted.'

'I see.' With care: 'You have a tendency to enter into personal relationships with women, during the course of a mission. I would like to ask – '

'I'd like to tell you that the success I've had in my work for the Bureau indicates a degree of intelligence that would hardly allow my judgement to be swayed in critical situations, but if you've got any doubts about it then you can send me straight back to London so that I don't have to sit here listening to bullshit.'

It was eighty degrees outside but I'm not absolutely sure there wasn't frost on the window. Look, I know I'm rather rude but this bloody man had been going to ask whether I was capable of carrying out the tasks of a senior shadow executive without selling the whole mission down the river at the first sight of a nubile woman and it made me cross, and if you don't understand what I'm talking about it's your problem.

The silence had gone on for an awfully long time. I caught a look in Monck's eyes that could have been amusement; then Ferris said evenly, 'Quiller came very close, sir, to losing his life in the early hours of this morning, and I think – '

'Civil of you,' I said, 'but I can manage my own buttons now.'

Didn't make things any easier, I know, and that was a damned shame. I waited for Croder to ask me for an apology as soon as the smoke cleared a bit, but he did a surprising thing.

'Thank you,' to Ferris, and then to me, 'at this stage of the mission you'll have certain questions in your mind concerning the background, and I think you should have the answers. I'll be brief. Proctor is a British subject and he's become involved in some kind of subversive activity on US soil and seemingly in connection with Senator Mathieson Judd's presidential election campaign.' Waved his steel claw – 'I'm taking this from the debriefing notes and partly from my own information from other sources. The notes, by the way – ' to Ferris now – 'for the most part provide a very direct focus on the background data that's been coming in from international sources. You are both closer, I believe, to success in this mission than you're at present able to appreciate.'

I thought that was extremely doubtful because we couldn't get anywhere near the end-phase until we'd found physical access to Proctor. But of course Croder could see the whole picture and I couldn't.

'The fact of Proctor's involvement in US affairs gives us concern that he might cause harm to our ally. It could at least cause embarrassment on a diplomatic level. The American people are at present engrossed and engaged in the elections and any interference by the UK, however unintentional, could hazard the relationship between the two countries. That is one reason why you were sent out here, Quiller, to find Proctor and get him out of the USA as soon as possible and in secret. Another reason is that we cannot warn and advise either the CIA or the FBI and let them take care of the matter, because we've been informed that both those services may have been compromised. Even if that were not so, we are able and prepared to question Proctor, once in our hands, more effectively than could be done in the US, where special methods of inducement could not be practised. And on that subject I have a question. You've been through two missions with Proctor, isn't that so?'

'Yes.'

'I realise he might have undergone some sort of change in personality since then, but would you say he'd be liable to offer information, sufficiently induced?'

In a minute I said, 'I don't know. I can't say.'

They don't get out the cutlery in that particular room at the Bureau. I mean they don't use curling tongs, anaesthetics on the eyelids, needles in the urethra, that sort of thing. But they use the hood.

'You mean you're unsure of his present mental condition?'

'Well, yes. It's a bit complex now. His head's full of strange ideas and his nerves are possibly strung out on coke, and I'd say he's more like a dangerous psychopath than an intelligence agent. You could try hooding, of course. It might break him.'

Croder called it 'sufficient inducement' because in a trade as uncivilised as ours we reach for euphemisms for the same reason that a coroner reaches for the smelling-salts. Hooding doesn't cause pain and it's physically non-invasive and all they do is shut you in that particular soundproofed room with a black bag over your head until you're ready to tell them what they want to know. The sanitised term is sensory deprivation and I went through a bit of it in Turkey and it's a lot less pleasant than it sounds because after two or three days you start floating about in a mental vacuum until finally the panic begins and then you're done for because when they come to take the hood off you'll either tell them what they want to know and keep your psyche intact or you'll keep your mouth shut and go right over the edge and if you're lucky you'll finish up in the funny farm. Neither of these things happened to me in Turkey because one of the people looking after things came close enough for me to reach his throat and he'd got the keys of the handcuffs on him.

'One way,' Monck told Croder, 'might be to keep him short of cocaine, catch him while he's screaming his head off.'

Ferris was making a note.

'Thank you,' Croder said, 'we could indeed try that.' Turning the sheets of the debriefing book, 'From what I've just told you, then, Quiller, you'll know that if at any time the CIA or the FBI get wind of us and ask you what you're doing in Miami, you'll need to stick closely to your cover. If they decide to detain you on suspicion, your director in the field will ask London to make representations through private diplomatic channels.'

There is always, for instance, a certain amount of suspicion aroused if you're seen crawling out of a burning car with bullet holes in it, or climbing out of the water a hundred yards from a wrecked Mafia boat at three in the morning. That's why I'd avoided questioning on both occasions.

'Understood,' I said.

'Ferris?'

Ferris nodded and turned to me. 'You also need to know that we found a micro-transmitter concealed in the ceiling fan in Proctor's flat. We've sent it to London for them to look at, but in the meantime Parks has told us he thinks it's designed to broadcast subliminal material from a remote source, buried in the wave structure of any kind of electrical hum – fan, refrigerator. It would also work in a TV set whenever it's receiving a signal. Parks is still taking Proctor's flat to pieces, looking for more electronics.'

Croder was going through the debriefing book again. 'I'd like some elaboration on this *Newsbreak* anchorwoman Erica Cambridge. You've reported that she's "anxious to find George Proctor".'

Ferris had debriefed me on this in the air, but there was a lot I hadn't been able to say. 'She told me she wanted to find him "very much", but that it wasn't for any personal reason.'

'Do you think that's true?'

'Yes. I think they were close – in fact she said so – but I sensed that when they broke up there was a lot of unfinished business, political business. She asked me what we were going to do with Proctor when we found him and I said we'd get him out of the country right away.'

Ferris was making notes again. Croder asked me: 'How did she react to that?'

'She wanted a meeting with him before we got him out, and I used that as a trade-off – '

'Yes, you guaranteed she should see him, provided she helped you find him. Perhaps it's not important, but do you feel it's a guarantee we should keep?'

'Ethically?'

'Yes.'

'Your ethics might not be mine. I've been trained to play it rough. But a meeting between those two, suitably bugged, would probably give you a *lot* of information. If we can find him.'

I suppose Ferris was making those notes for Purdom, keeping the bastard briefed, ready to take my place. Over my dead body. Joke.

'If we can find him,' Monck said, 'yes.' He was watching me steadily. 'What do you think the chances are? It would help us to know your feelings on that.'

Not really. My feelings weren't terribly sanguine.

Phone again, and Tench picked it up.

'Proctor is a professional,' I said. 'A top professional. He's trained and he's dangerous and he's apparently got the whole of the Miami Mafia behind him, and that gives him God knows how many places he can hide.'

Ferris was on the phone: Tench had passed it to him. Croder said to me, 'You don't think our chances, then, are very high.'

I tried to keep the tone under control, didn't quite manage. 'Oh for Christ's sake, d'you want it in letters of blood?'

Then one of those silly coincidences happened, you've known them, I'm sure, because Ferris was saying, 'I'm sorry to break in, but they've checked on that phone number in the diary, the one with the initials G.R.P., and I think you've located Proctor – he's on board the *Contessa*.'

17

RISK

'I want a twenty-four-hour watch,' Ferris said on the phone, 'on the cutter for the motor-yacht *Contessa*. It normally ties up at Quay 19, the Bayside Marina.'

I noticed Croder's assistant, Tench, watching me obliquely. He'd obviously gathered I'd made some kind of breakthrough; when I caught his eye he looked down, stroking the back of his head. He did that a lot, frightened, I rather think, of Croder and his responsibilities, and the stroking was meant to show how relaxed he was.

'You'll need four men, two for each shift. I want a photograph of everyone who boards that cutter or disembarks from it, and I'll tell you by radio if I want anyone tagged. Questions?'

Purdom hadn't reacted. He sat with his head down, waiting for doom. I think he'd made up his mind I was going to finish up with a dum-dum in the left ventricle and his feet were already on the starting blocks. The fact that we now knew where Proctor was didn't guarantee I wouldn't bite the dust at any given moment, according to the terms of the contract the Mafia had put out on me. But I wished he wouldn't sit there with his nerves twanging like that; it didn't help.

'Starting immediately,' Ferris said, and gave the phone back to Tench, looking at Croder. 'Signal, sir?'

'Yes, before we leave here.'

Signal the board for *Barracuda*, for the eyes of Bureau One. *Executive has located objective. C of S informed.*

Mr Shepley would be pleased, and so would Holmes, standing there in the shadows between the floodlit signals boards: it'd take the edge off his nerves, be okay to get himself another cup of coffee, celebrate, so forth, but it might be all that caffeine inside him that keeps him at such a pitch, you know, I've never thought of that.

'Congratulations,' Croder said, watching me, dark-eyed, brooding, busying his mind already with the future, because it was one thing to locate the objective and another thing to get him away from that privately-owned and well-protected vessel out there and take him to London and fry his brains out under a hood.

'Now I'd like to talk a little more about the anchorwoman. There's now an obvious question in our minds, isn't there?' Yes indeed. When she went aboard the *Contessa* last night, had she known Proctor was there? 'Your report was necessarily brief. Can you remember what she actually said about Proctor?'

'Yes. One thing was, she said it would help us if we let her see him before we got him out of the country. She said she'd got a great deal of information on him.'

It took another ten minutes to give him a replay of the scene in Kruger Drug last night; then I called up the other material that hadn't been specifically about Proctor. 'She told me I'd caught her at a critical – no, a *crucial* time, and that she needed help. There was no one she could trust.'

'She has no friends?'

'She didn't know if they'd be strong enough – I quote.'

'For what?'

I asked him to give me a minute.

I don't know how strong they'd be if things got really rough. And none of them know about George Proctor. Okay, we were close, yes, but they don't know about this thing that's happening.

Told Croder.

'Thing.' He dropped the word like a stone into the silence.

'I don't know,' I said, 'what the *thing* is. But she began talking about Proctor again before we left Kruger Drug.' Pictured her face, her hands spread on the marble-topped table, listened for her voice. *He still had a reserve I couldn't get through, and I believe he was doing things unknown to me that would have surprised me – correction, alarmed me, frightened me – not just personally, I mean on a geopolitical scale. I want to get this right – on a* clandestine *geopolitical scale.*

Told Croder. He didn't comment, and I kept on going. 'She said something interesting about the late Howard Hughes, that he had a mad dream about buying America, by getting control of the industry, the machinery behind the throne. She said there was an easier way, that to buy America all you had to do was buy one man: the president.'

I sat back.

'You must have asked her to elaborate on that.'

'I would have, but her bodyguard brought her a remote phone. She had to go.'

'Who was the caller? Did you –'

'A Mr Sakomoto.'

'Was he the Japanese you saw boarding the cutter with her?'

'I don't know. He – '

'You tagged Cambridge – ' Ferris – 'from Kruger Drug to 1330 Riverside, and she came out of the house with the Japanese and you tagged them to the quay, is that right?'

'Yes. But he wasn't necessarily Sakomoto.'

'There could be several Japanese,' Croder said, 'in that house.'

'Yes.'

'And how did you leave the Cambridge woman?'

'Leave – ?'

'At Kruger Drug. What was said, do you remember?'

'She asked me when we could meet again, and I said I'd phone her the next day. She – '

'Today.'

'Yes. She said it was vital that we met again as soon as possible, and that she'd stay at her phone until noon.'

Croder scuffed through the book. 'You didn't telephone her.'

'I was on board Harvester's boat all the morning. At that time I wasn't certain I could trust her, and I only used the phone once, to call Ferris, just a two-word signal.' *Shadow safe*.

'It looks,' Ferris said, 'as if you'll need to meet Cambridge again.'

'Especially now.'

'Now that she's been on board the *Contessa*, and may have seen Proctor.'

'She may be still there,' Croder said. 'On board.'

'I doubt that. She goes on the air every day.'

'In a minute from now,' Monck said. 'Tench, is

234

there a TV in that cabinet?'

He pulled open the double doors. 'Yes, sir.'

'Turn it on and cut the sound down and play the channels. We're looking for *These Are My Views*, you know the one?'

'Erica Cambridge, oh yes.'

'Channel 6,' Monck said. 'Half past nine.'

'Thank you, sir.'

Flick, flick, flick, and the juiciest cheeseburger you ever saw, dripping with some kind of sauce, then lots of them with lots of people with big white glistening teeth all biting into them with the cheese pulled out into strings, fade out, fade in some shadowed cleavage.

'No,' Ferris was saying on the phone, 'but you can leave a signal there. How is Jowett doing?'

'Tench,' I said, 'use that other phone and get me the number for *Newsbreak* studios, Miami, will you?'

'Jowett?' asked Croder when Ferris had rung off.

'There's no news.' Jowett had run *Cocktail* into the shit in Sri Lanka.

Knocking on the door. Tench went across and opened it. The security guard and a man in a khaki suit and carrying a worn leather bag, looking around. 'Who's the patient?'

'This is Dr Hornby,' Ferris said. *Bloody* doctors. He must have sent for him. I pulled my shirt up and Hornby came over and looked at the dressing and began loosening it.

Tench asked me if I wanted him to get *Newsbreak*.

'Yes. I want to leave a message for Erica Cambridge.'

'It's good of you to turn out,' Ferris said, and took a look at the wound.

'I was only mending a rod. Fishing rod. Was it a clean knife, or dirty?'

'I'd say clean.'

'Woman did these? These stitches?'

'Yes.'

'Thought so. Wonderfully drawn. Nurse?'

'Yes.'

'They're underrated, you know.'

'She'd like to meet you.'

Good evening. I'm Erica Cambridge, and these are my views. The violet eyes, the brilliant smile. Shuffling the papers. *Yesterday in New Hampshire it looked as if Senator Mathieson Judd was, for the first time, pandering to the dictates of those on his campaign staff who have been trying to persuade him –*

'I've got *Newsbreak* on the line, sir. Her show.'

I took the phone. 'Who is this?'

'Bennie.'

– Has put it, to counterbalance the Republican candidate's serious and perhaps solemn approach to the matter in hand. But in my view, ladies and gentlemen –

I thought she looked a degree nervous, just a degree.

'Bennie, this is Richard Keyes. Ask Miss Cambridge to telephone me, would you, as soon as she comes off the air? She can find me at – '

'She's not here, Mr Keyes.'

'She taped the show tonight?'

'That's right.'

'Look, if she happens to call, give her this number.'

'See me in four days,' Hornby said. 'Here's my card.'

– His respect and regard for the electorate. So what

happened in New Hampshire was not rehearsed, was not premeditated. It was real. Some of you were there, I believe.

I thanked Hornby and tucked my shirt in again. *Had she met Proctor on that yacht?* That would make her nervous, a degree nervous. Unless of course she'd been lying, unless she'd known already that he was there.

I phoned her apartment.

'She's not here, Mr Keyes, I'm sorry.'

'Can you tell me where I can find her?'

'She just went out, that's all I know.'

I left both numbers where she could find me and Ferris picked up the other phone.

Monck told him, 'Ask your people if they saw her come off the cutter.'

'But of course.' The tone acid. Ferris can get touchy when people give the impression he can't think straight.

'We need that woman,' Croder said. 'We need her badly.'

'Yes,' I said.

We'd begun feeling jumpy now, all of us, especially Purdom. When we'd parted company at Kruger Drug last night she'd told me it was vital we got together again as soon as possible and since then she'd gone to 1330 Riverside and she'd gone aboard the yacht out there and if she still wanted to talk to me she might give me the evidence we needed to push *Barracuda* straight into the end-phase.

'She is our new objective,' Croder said, 'for the mission,' the thin body buried in its clothes, the gaunt head sunk onto the shoulders, the obsidian-black eyes watching me to see if I understood how *very* important Cambridge had suddenly become to us all.

237

'If she'll cooperate,' I said.

'We shall do all we can to persuade her.'

The bleak, bright, bare-walled scene of an interrogation cell flashed across my mind, triggered by the word *persuade*. But of course he didn't mean that. We would approach Erica Cambridge, if we could, with civilised blandishments and exhortations, like the gentlemen we are.

'What time was that?'

Ferris, on the phone.

'You said she uses a bodyguard?' Croder asked me.

'She was using one last night.'

'I need two people,' Ferris said, 'on the *Newsbreak* building, front and rear, and I want you to keep a watch for her limousine. You've got the number. If she's seen *anywhere* at *any* time I want to know immediately, and don't let her out of your sight. This is – '

'Ferris,' Croder said.

'Hold it,' looking across at him.

'If she's not using a bodyguard, tell them to give her protection.'

Ferris repeated that and said it was fully urgent and rang off and then everyone was standing up and Monck said, 'Don't waste any time,' and I tied my shoe-laces and Purdom opened the door and we were on our way out when one of the telephones began ringing.

I went back and picked it up.

'Is Mr Keyes there, please?'

'Speaking.'

'This is Erica Cambridge.' The tone quiet and urgent. 'I'm speaking from the limo. They called me with your message. Why didn't you call me? I waited until noon.'

'I was prevented.' They were all watching me and I gave a slow nod. 'Where can we meet?'

'I'm on my way to the party at the Marina Yacht Club. They're giving it for Senator Judd – that's why I had to tape my show for today. Did you catch it, by any chance?'

'I was at a meeting.'

'I'm sorry you missed it. Some of the things I said were a little different. A lot of things are different now, Mr Keyes. I want to tell you about them. Can you get to the party? You're in Nassau right now, aren't you?'

She knew by the number. 'We need to meet somewhere more private than a yacht club.'

'Afterwards. Look, if you can get here before, say, midnight, you should do that. This is a campaign party and it'll go on till the morning, and there's a man I want you to meet. I'll keep him here as long as I can. It shouldn't be too difficult – he has the hots for me.'

'What's his name?'

'Stylus von Brinkerhoff.'

'I could meet him somewhere privately.'

'It has to be low key, a casual introduction.' A beat, then because I hadn't said anything she went on. 'It's really very important for you to meet him, Mr Keyes. And there are some things I have to tell you. One is you don't need to look for George Proctor any more. You know what I'm saying?'

I didn't like the pressure she'd started to put on me. Or it could be nerves, a touch of apprehension before *Barracuda* was pushed headlong into a new phase.

'Look, I have to pick someone up and take them along, and I won't be able to talk in front of them. I don't have more than a minute. I'm going to leave you an invitation at the desk of the Marina Yacht Club and you can ask for it there. It's black tie. Mr Keyes, you just don't appreciate how important it is for you to be there tonight. All you have to do is trust me.'

The line went dead and I put the phone down.

'That was Cambridge?' asked Croder.

'Yes.' I filled him in, verbatim.

'How does it strike you?' This was Ferris and he spoke before anyone else could. The ranking here went from Monck through Croder to Ferris and me, but Ferris was my director in the field and the mission was running and it was his sole and sacrosanct responsibility to look after his executive and he was making that quite clear.

'She used rather a lot of obvious pressure, don't you think?'

'When she said you had to trust her, did she sound hurt or indignant?'

'No. Persuasive.'

'Did she sound out of tune?'

Argot: he meant out of character.

'I've only met her once.'

Croder said, 'Can you bring it down to the odds?'

'That it's a trap?'

'Yes.'

Purdom had begun tapping the tips of his fingers together, not making any noise, just doing it quietly, not knowing he was doing it, wished he'd stop. 'The thing is,' I said, 'we've taken a lot of trouble keeping me under cover since the Mafia thing last night, and we'd be coming right out into the open again if I went there. To the party.'

Monck had been shuffling around the room and now he stopped and said with his head on one side, 'Let's try it this way. How much do you think you could learn, if you met her there?'

'A lot. If she's genuine. If it isn't a trap.'

Beginning to feel the chill a little. I've walked into traps before, knowing once or twice what I was doing, but they'd been the kind where you stood a chance of doing something very fast or very deadly, a chance of getting out again with what you'd gone in for, the product, some kind of information, dragging a man back to base for interrogation or bringing away papers, photographs, tapes. I don't mind taking a risk as long as it's calculated, as long as it's worth taking, but the problem we'd got here was that we couldn't tell what the odds were, whether it was worth it or not, whether it was worth walking into the Marina Yacht Club and hearing, a long way off in the distances of the mind, the swinging of a hinge and the closing of steel doors and the dying away of the echo in the dark.

'Ferris?' This was Croder, asking for a decision from the DIF, from the man who knew the field better than anyone, who knew the executive and what he could do, what he couldn't do, couldn't be asked to do.

'If you went in there,' he spoke directly to me, 'you'd have all the support we can raise. Fifteen or twenty people.'

Trained, talented, armed and strategically dispersed.

'They couldn't stop a long shot.'

'They would check the environment, very carefully.'

Purdom was still tapping his fingertips together and it worried me and I turned my head but Ferris got in very fast and made a gesture and Purdom froze and looked down suddenly, turned away, hadn't known he'd been doing it, and I saw Monck and Croder pick up the score, all very nervy, we were all very nervy because if I walked into that place and we'd got it wrong we'd lose *Barracuda*, lose it to a single shot.

Sweat beginning, cold on the skin.

Said to Ferris, 'Do you think I should do it?'

With his customary care: 'I think you should consider doing it. But consider well. The chances aren't very good, and the last word, of course, is yours.'

Car going past in the street, someone calling out, faint laughter.

La dolce vita.

'I think it's worth the risk.'

18

BALLOONS

'If von Brinkerhoff is there, we'll have him tagged, of course.'

There was a heat-haze right across the city as we swung into the approach path, and the lights glimmered through it, brightening as we lowered.

'Ask her about that script she was using for last night's show,' Ferris said. 'Does she remember working it out according to campaign logic, or did it just come to her from out of the blue, as a flash of inspiration? But I wouldn't suggest she might have been under subliminal direction, or that she might still be.'

'Why not?'

'It's delicate ground, and it might panic her. It panicked you.'

Flaps down.

I was feeling all right. He hadn't asked me how I felt because he'd got a pretty good idea. When I say I was feeling all right I really mean I was feeling normal, normal for this particular situation. I was going straight into a red sector and we couldn't hope to cover all the contingencies because a gun is a gun and they don't have to be very big and they can be quite accurate if people know how to use them and they can drop a man from a distance even in a crowd, even with a silencer in place.

'Ask her if she'd be willing to meet Mr Croder and Mr Monck.'

I half-listened. He wasn't really briefing me; he knew I'd got a rough idea of what we wanted out of Erica Cambridge. He was making conversation, covering the important points to see if I had any questions, yes, but giving me comfort at the same time, giving me someone to talk to as we levelled out and the blue lamps flickered past the windows and the bump came, the first of three, because what we were doing was executing a trade-off, balancing the odds and deciding that the life of the executive for the mission was worth putting at risk providing the chance of getting vital information was high enough.

So I was feeling normal for the situation, a hollowness in the stomach, a chill on the skin, the palms slightly moist. The feeling that I was on my way to an execution wasn't new: I'd had it a hundred times and as recently as last night when little fat Nicko was taking me across the darkling main to a rendezvous with the grim reaper, God rest his stinking little soul, I did not *like* that man, execution, yes, nothing new, but this was different because everything looked so civilised and I was sitting here in Monck's dinner jacket and there was going to be an invitation left for me at the Marina Yacht Club for this very plush party and I was meeting a rather attractive woman there, so forth, different but no better, no better, my good friend, because a trap is a trap and in this trade you don't often get out alive.

'You'll have immediate contact, of course, whenever you need it,' Ferris said, and pulled his valise from under the seat in front. He meant I could signal any one of his people in the environment and talk to them, tell them what I wanted, pine veneer and simple handles, nothing fancy, joke.

Draughty out here on the tarmac. Ferris had phoned from the plane for a chopper to stand by for our arrival in Miami and take us to the shuttle pad by the Yacht Club because the timing had been tight and it was now 11:43 and we didn't know how long Cambridge would be able to keep von Brinkerhoff there.

A Customs and Immigration man was waiting for us and we stood there showing papers with our hair all over the place and then he said everything was okay and we got into the Hughes 300.

Lift-off, 11:48.

'Croder will be following on,' Ferris said, 'and he'll be available for a meeting with Cambridge if she seems amenable.' A tuft of his thin straw-coloured hair still sticking up. 'At this stage anything can happen, and with a bit of luck she might be ready to give us the whole thing and we can wrap up the mission.'

Keeping things cheerful, you understand, knows his job, Ferris.

Down at 11:57, lowering across the masts in the marina, heeling a little as the pilot brought most of the power off and turned through the last few degrees and then settled her carefully on the skids. A nice enough building, the Yacht Club, as you'd imagine, pale red brick and white window frames, pillared portico and wide green lawns, people standing outside on the balconies with drinks in their hands, the women in long colourful dresses, I'm not, if you want to know, particularly keen on parties because you can't hear what people are saying with all the noise and that wouldn't matter so much but you've got to put in some kind of answer here and there for the sake of politesse, Ferris opening the door and dropping onto the pad and waiting for me, a last-minute rush of apprehension as I followed him, ducking under the rotors and already seeing some of them not far away, some of his people, one of them the man who'd got me into that cab on the quay when the shed had caught fire two days ago, good people, well trained, a comfort, yes.

I swung the door of the chopper shut and turned round and faced the building and blew the cover they'd been giving me since they'd taken me off the tug last night, blew it to the winds. The Mafia had got a contract out on me and Toufexis's people had been given my photograph and there'd be some of them here tonight and I felt the sudden air-rush and the bloody thing droning into the skull and then it was over and I was back in control.

'Eighteen men,' Ferris said, 'your own little army,' and touched my elbow and turned away and I walked along the tiled path between the massed geraniums, not hurrying because I was here now and the party was far from over by the look of things, a crowd of black polished limousines in the car park on my left with chauffeurs standing around and two of our people near the wrought iron gates. I didn't know exactly what orders Croder had given for tonight but he wouldn't have put this amount of support in the field just to keep things jolly, so I suppose he'd told them to watch for a gun hand moving and make a killing drop in time to protect me. They'd carry official bodyguard licences to keep the fuss down when the police wanted to know what was happening: this was routine Bureau procedure.

Skin beginning to itch because the warmth of the night was heating up the Teflon I was wearing under the dinner-jacket, people crossing the portico on their way to the car park, only half a dozen police officers standing around so I suppose Senator Judd had already left: it was midnight. If he'd still been here there would have been fifty of them.

But there were a great many other people also standing around, most of them in blue serge suits. There would be a lot of high-echelon guests here tonight, targets for political activists and weirdos.

'Hi! Can I help you?'

Brilliant smile, a small corsage of carnations, one bare shoulder, Florida chic.

'There should be an invitation here for me. Richard Keyes.'

The name for the face in the photograph. They would know my name too. Shortening the odds, yes, on the other hand –

'Sure, Mr Keyes, I have it right here. I'm sorry you missed the Senator.'

'Was he good?'

'O-h-h-h . . .' with her eyes shining, rolling to heaven, every hormone in her slim preened body lining up to vote for Golden Boy.

– On the other hand, it wouldn't be easy in a crowd this big to squeeze off a shot and get clear with all those chauffeurs and police officers and bodyguards standing around, and less easy still to pump out some rapid fire from an Uzi: that would attract even more attention and they wouldn't reach the car before the police dropped them with a fusillade. Seek comfort, my good friend, seek comfort where ye may.

'Enjoy what there is left, Mr Keyes.'

The smile shimmering, the corsage quivering slightly to the body language, what there is left of what, my little darling, you mean my life?

247

'Champagne, sir?'

'Thank you.'

Cutting quite a dash in my borrowed plumage, glass in hand, the truth of the matter concealed beneath silk lapels, the Teflon itching on the skin, proof against anything up to armour-piercing grade, but if they were professionals they'd go for the head.

YOU'LL MAKE IT, MATHIESON! strung out in huge gold letters on a banner across the podium where the band was playing, a dozen couples still on the dance floor, their shoes brushing through coloured streamers, two waiters on their knees picking at the carpet where a glass had fallen and smashed, three Japanese talking together by one of the tall white-framed windows, and Erica Cambridge.

'Well hello, Mr Keyes.'

Slight, cool-looking in a sheer white silk gown with a lamé belt, lamé shoes, her violet eyes watching me as the smile was flashed on for the occasion.

'You look stunning,' in fact, did.

'Thank you. Did you just get here?'

'Yes.'

'Did you come alone?'

'Yes.'

'Then you didn't see Mathieson.'

'I heard he was very good.'

'He's – ' looking away, looking back – 'I have a lot to tell you. Why don't we go outside where it's quieter?'

'It's like a Turkish bath out there.' I led her towards the white moulded archways opposite the windows, giving my glass to a waiter. 'I got here as soon as I could.'

The slapping sound of a rotor cut across the music

as another chopper landed. *Croder will follow on*, Ferris had said; or it could be picking up some of the guests.

'Stylus couldn't stay,' Erica said. 'He had to get back.' We found a couch, blue linen with white rope trim, where it was quiet enough to talk. Someone had left a brocade bag.

'Back to the *Contessa*?' Stylus von Brinkerhoff.

She looked at me sharply. 'You're well informed, Mr Keyes.'

'My first name is Richard. I'm sorry I missed him.'

'What do you know about him?'

'You said you had a lot to tell me.'

'Ma'am, is this your bag?'

'Oh my God, I've been frantic. Thank you so *very* – you're Erica Cambridge! I just *love* your show!'

'Thank you.'

'Well I'm – interrupting.'

'How is Proctor?' I asked her when the woman had gone.

She looked surprised again, wary. One can't always remember, but I think I've never seen a woman so frightened, beneath the *maquillage*, so close to some kind of brink. 'I didn't see him,' she said.

'But he's on board the *Contessa*.'

Reaction after reaction, and I began worrying that all she had to tell me was what we already knew.

'I believe I mentioned, Mr – Richard, that I have no one I can really confide in, really trust. I – I suppose I've gone through life antagonising people; at least that's my reputation. So why should I confide in you? Why should I trust you?'

'No earthly reason. You don't even know me.'

'You're not making it easy for yourself.'

I was.

'I didn't ask you to trust me, Erica. There's no obligation. But if you want my guarantee that I won't divulge anything you have to tell me, without your permission, I can give you my word.'

'How much is it worth? I'm sorry, that's not very – '

'It's unbreakable. Would you be prepared to talk to my people?'

'Who are they?'

'Officers of the British government.'

Her hands were on the move again, as they'd been when we'd sat at the table in Kruger Drug. Correction: not *frightened* beneath the *maquillage*. Awed. Awed by what she knew, what she'd found out at 1330 West Riverside Way and on board the *Contessa*.

'The British government,' she said, 'is involved. The entire world is involved. I – '

'Look, if you're willing to see my people, I can arrange it. You'd have more confidence in them than just one stranger. They're much higher than I am.'

It was a get-out but it was logical. If she was ready to talk to Ferris and Croder and Monck I could walk out of this thing and go home with a whole skin and let them put it down in the records, *Mission completed, executive debriefed*, because if this woman had the information we needed, that was exactly what I'd be doing – completing *Barracuda*. She was our new objective and I was close to handing her over.

'Whether I agree to see your "people" or not, I've decided to go to the State Department.' Running one violet-lacquered finger-nail along the white rope trim, unable to keep still. 'It would then be for them to consult with the President, and for him to decide whether to summon our allied ambassadors. But I don't know, Richard, this whole thing is – ' her hand brushing the air – 'it's so far-reaching. And this is what scares me – I want to help Senator Judd get into the White House and in fact I'm already helping him do that, but now that I've learned what I have, I don't know if it isn't the most dangerous thing I could do. For everyone. For the United States and the rest of the world.'

I didn't say anything.

'I *know* he went thataway, Simon.' Gusty laughter, much champagne. 'He said the men's room.' Trotting past with uncertain feet, arm in arm. 'But *where* is *Nancy*?'

'*Not* in the men's room, let us hope!' More laughter.

'There are some people I have to talk to, Richard, before I can leave. But not about this. Let's meet on the front porch in fifteen minutes. We'll go to my apartment and I'll show you what I'm talking about. It's actually on paper, duplicated. You know what I'm saying? A whole *brief*, do you understand?'

The product. Mission completed.

Unless it was a trap.

I didn't know how good an actress she was. I didn't know if the fright in this woman, the feeling of awe, didn't derive from the knowledge that she was about to do what they'd briefed her to do when she was on board the *Contessa*: lead a man to his death. *Proctor* had been there on that yacht. Let that be borne in mind, because yesterday he'd asked La Cosa Nostra to put out a contract on me, and they'd come so very close to a kill.

Don't go with her.

You have a point.

'I need to know a little more,' I told her.

251

'We can't talk now. I asked you to come here to meet that man, not to discuss what I know. My apartment has a security guard, and you'll be absolutely – '

'I'm used to looking after my own security. That's why I need to know more.'

She looked hunted, glancing around her. 'But in a public place like this – '

'It's very private, actually. There are no bugs in the walls. Give me the gist. I need to know how serious this thing is.' Whether, in fact, it was serious enough to force me to take the risk of going to her apartment.

She looked around her again, pressed, frightened. That was my impression. 'All right,' she said in a moment, 'here it is.' She moved back against the wall, against the big mural of sails heeling across a choppy sea with spindrift blowing, and said quickly and softly, 'I told you there were plans, with Senator Judd as the prime mover, to buy America. I know more about it now. On board the *Contessa* there's a faction calling itself the Trust, frighteningly powerful, awesomely influential in world affairs. It has people like Apostolos Simitis, the shipping magnate, Lord Joplyn of Eastleigh, who controls more than half the mineral deposits in South Africa, Takao Sakomoto, the leading industrialist in Japan. Maybe you haven't heard of these men – '

'No – '

'Then take it from me, they're the puppet masters behind the scenes of international finance. People like Stylus von Brinkerhoff, the Swiss banker – the man I was hoping you could meet here tonight. They – ' she broke off as someone came through the arches towards the rest rooms, passing within a dozen feet of us. In a moment – 'My God, this is so dangerous, talking in a place like this. But you wanted the gist, and it's this, Richard. These men plan to buy America – and sell it to the Soviets. In the declared interests of the final and permanent laying down of arms among nations, they propose the creation of a single world government, behind whose public throne they can exert their private power. And to meet the enormous demands of demographic reorganisation they envisage the setting of that throne to be in Moscow.'

Watching me for my reaction, didn't see anything. But my pulse was elevated: I could feel it. It was going to be worth it, then, worth going to her flat, taking the risk, because she couldn't be making this up: it had the appalling ring of truth.

'We'll go there separately,' I said.

'To my apartment?'

'Yes.'

'I have the limo here. We can talk – '

'No,' I said. 'For the sake of security.'

'Yours, or mine?'

It seemed to worry her.

'Both.'

Mine, if this whole thing was a trap. Hers, if they put me in the cross hairs out there and missed, and hit her instead. It wasn't a night for taking chances.

'Okay. You have my address?'

'You gave me your card.'

She got up, straightening the lamé belt. 'I'll be there inside of forty-five minutes, depending on the traffic. You'll be alone?'

'Of course.'

She left me.

Setting me up.

She's setting you up.

Probably.

This is a trap, you know that.
Probably.
So don't go there. Don't be such a –
Oh for Christ's sake shut up. I know what I'm doing.
It's a trap, it's a trap, it's –
Shuddup.

Snivelling little bloody organism, scared of its own shadow, one of them over there by the french windows, he'd been there since I'd first come in, another one by the doors, talking to a girl, chatting her up, good cover, another one on the dance floor, engrossed, or seemingly engrossed until he saw my signal and said something at once to the girl and she laughed quickly so I imagine he'd said if he didn't go and wring out a kidney *soon* there'd be an accident, because he was coming towards the men's room and I went back through the archway and cut across him in the corridor, a small neat-looking man with glasses, never look at him twice unless you noticed his eyes, cold as the eyes of a reptile, the kind of man I like to see when they're meant to be keeping me as far as possible from the slab in the morgue, stretched out under the shroud and stinking of formaldehyde, *it's a trap*, oh for God's sake bugger off.

'Have you seen Lucas?' he asked me.

'No, but I've seen Baldwin. The way I want it is like this. She's leaving here in about fifteen minutes and it's going to take her another thirty to reach her flat. Here's the address. I'm – '

'I know the address.'

'I'm going over there by the bar and wait until I see her leave. I want her tagged and I want you to see if she makes any kind of signal and if she does

I want you to see who gets it and what he does, where he goes, if he – '

'Normal routine,' he said.

Starchy bastard, as bad as Ferris, put on a pout when they think they're being told how to do their job, but I liked that because only the real professionals have got that degree of pride and tonight I wanted real professionals about me, my good friend, not yonder Cassius.

'Whatever happens, I'm going to follow her to her flat as if I didn't know any better, and if you people find you've got a lot to deal with I want you to do exactly as much as you need to, including deadly force if you think I'm endangered – has C of S cleared you on this?'

'Yes.'

'What have you got for me out there? Something with smoked glass?'

'A limo, yes.'

'I'll sit in the back. Providing – '

'As long as you don't tell *Nancy*, you know what I mean?'

'She thinks you don't sleep around?'

'That's exsh – ex*actly* what she thinks.'

Peals of restrained mirth, their voices fading.

'Providing I reach her flat without any diversions, I want all the cover you can give me at the moment when I get out of the car. How many people are there outside her flat now?'

'Four. Crosby, Mace – '

'Where will you be?'

'Following your limo, two cars behind. Black Honda coupé, Florida plates.'

'All right, when you – ' broke off to let him concentrate on the two men over there by the reception desk. He turned his head an inch and got a signal from the man standing by the curtains picking at his nails.

'They're okay.'

'Have you seen any Sicilians here?'

'Nine. They haven't seen you, not to recognise.'

'Where are they?'

'Five outside, two of those are in the car park. The others are in here, that one over there, the one on the far side with the cummerbund, those two by the bar.'

He meant he'd seen them before or they'd been seen before by one or more of the other support people here tonight, seen and recognised. There could be a dozen more of them, a hundred, they've got a vote too, got political views, go to political parties, eat cookies, crap, close in on you, aim for the head, splinters of bloodied bone from the site of exit in the skull, *you're taking a risk, you're playing Russian roulette again, you* –

Oh for God's sake piss off.

'When you see me getting out of the car I shall want your personal signal as to whether you think I should go into the building. You're Hood, aren't you?'

'Yes.'

Seen him before, North Africa, Loman had put him into the field for *Tango*, he'd impressed me, knew how to drive, how to subdue a man, how to make no noise, ask no questions, I wouldn't be surprised if they didn't send him up to Norfolk for training as a shadow if he lived long enough, though it's a fraction chancy for the troops, as you know, look at the one they got last night in Riverside Way.

'All right,' I said, 'tell someone to get my car moved within sight of her limo. She – '

'That's been taken care of. You're on the west

side, three rows from the gates and five cars along from the middle aisle. She's on the same side, two rows from the gates and six along, the gaps counting as cars, because there's a lot of movement down there now with people still leaving. Your driver's waiting for you there, name of Treader. I'd better fade.'

I moved round the room, keeping behind people when I could, watching for Erica. In ten minutes she came through one of the arches with a man, talking intently. I hadn't seen him before. Hood was watching him from the bar. I moved again, this time towards the reception area, and I was outside by the time she came across the porch. She was still talking to the man, listening to him, neither smiling, nothing social, and when they parted she simply turned away and he went back inside.

There were other people drifting across the lawns and along the pathways, dinner jackets, bare suntanned arms, cigars, the glitter of jewellery, sudden laughter, a drunk getting rather loud and then being hushed, chauffeurs coming forward, some of the men in blue serge moving into the crowd, music still coming from the building through the open french windows, a three-quarter moon afloat in a clear sky above the turreted roof, a fine night, windless but close, oppressive.

I didn't know where Croder was, or if in fact he was here by now; he hadn't necessarily been on board the shuttle chopper I'd heard earlier. There was another one on the pad with its rotor turning but I think it was taking off, not landing. Croder might not be here at all, though I assumed he'd be somewhere in Miami by now. There was still a chance that Erica would agree to meet him, give him the whole thing.

That had been Ferris, I think, doing his homework, going through my debriefing on the Kruger Drug meeting and suggesting that Croder follow me in to Miami in case Erica was ready to talk.

She was walking down to the gates, another man with her now, a bodyguard, keeping pace from a short distance behind, his head turning the whole time. Someone was laughing in the little group on the west side of the car park – the chopper was airborne over the pad and some balloons were blowing across the people's heads in the down draught.

I went through the gates not far behind Erica and peeled off to the left, walking five cars along and three rows down. I was in a small open space now, with no one near me, and I saw the man signal me from the limousine. I didn't see anyone looking in my direction, but I'd seen Hood over towards the aisle, covering me, and I felt the pressure coming off, the pervasive fear that had been with me since I'd arrived here.

My shoes – Monck's shoes – slipped a little over the brick-red tiles; I suppose they were new ones. The chopper was passing overhead now and some of the coloured balloons were sent blowing to the ground and bouncing and flying up again in the draught from the rotors as the chopper slowed, hovering, and I looked up and saw the door coming open a few inches and the submachine gun poking through the gap and the dark orange flame as it began firing.

19

MAZDA

Picked up the phone and dialled.

'Yes?'

Voice I didn't know.

'DIF.'

'He's not here.'

'Then give me the number.'

Rage, great rage.

'Parole?'

'*Barracuda*. Give me that *number*.'

'He's mobile. Here it is.'

Wrote it down on the pad. 'Christ,' I told the driver, 'is this the best you can do?'

'We're jammed solid,' he said. Treader.

Ringing tone.

Smoked windows, I couldn't see much more than highlights outside, glass, chromium, police cars with their roofs lit up. Sirens fading in, a fire truck, an ambulance, rage, great rage.

'Yes?' Ferris.

'Listen,' I said, 'they've hit Cambridge.' Get in control, accommodate it, but Jesus *Christ* we should have seen it coming. We –

'Where are you?' Ferris asked.

'In the limo, outside the Yacht Club.'

Good evening. Brilliant smile. *This is Erica Cambridge, and these are my views.*

The bloody thing pumping out rapid fire and her white silk dress turning crimson and the bodyguard trying to reach her but going down too, his body humped and jerking as the shots went in, then the chopper lifting suddenly and very fast, leaving the balloons blowing across the car park, blue and green and red and yellow, whirling in the wind above the people's heads as some of the women screamed and went on screaming until a kind of silence came, the sound of the chopper fading across the sea.

'*Get in!*'

Treader, dragging me to the car and hustling me into the back, slamming the door and getting behind the wheel and starting up and moving off, someone hysterical in the crowd just here where the woman was lying, the woman and the man, their blood pooling in the moonlight.

Rage, fierce rage.

And these are my views.

Let them stand.

'You saw it happen?' I heard Ferris asking.

'Yes. I saw it happen.'

Get in control. It was nasty but the executive in the field is reporting to his director and there is the need for control, for decorum, you understand, there is no room here for personal feelings.

'How did it happen?'

You're perfectly right, how indeed did it happen, they'll want it for the signals board in London. 'A chopper took off from the pad here and came across the car park and someone opened the door and used a submachine gun at a range of fifty feet.'

In a moment, 'Where were you?'

'Not that close. They weren't making any mistake.

It was a straight, accurate hit.'

We moved forward, slowed again. The cars were jamming at the stop sign where the Yacht Club drive met the main road. Police whistles blowing – they were trying to clear the exit roads but it was difficult because a lot of people had obviously stopped their cars to see what had happened, some of them standing on the roof.

'They didn't know you were there,' Ferris said. 'The chopper didn't shift its – '

'No. This was just for her.'

We'll go to my apartment and I'll show you what I'm talking about. It's actually on paper, duplicated. You know what I'm saying? A whole brief, do you understand?

The product. Mission completed.

Not now.

'All right.' Ferris sounded a touch over-controlled, very cool, his articulation precise. We had come, after all, so very close to wrapping this one up and going home. 'Your instructions are to – '

'Listen,' I said, 'her phone must have been tapped. They picked up her call to Nassau tonight.'

'You think so?'

'She'd been on the yacht and she asked me along to the club to meet Stylus von Brinkerhoff and said it was very important for me to meet him. She also named Proctor. We were bugged. We must have been.'

'It didn't cross your mind,' Ferris asked carefully, 'at the time?'

'All that crossed my mind was that she could be trying to trap me.'

Scared for my own skin, it doesn't do, you know, it doesn't get you anywhere except on the bloody slab, but the problem was that I was *still* scared

261

because I was *still* in a red sector and we were jammed solid in a pack of cars and if one of Toufexis's hit men had seen me leaving the club and going down to the car park they'd come for me and it wouldn't do any good keeping the doors locked because they'd just smash a window with the muzzle and start pumping.

Control, yes. There must be a modicum of clear thinking. 'Listen,' I told Ferris, 'this won't wait for debriefing. There's an international syndicate called the Trust, and von Brinkerhoff is a member. Their objective is to "buy America and sell it to the Soviets" – I quote.' I gave him the other names she'd told me, and filled in the details. 'She said she'd got it all on paper, a whole *brief*, she called it, at her apartment. So if you can get permission to go and look around – '

'Someone broke in there, half an hour ago.'

Merde.

'How do you know?'

'I had some people stationed there in case it was in fact some kind of trap. Two patrol cars arrived and they followed the police inside the building and said they were reporters. The doorman told them he'd been attacked and tied up, fifteen minutes before. They found Cambridge's door open, with the lock smashed.'

The place ransacked, every drawer pulled out, the pictures dragged off the wall to find the safe, the bedding all over the floor, the mattress ripped, and in the end they'd found it, the brief, they must have, because she hadn't even thought about checking for bugs on the phones in her flat or the phone in her car, she wasn't intelligence, she was political, didn't understand things like cover, had probably just

dropped the brief onto the coffee table or somewhere and they'd looked right past it at first and
then they'd seen it and there was *nothing* we could
do about it now.

We were moving suddenly, free of the jam, going
north-east along Bayshore Drive.

'It could have been Proctor,' I said.

'That is our thinking.' His and Croder's. 'He was
seen landing from the yacht's cutter.'

'When?'

'Earlier tonight, just before eleven.'

Slight jolt to the nerves.

'They lost him?' They must have, or Ferris would
be telling me where Proctor was now.

'Within minutes.'

Support people are exactly that: they are troops
in the field and they lack the refined, exhaustive
training of the shadow executives. Even if I'd tagged
Proctor myself he would have made it difficult for
me because he was on my own level, competent and
seasoned.

So Proctor was off the *Contessa* and back in the
streets of the city and he'd probably conducted the
break-in himself because he was very good at it and
he'd been looking for a vital piece of product. He
had also cut right across the potential end-phase of
Barracuda and put us back onto square one.

'If he landed at 10:45,' I said, 'that was about
an hour after Cambridge phoned me in Nassau. It
would've taken him about an hour to reach land
from the *Contessa*. That call must have been bugged
and Proctor himself could have been listening in.'

The thought of it gave me another jolt. 'Hold on,'
I told Ferris. 'Treader, how far are we to the safe-
house?'

He half-turned his head. 'Ten minutes, bit more.'

'Don't go any closer. Keep on the move but don't circle that area.'

'Got it.' I saw him checking the outside mirrors.

'Is Hood with us?'

'Two cars behind.'

12:41 on the digital clock.

I said to Ferris, 'She must have taken that brief without their knowing – they wouldn't have given it to her. There would have been several copies, and they didn't know that copy was missing until she phoned me in Nassau over a bugged line. Then Proctor knew.'

'We considered that.' His tone still had its cutting edge. I'd heard it before, in *Mandarin*, in *Northlight*, when the mission had gone dangerously off track. He wasn't of course furious with Proctor tonight; he was furious with himself for letting it happen, furious with his own incompetence, as competent people often are when a wheel comes off. 'We also considered that it might have been Stylus von Brinkerhoff who'd shown her a copy of the brief. He was at the party tonight.'

'That's possible. She said he was attracted to her.'

'I would think most men were.'

'Where's von Brinkerhoff now?' I asked him. Perhaps we could turn him.

'We're watching for him to take the cutter back to the yacht. Monck suggests that if Cambridge wanted you to meet von Brinkerhoff, he might be ready to back out of the project, or even blow the Trust. We've sent someone to Quay 19 to wait for him and offer your apologies for not being in time to meet him at the Yacht Club, and see what he says, see if he's ready to take it further.'

Treader went through some lights on the yellow

and checked the nearside mirror. 'There's a Corvette moving up on us,' he said. 'I've been trying to lose it.'

'It he right behind?'

'No, there's a Buick right behind but the Corvette's buzzing it.'

There is the moment when you are sitting comfortably in a sumptuously-appointed limousine with a telephone in your hand and a cocktail cabinet in front of you and pile carpet under your evening shoes and there is the moment when you are suddenly aware that you have become prey to a hunter not far behind you who seeks your death, and aware also that you cannot hope to run fast enough to escape him, and the contrast between these two moments is so violent as to numb the mind, because in this instant the trappings of civilised life are stripped away to leave you in a different world, a different creature, crouched barefoot on rough ground with the hackles raised and the teeth bared as the terror courses like cold fire through the blood.

Proctor was in this city again and he'd come here to retrieve that brief and he'd asked Toufexis to make the Cambridge hit for him and he knew how close the executive in the field for *Barracuda* had come to infiltrating his operation and he knew I'd be at the Yacht Club party because he'd bugged Erica's phones and he had *not* asked Toufexis to hit me too *because he wanted to do it himself*.

It had become *personal*. My meeting with him on the day I'd arrived in this town had forced him out of his apartment and sent him straight to ground and he'd used his connections with the Mafia and got Toufexis to put out a contract on me and they'd tried twice and I was still alive and was still a threat to him, and it had hurt his pride and he'd told

Toufexis's hoods to hold off tonight because he wanted this kill for himself.

Lights swung in the mirrors but I couldn't see from this angle what Treader could see. 'I want instant replay,' I told him.

'We've lost the Buick. I think he got scared.'

'The Corvette's right behind us?'

'Yes. Close.'

'Ferris,' I said on the phone, 'are you still there?'

'Yes.'

'We're heading north on 22nd Avenue and crossing Coral Way. I think Proctor is right behind us.' I let him absorb that while I spoke to Treader; then I came back on the line. 'He's in a black Corvette with a Florida number plate. You've got that?'

'Yes. I'll do what I can.'

'Thank you. Have you got a second line there?'

'Yes.'

'Then leave this one open.'

He said he would.

Flashes on the roof-lining, quick and regular. Proctor was signalling for us to pull up.

'Treader. Where's Hood?'

'Behind the Corvette. And there's a red Mazda behind the Honda.'

Whole bloody parade, Proctor right behind us and a Toufexis hit man following Hood in the Mazda, light traffic coming the other way, the night clubs still open, this town never sleeps. Proctor was still flashing us and it was the sensible thing to do because he didn't want to make any noise, attract any attention: none of us wanted the police in our way. It would be very nice to tell Treader to put his fist on the horn and leave it there till a patrol car picked us up, officer, this nasty man behind us wants to kill me so you'd better do your duty, so forth, nothing so cosy because it would lead to a lot of awkward questions and making charges and that would stop *Barracuda* right in its tracks, and in any case there's a strict injunction in the rule book against a shadow executive's calling upon any police officer – it's quaintly written, don't you think – for his assistance, and yes, I take your point, *Barracuda* is going to get stopped right in its tracks in any case just as soon as Proctor gets into the back of this sumptuously-appointed limousine with his Heckler and Koch P7 9mm and its Wilson sound suppressor and starts tickling the tit, which he is very likely to do for the simple reason that he can outpace this ornate tart trap by a factor of three to one and if you think this looks like a car chase you're dead wrong, it's a funeral procession.

First shot and I slid down against the soft leather upholstery to bring my head below the rear window and saw Treader doing the same thing, settling back against the head-rest, wouldn't help him much because Proctor would be using heavy armament against a car like this or he wouldn't have started firing at all, though Treader could get away with it if the slugs had to plough through the rear panel of the boot and then the back of the rear seat before they hit the head-rest with most of their momentum gone, he was just making things as easy for himself as he could, never say die, so forth, take what cover you can get.

'What do you want me to do?' he asked me, and I liked that, we were having a conference, and if we needed advice from headquarters we had a line still open for signals, you can't say, you can't say, my good friend, that the situation was not under control.

Slug hitting the boot and bursting its way through

the seat-back *very close* to my left arm the bastard, oh the bastard he's going to put the next one straight into the spine and that means a slow death with unbearable pain or six months' rehabilitation and a wheelchair, *put it into the head you bastard don't forget your bloody manners*, chipping away at the cocktail cabinet with splinters flying up from the woodwork, rattling against the windscreen with not enough momentum left to smash a hole in it.

'Situation?'

Ferris.

'He's firing on us.'

'I've ordered three cars in. Where are you now?'

'Still going north, past Shenandoah Park.'

'You're still on 22nd Avenue?'

'Yes.'

'Then don't divert. I'll route them to intercept.'

I told Treader.

The flashing through the rear window had stopped. Treader wasn't going to pull up because if he did that it would finish me off and it was his job to keep me alive for as long as he could or God help him when it came to debriefing. There was a bit of noise from behind us and I asked him about it and he said he thought Hood was using the Honda to worry the Corvette, ramming it obliquely to burst a tyre. It looked as if Proctor was alone in his car because I didn't hear any shots going off that weren't putting slugs into the limousine.

Proctor had decided how to handle the police thing: the gun was making a noise and it wouldn't be long before we brought a patrol car zeroing in but he was now relying on a quick kill with enough time to get him clear. He –

Pock-pock in quick succession as the next one hit the boot and then the three-ply bulkhead and began nosing through the upholstery and I shifted to the right and felt the bloody thing ripping into the sleeve and saw the starburst on the windscreen as the glass frosted over.

Very close and I crawled across the seat to the other side because he'd shifted his aim six inches to the right every time, feeling for me with his gun. Sweat on the skin and the scalp creeping because the situation was not in fact in control and there was *nothing* we could do and he was going to get fed up in a minute and pull out and gun up alongside and aim for Treader and send this barouche into a shop window and get out of his car and walk across and kick the glass in and empty the whole chamber into the side of the head, unless of course Ferris could bring in his interceptors somewhere north of here and do something useful.

By the look of things we were doing approximately sixty mph and Treader was using the traffic lights as best he could, slowing enough to bring him to the next intersection still fast enough to gun up and go through on the green without losing too much speed. We could –

Pock-pock and the thing glanced off the door pillar and buried the last of its momentum into the sun visor on the forward passenger's side and I moved again, crawling across the seat to the right, little tufts of nylon padding lying around like puffs of smoke, torn away from the leather.

Treader saying, 'OK?'

'Yes.'

Quite a lot of noise suddenly from behind us and I saw headlight beams sweeping across the face of the buildings on the other side of the street and the flush of light under the roof didn't change so it must be Hood in the Honda, some kind of trouble.

'He's lost it,' Treader said.

'Hood?'

'Yes.'

Crumpling noise, a roll-over, the headlights flickering across the shop windows and then going out.

'Ferris?'

'No, sir. he's on the other line. This is Tench.'

'Tell him we've lost Hood. He's crashed.'

'Will do.'

Pock-pock and the door of the cocktail cabinet buckled and glass smashed inside it. I got onto the floor and asked Treader, 'What made him crash, did you see?'

'It could've been the Mazda behind him, sideswipe or something.'

Treader couldn't see all that much because he was hunched down against the seat squab and could only use the outside mirrors and from his angle they wouldn't be showing him a lot more than the top half of Proctor's Corvette, but it was logical to assume that the Mafia hit man in the Mazda had got the Honda out of the running because it had been a threat to Proctor.

We were leaving the park on our right and crossing 16th Street as the yellow turned to red but the Corvette and the Mazda came through without stopping and I gave it a minute, another two minutes at most unless Ferris could get his interceptors into the action because we were a sitting target and it was simply a matter of time.

'Listening?'

Ferris.

I said yes.

'Change of plan.' He sounded quietly impersonal. 'My instructions are to call off my people.'

'To call – '

'They won't be intercepting. You're expected to deal with the situation by whatever means. Stay in contact.'

Finis.

I told him I understood. It did not in point of fact take a lot of understanding: Ferris was speaking from his base and Croder must be there too and either he'd only just found out that Ferris had ordered mobile support into the area or he'd given the order himself and then changed his mind. The Bureau gives a great deal of licence to the executives and their directors in the field but there are some rather strict guidelines and one of them is that we don't fight a running battle through the streets of any given city and place the citizenry at risk, and – *sirens* – and that was precisely what we would have started doing if the interceptors had been sent in.

Shot and then a secondary bang that sounded right underneath us and the limo gave a lurch and Treader said, 'Got a tyre,' and we began weaving and then straightened. There was a lot of noise now as the rubber wrapped itself around the rim and started heating up. The sirens were fading in from behind us, I suppose because of the Honda thing – someone had seen it roll and they'd got on the phone.

I said, 'Treader, we're not going to get any help. They changed their minds.'

'I see.' Trying to sound cool. He knew the score now, too.

Stink of burning rubber coming into the car, I hate that smell, gets on your guts, *shot* and the rear window frosted over as the slug came through and drilled a hole in the roof, he wasn't firing wild, I think, it was just that the limo was lurching about quite a bit, difficult target at sixty mph with the steering affected. Siren again and this time ahead of

271

us, a patrol car picking up the Honda call from the despatcher and turning south, its lights starting to colour the polished surfaces inside the limo and the siren growing louder. I didn't think it would ignore a limo doing this speed with a burst tyre so I spoke to Treader again.

'Listen, I want you to ditch me. Look for an alley between the buildings or the gates of a yard or a car park – ' bright lights now as the police car saw us and started a U-turn with the siren howling – 'anywhere with enough cover to let me run, all right?'

He said he'd do what he could and I found the little chrome lever and got the right-hand door unlocked and waited, pulling out my handkerchief and wrapping it round my right hand, waited, watching the coloured lights reflecting from the inside of the windows, waited, holding my breath against the sickening reek of rubber, sweat on the left hand, the phone slippery with it, waited until Treader told me to get ready and I signalled Ferris that I was making a run and pitched sideways against the division as the brakes came on and the tyres whimpered and we lurched once, twice as he lost the front end and dragged it straight again as the burst tyre came off the rim and the metal screamed on the tarmac and I heard Treader's voice in the background.

'*Ditching.*'

Pulled the door-lever and hit the door and went through as it swung wide and I rolled into the *ukemi* with the edge of my right hand making contact with the pavement and the arm and shoulder following and then the whole body curving into the roll and coming out of it with my feet to the ground and enough balance to get me running.

He'd found an alley for me and I checked the

environment as I ran because I didn't want to present a silhouette against the lights of the street at the far end: it was a mess back there and I didn't know if Proctor or the man in the Mazda had seen me leave the car but if they'd seen me they'd follow me on foot and I wouldn't have more than a fifty-yard lead and there were high walls here and no cover that could shield me if he came close enough to use his gun.

The alley looked endless ahead, the length of a city block, with the lights of the next street making a bright niche in the shadows. I didn't turn my head to look behind me because it would slow me and if I saw Proctor coming there was nothing I could do – he'd have ample time to break his run and go into the aiming stance and make sure of the shot, *shadow down*, the slug ripping into the back of the dinner jacket and shattering the spine and leaving the nerves in catastrophic disarray, the muscles of the legs cut off from the brain and the body tilting forward, *shadow down*.

I was nearing the street ahead but the scene in the mind's eye had brought fear with it and I had to look behind me and I saw *nothing*, no movement anywhere in the whole length of the alley, so I slowed a little as the brightness of the street came flooding against me and a car slid to a stop with its tyres squealing and a door coming open.

Mazda.

20

MONIQUE

'You don't trust my driving?'

'It's not that,' I said.

Buckle wouldn't work.

'You know something? I bet I dropped a dime down there in the slot. I'm always doing it.' She leaned towards me, scent of *patchouli*. 'Hit it. Hit it like this.' A ripple of laughter, 'See what I mean? You can keep it, buy yourself a yacht.'

I got the buckle fixed and sat back and pulled it tight and tried to think.

'Ride around a little?'

'That would be nice.'

She turned left again at the lights, driving cleanly, sitting there in her black leather skirt and tunic, gold belt, rings on her fingers and long gold nails, tiny feet half-naked in gold sandals poised over the pedals, the curve of her body cut like a black crescent moon.

'Monique, I believe it was.'

'That's right.'

'What happened,' I asked her, 'to the Honda?'

I wanted to know where we stood.

'He got him kinda shunting. George Proctor is a real mean man. He got him kinda shunting and then

I think the guy in the Honda must have swung the wheel at the wrong time and he wasn't going too slow and bingo, he went rolling like a barrel. Who was he?'

'A friend of mine.'

'He in drugs too?'

'No.'

'He was trying to look after you, right? Didn't want Proctor to get you.'

'You could say that.'

'Proctor's real mad at you, right? You cut off his supplies or what?'

'I'm not a dealer,' I said.

'Nothing like that.' I watched the flash of her smile reflected in the windscreen. 'That's why Nicko was going to feed you to the sharks.'

'Thank you,' I said, 'for trying to stop him.'

'Usual way,' she said, 'I don't give a shit if a dealer gets his, providing of course he's not working for Toufexis. But the execution thing, I dunno, it kind of involves *judgement*, right? Kind of cold-blooded, different from just some guy gets in the way of an AK–47 and *kerboom*. You British?'

'Yes.' She still hadn't answered the question. It hadn't had anything to do with judgement.

Is this the guy? Nicko, pushing his flashlight against my face.

No.

Don't give me that shit! Shaking the photograph in her face.

I haven't seen him before.

Well Jesus Christ this is the face of the guy in the photograph!

You'd better take care, Nicko, she said. *Don't kill too many*.

Her face hidden by the glare of the flashlight, but

I'd caught the scent of *patchouli*.

'So why did you get in the car?' She was watching my face, too, in the windscreen.

'Which car?'

'This one.'

'I didn't have time,' I said, 'to find a taxi.'

'With Mr Proctor right up your ass!'

'That's right.'

'So what's a Britisher doing over here in God's country, muscling in on the game?'

'It's like calling you an Americaner, which sounds awful, don't you think? A British subject is actually a Briton.'

'You real cool cat,' tossing her head back, laughing, the big gold earrings flashing as they swung. 'So what's a *Briton* doing over here messing around on our home ground?'

She swung the wheel and gunned up through the intersection with an expertise that I found sexy. 'I work for the Foreign Office in London,' I said, 'and the reason why Nicko intended to kill me was because Proctor had asked your friend Toufexis to put out a contract on me, as you know.'

'Maybe I do, maybe I don't.' Not smiling now.

We were going very carefully, she and I. As far as I knew she worked for Toufexis and looked capable enough of making a hit if I said something wrong, despite her alleged aversion to making judgements. As far as she knew I was opposed to Proctor and Toufexis to the point where they'd put a price on my head.

'Foreign Office,' she said. 'What's that?'

'State Department.'

'See your ID?'

And the tone was unmistakable. I gave her my card.

'Looks authentic,' she said. 'Could even be.'

I took it back. 'You can flash your badge,' I said. 'I won't tell Toufexis.'

'What badge?'

Said it too fast.

Watching me in the windscreen, 'You know what I find so interesting about you? First time I see you, it's in George Proctor's place, visiting. Next thing, he vanishes like a bunny with a bee in his ass. Then you're down there on Quay 19 and Nicko's going to cream you, execution style, which is the only way he knows. Next thing, I see you tonight in that place talking with the highest-paid anchorwoman in the US of A like you knew each other all your lives, when you shoulda been out there in the ocean feeding the sharks. I don't get time to catch my breath before La Cambridge is lying dead on the ground just a hundred feet from where you're standing, just like you were the spotter for those guys, ain't actually saying anything. Then before I can blink you're tooling through the town in a limo with Proctor drilling holes in the bodywork, busy as a riveter. So I find you a very interesting man.'

She used the gear shift, the heavy gold bracelet shimmering in the glow from the facia panel, and we turned again, eastward towards the Bay.

I didn't say anything. I'd had to roll twice on the sidewalk back there and the stitches must have pulled because my shirt was sticking to the wound and the right shoulder was bruised because it had taken the impact but the worst of the shock was over by now and I was beginning to feel the heady lightness that suffuses the organism when it comes to know that life is sweet and that it has not been taken away.

Proctor had come very close to doing that, and it

was nice to be driving through the late night streets of this fair city with a pretty little undercover agent of the Miami Police Department.

She was still watching me, and I suppose it would have been rude not to answer.

'One has to keep busy,' I said.

'It's this Foreign Bureau thing I don't get. It doesn't gel with all that.'

'Office.'

'Huh?'

'Foreign *Office*.'

'Oh, sure, yeah. Maybe intelligence?'

'I was afraid you'd never catch on.'

Proctor knew; Toufexis and the mob knew; it was practically in the papers.

'Okay,' she said in a minute, '*that* makes sense.' She turned her head to study me. 'Yeah, you got the look. Mean, hard as a nail, sell your own mother and not for much.' She slipped a slim dark hand into the gold bag on the seat. 'You mean this one?'

'Yes.' A lieutenant, yet.

'Just a bit of gold tin, but I like the life.'

'It suits you. Does he deal? Proctor?'

'No. He smokes crack, that's all. But he's in with Toufexis like you said. We go to your place or mine?'

'Yours.'

'Okay. Fix you some protein. You gotta be feeling hungry after a ride like that. I been there.' I suppose she meant the Corvette thing.

'I can imagine,' I said.

'See, I moved in on Proctor to find out what he was doing. I knew he was in with Toufexis.'

'And Toufexis is your assignment.'

'Absolutely. Pull him in, I pull in the most powerful branch of the mob in Florida, that don't get me captain, nothing can. Proctor, he doesn't deal, no, but tell you this, he's into something bigger than that. Political. And very sophisticated. Like when I move in on him I have to move La Cambridge out, and she's – she was really quite attractive. So what happened, you going to tell me Nicko got a sign from heaven to spare you out there in that boat, or what?'

She'd done a lot of interrogation in her time, been taught how to drop a subject for a while and then snap back to it, catch you by surprise.

'They weren't professionals,' I said.

'You bet your sweet ass they were professionals, man. They – '

'I mean they weren't trained in close combat.'

'Oh, come on. You mean you had a teeny weeny XM–177 assault rifle tucked in your sock and they never frisked you.'

'I never carry a gun.'

She stopped at the lights, hand on the gear shift, her head turned to look at me. 'You never carry a gun. But there were four of those guys out there with – '

'Look,' I said, 'this is very embarrassing. I had some luck, and that's it.'

Watching me, a shimmer of dark eyes between smoky lashes. 'You're really annoyed aren't you?'

'Yes.'

A soft explosion of laughter as the lights changed and she hit the gear shift and took the Mazda away. 'You real, *real* cool cat!'

Very annoyed cool cat. 'So why didn't you just flash your badge and call the police and get me put into protective custody?'

'Huh? Well see, it's this way. I thought you were a rival dealer horning in on his operation, or maybe you'd stashed away a little bit of Toufexis's merchandise when someone wasn't looking, and normally I don't give a shit if one of those mothers gets in the way of a spray gun, it lightens the load for us and it saves all that bullshit in the courts when we work our ass off for months on end and bring a bunch of those suckers into the court and see some bleeding-heart jury give them an acquittal on all counts and send them whistling on their way, happens all the time. But like I say, the execution thing gets under my skin a little, I mean I like to sleep nights, so I put in my bit for you and tried to cool Nicko off, but that was all I could do because you know what? I flash my badge and he'd have shipped me out there with you on that boat, you better believe me, and if he hadn't done that I'd have blown my cover, and I've been working more than six months getting closer and closer to Toufexis and I would've thrown the whole thing out the window for the sake of one little waterfront dealer, which like I say is what I thought you were, didn't know you were a real live dude in the British Foreign Bureau – sure, Office, right. But then, gee, big deal, you didn't need my help anyway.'

'All the same,' I said, 'it was civil of you.'

'Hey, any time.' White flash of her smile in the windscreen.

She turned again and headed south and started slowing along a street full of waterfront apartment houses.

'That was a Mafia hit?' she asked me. 'Cambridge?'

'I don't know.'

'Oh. That's a shame.'

We ran into an alley behind the houses and hit two speed bumps and she swung the Mazda alongside a broken-down fence and switched off the engine. 'I was kind of hoping you'd be able to tell me about that. You seemed to know her pretty well, the way you were talking to her at the party. See, narcotics are okay but she was a big time gal and that was a big time hit, and if I could get a handle on *that* operation I might take it straight to the FBI and who knows, they could offer me a job with them, change of pace, little more prestige, you know?'

She locked the car and we went across a concrete yard and into the rear of the nearest house and took the lift to the fourth floor, a broken strand of one of the cables twanging through the pulleys. At the third door along a dim-lit passage she got out her keys and opened up and went inside and I followed.

'You want some eggs?'

'That would be nice.'

'Make yourself at home. Bathroom's through there, you want to clean up. Boy, you got legs, you know that?'

'I'm sorry?'

Throwing her gold bag on to a chair, checking her hair in a mirror, 'I saw you get out of that limo so fast I thought you were going to mash your head all over the sidewalk. Then you were up and running and I figured you were going to keep on flat out right to the end of that alleyway, and I had to burn rubber through a red light and get the whole of that block behind me and make another turn and get my ass all the way down to where you were in time to catch you, is what I mean, I only just made it, you got legs.' Turning away from the mirror and facing me with her hands on her hips in her black leather skirt with her moist skin glowing in the light and her eyes half-hidden in her long dark lashes, 'I'm real glad I made it, you know? I don't have a man now

282

Proctor's taken off, you go for black gals?'

'Oh for Christ's sake, Lieutenant,' I said, 'we've got business to do.'

A flash of laughter – 'And just *dig* that accent – *leff*-tenant, wow! You want them boiled, fried, Benedict, sunny side up, over easy, two, three, four?'

'Whatever you're having,' I said and went into the bathroom, and when I came back she'd started frying them, the top half of her body visible above the counter dividing the big cathedral-ceilinged room from the kitchen.

'Like a drink?'

'I'm fine as I am.'

'Take a look around. That's my own art work on the walls.'

She meant the photographs, rows of them, black and white and most of them taken by flash, Lt. Lacroix with incident-number 3546, Lt. Lacroix with incident-number 1170, the positions mostly the same, a man stooping or leaning face to the wall or prone on the floor, a cop frisking him or putting the handcuffs on or keeping a locked arm-hold or pushing him into a squad car, Lt. Lacroix looking on, got up in short pants and a tank top or jeans and a tee shirt or a torn leather jacket, the same expression on her face in every shot, very alert, her eyes wide and missing nothing, giving me the impression that if the cop fumbled with the handcuffs or lost the arm hold or let the man slip away from the car she'd *be* there with a force of her own, because she hadn't spent the amount of time she had in nailing these people just to see them evade arrest.

'Kinda toast?' she asked me, 'rye, whole wheat, French?'

'Whatever you're having. So what would you do if one of these people tried to get away, Monique?'

'I do what it takes. I've been up three times this year on a police brutality rap, you beat that? Thing is, they're all in the slammer and I guess that's the name of the game.'

'How tall are you?'

'Five two, hundred and ten pounds, call me a fucking midget, but listen, the bottom line is just how hard you kick them in the nuts, because it really gets their attention.'

We sat at a black lacquered table under one of those hanging mirrored globes, with its reflections floating across the walls and the black net curtains as she flashed me a smile and passed me the ketchup and said in her light, husky voice, 'See, I don't personally give a shit if people decide to go to hell in their own handcart by smoking crack or shooting snow, they don't wanna live and they know how to die, it's their business. I just find it's a good game to play, it's fast and it's risky and I go into these houses and make a purchase and flash my badge and bring the rest of the guys in from the cars, scare the shit out of everybody and maybe sometimes shake a guy down for a couple of grand, I like nice things, look at this room, I like a nice watch and nice shoes, you know? And who do I steal from, the public? Shit, I steal from the dealers, see, I'm not like those fancy congressmen, charge the public for their plane trips and women and cruises and all that stuff, they're the real crooks but of course for them it's legal. They okay?'

The eggs. Said yes.

'Thing is, it triggers so much crime, and there's not much we can do to keep it down, the numbers are just too big. In this town there's maybe a thousand armed robberies and auto thefts and break-ins every *day*, and a big percentage of those are drug-related, those poor slobs sucking on the devil's dick and having to net a hundred grand or two hundred grand to support the habit – *that's* where the public pays. So I do my thing and like I say it's fast and risky but there's no way, there is no *way* we can stop the biggest growth industry in Miami – the stuff just comes dropping out of the sky in bales and canvas bags from the low-flying planes while the power boats are out there picking them up, same time as the body-packers in from Columbia are dying in the hotel rooms, found one of them today with a pound of cocaine in his stomach stashed away in eighty-two condoms, had to give him emergency surgery because, see, those things can burst and the coke paralyses the colon and this poor son of a bitch had been out and bought himself an enema and two packets of prunes and a box of Exlax, didn't do him any good, see, near dying when we got to him, went to Jesus two hours later in the post-operative room, things going on like that all over this town, the stuff comes in every way there is, planes and boats and pickup trucks and people's stomachs, you like some more?'

Coffee. Said yes.

'Anyway, Toufexis is my assignment, I mean my *personal* assignment, they wouldn't put just one little lieutenant to work on the head of the Miami Mafia, we've got a whole special unit on his ass, but that's why I moved in on George Proctor, see.'

'What caught your interest?'

'I saw him with Toufexis himself, talking in the lobby of the Gold Hibiscus, shaking hands and everything like real good friends, I took it from there. Had to get Cambridge off the stage but he liked the cut of my *whoops* or something and it only took a few days. Then I began working on him, you know? I mean once I'd copied the key of the apartment and he wasn't there. Diaries, phone-numbers, the regular routine, and one time I followed him to a place he often went to, and the next day I got myself invited inside, flashed my badge, nice and polite.'

'Where was that?'

'House on West Riverside Way, 1330, you know the place?'

'No,' I said, and put my coffee down, 'but tell me about it.'

21

FINIS

'. . . And the last time he went there was two days ago, but it's a dead end because I can't go in there myself a second time without an official backup and like I say, that place sure is no crack house.'

She was sitting on a black leather bean bag, one arm held straight out and resting on her knee, her hand hanging, the gold nails glinting sometimes as the light from the mirror-lamp floated across them.

'How many of the rooms did you see?'

'Maybe three or four, the big hall with the staircase and a couple of rooms either side and a small kind of den. See, you can't have just one cop go into a house and take the whole place apart, this was just a drop-by kind of thing, like I explained to them, they could have asked for a warrant if I'd tried muscling them. You okay there?'

On the floor. Said yes.

'The way it was, see, they *should* have told me to keep my ass in the street, a great big house like that and the guys got up in pin-stripe duds and everything, and it got me thinking a little bit, why they were so ready to show me around, but maybe I was just over-suspicious because Proctor went there.'

'You didn't see a Japanese?'

'No. Just these three guys, two of them American and one with a French accent – he was on the phone to someone. I took it to the point, see, where I could back out and leave there with my nose clean, said my despatcher had obviously sent me to the wrong address. I wanted them to forget the whole thing as soon as they could because I was taking a risk, they could mention a cute little black cop in Proctor's hearing and he could ask them to describe her and bing-go. But anyway he's gone to ground and unless he shows up again there isn't anything more I can do. But there's a couple of little things that've got my antennae quivering, see, though they're nothing to do with drugs, things like him calling the Soviet Embassy, that get your attention?'

'Somewhat,' I said.

'Somewhat, sure, you being in the intelligence game. But listen, this is a two-way street, you know? I show you mine, you show me yours. If there's anything you've got on Proctor I can take to the FBI, I want it.'

I got off the cushion and walked about, rolling the right shoulder to ease the stiffness. 'I can't promise anything.'

'Shit.' A bright, frozen smile.

'I can ask my superiors to give you anything they're able to. That might be nothing at all.'

'He's into something that big? Proctor?'

'Something rather sensitive.'

'The way you understate things,' she said, 'it sounds like an international spectacular.'

'I didn't say that.'

'It's the things you don't say, Richard, that I listen to the most.' The slim hand hanging from the wrist was moving a little, circling, restless. 'You can't show me yours, gee, why should I flash mine around?'

'Try this,' I said, but the telephone on the black lacquered cabinet began ringing and she went over there.

'Yeah. A half hour back.' She lifted her free hand towards the ceiling, very slowly, and as it reached as high as it would go she spread her fingers out, and the gold nails looked like fruit glowing on a tree. 'Then get him,' she said. 'I don't give a shit. Go get him. Bring him in.' Her hand was turning slowly, the gold vanishing and reappearing from behind her fingers as the floating lights passed over them. Her bare arm, stretched like this, looked like a slim dark vine, the muscle lit and shadowed. 'Okay, Maloney, can you hear me all right? Okay, I don't give a shit he's connected to Washington. Go get that mother-fucker and bring him in and I mean right now or I'll have your badge first thing in the morning, now move your fucking *ass*, man, those are my fucking *orders*.'

She dropped the phone and brought her other hand down slowly, watching it, turning it into a black and gold fan, spreading it across the shadows.

'You're beautiful,' I said.

'I know. I'm into dance, nights off. Those guys,' she said, 'they think just because some dude got a pass into the State Capitol they can't arrest him. You give me enough on a guy and I'll go and arrest him *inside* the State Capitol. Try what?'

'I'll give you as much as I can.' Told her, throwing in details, that Proctor was persona grata on board the motor-yacht *Contessa* and was involved in Senator Mathieson Judd's campaign for the presidency. That there was, yes, a Soviet connection and Proctor had already been reported as having telephoned their embassy. 'That's as far as I can go, Monique. It's practically all I know about his operation, except that it *has* got international dimensions. Now that Proctor's gone to ground, you should use the time to get as close as you can to the Cambridge hit, and work from there.'

She dropped onto the floor, facing me in the lotus position, her thigh muscles carved out of ebony, wrists across her knees and both hands hanging with the fingers wide, making a black and gold screen. 'You're taking a risk,' she said.

'Not really.'

'I go blabber-mouthing that to the FBI, trying to look good, trying to get in there?'

'That wouldn't be very intelligent, would it, at this stage? The FBI are going to be working on the Cambridge hit in any case, and I shouldn't think it'll take them terribly long to find the helicopter and start from there. Tell them if you like that it could be a Mafia hit. It's only my supposition.'

She watched me from the shadows of her lashes. 'Not too many people outside the Mafia go and make a hit like that. Takes money, and it's very exposed. Shows how cool they are, giving us guys the finger, part of Toufexis's personality, he's like that, always keeps just out of reach. So that's all you got to show me?'

'It's dynamite, and you know that. Because of the Judd connection. And the Soviet.'

'Jeeze,' she said in a minute, 'you seen the FBI badge?'

'No.'

'It's real pretty.' Looking down, frowning a little, 'Okay, show you mine. I knew he was calling the Soviet Embassy because once when we got in from the Black Flamingo Club there was a message on his machine and I was near enough to watch the numbers he touched on his phone, next day I checked them out and it was the embassy.'

'He was on coke at that time?'

'Sure, he was riding right along.'

Or he would have waited until he was alone before he made that call. He was still slipping, getting cocky in the coke fumes, some of the Mafia braggadocio rubbing off on him, perhaps it'd give me a chance, take him when he was high, if I could do it before he or the mob had another go and brought it off.

'What did he say on the phone?' I asked her.

'Nothing too much, no names or anything, he was just making a rendezvous.'

'Did you surveille it?'

'The timing was wrong – I was on duty.'

'You didn't sent someone else to cover it?'

'Send someone else and I'm giving the whole deal away, you don't watch your ass in this service you get kicked.'

'That was the only time you heard him phoning the Soviet Embassy?'

'Right. But there were other things.'

She told me she'd followed Proctor once to Quay 19 and saw him board the cutter, nothing new, and told me he'd been going with a girl named Harvester before Cambridge had moved in, nothing new, and then she began talking about the canisters.

'He used to bring them back from the *Newsbreak* studios, couple of times a week, and a guy came for them and returned them later. He – '

'Do you know what was in them?'

'Sure, I checked a couple for drugs, but they were just video tapes. It could be the guy that came for

them took them to Riverside Way, because I saw
one of them there that time I checked the place out.
It seemed – '

'Did you put them into a VCR?'

'I couldn't do that. They were sealed, besides
which, I was looking for a big stash of merchandise
and tapes didn't turn me on too much. Anyway they
were just commercials.'

'How did you know?'

'They'd got labels. *Honi-du, Syn* – '

'What's that?'

'Uh? Skin cream. *Syncrest*, that's an earphone
unit, *Pizzarita*, that's a chain of chic pizza stops.
Discreet, that's pads for gals.'

'Go on,' I said.

'What's so big?'

I was dead-pan, but it must be showing in my
eyes. 'It might be nothing,' I said. I didn't think so.

'Okay, there was *Orange Sunset, Yummies*, and
Tuxedo Junction, that's a soft drink and a junk bar
and a cologne for men. They're all I can remember.'

'They're all you saw.'

'You got it.'

In a moment I asked her, 'Where is Proctor now?'

'Last time I saw him he was climbing up your ass
in a Corvette.'

'If you know where he is,' I said carefully, 'and
don't want to tell me, I could understand that. But
if you know, and choose to tell me, I could give you
much more – '

'I ain't lying.'

She didn't put on any false resentment. I thought
it was probably true.

'Is there any way,' I asked her, 'you could go into
the house again, the one on Riverside?'

'Not without a warrant.'

'And you can't get one.'

'I don't have no reason.'

'There is no way, then, that you could get hold of one of those canisters.'

'No way. They're private property.'

It was nearly three o'clock when I looked at my watch.

'When are you back on duty?'

'Varies, on undercover. Maybe eight, maybe nine, report in.'

'Can I use the phone?'

'Go ahead.'

I went across the room and dialled.

'Yes?'

'DIF.'

'Hang on.' Tench's voice.

In a moment: 'Yes?'

'Just reporting in,' I said.

'Where are you?'

'Oh, not long.'

Any kind of answer will do, as long as it doesn't make sense. Means someone is listening. Then they've got to take it from there, asking suitable questions until they make a hit.

'You need support?'

'No.'

'Medical attention?'

'No.'

'Congratulations.' The last time we'd talked over the phone I'd been in the limousine, waiting to ditch. 'You need transport?'

'No.'

'A rendczvous?'

'Yes.'

Silence for a bit. 'It will have to be in the open.'

I didn't like that but I'd been expecting it. I'd

become a security risk. It happens a lot of the time, when the shadow executive becomes so exposed and so vulnerable that the whole of the field becomes a permanent red sector. He is then a danger to his director, and must keep his distance from every base and safe-house because he could be followed there. He becomes a pariah dog, unwelcome at any door and therefore without shelter. Ferris would have a bolt-hole for me but it wouldn't be an established safe-house because I could contaminate it.

'All right,' I told him.

He couldn't say *where are you* so he said, 'How far are you from where you ditched?'

'More explicit.'

'Five miles?'

'No.'

'More?'

'No.'

'Three?'

'Roughly.'

'Give me a minute.'

Getting a map.

She hadn't moved. Her reflection was in the black lacquered cabinet with the gold inlay, stylised pea-cocks. She was watching me. She would realise I was shielding the content of my talk with Ferris but I couldn't do anything about that. At worst, it was discourteous: we had established trust.

'You're without transport?'

'Yes.'

'You'll rdv on foot?'

'That's right.'

'Then I'll be at SW 21st Avenue and SW 11th Street, by the school. In ten minutes?'

'No.'

'More?'

'Yes.'

'Thirty?'

'No.'

'Forty?'

'Yes.'

'Right. Look for two vehicles, a dark blue Saab and a black Chevrolet Blazer van, both fairly new. I shall be in the Blazer, and you will therefore rdv with that. You'll take it over. Questions?'

'No.'

'Forty minutes, then, at 03:35.'

'Yes.'

I went back across the room. She was still in the lotus position, her hands spread like fans, a beam of light floating across one of her eyes, brightening its translucent orb like a jewel before it moved away.

'Will you dance more,' I asked her, 'as time goes by? And finally turn in your badge?'

'Think I should?'

'Yes.'

'Look,' she said, and unfurled her legs and rose with the grace of a swimmer surfacing, 'this is the body my spirit chose, but my spirit is feisty and assertive, and I hate men, because they've always called the shots. Most men, sure, not all of them. So it gives me a kick, see, to order them face down on the floor and then have them hustled into the van and sent to the slammer. And it gives me a kick because they're dangerous, and I've got to be good to beat them at the game we play. So maybe I'll dance more, as time goes by, but for now I'm the happiest little gal alive, kicking the shit outa those mother-fuckers. You going?'

'Yes.'

'You don't want to jump in the jacuzzi with me?'

'Of course I do.'

'But you gotta go.'

'That's right.'

'Some other time. Get you a taxi?'

'I'll find one.'

'Couple of minutes from here,' she said, 'right in front of the hotel, just go left on the sidewalk.' Turning to face me at the door with a quick swing of her hips that went through me like a wave, 'I don't know what it is about you. It ain't the looks – I prefer blacks. I guess it's the brand of phero-mones you send out. I'm in most nights, after twelve. Call me?'

I'd asked for forty minutes to give me time to get to the rendezvous absolutely certain I was alone. The taxi dropped me off at SW 11th Terrace and SW 23rd Crescent and I walked from there, covering two blocks and using doorways and double-tracking, making certain, making absolutely certain. Since I've been with the Bureau only three executives have inadvertently blown their directors in the field and the one who survived his mission was fired the day after debriefing.

The Saab and the van were already there and I gave it another five minutes, scanning the whole of the environment until I was sure. Then I walked across the street to the van and got in.

Ferris was alone, sitting at the wheel with his long body slightly hunched, held in on itself, and his hands folded on his lap. I hadn't ever seen him like this before, and I suppose I should have been warned. I began debriefing but he stopped me almost right away and got it over, said I'd been withdrawn from the mission.

22

WINDOW

'There are some new clothes for you,' Ferris said, 'in the back. I thought a van would be easier to change in than a car.'

The night was quiet. This wasn't one of the main streets that casino and night-club traffic used. There was only one light that I could see, in a window, apart from the street lamps. The only other vehicle in sight was the dark blue Saab, waiting to take Ferris away when we'd finished the debriefing.

'The programme is,' he said, still hunched at the wheel with his eyes on the street, 'to fly you by private jet to Nassau, and put you on a plane for London. You'll be smuggled – '

'Purdom can do *nothing*.'

First time I'd spoken since he'd told me the news. I think it sounded fairly normal, my tone. Bit of an effort, though, as you can well believe, my good friend.

'You'll be smuggled through to the London plane with great care. For one thing we don't want you seen and shot at before you can get out of the field, and for another thing Croder wants the opposition to believe you're still in operation, in the hope that Proctor will waste his time trying to find you, and

Purdom can proceed under the cover of your assumed continuing presence.'

And that is *exactly* the way that bastard Croder talks, *assumed continuing presence*, nibbling the words over in his small rat's teeth and then spitting them out.

'You'll be at the airport here,' Ferris said, 'at 06:00 hours, outside the private departure lounge. I'll get into the van and tell you where to go.'

'There is *nothing* Purdom can do. If I go, the mission goes. You know that.'

I realised I'd got my hands tucked under my folded arms, that I was feeling cold on this sultry Miami night. I suppose that was why Ferris sat hunched over the wheel. He'd directed me in five missions, major ones, and we understood each other, worked well with each other, had mutual respect and trust. It's not always like that – take bloody Loman for instance. But he'd got more to deal with than losing an executive he could rely on. He'd told me that if I got fired from *Barracuda* he'd go back to London too. I wouldn't keep him to that – it had been a gesture on his part, bit of civility. But it wouldn't make any difference: if he stayed on here he'd be stuck with a new executive who couldn't make a move. It doesn't always happen but it was true now: I was indispensable to the mission.

'We've *got* to get Proctor,' I said. 'And we've got to put him under a hood and sweat the whole thing out of him. He's the *major* objective, in fact the *only* objective, now that we've lost the Cambridge brief. And the *only* way we can get Proctor is to let me go on running till I get in his way and draw his fire, expose him, pull him into a trap. Stop me running and *Barracuda*'s dead.'

It didn't hold water but I thought I'd at least try.

I wasn't sure Ferris would trouble to answer, but if he just sat there and let the silence go on it'd leave me looking stupid, and he wouldn't do that.

'It would work,' he said, 'yes, if Proctor were the only danger. But the pre-eminent Mafia family in this town is actively searching for you and they've got your photograph. They total, by the way, ninety-four members. So if you go on moving in the streets it's going to lead to another situation like the one we saw tonight, and *that* is what brought Croder to his final decision.' He sat back at last and turned his head and watched me with his expressionless amber eyes. 'You've become a danger to yourself, to the mission, and to the overseas Bureau network on this coast, whose main task is to assist the Americans by monitoring British and European underground activity. You are therefore a danger to our hosts, and that is also why Croder has come down on you. It's not London's policy, I hope you'll admit, to run a mission to the point of open street battles inevitably involving the police, which is why Croder had second thoughts on sending in interceptors tonight.' He waited for me to say something. I could think of nothing to say. 'In my opinion he's justified in withdrawing you and sending you home. At least you'll have survived the mission.'

The light up there, the light in the small high window, went out. I'd been watching it, and the thought had been in my mind that as long as it stayed there, as long as it didn't go out, I would somehow manage to stay with *Barracuda*. So you will understand the state of my mind, my good friend, as I sat there with my director in the field in the small black Chevrolet van, lost in the vastness of the night-quiet streets. I had descended to rabid superstition.

The silence was drawing out, so I asked him, 'What happened to Hood?'

'He's in hospital with concussion, nothing major.'

'Treader?'

'The police booked him for speeding. He told them he thought he was being chased by a drug gangster who took him for someone else. He'll be all right.'

'I'm sorry,' I said in a moment, 'for Purdom.'

'I'll tell him that.'

'Tell him I wish I could have left him with at least a direction to take. I've done nothing, you know, since I came here, except stay alive. So I can quite see Croder's point of view.'

Got *that* over. It hadn't been easy but had to be done, for the sake of the records. The shadow executive is the most important member of a mission, and his personal views are sought at critical times. What I had just said would go down as: *The executive has evaluated the decision made by the Chief of Signals and fully understands its necessity*.

From the Chief of Signals himself I expected no comparable manners. He could have sent for me and personally explained the situation but had simply told Ferris, instead, to order me out of the field. But then Croder was a worried man, and I didn't envy him. In the normal way he doesn't lack common courtesy.

In a moment Ferris said quietly, 'Final debriefing?'

'What? Yes.' I thought for a minute to get it straight. 'It doesn't amount to much. There's a policewoman on undercover work in the narcotics division, name of Monique Lacroix, a lieutenant. She took up with Proctor in the hope that he might lead her closer to Toufexis, the Mafia chief. She confirms that he telephoned the Soviet Embassy in Washington at least once. She would be helpful to you in finding Proctor, and you should consider letting her have any information on his connection with the Trust. She'd like to get into the FBI.'

'All right. Do we need a recorder?'

'No. All I've got for you is this. Proctor brought canisters of video tapes back to the apartment from the *Newsbreak* studios and someone called for them and brought them back later. Lt Lacroix said they contained video tapes of commercial ads. You'd better note these.' He got the mini Sanyo out of his pocket and pressed for record. '*Syncrest, Honidu* – ' I spelt that one for him – *Discreet* – *Pizzaria* – no, *Pizzarita* – wait a minute.' I had to recall her voice, light and husky, as a context for the mnemonics. '*Orange Sunset, Tuxedo Junction.*'

The light in the window went on again, and the nerves leapt for an instant as hope came, touched off by superstition. It's remarkable, it is quite remarkable, how sensitive the web is, where we sit enmeshed with our environment: someone up there had pressed a switch and activated the nervous system of a man down here in the street, hidden inside this little black van. The superstition itself, of course, rated no more than a cheap laugh: the stranger up there behind the high window hadn't intended to rekindle hope in this poor creature's breast; he'd intended simply to have another pee.

'Is that it?'

'What? Yes. No, I've missed one.' In a minute, '*Yummies.*'

'*Yummies*?'

There was an odd sound coming from my throat, presumably a kind of strangled laughter. If there's

301

anything that makes me fall about more than a prat-fall it is bathos.

Watching me, Ferris said, 'You're in better condition than I thought.'

He meant that as an executive just thrown out of the mission and ordered home I didn't appear to be ready to cut my throat.

'Never better,' I said stoutly.

'So what's your thinking on these commercials?'

I believe he'd got it, but had decided to leave the big number to me, which was nice of him. I said, 'It could be a long shot, but if you had those ads analysed on the screen for subliminal content, at either visual or audible wave lengths or even both, you might possibly come across things like *Vote for Judd* in any number of variations. And if you did, you could then work out the potential impact of those programmes on the American population, to the nearest hundred million.'

He let the silence go on for a bit, then said quietly, 'If you're right, this would go down in your records as a major accomplishment.'

'Fuck the records.' I didn't want a pat on the back from those superannuated old farts in the hierarchy, I wanted the mission, I wanted *Barracuda*.

'I take your point,' Ferris said. 'You think this has been Proctor's main operation?'

'No. This is an educated guess. I think he began using cocaine, lost control, and was got at by scouts working for the Trust, to give them access to a major television network as an outlet for their subliminal signals.'

'Sorry,' Ferris said, and pressed for record. 'Again?' I did it for him and went on, 'I think the Soviet connection began as a developing relationship between Proctor and a KGB agent in Washington, one of the people he would normally meet in the international intelligence watering holes, such as the Gold Hibiscus in Miami. And I think his major operation is working for both the Trust as an active tool well-versed in subterfuge at high levels, and someone in the Kremlin who needs the Trust monitored without its knowledge.'

Ferris pressed for off and sat for a bit without talking. I let the silence go on. There was a lot more I could give him if I felt like it but they'd ask for it in London at the end-of-tour debriefing – that reads end-of-*tour*, my good friend, and not end-of-*mission*, you will please understand, there is a difference.

'I wouldn't say,' Ferris said at last, 'that you've left Purdom without a direction. This is very good product.'

'Mostly assumptions.'

'By a highly experienced agent.'

'Civil of you. But the major objective for the mission is still Proctor, and he's still out of your reach.'

We talked about that for a few minutes but it was a dead end and he put away his little Sanyo and we compared watches and he said, 'I'll stay in Miami until they send out someone to direct Purdom, and then – '

'You don't have to,' I said. 'You can direct him better than anyone.'

'He's not quite my type. I'll have to brief the new man, then I'll get a plane.' He looked at all three mirrors and got out of the van and stood for a moment looking down and around him, hoping to find a beetle to tread on.

'They're all asleep,' I said, 'this time of night. Christ's sake leave them alone.'

He looked up at me with a faint unholy light deep

in his eyes. '06:00,' he said, 'at the airport, private lounge.'

I watched him going along the pavement, a tall reedy figure with its wispy hair catching the lamplight; his head was down again, looking from left to right, as I'd seen him in Las Ramblas in Barcelona and at Tegel Airport in Berlin and in Monkey Street, Hong Kong. I do wish he'd leave the poor little buggers alone; the sound of that small crisp explosion sickens me.

When he got into the dark blue Saab and it drove away I waited for a little while to let things settle in my mind, and gradually the panic diminished, the panic of finding myself suddenly isolated, abandoned, cut off from the signals board in London, with nothing more important to do now than change my clothes and get a couple of hours' sleep and drive to the private lounge at the airport, there to be led away and smuggled out of sight, the discomfited embodiment of a fall from grace.

Then I shifted behind the wheel and started up and moved off, and when I passed the tall balconied house the light in the dormer window was still burning, so I stopped again and fished for a map in the glove pocket and found one and looked for Chucunantah Road and moved off again and turned east and then south, with the thought in my mind of seeking Parks.

You don't remember him, I know, but I'll tell you this. He was my only chance, and the opera ain't over till the fat lady sings.

23

SING

'Will this do you?'

'Yes.'

It stank of rotten eggs or something, and seawater was lapping at the side as the swell moved against the harbour wall. Flotsam made a multicoloured scum on the surface beyond the rail.

'It's not for long,' Kim said. 'Is that right?'

'Twenty-four hours. Did the hurricane do all this?'

'Most of it.' She ducked her head under the shattered boom and crouched beside me in her frayed sunbleached shorts. It was almost dark here, in contrast to the glare of the morning sun across the water outside. 'The harbour's becoming abandoned, pretty well. Other storms began wrecking it, and people began bringing their boats here, those that were still afloat. Their idea is to do them up, given enough time, but the thing is they haven't got enough money. They're allowed to leave them here; they don't pay dues or anything.'

She pulled a loose timber and shoved it into the flooded hold behind us, then moved away to work at the jammed door of the cabin. Two of the berths were still intact, and she'd brought oil lamps and a keg of water.

She'd been asleep when I'd telephoned the tug just before five this morning from Parks' place, but she'd said straight away that she'd pick me up at the Exxon station three blocks from the harbour and find me shelter. I'd telephoned Avis and told them where I'd left their van.

I would go down in signals as missing.

All instructions to the executive in the field will be followed except where extenuating circumstances are seen to exist, as determined by Administration at the time or at a later date.

Failure to report to a rendezvous was technically a breach of contract and if I ever managed to get back to London I would face a board of enquiry. I hadn't telephoned Ferris from the Exxon station to tell him I was going to ground because that would have put him in an invidious position: technically he would have been expected to inform Croder but he wouldn't have done that; he would simply have accepted the fact that his executive had become a rogue agent and reported to Croder only that I had missed the rendezvous. He would first, of course, have done everything he could to persuade me to change my mind and follow instructions, but there would have been no point in letting him go through an exercise in predetermined futility.

And if I'd told him what I planned to do he would have tried everything to stop me.

Soon after 06:00 hours today the executive in the field for *Barracuda* would be posted on the signals board in London as missing. Soon afterwards his name would be removed from the board and replaced by Purdom's.

In the meantime there would be a man holed up in the stinking cabin of a wrecked schooner on the Florida coast, awaiting the coming night with the patience of a saint and the conscience of a sinner, while hour by hour the terror would grow in him until at the long day's end he would surely come to know that he was mad.

'I can't borrow a boat,' Kim said when she came over to me again. 'It'd involve other people, and we don't want that. So what I'll do is take the tug out to deep water and hang around and see if anyone's followed me. If I'm clear I'll head back to the coast where there's not much shipping, and come into the harbour here as soon as it's dark.' She sat next to me on the splintered bunk, touching, her bare arms folded across her knees. 'Does that sound all right?'

'It sounds very good.'

I offered her a couple of hundred dollars to defray expenses, the diesel oil and the three diving lessons she'd had to postpone, but she said she often went out deep-sea 'just to be there', and the lessons were no big deal. 'This ride's on me,' she said, 'and that's the only way you can get it.'

During the heat of the day I slept, woke and slept again. Voices came sometimes, but not close. This place was a graveyard, and there was no sea-borne traffic.

In the evening I opened a can of sardines and had them with a piece of bread, and drank some tea from the thermos Kim had left for me. The blood-red remnants of the sun were paling to a grey wash and then darkening as night came down across the littered sea, and I heard the straining of rowlocks not far off, then the bump of timbers.

She came aboard quickly and on bare feet, without a sound. The moon, in its third quarter, cast an ashen light across the harbour, and reflections pooled on the planks above our heads. I hadn't lit the lamp.

'There was no one,' she said, coming beside me, 'absolutely no one.' Her hands smelled of oil and rope and seaweed; the pale light frosted the salt along her arms. 'Being not quite certain isn't a risk I'd take. I mean – '

'I know what you mean.'

Her breath was coming a little fast, and she tried to slow it, talking about the tides for a moment and the state of the sea, until she finally said, and had not been willing to say, 'All right, when you're ready.'

By the brass chronometer in the cabin of the tug it was eight in the evening when we anchored over deep water, a few minutes after eight, though time had lost its meaning now, and there was no hurry.

'How far are we?' I asked her.

'Two sea miles, give or take a bit. That's what you said you wanted.'

'Are we under their radar?'

'Yes. But we're only a blob. They don't know what vessel she is.'

The sea was dead calm, and the lights between here and the coast were motionless. The moon hung among hazy stars, and you would have said it was a night for magic to be made across this vast unfathomable stage, a night for sorcery, its reaches peopled by warlocks, witches and diabolists, casting their spells and conjuring phantoms from the very air. I told you, my good friend, that by nightfall I would come to know that I was mad, and here was the night, and here this madman's tale.

Here too of course the appalling urgency to turn back and gain the shore and find a telephone and offer myself to be led like a lamb to London.

'Did you eat anything?' she asked me.

'Yes.'

'Not too much.'

'No. Some sardines.'

'Time to go to the loo.'

When I came back she helped me on with the wet-suit, and I asked her, 'All right, what am I up against?'

I heard her take a breath. 'Bad news first. They feed by night, and actively. There are a lot more rods than cones in the retinae, so they can see quite well in dim light. The moon isn't a help, though you'll need it to see what you're doing.'

I pulled the front zip and began strapping the ankles. She helped me, crouching at my feet, her hands quick and deft. 'The things that attract them are light, noise and rapid movement. I suppose that's true for most creatures, it's nothing special. But watch out if you see garbage being thrown overboard, and keep well away from it. They sometimes move about in packs, as you saw yesterday, but ninety per cent of attacks are made by a single shark. The attack's usually direct, straight on, without any close passes beforehand.' She straightened up and began helping me with the gear and the floats. 'Statistically, which is really all I'm talking about, only a third of the vic – of the people attacked have reported seeing the shark. It's usually what we call a blind hit, before you can see anything.' She stopped talking for a minute; I suppose she was having trouble with a buckle or something.

'That's all I need to know,' I said. 'You've – '

'They're also attracted to fish moving in a shoal. If you see a shoal, steer clear of it or try to swim towards it to turn it away. Most of the strikes are made at the extended arms and legs; try to remember to swim with your flippers almost together; just paddling slowly, with your arms close to your sides.

I wish to God – ' she said and broke off and for the rest of the time she managed to sound almost normal, with her voice no more than subdued.

'What's the best weapon?'

'I'll come to that,' she said. 'These things have got large olfactory sacs, and their sense of smell is acute. A test they made at Lerner's showed that a shark can detect one part of tuna juice in twenty-five million parts of sea-water. When they smell anything that interests them, they turn upstream and home in on it. So if you feel any current running and you see a shark upstream of you, you're in better shape as far as your scent is concerned. I know you probably won't have to use *any* of this but if you do run into problems it's going to give you an edge.' She was standing in front of me now, fastening the last strap of the scuba harness, her eyes watching me in the light from the binnacle, the green pupils iridescent, darker than I'd seen them before, more concentrated, and I had the passing thought that she was looking at me for what might be the last time, but if that kind of thing was in her mind she would be wrong, she would of course be wrong.

'Does everything feel okay?'

I shrugged the harness a bit higher and she took up the slack on the buckles. 'Okay now?'

'Fine.'

She turned away and got a metal cylinder from the cabin, black-painted with a fire-extinguisher type lever. 'That was all the bad news, as I said. This is the only good news we've got. It's a concentrate from the Moses sole fish, gives out a milky fluid, but the toxicity's only potent enough if it's released into the shark's mouth.' She buckled it to the left side of the harness at the hip. 'Don't forget you've

310

got it, for God's sake. Everything comfy?'

I said yes and walked to the rail and she held the gear steady while I climbed over and turned my back to the sea and looked up at her as she offered me the unexpected miracle of a quick, flashing smile and I let go and the cylinders hit the surface and spread bubbles around me like a veil of white lace as I turned over and began swimming.

It was huge, a long shadow lying under the surface.

I'd heard someone say it was two thousand tons, the size of a destroyer. It looked even bigger than that, its outlines etched by the play of moonlight through the water, broken by a shoal of fish swarming near the twin screws aft, flashing as they turned, darkening and flashing, their quickness mesmerising.

There were sounds here, muffled but not distant, the sound of generators and voices and music, so faint sometimes that I believed that silence had come, then getting louder as the current swirled and I rose through the water, breaking the surface under the dark slope of the keel. There was no music now; it hadn't been a party on deck or anything; I think it had come from radios in the crew's quarters, aft, where I'd approached the target, the motor-yacht *Contessa*.

I began work straight away, and fixed the first one a foot above the surface on the starboard side. The magnet was strong, and made a sudden ringing sound as its field pulled it to the hull with the force of a hammer blow.

I hadn't been ready for that. I didn't like it. A fish, even a big fish, moving at speed and turning, hitting the hull obliquely, wouldn't make a sound like that. I think it would have been heard, inboard,

I think it would have been heard by people in the well of the ship.

I used the flippers to drive me below again so that I could take sightings. I didn't feel comfortable with the lower half of my body dangling below-surface. Looking down the length of the hull I could see the shoal again, a swarm of two or three hundred small fish, flashing silver as they turned and turned again with a speed that gave them the semblance of an illusion.

They're also attracted to fish moving in a shoal. If you see a shoal, steer clear of it or try and swim towards it to turn it away.

I was all right here: they were as distant as the length of the ship. There was no other movement anywhere, except for bubbles rising from vegetation on the sea bed. The anchor chain hung in the water not far off, under the bows, a rope of black pearls in the filtered light of the moon. In the other direction the twin screws bloomed like dark flowers, their rounded petals silvered at the tips. The moon was above the port beam, so that one half of the hull was dark, the other barely visible, lit from the surface as brightly as the sea itself and merging with it.

I moved slowly to the other beam, and spread one hand against the painted metal, palm towards me, and laid the next unit over it; but the magnet was stronger than I'd thought and it was a job to pull my hand free, and when I did there was still a slight hammering sound as the unit met the ship's plate. I would have to do better than that.

In the next half-hour or so I fixed four more of them, using a fabric strap as a buffer to deaden the sound, and then duck-dived to take another sighting below, and saw the shark.

It was half the ship's length away and looked

motionless, a ten or twelve foot grey cylinder, flattened a little horizontally. It was just below the surface, its profile silvered by the moon and not easy to see, except for its size. Then it began moving, at first across the beam of the ship and then turning to stand off again, nearer me but not close yet. It was pointed now towards the stern, and did nothing for a while; then the long tail-fin moved suddenly and it was streaking the length of the hull and hit the centre of the shoal before the fish had time to scatter. It looked like a big window being smashed, with the bits of glass exploding from the centre.

I was about midship, and needed to move aft. The shark had turned and was facing towards me, but at a fair distance. What was left of the shoal had regrouped and was shimmering in the water near the hull again, apparently unable to learn.

Itching on the skin, the nerves shaken and sweat springing, not unexpected. I'd done most of the work down here in comfort, free of any concern except for the noise of the magnets jamming home, but now things had changed.

I know you probably won't have to use any of this but if you do run into problems it's going to give you an edge.

It was time to remember the other things she'd told me, and I kept my arms close to my sides and my legs together, drifting closer to the hull. There was so little movement of the water against my hands that I wasn't sure there was a current at all; but if there was, I was downstream of that bloody thing and it couldn't smell me. But of course it could see me: she'd said they could see well enough in dim light, and the moon was bright enough through the clear water to define the shark's dorsal fin even at this distance. It could see me very easily.

313

You've placed six of those things. Now get out.

We need eight. That man Parks recommended eight.

Six are good enough. For God's sake get out while you can.

Panic will get us nowhere. I shall stay exactly where I am.

But it wasn't easy. It was not easy, my good friend, to stare at that hideous two-ton killing machine while it stared me back. It had kept still like this, just like this, before it had suddenly shot forward and hit that shoal like a missile.

For the sake of Jesus Christ get out, get out, get out.

Sweat crawling on the skin under the wet-suit, itching, making me want to move, to pinch the flesh through the rubber, the only way to scratch. But let us be reasonable; nothing much has changed, when you stop and think. I knew this was dangerous, and I knew Ferris would have tried to stop me if I'd told him what I meant to do, and I knew that by the end of this long day I would come to realise that I was mad, and that when she had given me that wonderful smile, when she had mustered all the courage she had needed just to do it, to give me that flashing beatific smile, I knew that she hadn't thought much of my chances, that she was in all likelihood looking upon this vain and ambitious madman for the last time, and had managed to bring herself to offering him everything of life she could, the gentle valedictum, the grace of her womanhood. I knew those things.

But somewhere along the line, as they say, I'd been lulled into thinking it was going to be cushy down here after all, because they wouldn't come, the sharks, wouldn't seek me out, wouldn't decide

to make of this impudent clown a snatched meal,
the jaws coming open as the great body turned with
the tail driving it towards the kill, the jaws locking
shut on impact and the flesh becoming shreds, the
bones –

Out, get out for Christ's –

Yes, I'm afraid I got carried away a little, didn't
I, and if you weren't quite so shit-scared I wouldn't
have to suffer your pusillanimous bloody whining,
I'd have a better chance to think.

Think.

Move very slowly, paddle with your flippers, arms
to the sides, move towards the stern, towards that
great grey fish with its tiny eyes, keep close to the
hull, just underneath it, part of the ship, just a piece
of equipment, nothing alive, nothing of flesh and
blood, the jaws coming wide open as it – steady,
lad, we came here to do this and we are going to do
it, the sweat crawling, ignore it, ignore the itching,
driving me crazy, ignore.

Then it moved and grew enormous as it drove
past me and hit the shoal again and the fragments
scattered and I held still with the breath blocked in
my throat and my senses numbed, held still, a piece
of equipment, nothing alive like the little fish over
there, some of them crushed but slipping out of
that cavernous mouth again, floating to the surface,
awkward-looking, their blood trailing in the light of
the moon.

Door banged somewhere, some kind of door, the
clang of metal, and then the light was dappled with
movement as things began drifting down, touched
with silver and sending out small bubbles, some kind
of *things* I didn't know what, my mind was too
occupied with the shark over there, nosing through
the water while the *things* went on drifting down,

315

surrounding me, an apple-core moving against the face-mask, an *apple-core*, mother of God, *the things that attract them are light, noise and rapid movement, but watch out if you see garbage being thrown overboard and keep well away from it.*

Egg-shells, a chicken carcass, potato peelings, drifting around me and I started moving forwards, keeping horizontal and just below the hull but too close and the air-bottles banged against the plates and I froze and waited for the shock to pass and then put my head down and went lower, fanning with the flippers, not looking to see where the shark was because it would mean turning and I didn't want to turn, to move more than I had to. It was somewhere behind me now, the big grey fish, but I didn't know how far away. *Only a third of the people attacked have reported seeing the shark. It's usually what we call a blind hit.*

But suddenly it was in front of me, small in the distance, and I hadn't seen it go by. It must –

Two. Two sharks now.

A vessel of this size, I suppose, would attract attention at night, at feeding time. The memory cells inside those tiny brains would automatically steer them towards garbage. With this amount of light –

Three. Four.

They were zeroing in from the featureless expanse of water wherever I looked, and the big one behind me went past at a distance of a dozen feet as I floated just beneath the hull, a part of the equipment. The thing hadn't accelerated this time; it knew that garbage doesn't scatter when attacked. Two others – three others came in much faster, competitively, and went for the debris, brushing one another, making tight turns with their jaws wide, taking in what they could get.

The metal door clanged again and more garbage mottled the surface, dark at first and then catching the light as it sank, and the four sharks – five – became excited, dog-fighting their way through the debris, and one of them broke off and brushed against the propellers, jaws open, ready to attack anything, any shape at all, then it turned very fast and came for me head-on and I held still for as long as I could and then I was looking directly into the gape of the jaws and brought the cylinder up and squeezed the lever and felt the coarse hide graze past my shoulder as the toxic fluid clouded the water like milk and the tail fin hit me and the air-bottles rang against the hull.

Sake of Jesus Christ get out, get away.

Things not good, a degree of concussion, it had been a blow to the head, but I was aware of what was going on, though not terribly interested, blood in the water now ahead of me, 'a blossoming of crimson, perhaps one of them had gone for another, becoming frenzied, I didn't actually care whether –

God's sake get out, get out –

Yes, the voice of reason, moved my head down and turned with the flippers fanning, clear water now in front of the mask, fast as we can now, yes, *usually call a blind hit*, keep a cool head, so forth, blood again and the whole scene flashing and swirling in the moonlight as they circled just aft of the ship, the drift of milky toxin still hanging in a cloud, the blood worse now, a mist of crimson, *you've turned, you shouldn't see them any more, you're not going straight*, this was true, yes, I was wallowing, I think, not able to steer too well –

God's sake turn again, turn and go straight –

Using one arm, paddling, turning and seeing clear water ahead, moving faster now, feeling a little

317

brighter, *thing hit me like a train and I blacked out* –

Blacked out, the music, the music of the spheres, *a blind hit*, that was what had happened, and the organism was trying to run on its own now, autonomically, the eyes still open and watching for clear water, the balance mechanism of the inner ear correcting, adjusting, but there was redness in the water and my feet were not moving, the blind hit had ripped the wet-suit away at the shoulder and broken the skin, *the feet not moving*, we need to *move*, my feet just lying in the water, *move* them, it is necessary.

Life is necessary, we are moving ahead again, fanning slowly, and the truth is that one of two things will happen, I will continue to move, to leave behind me the frenzied dance of the big grey bloodied fish, or one of them will come for me again and this time use its jaws to better effect and close on my body and shake me, crush me, with my arms and legs obscenely sticking out from that great shape like the legs of a frog I had once seen in the mouth of a golden carp, and then shall it be written, *finis, finito*, on the final pages of this man's life –

Move your feet, keep moving –

Philosophy, a rush of cheap philosophy through this semi-conscious mind, I agree, will get us nowhere.

The water was still clear ahead of me through the mask, and I rose a little and broke the surface and let the full light of the moon strike down against my eyes. The Coral Rock, she had said, would be my marker to the east, and there it was, a red winking eye in the night, and behind me, as I turned my head, the lights of the motor-yacht afloat on the sea, quite a distance from me already – I'd come farther than I would have thought. I went down again, to swim below the surface for a time, the legs feeling stronger now and the head clearing.

Six of them. I had set only six of them, not eight, but the fish had come and there'd been no choice. It might be enough, six. let us hope so.

Fat lady sing, now.

Fat lady sing.

24

BOMB

It's all very well for them. I haven't had a woman in three weeks, they think we're bloody robots?

All day.

I haven't seen him, sir. He said he was going on deck.

We'd been here all day.

I asked him, 'How long will those batteries last?'

'Thirty-six hours. That's their normal endurance.'

They'd been running since midnight and it was now seven in the evening. They'd been running for nineteen hours. We'd got until noon tomorrow.

So the judge asks him, what makes you rob banks, then? And this guy says, that's where the money is.

Laughter. TV show.

The shivering hadn't stopped. I don't know if Parks had noticed. It felt like a fever, without the temperature, cold, if anything, the skin clammy. I'd had a row with Kim: she'd said, 'You've *got* to sign in at a hospital for a bit. Shock needs *treatment*. It's as important to *treat* shock as if you were bleeding to death. I *know* this, I've been *trained* and I've *seen* what happens if people neglect shock. It can *kill*.'

The worst of it was that she probably thought I was carrying on out of bravado, but that was not the case, it was not, my good friend, the case at all. I would have given a great deal to report to a hospital and flop out onto a bed with nice clean sheets and a gentle nurse to wipe my fevered brow and hold my hand, a very great deal. But this, if you remember, was the last chance I'd got of bringing home *Barracuda*, however thin, however desperate.

We'll talk about that when we meet. Apostolos doesn't want anything said before then. We need to keep open minds.

Apostolos Simitis.

The voices coming in to the recorder weren't always as intelligible as that. They were coming through a mass of unrelated and conflicting sounds – other voices, music, static, interference, coming in on six channels from the six transmitters, and Parks was doing what he could to keep them separate and edit them before they went onto the tapes. He was sitting like a spider in the middle of a dense array of equipment – amplifiers, modifiers, input balancers, audio monitors, with signal-strength needles swinging across the dials the whole time.

He'd started editing and recording the moment I'd placed each transmitter and pushed the contact under the rubber shield; by the time I'd reached here at three this morning he'd filled three sixty-minute tapes, with nothing much on them in the way of voices: most of the crew and passengers had been asleep.

'You all right, are you?' he asked me.

'I'm fine.'

He'd noticed the shivering, then, but of course that wasn't all: I must have looked like something out of a car crash when I'd got here. She'd said the blood loss wasn't critical but I'd need to have the dressings changed in twelve hours. That thing had

322

ripped flesh off the whole of the upper arm and left the triceps exposed. 'I'm not a *doctor*,' she'd said, 'I could be up on criminal charges, practising medicine on you and not even reporting it.'

I don't think the shock was because of the wound; there was the lingering horror of having been out there with the huge dark shape of the vessel blotting out most of the surface overhead while those bloody things had come at me through the open expanse of water like the angels of death.

'More tea?'

Said yes.

He was looking peeky himself, hadn't slept since transmission had started nineteen hours ago, hadn't taken a break, because I'd told him we mustn't miss anything, mustn't miss a word.

'Don't fancy anything to eat?'

'No. Don't let me stop you.'

I didn't think I'd ever want to eat again; I was just this side of nausea, slumped here in the big lopsided armchair stinking of iodine and God knew what else. 'It's normally the dog's bed,' Parks had said, 'but I've put him in the kitchen.'

But you shouldn't have come here, darling. This is a terribly small ship. I told you, I'll come to your cabin whenever I can.

That had been in French. So far we'd heard English, French, German, Russian and Japanese coming in to the tapes. There were five women on board, three of them secretaries. We'd heard several people identified by name during conversations: Takao Sakomoto, Simitis, de Lafoix, Lord Joplyn, Abraham Levinski, Stylus von Brinkerhoff. We'd heard only the first names of the women, except for Madame St Raphael.

He said he'd cover that sort of thing at the meeting.

I couldn't make him budge.

Parks was watching me, and I nodded. It was the third time we'd heard people mention a meeting.

'I wish they'd say *when*,' I told him.

'That's what we're after, is it? Some kind of meeting?'

'We're after anything we can get.'

'I see.'

His tone told me he thought I was playing it close, shutting him up, and that was true. Anything at all going onto the tapes from the *Contessa* was by its nature ultra-classified, except for the private conversations, and if the batteries held out long enough to give us the scheduled meeting we could be listening to material as vital as the briefing that Erica Cambridge had brought off the ship. It could give us the whole of *Barracuda*.

'If we get what I'm hoping for,' I said, 'they'll want you to come with me to London for special debriefing. Consider this stuff Ears Only for Bureau One, you know what I mean?'

'Crikey.' The kettle was whistling and he said, 'Look, could you – '

'Stay exactly where you are.' I got up and went over to the stool where he'd set up the makeshift canteen, and the ceiling came right down at an angle and I threw a hand out behind me and broke the fall and lay on the floor listening to the constant rush of static and voices, and Parks got off his stool at the console and I told him to sit down again and get on with what he was doing, we mustn't miss, floating in front of me, the canteen floating in front of me, miss a word, not a word.

Got up and tried again.

'You ought to have something to eat,' Parks said.

So I found some bread and made the tea and went back to the armchair. 'Bread?' I asked him.

'Not just now.' Sitting there like a leprechaun on his toadstool, face pinched with fatigue, eyes flickering as he monitored the signals, all I'd offered him was some bread, poor little bugger, as soon as I felt a bit better I'd go and find some eggs or something.

. . . He is to be eliminated.

But how can that be done? Toufexis is protecting him.

We own Toufexis. He will be given the task of eradicating crime throughout the United States, once the new order is established. He'll do as we tell him.

Interference came in and saturated the voices, then cleared a little.

. . . He's too dangerous now. We used him to work on the tapes for the selected commercials at the studios and that was fine, but then Apostolos brought him aboard here and gave him too much trust, in my opinion. He's now privy to very sensitive information on the whole project, and his behaviour is becoming a little irrational, as perhaps you've noticed. Brink agrees with me. He is to be allowed to go ashore once more, and Toufexis will be given instructions . . . This is . . . but no later than . . .

We were both crouching, Parks and I, watching the console, but static was coming in in overwhelming bursts.

'Talking about Proctor?'

'It sounds like it,' I said.

Parks knew about him; Ferris had sent him in to search Proctor's flat for bugs the day after he'd cleared out and gone to ground. I wasn't surprised they'd decided to put him out of the way. The last time I'd talked to him he'd looked perilously near the brink, with his psyche undermined by cocaine and subliminal indoctrination, and by now he could be coming slowly apart.

. . . You brought me aboard as your mistress, Baptiste, not as your servant. I would like some sleep, if you'll be so kind. . . . When I have . . . Otherwise . . .

Eight. Eight in the evening.

At nine Parks showed me how to adjust the volume and selector controls to keep the stuff channelled as it came in, and went into the kitchen and made us some eggs on toast and some coffee.

By midnight I was feeling stronger, and took over from Parks while he got an hour's sleep. The signals flow was down to a trickle now, mostly comprising private conversations and snatches of speech from the bridge.

I slept between two o'clock and six, and then went through the only tape that Parks said might interest me; but it wasn't anything to do with the project and there was only one reference to a meeting, with no time mentioned.

. . . And in that case you have my full authority to arrange the takeover. If they wish to contest our offer of three and a half billion US dollars, I'm prepared to listen to a counter offer, but the bottom line must be three and a quarter billion. I am calling Weiner today, to get his opinion . . .

Ten in the morning.

'Doesn't look too good,' Parks said.

I *do* wish people wouldn't state the *obvious*. Of course it didn't look too bloody good when we'd got two hours left, *two hours* before those bloody batteries ran out, did he think I didn't know the situation? Those bloody things coming at me with their jaws wide open and putting the fear of Christ in me and in the end what'd we got, nothing, *nothing* I could take to Ferris.

Eleven.

Eleven o'clock.

Most of it was useless. Talk of corporate infrastructures and aggressive trade policies, snatches of talk shows and dirty stories below deck, the imbecilic beat of heavy steel and the rise and fall of the Dow Jones Average on the financial services programmes, long discussions on the advisability or otherwise of asking the Vatican if it wanted limited participation in order to persuade the South American states to accept the proposed status quo without the inconvenience of rebellion.

Nothing I could use, no statement of aims, no commitment to illegal acts, no material on rigging the imminent elections, nothing on Mathieson Judd, nothing on the Moscow connection, nothing, nothing, *nothing*.

Noon.

Fifteen minutes later Parks said, 'The first one's starting to fade.' He was fiddling with a volume knob, watching a dial.

'Batteries?'

'Yes.'

'You can't amplify?'

'You'd just amplify all the slush as well.'

I let my eyes close, shutting out the glare between the slats of the blind. My arm had started throbbing, and I remembered she'd said I'd have to get the dressing changed in twelve hours. She'd given me some antibiotics but I hadn't swallowed them because I needed a clear head.

. . . *Or not at all. Spain, of course, must be invited.*

At twenty minutes past noon the next transmitter began fading and went out.

Limpets.

They were becoming no more than limpets out there, clinging to the hull of the motor yacht *Contessa*, where the shoals flickered silver in the underwater light and the anchor chain hung like a rope of black pearls.

. . . And let me reiterate the salient points for you, so that we can go over them later in more detail. The key agent is of course Gordon Schaffer . . .

The voice of Apostolos Simitis.

. . . We have persuaded Senator Judd that Schaffer is the best man, by far, to assume the post of his premier aide at the White House. It will be for Schaffer to install the radionic transmitters in the Oval Office itself, in order to bring President Judd under the continuous influence of our directives . . .

'Parks,' I said, 'stay with that. Don't lose *that*.'

'If the batteries go, there's nothing – '

'All right. All right.'

It was a time for praying, for what it was worth.

. . . Hellstrom has estimated that it will require something in the region of twelve months' continuous subliminal suggestion to inculcate the main schema into the President's subconscious, and if that seems a rather long time we should bear in mind that the changes we envisage for the social environment of humankind are greater than any seen since the beginning of man's history.

A thin bar of light leaned from one of the shutters to the linoleum, and motes of dust floated through it, brightening suddenly and going out again as they passed on, in a microcosmic mimicry of the constellations, each star moving from light to darkness, from life to death.

. . . We will remember that there are certain factions within the Kremlin who could not be counted

upon, to say the least, to lend their influence to our project. We have begun to suspect that the Englishman, Proctor, may be in the process of breaking our trust in him, and working for those factions in the role of what may be called a double agent. We have agreed to eliminate this problem at the earliest opportunity.

There was a pause, and we were left with the rush of static and interference, and I looked across at Parks.

'We're starting to lose it,' he said.

'Get the volume up. Slush and all. Keep it *up.*'

. . . Joplyn, can you assure us that Great Britain would ally herself to our aims?

I can assure you that once President Judd has persuaded the United States . . . and the end of war on . . . no option but to ally herself . . . impossible for Europe to stand on its . . . massive dimensions of this enterprise, but . . . on the understanding . . . we may assume . . . not . . . interests of military . . . when it . . . compromise . . . outset . . . if only . . .

Slush, a deafening tide of slush in the room as Parks brought the amplifiers up to full strength and sat watching me and I lifted a hand and he cut it.

'Leave the others going,' I told him, 'while they last. Can you start making duplicates of that one at the same time?'

'How many?'

'Six.'

'No problem.'

The last transmitter went dead soon after one o'clock, and Parks hit a switch and all we could hear was the dog in the kitchen scratching to get out.

'Sounded heavy stuff,' Parks said hesitantly. 'That what you wanted?'

I suppose I was a bit groggy, and not quite able

329

yet to realise what we'd got on that tape, because I just said, 'What? Yes, I think so. Look, is there any way that stuff could get wiped out, in here or in transit?'

'I'll take good care, and put it in a shielded box, if that's what you mean.'

'Do that, yes. Do that. Handle it,' I said, 'as if it were a live bomb, because that's pretty well what it is.'

Half an hour later I asked him if I could use the telephone, and he showed me where it was.

I hadn't even attempted to work out the risk, but at the back of my mind I knew of course that it was appalling. But it was something that had got to be done, so that made it easier, in a way.

25

GIRLS

The black Cadillac had been there for more than fifteen minutes at the kerbside. No one had got out.

It was a quiet street, residential. Other cars were parked there, under the lamps or in the shadows between the lamps. I had got here thirty minutes ago. Now that I was here, I could only wait. I needed to see his face, to know that he was here.

If he weren't here, if there were something else in the black Cadillac, I would get out of my car and walk down the street into certain gunfire. I knew that.

I'd picked up a Lincoln an hour ago from Avis, nothing very fast, because we weren't going anywhere, just a car he could recognise easily, if he came, if Proctor came. I sat waiting.

I had telephoned him from Parks' flat, suggesting a rendezvous. He hadn't asked questions; he was a professional and he knew three things. One, that I wasn't trying to bring him off the *Contessa* into a trap, because I couldn't hope to do that, with the massive armed support he would ask Toufexis to put into the field. Two, I wouldn't suggest a rendezvous unless I'd got something to tell him that would interest him, and interest him to the point where he'd consider sparing my life. Three, that I was ready to trust him with that same life, or I wouldn't be here at all.

It was six minutes before the appointed time. In six minutes I would know what he'd decided to do, and there were only two possibilities. He was either sitting there in the Cadillac and would walk up the street to meet me, or he had let me believe he'd be here and simply told Toufexis that I was set up for the kill at this time and in this place.

If, in six minutes from now, I tried to drive away I would receive a fusillade before I'd gone fifty feet. The same thing would happen if I walked up the street and Proctor wasn't here.

The Cadillac had arrived with an escort of five vehicles, two of them armoured, with door pillars thicker than standard and smoked windows and massive front bumpers and heavy-duty tyres.

Five minutes.

Even if he were here, and we met, and talked, he might not be interested in what I'd got to say. He might disbelieve it, counter it or ignore it. And when he left here he would give the signal for the kill: he wouldn't let a chance like this go begging.

Four minutes.

There was another risk. Even if what I told him made sense, and would normally have interested him to the point where he would decide to spare my life for his own sake, he might be so far gone by now, so subliminally indoctrinated or so high on cocaine, that he would behave irrationally, as they'd already noticed him doing on board the *Contessa*, according to the tapes.

I don't think there were any other risks. There may have been, and I could be missing them. I was very tired now, dangerously tired, pushing my luck.

And you can't get clear now, even if you wanted to.

I know that. Shuddup.

You're locked in.

It was the only way. Leave me alone.

The minute you get out of this car –

God's sake leave me *alone*.

That familiar feeling.

Three minutes, two, one.

Familiar feeling, ice along the spine, the hairs lifting at the nape of the neck, the breath quicker and the pulse accelerating, felt it so many times before, never got used to it, always as bad, the mouth dry and the eyes ready to flinch at the crack of a twig or the creak of a door or the click of a rifle bolt, thirty seconds and time slowing, slowing.

Nine o'clock on the facia, nine o'clock and no movement anywhere, no one getting out of the black Cadillac, *we'll say nine*, he'd said and I had agreed, and now it was nine, the appointed hour, and it would be up to me how long I waited before I realised he hadn't come, before I decided to get it over with and started the engine and pulled away from the kerb and drove into a burst of deadly hail, *finito, you were a fool after all, you could have gone home, they had a plane for you*, the hail shattering the windscreen and ripping into the bodywork and into my head, my face, my lungs, fool after all, there's one born every –

Door of the Cadillac opening.

Didn't have, it didn't have to be Proctor, just one of Toufexis's –

One man, only one man, getting out and slamming the door and looking in this direction and starting to walk, *Proctor*, his hands hanging loosely by his sides. I couldn't see his face but I know people

333

by their walk and this was George Proctor and I got out of the car and shut the door and started along the sidewalk, picking my feet, having to pick my feet up and put them down again, felt like a marionette, did it show, felt like a marionette under slack strings, step at a time, one step at a time, you'll get there, a leaf, a leaf here and there underfoot, the trees breaking in high green wave against the city-bright sky, the shadows deep enough here to conceal –

'It'll have to be good,' he said, Proctor, halting in front of me.

'What? I told you to come alone. You don't listen.'

He studied me, dark eyes shimmering between narrowed lids, the heavy mouth pursed in a false smile. 'You look a bit under the weather.'

'It's just indigestion.'

He didn't laugh. 'I haven't got long.'

I went and leaned my back against the railings of the garden, hibiscus in bloom, red in the lamplight, brought one foot up to rest on the low stone wall, where to start, where are we going to start? 'You know I didn't get you here to waste your time, Proctor, or mine, so you'd better listen, because it's true.' I turned my head and saw men standing beside their cars, turned and looked the other way, same thing, a small army, I just wanted to know I'd been right: he'd asked Toufexis to bring a small army here. Turning to look at Proctor, 'You were very good, once, first class, we did two big ones together, didn't we, and then you had a bit of bad luck with that bullet and it brought you out of the action and you've been getting so bloody frustrated that you finally hit the drugs and let the Soviets turn you and now you're deep in all that shit they're peddling on

334

the *Contessa*, and that is absolutely true. Were you listening?'

'For what it was worth.' The eyes very bright, not with anger or anything but worse, with amusement.

'I came here to take you home,' I said.

His eyes changed very slightly, and he was lifting his head back a degree, sighting me, and I realised something I hadn't ever thought of. He was thinking that *I* had lost my reason.

Perhaps I had.

'Home,' he said, 'I see.' Watching me carefully, 'You missed out, you know. You should have joined forces with me. It's an incredible thing they've come up with, a real master plan, a – '

'Call it world dictatorship.'

He shrugged. 'If you like. But a benign dictatorship. A new order, with – '

'The Thousand Year Reich,' I said, 'lasted twelve years.'

'This is so very different. This isn't socialism.' His hands began gesturing and his eyes brightened again. 'This is *one world* in the making, and we're – '

'Happy for you,' I said. 'Another thing you should listen to, Proctor, is this. You've been influenced by subliminal suggestion, ever since those people picked on you to work the Soviet connection. They've turned you into a robot.'

Stood waiting, letting it sink in. It had got home, I'd seen that. He knew all about subliminal suggestion: he'd had those commercial tapes doctored for the Trust.

In a moment he asked me, 'How much do you know?'

'About what?'

'About the Trust.'

'The whole thing.'

He took a long time now. He didn't think I was mad any more. 'If you know everything, why do you want me to go home?'

'That's the mission. Always has been. You're the objective. You're out of your depth here.'

He asked suddenly – 'What makes you say they've had me under subliminal suggestion?'

The focus was here, then.

'We found a transmitter in your flat.'

'A bug?'

'No. A transmitter, putting out information. It was very powerful – I picked up some of the stuff when I was there that night, political stuff, and instructions. They were for you, of course, not me.'

His face was dead-pan, a trained face, conditioned to express nothing; but his eyes were changing all the time now, glittering, excited, then deadening, darkening. Perhaps it was the cocaine, but I didn't think so. I'd started some kind of struggle inside him.

'What were the instructions?'

'To go to 1330 West Riverside Way.'

Quickly – 'Did you go there?'

'No.'

I waited, thinking there was a chance still, but he said, 'Whatever happened, I've become a valued member of an organisation that can give us a new world. And all you can offer me is the old one, if I come home. They want me for debriefing, don't they? That's what your real mission is – you're here to blow the Trust. That bloody woman Thatcher's given this one to the Bureau to look after.' He left his eyes on me for another five seconds and then looked at his watch.

'You're wasting my time.'

'I haven't finished.'

'Yes,' he said, 'you have.' He swung his head and stared along the perspective of the street. A man was standing by the nearest vehicle, an armoured limousine, smoke curling from a cigarette under one of the lamps.

Ice in the blood, the scalp shrinking.

I don't like it when there's only one last throw.

Turning back to me he said, 'You knew the risk. Have you got a capsule on you?'

'I don't need one.'

'It'd be less noisy,' he said.

I brought my foot down off the little wall and leaned away from the railings, wanting, I suppose, to be standing up straight when they did it, or perhaps I was just stretching my legs, felt so bloody tired. 'There's something I meant to ask you, Proctor. How far do you trust those people?'

'Toufexis's?'

'No. Simitis and Lord Joplyn and the others.'

His eyes were excited again. 'Why?'

'You think they're putting you in charge of their intelligence, don't you? Their *global* intelligence network.'

It had been on one of the tapes.

'*How do you know*?'

'I know everything. But look, work it out for yourself, for Christ's sake. That's a job they'd offer Bureau One, yes, or Croder, even Loman, or the chief of MI5 or MI6 or the CIA. But a shadow? A ferret in the field? You're not even thinking straight.'

He watched me without saying anything for so long that I thought the coke had phased him out in some way; but his eyes were still very bright. God knew what was going on inside his mind, but I think

I'd found another focus, and this time it was *trust*.
It had got to be.

'Think about it, Proctor. The minute you've done
what they recruited you for they'll throw you to the
dogs.'

Very quietly, 'You can't say that.'

I'd hit the nerve.

He'd already suspected it; he'd seen the signs and
chosen to ignore them. We believe what we want to
believe.

'You're trusting those people with your *life*, you
know that?'

I think he might have started listening, at that
point, but the months of continual indoctrination
had left him unable to think for himself. He looked
along the street at the man standing by the limousine, and said again, 'You knew the risk,' and turned
away.

Last chance.

'Proctor, you'd better have this.'

I went for my pocket and then froze, not thinking
fast enough: God knew how many guns were trained
on me here.

'Get it out of my pocket. This one. Tape
recorder.'

He hesitated, his dark eyes narrowed, then did as
I'd told him.

'Push the play button.'

Last chance, yes. It would depend, really, on how
much control he'd still got, control of himself, his
persona, how much he'd be able to understand what
he was listening to.

He is to be eliminated.

Lord Joplyn.

'You recognise the voice?'

'Yes.'

The lamplight pooling in the street, the men watching us from their cars.

But how can that be done? Toufexis is protecting him.

His eyes darkening as he listened.

We own Toufexis . . . He'll do as we tell him.

I'd asked Parks to make a new tape, this one, putting it all together and bridging the gaps, all the stuff about Proctor.

He's too dangerous now. Apostolos brought him aboard here and gave him too much trust, in my opinion.

It began just then, a kind of fever in him, in Proctor. He'd suspected this already: he was an experienced shadow, trained to look into mirrors within mirrors, and he'd caught an incautious glance, picked up a careless word, and begun piecing things together. All I was doing tonight was giving him the substance and the proof, and he was shaking now, swinging his head, and I felt the energy coming off his thick strong body as the rage took hold.

He's now privy to very sensitive information on the whole project, and his behaviour is becoming a little irrational, as perhaps you've noticed.

He turned from side to side, swinging like a trapped bear, and I took the recorder from him as he went to the railings and took hold of them, the knuckles of his big knotted hands going white as he shook the bars.

Brink agrees with me. He is to be allowed to go ashore once more, and then Toufexis will be given instructions.

Shaking the railings, not saying a word, returning to the primitive, a wounded animal. I was worried that he might turn and vent his rage on me; he was a big man, strong, and at the moment I could hardly

339

stay on my feet, lost more blood than I'd thought, lost too much sleep, call it accumulated mission fatigue, it had been a hard five days since I'd flown out here from London.

Let the matter rest with me . . .

Von Brinkerhoff and I will take full responsibility, if any question arises afterwards . . .

When it was finished I put the recorder away.

'You'd better get control, Proctor. They're watching us.' I looked along the lamplit perspective of the street, and saw the man by the limousine turn and reach through the window. 'Listen, this is your last trip ashore and they can get those instructions any time now and that man down there is answering his phone. We're playing it too bloody close – get in the car.'

We stood at the corner of Bayshore and 22nd street, traffic going past, long hair blowing in open cars, the night still young under the bright Miami moon. There was a club just here, with music floating out across the sidewalk.

'We'll be going home,' I said, 'through the Bahamas, take it easy round the pool for a couple of days.'

He stood shivering, head down, buried in himself. God knew how long it was going to take them to straighten him out, but that'd be their problem, in London.

Then he said an extraordinary thing.

'I apologise.'

For making life so difficult for me, I suppose. Civil of him.

'That's all right. Happens in the best of families. You know Monck, don't you, in Nassau?'

'Yes.'

'We'll be looking in on him while we're there.'

For major debriefing, the definitive debriefing on *Barracuda*. Then I'd drop those tapes on the table. I didn't think there'd be any trouble with Proctor, but one man's testimony wouldn't be enough to blow an organisation that size. They'd need first-hand evidence, recognisable voices, and that's what we'd got.

'Good club,' I said. 'Popular.'

Didn't answer, head on his chest, perhaps didn't hear.

Cabs pulling in, dropping people off at the marquee, some of them in fancy dress, some sort of gala. Then a car stopped by the kerb and Ferris got out and came across to us, people going by, a flurry of girls, giggling, covered in streamers, pretty dresses, silks and coloured plumes, a bit tiddly, I wouldn't wonder, one of them touching my arm as she trotted past – 'Oh *boy*, have *you* had a hard day last night!' A gust of laughter.

'Hello Proctor,' Ferris said, 'long time no see,' and we got into the car.

A selection of bestsellers
from Headline

FICTION

RINGS	Ruth Walker	£4.99 ☐
THERE IS A SEASON	Elizabeth Murphy	£4.99 ☐
THE COVENANT OF THE FLAME	David Morrell	£4.99 ☐
THE SUMMER OF THE DANES	Ellis Peters	£6.99 ☐
DIAMOND HARD	Andrew MacAllan	£4.99 ☐
FLOWERS IN THE BLOOD	Gay Courter	£4.99 ☐
A PRIDE OF SISTERS	Evelyn Hood	£4.99 ☐
A PROFESSIONAL WOMAN	Tessa Barclay	£4.99 ☐
ONE RAINY NIGHT	Richard Laymon	£4.99 ☐
SUMMER OF NIGHT	Dan Simmons	£4.99 ☐

NON-FICTION

MEMORIES OF GASCONY	Pierre Koffmann	£6.99 ☐
THE JOY OF SPORT		£4.99 ☐
THE UFO ENCYCLOPEDIA	John Spencer	£6.99 ☐

SCIENCE FICTION AND FANTASY

THE OTHER SINBAD	Craig Shaw Gardner	£4.50 ☐
OTHERSYDE	J Michael Straczynski	£4.99 ☐
THE BOY FROM THE BURREN	Sheila Gilluly	£4.99 ☐
FELIMID'S HOMECOMING: Bard V	Keith Taylor	£3.99 ☐

All Headline books are available at your local bookshop or newsagent, or can be ordered direct from the publisher. Just tick the titles you want and fill in the form below. Prices and availability subject to change without notice.

Headline Book Publishing PLC, Cash Sales Department, PO Box 11, Falmouth, Cornwall, TR10 9EN, England.

Please enclose a cheque or postal order to the value of the cover price and allow the following for postage and packing:
UK & BFPO: £1.00 for the first book, 50p for the second book and 30p for each additional book ordered up to a maximum charge of £3.00
OVERSEAS & EIRE: £2.00 for the first book, £1.00 for the second book and 50p for each additional book.

Name ....

Address ....

....

....